AGAINST
DESTINY

REVIEW

Alexander Dolinin's *Against Destiny* is a striking and powerful novel that maybe occupies a unique place in English, translated, and also Russian literature, in which it has its roots. There have been numerous documentary and fictionalized accounts of life in the Stalinist GULag, but this is virtually the first full-length story of one of those rare but still conceivable escapes from the Soviet punitive system. The escapers, together with their fellow prisoners, their guards and pursuers, as well as various personalities they encounter en route, offer a microcosmic view of Soviet society in the postwar years, reminding one of Solzhenitsyn's *First Circle* and *Cancer Ward*. Although a work of fiction, every detail of the novel and its background has been minutely and scrupulously researched, in a manner reminiscent of Frederick Forsyth. The result is a novel that has a cogency, a sense of psychological and documentary realism, and an ideological message that place it among the best writings in any language on this harrowing subject matter.

Christopher Barnes
Department of Slavic Languages and Literature
University of Toronto

REVIEW

I read *Against Destiny* with pleasure . . . Hitler's crimes are recognized by the whole world and definitely condemned. But the unconditional condemnation of Communists' crimes, which are more horrible, is still not part of the Western psyche . . . To preach Nazi ideology is a crime in many countries; but in no country is it a crime to preach Communist ideology . . . *Against Destiny* constitutes an important contribution to the cause of the defense of our civilization. I have no doubts that, for any reader, this novel will be an eye-opener.

Igor Melcuk
Professor, Fellow of the Royal Society of Canada
University of Montreal
Dept of Linguistics and Translation

AGAINST DESTINY

A NOVEL

ALEXANDER DOLININ

KÜNATI

CLEARWATER | FL | USA

For information, contact Kunati Inc., Book Publishers in Canada.
USA: 13575 58th Street North, Suite 200, Clearwater, FL 33760-3721 USA
Canada: 75 First Street, Suite 128, Orangeville, ON L9W 5B6 CANADA.
E-mail: info@kunati.com.

F I R S T   E D I T I O N

Designed by Kam Wai Yu
Persona Corp. | www.personaco.com

ISBN 978-1-60164-173-1   EAN 9781601641731
Fiction

Published by Kunati Inc. (USA) and Kunati Inc. (Canada).
Provocative. Bold. Controversial.™

http://www.kunati.com

TM—Kunati and Kunati Trailer are trademarks owned by Kunati Inc.
Persona is a trademark owned by Persona Corp.
All other trademarks are the property of their respective owners.

Library of Congress Cataloging-in-Publication Data

Dolinin, A. (Aleksandr)
Against destiny : a novel / Alexander Dolinin. -- 1st ed.
  p. cm.
Summary: "A fictional account of an escape from a Stalinist labor camp,
showing the harsh and inhuman conditions of the Gulag and the heroism of the
five unjustly condemned prisoners as they cross Siberia in a bid to reach
America"--Provided by publisher.
ISBN 978-1-60164-173-1
1. Glavnoe upravlenie ispravitel,no-trudovykh lagerei OGPU--Fiction. 2.
Political prisoners--Soviet Union--Fiction. 3. Labor camps--Soviet
Union--Fiction. 4. Escapes--Soviet Union--Fiction 5. Siberia
(Russia)--Fiction. I. Title.
PS3604.O433A7 2009
813'.6--dc22

2008049555

This novel is dedicated
to the memory of those who,
during Stalin's tyranny,
were courageous enough
to challenge fate
and the Soviet terror machine.

PROLOGUE

A lone man stood on a pier in a vast harbour. He watched the sun set over the enormous sea. The man was tall, still young, but his chestnut hair was touched with early grey. Despite his civilian jacket and jeans, his bearing revealed a military background. Any participant in World War II, now five years in the past, would at once recognize a fellow veteran. There was deep sadness in his grey eyes. Was it from the war? Or something else?

By day, the harbour was full of life and commotion. Now it was almost empty, just a couple of ships by the piers, and hardly a person in sight. On the horizon, the sea blended with the sky; only to the west did the purple-red sunset shine. The rays of the setting sun fell on the clouds, turning them from dark grey to lilac-violet. There, westward, beyond an ocean a thousand miles wide, lay this man's native land, a land both great and miserable.

It had been a tough and dangerous passage. They had started as a group of five. Only two made it, and he had just bid farewell to the only other survivor. Had the whole enterprise been worth it?

Yes, yes, it certainly had. Otherwise they were doomed to die a miserable death. Instead, they chose to fight their grim destiny. Those who did not make it died fighting as soldiers, better than to fade away slowly and painfully, destined for an unmarked mass grave in the permafrost.

Alexander Trofimov opened his eyes. Was it day or night? The small barred window was covered in dirt and cobwebs and let in no daylight. A dim electric lamp burned around the clock. The borderline between day and night was marked by turns of a key in the lock—waking time, breakfast, dinner and retreat. Trofimov remembered retreat being announced, but he could not recall being wakened. That meant it was still night.

He tried to stretch and moaned. His body was a pool of pain. After several weeks in Lieutenant-Colonel Razzhivin's dungeon, there was hardly a cell in his body that did not ache. His kidneys, groin and stomach, and all his limbs were racked by agony. His skin was covered in bruises and lacerated from the iron bars used in endless beatings. The joints of his hands and shoulders were dislocated after hours of hanging on the rack. All the time Razzhivin's underlings did that to him, he had prayed to die. How long ago was it? A month? A week? A couple of days?

Trofimov could not remember when he was brought here from the pit-jail where the counter-intelligence department of his division had held him. Nor had he any idea where his present jail was. Was he still in Jekabpils? Had he been moved to Riga? At least there was no more torture or interrogation. That meant the investigation was over, and he was to face a court martial. As a captain in the guards, he was entitled to appear before a military district court martial. That meant Riga.

He opened his eyes and looked around. He was alone. When they brought him in, a dozen people had been crammed into the small space. They were mostly Latvians, and their faces clearly showed their hostility toward a Soviet Army officer. Rumour soon spread that he was one of those who had helped their Forest Brethren partisans, and his Latvian cellmates believed it when they saw how he had been tortured. They treated him as a comrade and gave him the best place on the bunks. Who had told them? Certainly not the authorities: most likely they would have claimed he came from a Soviet penal battalion that had butchered several Latvians and was now being punished for his barbarity. Wherever the information came from, Trofimov's cellmates believed it and they treated him accordingly. Soon, however, they were removed one by one, and they never came back.

Trofimov tried to concentrate. There was no way of telling how long he was to stay there, but one thing was clear: at any moment he could be taken away to face trial. And then "it" could come— either straight after sentencing, or later on, the next night, the next morning, or even next month. He was not one to seek comfort in empty, unfounded hopes. After all he was a combat officer and had recently fought his way from Moscow to Berlin. It was best to face the inevitable and dismiss illusions. The charges against him were extremely grave, just short of high treason. He should be ready, so as not to lose face whenever "it" happened. After all, it was not painful: a shot in the head then oblivion. That at least he could face with dignity.

There were rumours that sometimes they shot you not in the head but in the stomach. Then they might bury you alive, or fling you into the furnace. Even so, he must not lose face. He must not give those scumbags pleasure.

And who was to blame for what was happening to him and to other war veterans? It was their own fault, he told himself. There were more than ten million of us. We had guns and mortars, tanks and planes, courage and experience. Who could have stopped us if we had turned on those bastards from SMERSH there and then, back in Germany? We could have slaughtered every one of the scoundrels and gone back to Mother Russia, to Moscow. On our way we could have routed the MGB secret police troops, and then we'd have dealt with the Great Leader himself and his henchmen. We could have gone home not only as victors but as liberators. Instead we relaxed and celebrated the end of the war. We drank with the Allies on the River Elbe. We dreamt of being demobbed, of laying down our arms and going home. Idiots! We were convinced that a happy new life awaited, by the grace of Comrade Stalin. Why on earth did we trust that lot? How blind we were not to realize that these men were enemies of the Russian people no less than the Nazis were. Stalin's henchmen watched us and singled us out one after another in this round of purges. We got our due. All that was left was to preserve our dignity.

"Trofimov."

The door of the cell opened, and an unfamiliar guard stood framed in the entrance.

Trofimov sat up, overcoming his pain.

"Come out and bring your stuff."

Gritting his teeth, Trofimov tried to rise to his feet but fell to the ground. The guard cursed but helped him. "And don't forget your trash. I ain't gonna mess with it," he said.

The large office was bathed in sunlight. Sunlight! When had he last seen it? A general and two colonels sat at the desk. On the wall behind them hung a portrait of Stalin. The Great Leader smiled. Trofimov stood in front of them, trying hard to remain on his feet. He dimly heard the questions put by the board members and answered them automatically. The sound of his own voice reached him from afar. The questions were trivial. It was only when the general asked whether he pleaded guilty to the charges that Trofimov forced himself out of his somnolent state and uttered a firm "No" although he realized that nothing he said would affect his fate in the slightest. His fate had been decided on high. A few more questions followed, after which the guard escorted him out of the office. He stood outside, collecting his thoughts. Death was the most likely sentence, and he wondered what he should do. Pray? If so, what should he pray for? For the salvation of his soul? For his poor parents about to lose their last surviving son? But he found he could not concentrate even on this. He was consumed by pain and exhaustion.

At last he was called back into the office. The general wore a familiar expression of virtuous severity, the demeanour of a man performing his noble and solemn duty, to purge society of filth and corruption.

"In accordance with the USSR law of 1939, concerning high treason, and the USSR law of 1934, concerning conspiracy, the Court Martial of the Baltic Military District has found Trofimov, Alexander Ivanovich, born 1922, Russian, former captain of the Soviet Army, guilty, in respect of Article 58/1b, activity undermining Soviet military rule; Article 58/6, espionage; and Article 58/11, conspiracy. The said Court Martial sentences him (Trofimov held his breath) to twenty-five years of imprisonment in corrective labour camps. This verdict is final, and the accused has no right of appeal."

PART I: THE CAMP

1

The guard's hammer struck the metal rail with a resounding clang, breaking the silence of the barracks hut and mercilessly wrenching its inhabitants out of their slumbers. Even on bare benches, and no matter how brief, their sleep was blissful. It always ended abruptly, just when they were most completely enveloped in peace and calm.

The prisoners scrambled from their three-storey bunks, and within a minute the narrow passage between the cots was crowded. Trofimov jumped down from the middle row and felt sharp pain in his frostbitten toes. Pain or no, he had to put on his boots and adjust the bindings, then join the lineup at the washstand and rinse his face before his work team went to the canteen for breakfast.

"No, fella, that won't work," Bondarenko's voice barked in his ear.

"What won't work?" Trofimov raised his eyes.

"If you bind your foot like that, you ain't gonna last one hour at work," Bondarenko replied. "And if you fall over, some fucking screw's gonna beat you to death. Frostbitten feet like those need special binding."

Bondarenko sat down by Trofimov's side and rebound his foot with the skill of a seasoned camp inmate.

"Now try the other foot yourself," Bondarenko said.

"Thanks, buddy." Trofimov tried to repeat Bondarenko's technique with his other foot.

"Fourth barracks! Out to breakfast!" The guard's harsh voice sounded like another hammer blow.

"Damn!" Trofimov cursed. "No time even to wash my face."

"Donna rush," Bondarenko warned him. "If you ain't tie your foot bindin' properly, it'll give you hell once you're down the mine."

"You scumdog! Need a special invitation?" The butt of a rifle hit Trofimov on the collarbone.

The prisoners, or "zeks" as they were called, looked alike in their overcoats as they stood outside by the canteen entrance. The icy wind blew in biting gasps. How long would they have to wait? No one knew. The convicts wore no watches.

"Shit," Ignatyev cursed. He was a blacksmith from the Don and a member of Trofimov's work team. "Are they trying to freeze us to death?"

"This ain't freezing, man," Bondarenko answered. "It's only November. By January it'll be three times colder than this."

"Why are they keeping us?" asked Trofimov.

"Could be anything. Some of the staff might be off to work in the fields."

"Work in the fields?" Goldberg protested. "There's snow everywhere."

"Oh, that's just an example," Bondarenko grinned. "They could be doin' road repairs, say, or buildin' a barn, or diggin' a ditch."

"A ditch? What the hell for?"

"What for? For no reason. Just to remind us what a cosy place the canteen is. Or maybe all the waitresses are busy, 'cos the guards got the urge for a fuck all at the same time. Their duties are so important, you understand?" Bondarenko giggled. "Their slightest cravings have to be satisfied, to maintain high morale, you see."

"Yeah," Trofimov chuckled. "So camp trash like us have to wait while the men of our glorious Cheka satisfy their noble lust. Is that it?"

"Oh, don't begrudge them, man," someone said. "The longer we spend here, the less time we have to slave down the mine."

"You're kidding," Bondarenko grinned. "They'll cut our sleep, not our work hours."

At last the canteen windows lit up, the doors were opened, and the prisoners poured inside.

Trofimov sat squeezed between Bondarenko and Goldberg, and gulped down the liquid skilly with thin threads of fish floating in it.

"Water again. Not a single real piece of fish," he complained.

"That's how things are here," Bondarenko shrugged. "The manager and the cook swipe most of our rations. They have to share with their underlings, or they'd rat on 'em. Everyone has to grease up to the bosses or go down on mine duty. To get money or vodka, they trade our food off to the geologists working outside the camp. After all that, what's left for the likes of you and me?"

"How are we expected to complete our work quota?" Goldberg complained. "We're always hungry. What master expects his horse to work without food?"

"No master expects that," replied Bondarenko, "'cos the horse belongs to him. If the goddamned critter dies, where the hell will he get the money to buy another? But we cons are different. The camp commandant doesn't pay a fuckin' penny for us. If you kick the bucket, he'll just get a replacement from the MGB, free of charge."

"And he won't even be held accountable," Trofimov said.

"You got it," Bondarenko nodded.

"Well, a long time ago Karl Marx proclaimed that 'being determines consciousness,'" Goldberg stated. "And conscience, as one can see—"

"Finish your breakfast! Line up!"

The convicts sighed and got up from the benches. Some tried to bolt down the last few precious drops of skilly, while others saved hunks of bread and hid them under their pea jackets.

The entire camp population gathered in front of the main office building and drew up in columns for the morning roll call. The camp authorities emerged: the commandant, Major Avdeyev, MGB security officer Klimenko, nicknamed the "Godfather" and various other lieutenants. These were followed by the leading camp trusties, those who assigned the work and the quotas, and the various foremen. Guards with submachine guns took up position alongside the prisoners, and the foremen checked off the members of their work teams.

"We gotta have Ananyev here. Bondarenko, Goldberg, Trofimov, Zabelin." Gusev the foreman counted one man after another. "And Zybkov. Where the fuck's Zybkov?"

"He died last night," Vaskov, the orderly from barracks number four, announced.

"Did he now? So soon."

"Why soon, Gusev? He was a goner. He'd been on his way out for a long time."

"Here, you scum." A screw emerged, dragging a man who was

scarcely able to stand.

"But I … I have a note from the doctor," the man protested.

"You and your doctor's note. You're just a lazy skiver, that's what you are."

Trofimov hoped there would be no body search, not in this wind.

"You, there. What's your name?" a screw barked right into his ear.

"Convict Trofimov, Alexander Ivanovich."

"Unbutton your overcoat. Quick about it."

Trofimov cursed under his breath. Any loud protest could cost a heavy beating or a couple of weeks in the Black Hole, or both. He unbuttoned his coat. An icy blast stabbed at his body, and his scars ached. The guard ran his hands over him, checking the pockets, then moved on to his pea jacket.

"Unbutton your jacket."

Shivering with cold, and with his body open to the biting frost, Trofimov hardly felt the screw's hands as they fumbled him.

"All right, button up."

Trofimov hastily buttoned, trying to shut out the cold. Hell, that was nasty, he thought. What sadism, forcing men to strip to their underwear in this cold. How those guards must despise us. To them we're not even humans, just like the Nazis treated the Russians.

"Citizen Guard, please listen. I'm a good worker, but I need to build up my strength. I won't manage otherwise."

"Hold your tongue, scum. You should eat your bread at breakfast."

The screw grabbed a man's bread ration, threw it on the ground and squashed it with his boot.

God. An entire bread ration. The sort of thing men fought and killed for.

"Comrade Lieutenant, I found one with a knife."

"A knife? Put him in solitary."

Tough luck, Trofimov thought. Poor chap, to get caught that way. Probably it wasn't even a knife, just part of an old saw blade, the sort of thing used in the camps in place of a knife. That was enough to pin a charge of terrorism and send a man to the "isolator," the punishment or solitary confinement cells. The man would likely catch pneumonia, and then …

"Attention! All work teams proceed to your workplace."

"C'mon, let's go." Foreman Gusev stepped up in front of his men and led them off to work. Trofimov, Goldberg, Bondarenko and twenty-seven others made up the team that joined the other mining brigades. Off they marched, escorted by a dozen screws with submachine guns and dogs.

"Attention, all prisoners! Follow your guide! One step to the left or right counts as an escape attempt. The guards will shoot without warning."

It was a routine formula, repeated everywhere in the camps several times a day, but the words chilled the soul of any newcomer. Any one of those well-fed young thugs could raise his submachine gun and wipe you out. The camp veterans knew it was no empty threat. They had seen it happen. Trofimov was not yet an oldtimer—one month was not enough to qualify. But after Razzhivin's ramrods, and several months in transit, nothing surprised him. He could well imagine the young thugs shooting the whole column dead, if the camp authorities saw fit to require it.

Meanwhile the column marched out of the inner compound and moved toward the outer gates of the camp. The mine was about three kilometres away, half an hour's walk, close enough to avoid complete exhaustion.

The workday was in full swing. Everywhere was the clangour of crowbars, picks and spades, and the creak of wheelbarrows. Some hacked the rock left by the dynamite blasts into small pebbles. Others, Trofimov among them, loaded the pebbles into barrows. When a barrow was full, it was hauled away and replaced by another, and the work went on and on without a moment's rest. This was the so-called "Kolyma conveyor belt," the revered achievement of miners in the Kolyma region, at least according to the front page of the newspaper *Soviet Kolyma*. Not a moment of work time was wasted.

Trofimov was worn out. His back ached, his arms and knees were numb. His whole body screamed: "Drop your spade! Lie down! Stretch your legs!" But that would count as sabotage. In the twelve-hour working day, they had one thirty-minute break for dinner. That was all, not a single pause even for a smoke, non-stop slave labour. When an overseer appeared, they had to put on a special display of vigor and energy, or their ration could be cut to 300 grams as punishment. They could slow down once the overseers disappeared. That was the advantage of being a face worker. The haulers were not so lucky. They were always in sight of the authorities and had to do everything at a run.

Trofimov was no stranger to hard work. As a high school student, he had worked summers on construction sites. Between school and starting at the automobile institute, he had spent a year digging the foundation pits for a large construction project. There he dug frozen ground in severe frost. At that time the end of the workday was a time for fun—songs around a bonfire, jokes and merry-making. It was a time of great hope and pride. The iron produced at that plant would make machines to fulfill the Five-Year Plan and transform the life of their Soviet Motherland. Everyone on the site was happy and strong and well fed. The working day was a long one, twelve to fourteen hours, and he got tired, but the day ended with a happy sense of achievement: he was building socialism!

Later Trofimov served in the army. He knew the squelching mud of the trenches, and he had crawled on his stomach under enemy fire. Even then everyone was full of faith and believed that soon a happy life would begin for them again, a reward for the hardships of war. Throughout his previous life, Trofimov had been filled with hopes for a better future, a future that did not envisage prison camp barracks or slave labour in a goldmine.

All of Trofimov's past—the small factory town of his childhood, his work as a builder, his student year in a Moscow college, the war, followed by a few months of peace on the Elbe and by the anti-guerrilla campaign in Latvia—all that was in another life. The only reality now was the camp and the mine. The only dream was of the end of the workday, returning to the camp zone, eating supper and enjoying the warmth of the barrel stove in the barracks hut. At the moment, that small pleasure seemed very far away.

Time had always seemed to be on his side, but not any more. Here the toil and semi-starvation wore you out. As the days went by, you became more and more feeble, and eventually you turned into a "goner," a living skeleton with a frostbitten face, arms and legs like matchsticks, bleeding gums and rotten teeth. Like the two guys from Gusev's team who ended up as invalids with just

400 grams of bread as their daily ration, waiting for death, which, if they were lucky, might overtake them as they lay in one of the Medical Section cots.

A loud commotion from the main gallery followed by angry cursing suddenly broke the steady noise of the mine works. A man wept and pleaded for mercy.

"You ass-wipes! Get back to work! Quick!" The foreman's voice roared. Several minutes later Goldberg emerged with an empty barrow.

"What happened?" Trofimov asked.

"One of the haulers dropped his barrow from the runway and spilled the gravel. The foreman laid into him."

"Was it Gusev?"

"No, Melnichenko."

"Damn." the word burst from Trofimov's mouth.

Melnichenko was one of the cruelest foremen in the camp. During the war he had worked in the Polizei in Nazi-occupied Ukraine. He had murdered more than a dozen people, Jews and other locals suspected of helping the partisans. For some reason the Soviet court martial had spared him. Now he was a camp foreman, heading a large gold-mining brigade. All this, despite a charge of high treason and a twenty-five-year sentence. He enjoyed his privileges and was famous for beating men into making their quotas. In the mine he walked around with a pickaxe handle and knocked the shit out of the labourers. On hearing the name of Melnichenko, Trofimov raised his hack and rushed toward the main gallery. Bondarenko hardly had time to catch him.

"You crazy shithead. If you so much as touch him, you'll be up on a charge of terrorism. They gonna shoot you in a wink."

"I'm sorry." Trofimov's fury receded. "Why didn't I meet him back in 1944? I'd have hung him on the highest birch tree."

"Yeah, I wouldn't have spared him either. When I was with the partisans, we shot the likes of him. Now those scumbags boss us around."

"Could we ever have imagined that during the war?" Trofimov reflected bitterly.

"To tell the truth, I know why they cracked down on us war

vets."

"Chatting again? You lazy loafers." Gusev emerged from nowhere.

"Yeah, boss, okay, donna worry," Bondarenko answered, plying his spade.

It was dark. An occasional star glinted through the patches of cloud as the exhausted prisoners slowly gathered by the head-frame of the mine and drew up in columns. They craved that long awaited supper, the small stove in the barracks and rest on the bunk. For some the day's work was not over. Some would be selected to fetch firewood for the barracks stoves. It was a daily ritual. In fact, it was not the workers' duty but that of the orderlies, but what self-respecting orderly would carry logs for prisoners? The orderly was a "trusty," on the very lowest rung of the bureaucratic hierarchy, but high enough to regard himself as exempt from any physical drudgery. So it was camp custom, rather than any rule, that the workforce provided firewood. Along the road, decent logs had to be found and carried back to the barracks.

"Lord, please don't let Gusev choose me," Trofimov whispered. "I'm too tired. I'll keel over and never get up again."

"Stop it. Donna you ever think or talk that way," Bondarenko gasped. "They'll shoot you on the spot. Or do you think they'll drag you and your log on their own shoulders?"

"Why don't they use a truck? We work such long hours," Goldberg sighed.

"Are you nuts? A truck indeed." Bondarenko laughed. "Waste precious gas on camp trash like us? It's cheaper to bring in a new set of slaves."

"No talking in the column." The screw's voice was full of lazy hatred.

"You four, go fetch firewood." Gusev pointed at a group of workers nearby.

"Lord be praised," said Trofimov. "My lucky day."

The camp and mines were located on a large barren plateau. All the taiga had been stripped off long ago for timber and firewood, and to prevent escape attempts. In a wooded area it would be hard to shoot an escaping con if he ran into the wilderness. On barren ground he made an easy target.

The logging site was beneath the plateau on a wooded slope, so the firewood carriers had to climb the slope with their heavy logs. There were enough cons in the fourth barracks so the task was never a frequent one, but it was quite arbitrary, and often used as punishment. A foreman could make one man do it seven days in a row if the poor wretch fell out of favour. Melnichenko was a brute. If Yakov Goldberg had been in his team, Melnichenko would have made him carry a tree trunk alone every day because he was a Jew. Trofimov clenched his teeth.

The column moved slowly towards the compound. The snow was deep, and the prisoners struggled with every step. The guards had skis and moved smoothly. They cursed and pushed the prisoners, but they cursed half-heartedly and seemed lazy and weary as they prodded their charges along. They moved through the silence of the Arctic night, broken only by an occasional exchange between the guards, or the subdued bark of an Alsatian guard dog.

Suddenly the column halted, and an angry yelp broke the silence:

"You! Get up, wretch. You're holding up the whole damned company."

"Yes, citizen Guard," an old man's voice moaned.

Everyone looked toward the sound of the voices. An elderly convict crouched on all fours and tried to rise to his feet.

"It's the same man who dropped his barrow off the runway," whispered Goldberg. "Melnichenko beat him terribly, and the other screws stood by and grinned."

"Looks like the old guy's unlucky day," Bondarenko observed.

The old man made another attempt to rise to his feet, but he was too exhausted, and the guard flew into a rage.

"Making fun of us? You lousy old sod." He kicked the man with his boot. The man moaned and tried to rise. The guard kicked him again and again, then he swung the Kalashnikov from his shoulder and hit the old man in the face with its butt. "I'll teach you, you dirty scumbag! I'll teach you to make fun of us, filthy old shitass!"

Blood streamed from the old man's face. The other prisoners watched with blank, lifeless eyes, used to such scenes. The screws' faces twisted in fury. This goddamned holdup delayed the welcoming warmth of their barracks. The lieutenant in charge of the escort approached.

"What's going on?" he enquired. "Can't you get this stinking skeleton on his feet?" He gave a sign, and two guards approached, took the fallen man by the armpits and propped him on his feet.

"Citizen Lieutenant," Trofimov did not know how he dared interfere. "Let me and a couple of other guys carry him. We'll get him back to the compound."

"What's that? Don't you know the rules? You have no right to address me." The lieutenant's voice was mockingly calm. One of the screws standing nearby punched Trofimov in the solar plexus. A sharp pain racked his body.

"You stupid idiot," Trofimov cried. "All you can do is beat and harass unarmed prisoners. If only I'd met you at the front."

"And what would you have done?" The lieutenant's lip curled in disgust.

"Shot him like the filthy turd he is."

"Very wise," grinned the lieutenant. "Just enough to win you a couple of weeks in the Black Hole." His face showed as much satisfaction as if Trofimov had done him a great favour.

Meanwhile the two guards had released the old man, and he fell again. They kicked and beat him with the butts of their rifles. His body shook with convulsions.

"I can't stand and watch this," Trofimov moaned. "If only I had my colt with me."

"And what then?" Baranov, another man in his team, grinned. "There's a dozen screws, each with a submachine gun. That's more than enough to rip your belly out before you had a chance to draw. It's useless protesting. Now you've earned a place in the Black Hole."

"See what happens if you fall?" Bondarenko commented. "If you fall in the Hole, they'll leave you there to freeze to death. Even if you're dying, you'd best drag yourself back to the compound somehow. There you can sleep it off, maybe even be lucky enough to have the doctor give you a discharge for a day or two."

The old man had stopped moving.

"Shit," the lieutenant cursed. "Looks like he's finished."

One of the screws leaned over the body:

"He's still breathing, comrade Lieutenant."

"Breathing or not," the lieutenant barked, "who needs the old geezer? Move on."

The company moved forward. After a short while the lieutenant ordered: "Kravchuk, go back and finish him off, or the boss will pin an escape on us." Kravchuk turned back.

"Well, poor old thing. He ain't the first, and he ain't the last," Vaskov the barracks orderly sighed. He sat together with Trofimov, Bondarenko, Goldberg and Timoshkin on adjacent bunks. They were enjoying a bite of bread and "chifir," the elite prisoners' favourite drink, made from a super-concentrated infusion of tea. "Who was in charge?"

"Makarov," replied Bondarenko.

"Then it's not surprising. Not with a bastard like him."

"Just like the Nazis," Timoshkin observed. "When I was captured on the Leningrad front, they locked us in a barn for a couple of days without food or drink. Then they lined us up in a column and made us march to the railroad a dozen kilometres away. You can imagine the state we were in. Within half an hour men started falling down in the road. The fascists just finished 'em off. They didn't beat them though. They just shot 'em."

"The Germans are passionless, like machines," Vaskov said. "They decide whether you can be used or not. If not they get rid of you."

"D'you mean to say Russians are more savage?" Goldberg asked.

"Yeah, in a way. Lazy more than anything."

"What has laziness to do with it?" asked Trofimov.

"Everythin'," Vaskov answered with a knowledgeable expression, as if surprised at the other man's ignorance. "Out here if a man dies along the road, the head of the escort has to prepare a Death Statement. That means at least an hour of writing. Makarov wanted to have the evening to himself. Maybe he'd planned a date or somethin'. So he tried to get the old guy to walk back to the compound."

"In the two and a half years I've been here," Bondarenko said, "I've seen at least half a dozen such incidents."

Trofimov said. "I saw similar things in Latvia. Our glorious Soviet state purged the local population to ensure greater security. Whole families were escorted to the railroad station. Those who couldn't walk were taken away by special detachments of soldiers."

"I bet they shot 'em," Vaskov sighed. "Or else they may have put them in a special work camp. You know, to sew or weave baskets or make lighters."

Suddenly the door banged open and a guard walked in.

"Fourth barracks. Attention." he roared. "Evening roll call. Line up."

Miserably the inhabitants moved toward the door.

"Trofimov." the guard shouted.

"Yes?"

"First of all, you reply with your full name, your article and your sentence, shithead."

"Alexander Ivanovich. Articles 58/1b, 58/6 and 58/11. Twenty-five years."

"Follow me."

"Where to?" Trofimov asked, and followed the guard out of the barracks.

"You can't guess?" the man grinned. "Who insulted the escort lieutenant today?"

"Oh, yeah, the Black Hole." Trofimov had not taken the lieutenant's threat seriously, and was too concerned about the fate of the old man.

"Two weeks?" he asked.

"Yep," grinned the screw. "Think you can just pick on lieutenants like that and get away with it?"

The screw led him in silence across the compound to the dark building of the penal isolator, nicknamed the Black Hole. The rumours Trofimov had heard were contradictory. Some said that two weeks in there ruined your health for good. Others grinned and claimed you could easily survive it, even enjoy a rest from work. Everyone agreed that the Black Hole was a holiday resort compared with the so-called Ice Hole, an underground dungeon carved out of the permafrost. Confinement in the Ice Hole was a death sentence.

The Black Hole turned out to be a cell with walls made of larch trunks and a high ceiling with icicles hanging from it. It looked like an ordinary cell. There was a lavatory bucket and a row of bunks by the wall, but no stove, no windows and no lamp. The temperature was only a little higher than outside.

"Here," said the screw, "take off your overcoat."

"But—" Trofimov pointed at the icicles.

"Off with your coat. And remember, you're lucky. Some guys get stripped to their underwear. Yeah, no shit. Now let's have your hands."

Trofimov stretched out his hands, and the guard slapped handcuffs on them.

"That's it," grinned the guard. "And that ain't so bad. The chain's long enough. At least you ain't gonna have a problem taking off your pants. Not so bad at all. See you." The door closed behind him and the light was gone.

Left alone, Trofimov decided to try sleeping. From his prison experience he knew they would not let him sleep during the day. He lay down on the bunk. It was made not of the usual boards but of the same fresh logs as the walls, only smaller and thinner. They were covered with the stumps of boughs and twigs, some of them quite sharp. He cursed—the camp officers' inventiveness was incredible. Fancy making a man sleep on something like this. He slapped the log wall with his fists then got down on the floor and lay there. The floor was ice-cold, and the chill penetrated. He jumped up again and tried to get warm by stretching, but his frostbitten toes were painful, and the handcuffs bit into his wrists. Tired and desperate, he collapsed on the floor and curled into a ball, trying to retain some warmth. Finally he succumbed to an overwhelming exhaustion.

2

Autumn 1943. In the darkness of his officer's dugout, Lieutenant

Alexander Trofimov, Third Company commander of the Twelfth Infantry Regiment, made love to Liza Burdenko, a radio operator who was at that time his "field wife." Having such a companion was one of the advantages of being an officer. No ordinary soldier enjoyed this privilege. There were enough women only for the officers, and only an officer had sufficient rations to reward his partner. Liza was a pretty woman. She could have chosen a major, or even a colonel, but she chose Lieutenant Trofimov. He was a hero, he had been decorated, and he was a surviving combat officer from the first draft of 1941. His generation had passed through fire and water, they had seen destruction and retreat, and hundreds of soldiers dying before their eyes. These men were the backbone of the army. Trofimov was a strong man, someone you could rely on, and Liza knew that.

Now they had a whole night to themselves. Tomorrow an important battle was in store, an operation to seize back the vital railroad junction of Unecha. Its seizure was crucial for maintaining ammunition supplies to the Red Army troops. It was no surprise that the Germans had fortified all approaches to the station with trenches, barbed wire fences and minefields. The fighting would be intense and, as for every other man in the regiment, this might be Trofimov's last night alive. In two years of war he had got used to such nights. He had little fear. As an experienced soldier he relied on his skills, and they had always helped him survive. Still, the likelihood of being killed was considerable, so he enjoyed this night.

Before going to bed with Liza, he had spent two hours lying on his stomach on the edge of the hill overlooking the station. He saw how tough the enemy's defences were, and he had no illusions about tomorrow's attack. But until the early hours of the next day, this night was his. At dawn the artillery thunder would explode, and a hundred soldiers of his company would engage in mortal combat without having enjoyed the pleasures of sex. He did not think that was unfair. It was a natural privilege, like his epaulettes, or his officer's food ration.

One of Trofimov's soldiers was young Vasya Ogorodnikov. He was barely eighteen years old, and he was spending the night cleaning the latrine. It was a legitimate punishment for going absent without leave. Yesterday afternoon, Vasya had gone to the neighbouring village to visit his mother. Trofimov could easily understand the youngster and failed to understand the platoon commander who refused the boy's request. Had Trofimov been asked to grant leave, he would have done so, but war was war, and discipline was essential. If Trofimov pardoned the youngster now, it would set a bad example to the others. And so, on the eve of his possible death, the young soldier was forced to dig in a pile of human excrement while his fellow soldiers slept in their bunks and their company commander enjoyed making love.

"Comrade Lieutenant." The voice of his batman Petrukhin interrupted them.

"Petrukhin? What's the matter?"

"Some of our men are out here—Kuznetsov, Volkov and others."

"Tell them to get the hell out of here, for Chrissake!"

"They say it's urgent, comrade Lieutenant. They insist."

"All right, I'm coming." Trofimov cursed and imagined what he would do to these intruders if it turned out to be something trivial. He dressed and emerged from the dugout. In the darkness he saw the faces of a dozen of his soldiers.

"What's the matter?" inquired Trofimov.

"Comrade Lieutenant." Volkov was an elderly collective farmer and a battle-hardened soldier, but it sounded as if he was sobbing. "Save Vaska, for God's sake."

"Which Vaska?"

"Vaska Ogorodnikov, comrade Lieutenant."

"Are you out of your mind?" Trofimov growled. "I've not sent him to a penal battalion, have I? Or made him strip naked in the frost. No one ever died from cleaning a latrine."

"It's not what you're doing, comrade Lieutenant. It's Vorotnikov and the SMERSH. He's going to shoot him."

"Nonsense."

"I swear it by Christ, comrade Lieutenant. He had 'im brought from the latrine, and now they're court-martialing him. After that they can shoot him on the spot. Please, comrade Lieutenant. Vaska is a kid. It's sacrilege to shoot one so young."

"Let's go," Trofimov said. "Petrukhin."

"Yessir?"

"Tell Liza I've something urgent to see to."

Trofimov approached the clearing. His company were formed up in rows, and in the center of the grassy area Lieutenant Vorotnikov, the head of SMERSH in their battalion, sat on a stool. Two of his junior lieutenants sat beside him on tree stumps. In front of them stood eighteen-year-old Vasya Ogorodnikov, the youngest soldier in the company, guarded by two soldiers of the commandant's squad.

"And therefore," Vorotnikov's voice was as calm as if speaking of something quite trivial, "the court martial finds the above-mentioned Private Ogorodnikov guilty of high treason, in the form of desertion during wartime, and serves on him the supreme sentence, execution by firing squad. This sentence is final and not subject to appeal."

"What's that, Vorotnikov?" Trofimov shouted.

"Can't you see?" Vorotnikov grinned. "We're meting out justice to a traitor."

"He's no traitor," Trofimov shouted. "You know that perfectly well."

"He's a deserter."

"He's not a deserter. He was absent without leave. And he wasn't caught, he returned of his own accord. I punished him."

"You call that punishment? That's a childish rebuke. There are special laws during wartime, and the country won't forgive any slackness on our part."

"How can you say that?" Trofimov demanded. "You've never fought in a single battle."

"Enough," Vorotnikov shouted. "You're poking your nose into something that isn't your business. We passed the sentence and we'll carry it out." He turned to the commandant's squad. "Carry out the sentence."

Two of them grabbed Vasya by the shoulder and turned him to face the soldiers of the company.

"Select the firing squad," Vorotnikov ordered Trofimov.

"Hell, never," exclaimed Trofimov. "I won't let this pass. This is lawlessness."

"Is that so, Trofimov?" Vorotnikov's voice became threatening. "D'you think that just 'cos you got your decorations, there's no authority above you?"

The blood rushed to Trofimov's face. He grabbed his pistol,

cocked it, and pointed it straight at Vorotnikov. "Listen, you jackal," he said, stressing every word. "If one hair falls from that boy's head, I'll empty this clip into your fat belly. Got it?"

Vorotnikov took a minute before he regained his speech:

"Treason," he yelled. "I'll have you arrested and court-martialed."

Trofimov appealed to his soldiers.

"This man calls me a traitor," he said calmly, addressing the company. "Tell me, men, does any one of you believe Senior Lieutenant Trofimov is a traitor?"

The company erupted. "How can he say that? You're a hero, comrade Lieutenant. The pride of Russia. It's him who's the traitor. Dirty jackal. Bloodsucker!"

"Give us the signal," a few men cried, "and we'll finish this butcher off on the spot. We'll throw him into the ravine. Nobody will never find out."

Vorotnikov turned to face Trofimov, and his lips muttered, "No, no, Trofimov. Please."

For Trofimov it was a sign that his opponent was vanquished, at least for now.

"No," he said to his men, "killing him would be an act of mutiny, and mutiny in time of war is tantamount to treason." He turned to Vorotnikov. "Did you hear what the men said, you bastard? These modest Russian heroes have shown their devotion to our country by fighting the real enemy, not by shooting defenceless teenagers. Now release Ogorodnikov."

"Yes," Vorotnikov muttered and motioned for his underlings to release the prisoner.

"And remember," Trofimov continued, "this entire company saw you plead for mercy. If you rat on me, that's what your bosses are going to find out, with all the consequences. D'you understand, you piece of shit?"

"Thanks be. You're our saviour," Volkov's voice trembled with relief. "Vaska is like a son to me since I lost my own son. I'm in your debt. You can send me out onto the minefield or wherever you want. Send me to my death if you wish."

"No, nothing of the sort," said Trofimov. "I'll only send you to your death if I go with you."

It seemed that Trofimov had got away with the incident. No senior officer mentioned it. Vorotnikov was in no position to go after him. If he did, Trofimov would tell how he had pleaded for mercy and his soldiers would confirm it. Weakness was an unpardonable sin for a counterintelligence officer. Vorotnikov would be demoted to the ranks, or might even face a firing squad. Besides, the SMERSH could not purge an officer without consent from a general in high command, and the general to whom Trofimov answered would never sacrifice a gifted combat officer like him, with his vast experience. The general, in turn, knew Marshal Zhukov personally from their times at Khalkhin-Gol. If pressed, he might appeal to Zhukov himself. Everyone thought that they had dumped the case for good. But how naïve they were. The Soviet "organs" never forgot or forgave anything. The file against Trofimov was carefully preserved and awaited a chance to settle scores with him. Like many others before and after him, he would pay for failing to be humble and subservient.

But had Trofimov been taught to be humble and subservient? As he now realized, this was the old paradox of "No, but yes." On the one hand it was drummed into his head that a young Soviet communist had to be a bold campaigner for justice and socialism, as well as a good friend who never failed you in danger or misfortune. On the other hand, he was expected to accept iron discipline and show unshaking devotion to Stalin, the Party and the Soviet Motherland. Stalin and the Party were the incarnation of Ultimate Good, the guarantors of justice and of a future paradise on earth. In this paradise was no room for oppression or domination, cowardliness or subservience. Terror was a weapon to be used against the enemy, never the innocent. Any present-day manifestation of these vices was alleged to be a remnant of capitalism. A good communist or member of Komsomol, the Young Communist League, was supposed to fight against these vices, not be subservient to them, yet he also had to obey the authorities placed above him by the Soviet rulers. Above all he was to revere the security organs that defended the country against spies and other enemies. The assumption was that these men of the "organs" were doing their legitimate duty. They were supposed to fight real enemies, not hound and slaughter the innocent.

This was what Trofimov believed. When he saw a security agent framing and sending to his death an innocent boy, guilty only of a disciplinary offence, he had no option but to oppose such action. By that time, however, he was no longer so naïve, and he fully realized that what he was doing was highly dangerous. Yet if he rejected the plea of his soldiers, who knew him as a stern but fair officer, and if he dissociated himself from the case, he would lose his self-respect. He would feel like a coward and a self-seeker, something that ran counter to so many years of psychological training. So Trofimov did what he did. And in consequence, a few years later, when the Soviet state no longer needed him as desperately as before, that same state exacted its revenge.

3

Trofimov had returned from the Black Hole a week before. Late one Sunday morning, Bondarenko, Goldberg, Timoshkin, and he sat with the barracks orderly Vaskov on the bunks beside the blazing stove and enjoyed the warmth. This was a pleasure every convict dreamed about during the severe winters in Kolyma.

"Well," said Goldberg, "it looks like this Sunday's going to be ours."

"Hopefully," sighed Timoshkin.

Every prisoner cherished a holiday weekend, although it was a luxury rather than part of everyday life. Last month there hadn't been a single Sunday when the camp inmates were not forced to work. Two Sundays were spent clearing the compound of snow, the third taken up by work at the mines and logging sites as if it were an ordinary workday. Granting or denying the prisoners a weekend holiday was at the discretion of the camp authorities.

"Well, it's only early afternoon," said Vaskov. "You know how it is. After telling us we can relax this Sunday they'll shout 'Fourth barracks, outside!' and set us to cut firewood for some boss's banquet, or clear the road of snow 'cos a VIP colonel's arriving from Magadan."

"Goddamn that tongue of yours," Trofimov exclaimed. He trembled at the idea of having to go out again.

"Don't you turn on me, man." Vaskov looked offended. "I'm just warning you. If I were in charge, I'd give you a whole month off. But I'm just a con like the rest of you."

"Yeah, Captain," said Bondarenko. "I know you're near the breaking point, but donna turn on old Yefimych. He's a decent old guy."

"Sorry, mate," Trofimov apologized. "My nerves are in shreds."

"No surprise," Goldberg observed. "You don't look well."

There was no mirror in the barracks, so Trofimov could not see how he looked, but his cheeks and nose ached with frostbite, his hands had a purple tinge, and his feet were racked by a constant dull pain. The Black Hole was a terrible place.

"He's finished." A voice broke in on their conversation.

"Who are you talking about?" Vaskov inquired loudly.

"Akimov," was the answer. "He got worse yesterday. He begged for bread, but where can I get it?"

"God bless him." Timoshkin crossed himself.

Akimov was a man from the same transit group as the rest of them, a peasant from Voronezh region. There was hardly a day in the compound without someone dying. Except for a few lucky ones who received food parcels, the camp population was slowly but steadily deteriorating. Usually within a couple of months of arriving, people suffered from severe frostbite. Faces became covered in suppurating ulcers, hands and feet swelled. But there was no release from work. Many looked like skeletons. In the worst cases, a man could no longer work and could hardly make it to the urine pail. Some were placed in the Medical Section, but to get there you had to give a bribe, so the majority were placed in the "dead men's barracks." There they stayed until one morning the orderly discovered their corpses. Those who had good friends to help them lived longer, but even they steadily faded away. Already a quarter of Trofimov's transit group had gone that way.

Vaskov turned to the convict who found the dead man.

"Don't tell no one for a couple days. I'll share his ration with you."

"Surely, Ivan Yefimych."

Trofimov, Bondarenko and Timoshkin exchanged glances. Barracks orderlies often concealed prisoners' deaths from the authorities in order to receive the dead man's ration for a while.

Sometimes they ate the bread themselves, and sometimes they sold it for tobacco or other things. Vaskov usually shared his food with Bondarenko, whom he kept as his bosom friend. Bondarenko had the reputation of being a tough guy with whom it was risky to quarrel. As a former scout with the partisans, he knew more than a dozen ways to kill a man. Of course he could never have maintained his strength for long on an ordinary prisoner's ration. But as an orderly, Vaskov used his rations and parcels to keep this tough guy afloat. This way Bondarenko had kept his strength up for two years. Others who had no right to receive parcels could only envy him. You weren't supposed to ask a fellow prisoner to share his food. Everybody cared only about himself and about other potentially useful people.

"Picking up the spoils, Ivan?" Timoshkin grinned.

"Well, he doesn't need it no more, does he?"

"No, he doesn't," Trofimov replied, "And it looks like plenty of us will soon be following him. Me, for instance. Hell knows how long I'll manage to stay on my feet. Just take a look at them."

Trofimov dragged his boots off, gasping at the pain. His feet and calves were swollen and covered in blisters.

"Looks real bad," Vaskov said. "Go to the medico and try to get off work for a couple of weeks. Maybe he'll put you on LPW, light physical work."

"Stop your fairy tales, Yefimych," Bondarenko scoffed. "The guy can't receive parcels. How can he bribe his way in? Without a gift, the doc won't even look at him."

"He can give some treatment though," Vaskov retorted.

"Only to get bad again in a month," Timoshkin commented.

"Donna you know what the thieves say? 'You die today, me tomorrow.' If the captain gets his legs treated, he'll walk for another month, instead of hobbling. And whatever happens after that, you ain't gotta care about it."

"What about tomorrow?" asked Goldberg.

"The same thing," Bondarenko said. "And the day after. Eventually you win another year or two of life. That's good enough, ain't it?"

"You mean to say we're all going to die here?" Goldberg wondered.

"Surprised?" Bondarenko shrugged his shoulders.

"Somewhat," responded Goldberg. "Can no one survive his term of sentence?"

"The trusties can," Bondarenko said. "They sit in their fuckin' offices and get three times our ration. You can survive on that."

"How many trusties are there?" Trofimov inquired.

"A good number," said Vaskov. "Clerks who assign the quotas, foremen, barracks orderlies, messengers, storekeepers, hospital and canteen workers. Then there's mechanics, chauffeurs, carpenters—around five hundred men, one fifth of the camp population."

"That's a lot," Trofimov said. "But still four-fifths are on general work. Do they all die?"

"No," said Vaskov. "Those on agricultural work have a good chance. There you can fill your belly with fresh vegetables—if you aren't caught. They'd all survive but for their tongues."

"Their tongues?" Goldberg echoed.

"Just that," Vaskov explained. "If they didn't discuss the camp commandant, or the nation's leaders or HIMSELF. Some are so eager to speak out that they don't care who listens, but camp is camp. There are stool pigeons everywhere. If you're assigned to mining or logging or road building or digging peat in the marshes, then ..." Vaskov sighed.

"Then you're doomed," Trofimov said.

"Yes," Vaskov nodded. "Unless you manage to get to a warmer place soon enough. If you've got gifts to offer, you can survive. Just grease the palm of the quota guys. Look at me. I used to be in the mines. I gave the guy who assigns the work a fur coat that my wife sent me. Otherwise you slave until you drop and they send you to the weaklings' brigade. The rations there are low, but the work's light. You can survive for a few more years. Especially if you get parcels."

"But afterwards you die anyway?" asked Goldberg.

"Of course. Like in the song 'There's no way back from Kolyma.' "

"Fourth barracks! Line up outside in three columns!" The roar of a camp guard burst on their ears like thunder from hell.

"Holy shit. Exactly what I feared." Bondarenko said in a half whisper.

"Shut your traps. You wanna me break my rod over your fuckin' backs?" the screw bawled.

"Filthy bloodsuckers," muttered Bondarenko as they moved towards the staff building. The screws goaded them with their submachine gun butts. The tall, well-built Senior Lieutenant Belyayev emerged in front of the column, followed by a dozen foremen.

"Attention!" Belyayev yelled. "In honour of the eleventh anniversary of Comrade Stalin's Constitution, the labour collective of our Fifth compound of the Administration of Seimchan Camps has volunteered to carry out a day of Sunday work, dedicated to the anniversary."

"Volunteered? What fucking crap." Whispers ran around the lines of prisoners.

"Who the hell is displeased?" yelled Belyayev. "Step forward." The column fell silent. No one moved. "Frightened? You scum! Who are you to go against the Party and the Government? And against Comrade Stalin himself? Next time you'll all be charged with sabotage."

The crowd split up into brigades, the foremen received their directions from the work assigners, and Gusev joined his men.

"Go to storage and get shovels and crowbars. We're going to clear the road. And hurry up."

The brigade members walked away, cursing under their breath. A large crowd gathered at the storage depot. Men pushed and jostled one another, trying to get the best tools. Elbowing his way forward, Trofimov managed to grab a spade and a crowbar. He looked at his pals and grinned.

"Well, here we are, guys, all set for another Sunday's work in the name of the glorious Stalin Constitution, the most progressive constitution in the world.

"How d'you feel, Captain?" asked Bondarenko. "Do your feet ache?"

"Like shit! At least I can walk. For how long though?"

"Don't worry. At least the evening's gonna be ours. Sunday work ends by about eight. After that, try the Medical Section. But hurry. Try and get in the first dozen. The doc might release you without a bribe."

At that moment a sergeant emerged in front of them.

"Who's Trofimov?"

"Me, Alexander Ivanovich, articles 58/1b, 58/6 and 58/11: twenty-five years."

"And Bondarenko?"

"Mikhail Savelyevich, 58/2, 58/4 and 58/10: twenty-five years."

"Follow me."

"Should we take our tools?" asked Trofimov.

"No, leave them here. Quick."

Trofimov and Bondarenko dropped their shovels and crowbars and followed the sergeant.

"To the Black Hole?" inquired Bondarenko.

"You guessed right," grinned the sergeant. "But not the Ice Hole at least."

4

Inside the penal isolator Trofimov and Bondarenko were separated. For Trofimov it was a disappointment. He was curious why he had again been sent to the Black Hole, although not entirely surprised. By now he was used to the fact that common notions of reason, fair play and retribution for a real offence meant nothing in the camp. Here he could be dumped in the Black Hole for anything—some camp officer disliked the look on his face, or he kept certain friends, or whatever. In fact he was not particularly distressed at having to return to the Black Hole. It was a release from that goddamned Sunday work and, if he were lucky, even from the following day's labour. By now he was accustomed to the constant cold, and to sitting and sleeping without any mattress on a hard rough surface. His feet hurt worst of all when he worked. He had hoped to enjoy his friend Bondarenko's company for a while, but those in high places had evidently figured that one out.

Trofimov had got to know Bondarenko back in the summer of 1944 in the woods and marshes of Byelorussia. The Red Army was by then steadily pushing back the German forces further to the west. Senior Lieutenant Trofimov and his company fought on a section of the front near Bobruysk. Their task was to penetrate the frontline and strike the Germans from the rear.

They crossed the front successfully, losing only two men, and made their way well into the wild country behind the German lines. Finding an approach to the German defences from the rear, however, proved extremely difficult. Intelligence data on enemy troop concentrations was outdated; evidently the German command had relocated them quite recently. Trofimov sent out a group of scouts, who captured a few locals working in the Polizei. These men said the Germans had taken off during the night, but had no idea where to. Uncertain how he was going to carry out his orders, Trofimov made a stop for the night in the woods and sent out another reconnaissance group. In the middle of the night he was wakened by a noisy commotion. Emerging from his tent, he saw his scouts had captured a medium-sized stocky man with wheat-blond hair, moustache and a short beard. The man cursed and demanded to see their commander.

"Who is this?" Trofimov demanded.

"We don't know, comrade Senior Lieutenant," replied the group leader. "We caught him on the way back, hiding in the bushes. He has a knife and a pistol. He broke Streltsov's jaw and almost ripped Kolka's guts out."

"Why the hell did you grab me from behind, you wise shitheads? How the fuck could I know you weren't Nazis or Polizei?" The captive concluded with another volley of curses.

Trofimov surveyed the prisoner and realized that he did not look like Polizei. He had no uniform, and the Polizei would hardly be crawling around in the bushes. Maybe he's a partisan, thought Trofimov, or a vagrant.

"Calm down, man," he said. "Sit down and tell me who you are."

"At last a normal person," the man said. "Tell 'em to untie my hands."

The man turned out to be Mikhail Bondarenko, a scout from Stavrov's partisan unit, which was active in the neighbouring woods. On his own reconnaissance trip, Bondarenko had found out where the German reserve troops were recently relocated. Trofimov was so happy that he hugged him and discussed the situation with him. Bondarenko suggested he could recruit his unit to help Trofimov in a combined attack on the Germans. By evening he returned with his commander, Stavrov, and the whole unit. Trofimov's company and Stavrov's partisans carried out the attack. The operation was a great success.

After that Trofimov and Bondarenko went their separate ways and never saw one another until the day when Trofimov arrived at the Fifth Compound in the same transit group as Goldberg and Timoshkin.

The punishment cell was similar to the one where he had been confined before. It had the same rime-covered wooden walls and no stove. The cell was crammed with prisoners. With difficulty Trofimov found a place sitting next to a thin old man with a half-bald head and a wrinkled frostbitten face. Maybe the man merely looked old. His eyes were sharp, and he had the vigour and strength to maintain his place in the crowd. Trofimov thought he had seen the man before, but could not recollect when or where. The old man noticed Trofimov's glance.

"May I introduce myself, young man?" The old man broke the silence. His voice was that of an educated person.

"Sure," Trofimov replied indifferently. "It seems to me I've seen you somewhere before."

"You're right, sir," the old man said. "I'm a tool carrier in Gusev's work team. You're from his brigade too."

"Yes, I am."

"First of all, I want to thank you," said the old man.

"What for? Sure you aren't mistaking me for someone else?"

"Not at all. I remember you. A month ago you stood up for my very good friend, God rest his soul. The old man fell and the screws beat him. You intervened on his behalf and as a reward you got two weeks in the Black Hole. That man was my old cellmate from Lefortovo jail in Moscow."

"I see," Trofimov smiled. "But you praise me too much. All I did was ask them to let me and a pal bring him back to the compound. That bastard Makarov finished him off. I never tried to shield him with my own chest."

"Nevertheless," the old man insisted, "what you did was an act of heroism. You know the two laws of the camp: 'You die today, and me tomorrow,' and the second one, pardon the language, 'If they don't fuck you, don't lie down and ask for it.' Those are the rules, and only an idiot or a hero takes the part of another person. But that's precisely what you did, and quite recklessly too." The old man lowered his voice. "You're rather a reckless guy altogether. Just now, for instance, talking to me, a complete stranger, you called Lieutenant Makarov a bastard. I heard you before talking like that about camp bosses. Don't you know there are stool pigeons in the camp? The Soviet criminal code has special articles about 'insulting Soviet officials.' "

Trofimov wondered about the old guy who hadn't even told him his name but lectured him about camp behaviour. Is he to be trusted? "Well," he sighed, "I don't care any more."

"You mean you don't care about living any more?"

"Why should I? I'll soon follow your friend. I'll fall down and some screw will finish me off. If they shoot me now for anti-Soviet propaganda, that'll be a favour. I'm not afraid of death. I've no future in this place, other than to kick the bucket. Every day brings nothing but suffering. What have I got to fear now?"

"Well," replied the old man, "that might be a reasonable sentiment, if the worst thing you had to fear was a shot in the back of your head."

"You mean, they could rip my guts out first?"

"Yes, in a manner of speaking. They could keep you in the Black Hole for a month with nothing but a tiny punishment ration. Or they could send you to Orotukan and stick you in a special tent jammed with people, with no heating and the frozen ground for a floor. They keep them there till they snuff it, then they just stick the corpses outside like a pile of wood."

"Hell," exclaimed Trofimov. "It's like Auschwitz all over again."

"Exactly. There was a Jew here from Lvov. He survived the concentration camp at Treblinka. After the war he was swept up in the purges in West Ukraine and found himself here. He said he saw no difference. There they used the gas chamber; here they have other methods."

Trofimov shivered. All this was beyond his imagination, even after being interrogated and tortured in that dungeon. Somehow he had assumed that death by shooting was the worst thing to fear. But it turned out there were many far more appalling things.

What, you bastard? Not afraid of death? Then try a load of this.

The old man looked Trofimov in the eye. "It looks like I've upset you. Maybe I can bolster your spirits with something more positive."

He thrust his dingy brown hand inside his pea jacket and produced a small paper package. He opened it with a neat twist of the finger and thumb. It was a packet of twist, black shag tobacco, in short supply in the camps. Trofimov had last smoked almost a month ago. This was the kind of small miracle that every convict craved. Trofimov often saw prisoners begging for a couple of drags on a home rolled cigar and here was a whole pack of the stuff.

"How'd you get it past the screws?"

"Let that be my little secret. Some time maybe I'll tell you. For now, help yourself to a cig. You're welcome."

Trofimov took the cigar, which the old man lit for him, and inhaled deeply. Blissful euphoria swept his hunger-crazed senses. It didn't matter whether the old man was a friend and wellwisher or just another stool pigeon. At that moment he was a man who gave him a new taste of life.

"Thank you," he smiled. "I think it's high time we were introduced. I need to know the person I have to thank."

"My pleasure, sir. I'm Vladimir Semyonovich Ganin, a surgeon. That is, a former surgeon, you understand." The old man proffered his hand.

"Alexander Trofimov. Infantry captain."

"Your patronymic?"

"Ivanovich."

From that moment the long hours of detention in the Black Hole no longer dragged. Trofimov and Ganin felt no inhibitions about telling their stories to one another. Ganin was of old intelligentsia stock, one of the so-called "former people." He graduated from the St. Petersburg Imperial Medical College in 1901 and worked as a specialist in lung diseases in one of the hospitals of the former capital. At the outbreak of World War I he was drafted into the army and served as a field surgeon.

Then came 1917, with all its calamities. Under threat of lynching by the revolutionary soldiery, Ganin fled to the Cossack region of the Don. There he joined Denikin's Volunteer Army, again as a physician, and took part in all the White campaigns in the south. In the end he fled from the Crimea along with other troops of the

White Army. Long years of exile followed. In the early 1920s the Soviet government allowed his wife and children out of Russia to join him. At first they lived in poverty, but he obtained work as a physician in a Paris hospital and later moved to Vienna. Life seemed to return to normal.

In Vienna he was caught up in the Nazi occupation and the new war. It did not greatly alter his position. He was not a Jew or a communist, not even a socialist, and physicians became even more valuable during the war. So he maintained his position in the hospital. As a Russian patriot, Ganin had no sympathy for the Nazis and felt frustrated that he could do so little against Russia's enemies. Eventually he made contact with a few resistance fighters. From time to time he helped by hiding concentration camp escapees and other outlaws in the hospital, and he allowed his flat to be used as a secret meeting place by a resistance group. But war was war, and that meant he had to treat wounded German soldiers. Not only could he not avoid that duty, but his medical ethics required that he treat all patients equally, regardless of who they were.

Then the Soviet liberation troops arrived, bringing a mood of patriotic enthusiasm that seemed to unite the Soviet soldiers and local Russian émigrés. The Soviet authorities made a public appeal to Russians living in Austria to return to their homeland. Many émigrés were persuaded, including Ganin. He applied to the Soviet commandant's office to be repatriated. The commandant was extremely polite and friendly, expressing genuine good feelings towards him, praising his collaboration with the resistance, and promising a warm welcome in Russia.

About a month later, Ganin was arrested in his flat at night. Then came a spell in the dungeons of the local SMERSH, followed by a cell in Moscow's Lubyanka prison, with beatings, charges of Nazi collaboration, sentence by a Special Board, transfer under armed guard, and finally this place, the Fifth Compound of the Seimchan camps in Kolyma.

Trofimov was impressed by Ganin's story. From his months on the Elbe he clearly remembered Soviet propaganda regarding former White émigrés. "The Motherland needs you and welcomes you. Let bygones be bygones." Initially Trofimov somewhat doubted the fairness of this policy. After all, there were so many former White officers who fought against the Red Army in the Civil

War, and against his own father. In all the books and films about the Civil War, Soviet heroes like Chapayev swore eternal hatred of the class enemy. But Trofimov was too young to challenge official attitudes. After all, times had changed. National unity was the main priority. Besides, many of those former enemies had participated in the anti-Nazi resistance. So it was only natural to reward them and allow them to return. Who was Captain Alexander Trofimov to question the decisions of Stalin, their Great Leader? Throughout the war he had led his soldiers into attack with the rallying call of "For Stalin and the Motherland!" If Stalin chose to approach these White émigrés, he evidently knew best. Probably the time had come for all Russians to put former hostilities behind them and unite behind the national leadership for the general good of their country. This was simply a manifestation of their Leader's supreme wisdom, as when he allied himself with capitalist Britain and America.

Even then, however, there were persistent rumours that spoiled the picture. There was talk of former Soviet prisoners of war being repatriated only to be sent off to the camps. Caught up in the euphoria of victory, however, Trofimov and his comrades-in-arms were not prepared to believe it. For them, the time had come to start a new life and to right all earlier wrongs.

This proved to be another deception. The former White émigrés joined the general population of the labour camps, together with yesterday's victors like Trofimov himself. The old system of party committees, secret police, collective farms and labour camps stayed in place. Those who might have questioned it, and even tried to resist, were in the camps.

"Dare I ask you for another cig?" Trofimov enquired next morning.

"My pleasure, Alexander Ivanovich." Ganin handed Trofimov another shag cigar.

"I'm too impudent, Vladimir Semyonovich," Trofimov said. "But I've hardly smoked at all this last month, and I'm not going to live long anyway."

"That's something I wanted to talk to you about." Ganin turned to face him. "You look in a really bad way. Pardon my frankness, but I'm a physician. You've got scurvy, you have problems with your lungs, and your hands look almost gangrenous."

Trofimov glanced at his purplish frostbitten hands. They ached permanently. Recently he had had them dressed with dirty bandages, but a screw at the camp entrance ripped them off, supposedly to ensure he was not hiding anything. A month ago he might have protested, but now it made little difference. If gangrene set in he might get released from general work. As for how he would survive without hands, that thought hardly concerned him. He would probably die before that happened.

Ganin continued, "Another month in the mines will definitely finish you off."

"I know."

"I could help you, or at least try to."

"Really?" In the camps hardly anyone ever helped anybody else, except for profit. "Because of that old guy I stood up for? Who was he, by the way?"

"Gilman was his name." Ganin said. "He was an engineer from St. Petersburg, an extremely nice, warm-hearted man. Unlike me, he stayed on in Russia after the Revolution, and he survived the Civil War and even the terror of 1937. But he fell victim to the post-war purges, and ended up here. God rest his soul. No one can help him, but I can try and do something for you. Till recently I was in charge of the camp hospital. My former assistant has replaced me, but he still needs my help. He's not all-powerful, and there's a strict limit on the number of patients in the hospital. The rules don't allow scurvy patients to be hospitalised."

Trofimov recalled some cases he had known. Mostly the patients dozed on their barracks bunks and got up only for basic necessities. They did not have to work, but they got no treatment either. They were left to die. They could not even walk to the canteen, and the barracks orderlies brought them food.

"But," Ganin continued, "the doctor never refuses me. I can ask him to take care of you. But of course, before we approach him," Ganin emphasized, "you must have a gift to offer him. Nothing out of the ordinary—a sweater, or some boots. Not camp boots, of course."

"In that case there's no hope for me," Trofimov sighed. "I'm banned from getting parcels."

"Well, that's a problem you'll have to resolve on your own, Alexander Ivanovich." The old man's voice was stern. "I don't get parcels either. I'll talk to the doctor, and hopefully he'll help you. But try and find a gift for Sergey."

5

"So he promised to help you in approaching the doc?" inquired Bondarenko.

"Sounds like it," Trofimov said. "I've no idea whether I can trust him."

"You're right, it's suspicious that he approached you. Stooges in search of a victim do that. All that fancy tale 'bout his past, serving in the White Guard."

"C'mon, Mikhail," Goldberg interrupted. "You sound like you can't trust a single person here. It's impossible to suspect everyone."

"Why everyone? You can trust me and Zakharych. We're old comrades. As for the rest of the population, none of 'em would bother helping a stranger. As they say, 'Donna shove your nose in somebody else's mess tin!' The old guy definitely wants somethin' from the captain. Unless he's a stooge, 'f course."

"So," Trofimov asked, "what am I to do? Rely on him? Or just tell him to shake off?"

"No, for Christ's sake," replied Bondarenko. "He may be helpful, and what he wants from you may be quite feasible. It's your only way of getting help. But you ain't gotta open up to him completely. I'll keep an eye on him. If he is a stooge, I'll sniff him out."

The barracks door banged open, and the guard yelled, "Fourth barracks! Out for roll call!"

The screw hustled them along. His eyes fell on one of the "goners" lying on his bunk.

"Another fuckin' corpse," the screw growled.

The prisoners approached the small square in front of the staff building and drew up in a column several ranks deep. They shivered in the biting wind as the officers began the roll call.

"Ananyev."

"Sergey Vassilyevich, 58/1b, fifteen years."

"Bondarenko."

"Mikhail Savelyevich, 58/1a, 58/2, 58/4, twenty-five years."

"Zybkov."

The column remained silent.

"Zybkov! Where the fuck is he?" inquired the sergeant.

"Dead, citizen Chief," replied Vaskov.

"Really? Petrov, go and check."

A screw made his way over to the Fourth barracks, followed by Vaskov.

Hopefully, there'll be no other search, thought Trofimov.

Evening roll calls were frequently accompanied by double searches: one group of screws searched under the prisoners' pea jackets while another group searched the bunks inside the barracks. They looked for banned items, especially homemade knives and other potential weapons. Trofimov had nothing to hide, but the prospect of unbuttoning in the frost was extremely unpleasant. Soon the roll call ended, and the prisoners sighed with relief as they looked forward to the warmth of the barracks stove.

Suddenly Senior Lieutenant Belyayev stepped up in front of them. A tall, well-built blond with a handsome Russian face, Belyayev was in charge of internal order in the camp.

"Attention. All prisoners, stay where you are."

Whispering curses, they stared at Belyayev. They were exhausted, they showed no interest in what the lieutenant had to tell them. "Listen to the following announcement from the Seimchan Camp Administration." Belyayev continued. "The Judicial Board of the Administration of the Seimchan camps having considered the cases of the following inmates of the Fifth Camp Compound:

Malinin, Pyotr Vassilyevich: Article 58/3, 58/4: twenty years;

Yegorov, Nikolay Dmitrievich: Article 58/6, 58/10: fifteen years;

Kamyshov, Alexander Petrovich: Article 58/1a, 58/10: twenty-five years;

Matveyev, Andrey Nikitich: Article 58/1a, 58/3, 58/10: twenty years;

Epstein, Mikhail Iosifovich: Article 58/3, 58/10: fifteen years; announces that the above-mentioned convicts have been found guilty of sabotage in the form of systematically disrupting fulfillment of the production plan, and of planning to escape. They are sentenced to the Supreme Penalty, that is, execution. The sentence has been carried out.

"This information concerns all of you." The lieutenant's voice suddenly rose. "All of you! The Soviet people will not tolerate enemies of Soviet society. You have all committed serious crimes against our country. The Soviet people, through their courts, have generously given you an opportunity to expiate your crimes. Those who continue in malicious defiance of their duties ..." Belyayev stared at the column with a menacing look, as if checking the attention of his audience. For a moment his eyes rested on Trofimov. "That's all." Belyayev's voice quietened again, and a sigh rose from the crowd.

"What news. Just to make sure we sleep well. Poor bastards." Timoshkin sighed when they were back in the barracks again.

"Perhaps not so poor," replied Vaskov. "Their torments are over."

"In that case, God bless their souls and forgive all their sins for the suffering they endured." Timoshkin crossed himself.

"I didn't get what they were executed for," said Goldberg. "He said sabotage and something about an escape attempt."

"Are you really asking 'bout the case, Yakov?" Bondarenko said. "The case is that they needed a few culprits to keep the rest of us in constant fear, so they picked up those guys for a show trial. I'm sure all those poor guys did was to fail to meet their production quota. And who can do that? No one. We could all be charged with sabotage."

"Then they should shoot us all," exclaimed Trofimov. "Who I wonder will dig their gold and cut their logs for them then?"

"That's just the point," Bondarenko replied. "They ain't gonna shoot us all, just a small bunch, so the rest of us quiver in fear. And it helps them to recruit stooges."

"How?" asked Trofimov.

"C'mon, Captain," said Bondarenko. "How the hell did you command a battalion, if you don't understand such things? Take our barracks. Most of the guys are weaklings, and a weakling trembles with fear. He feels he could be whacked at any moment.

What does such a person make of tonight's announcement? He hears that a few guys got shot for not making their quota, while he himself manages barely a third of it. He could be the next one up on a charge. That's what he thinks as he climbs into his bunk tonight. But tomorrow the Godfather offers him a chance to cooperate, and there he is, a stool pigeon, on the hook for all time, trying to save his skin."

"What about the supposed escape attempt?" Trofimov asked. "Is that true, or just another bluff?"

"Who knows?" Vaskov shrugged. "One of them might have told the others that he dreamed of escaping, and they all agreed and said they did too. Some stooge happened to overhear. Or they were provoked and set up to make an escape attempt."

"What for?" Goldberg asked.

"'Cos each time an officer uncovers or prevents an escape attempt, it's recorded to his credit in his career file. Every camp officer has one of those files."

That night Trofimov could not sleep. He thought about the five men whose fate had been announced at the roll call. Had they really tried to escape, or was it a trumped-up charge to boost Godfather's career. What if the guys really were ready to risk their lives to flee this hell? Trying to escape sounded crazy, but was hoping to survive in the camp less crazy? Wasn't it better to perish fighting your miserable fate than to succumb to it, fading away painfully in humiliation?

The idea of escape consumed Trofimov. At first glance, it looked impossible. The screws guarded your every move. They were ready to finish you off with a submachine burst for a single step out of line. But wasn't it a battle of wits? Trofimov was an experienced combat officer. He had more military experience than all the camp officers put together. He knew how to outsmart an enemy. Was there a way to divert the screws' attention then break out of the compound and the heavily guarded zone around it? If so, he and his companions would be in the vast Siberian wilderness: endless hills and mountains, heavily wooded valleys, rivers, swamps. Such lands could shelter scores of people from any pursuit.

What about the dogs? There were ways to neutralize them—rain, snowfall, whatever. One could not do it alone, but Bondarenko and Timoshkin and probably Goldberg would be the best imaginable companions, all of them veterans who knew how to fight and to survive.

But one would have to be physically fit, and he, Alexander Trofimov, was a ruin, physically and psychologically. As time passed, his condition would worsen. However tempting, escape was not for him. The very thought of leaving the warmth of the barracks for the icy winter woodlands made his body shiver. Even if he managed to escape, what kind of clothes did he have to survive the Arctic winter with fifty degrees of frost? Not in a pea jacket with minimal padding. But how could a con get a good winter coat? Nohow. Escape was anything but realistic. Forget it.

The next evening a staff orderly appeared.

"Is Trofimov here?"

"Yes, that's me," Trofimov answered.

"Sergey Petrovich is waiting for you."

"Who's that?"

"C'mon," grinned Vaskov. "Ain't you know the doc's name yet?"

"Oh, thanks. Let's go." With an effort Trofimov levered himself up off the bunk and followed the orderly out into the cold wind. He felt giddy and twice nearly fell, so the orderly had to help him.

"You lucky man." The messenger smiled. "If the doc hadn't singled you out, you'd probably have kicked the bucket in a week or two."

"It can still happen, old man," Trofimov wheezed. "I haven't any gift to offer him."

"Really? That's too bad. In that case I'm not sure he'll talk to you. It's the law around here: you pay for services rendered. He can't take you on just like that. Half the inmates are in your condition."

The Medical Section was a solid log building, the entrance of which was lit by an electric lamp shining on a red cross. As they entered, they found themselves in a long corridor with several doors. A large crowd of prisoners sat on the floor waiting their turn.

"Come along, we needn't wait," said Trofimov's companion, and led him in at one of the doors to the sound of loud curses from the men in the lineup. A young doctor sat at a desk.

"Here we are, Sergey Petrovich. This is Trofimov," said the messenger.

"Fine," smiled the doctor. "You can go, Sidorov. Trofimov, have a seat." He motioned toward the bench on the opposite side of the desk.

Trofimov sat down, full of pleasure at the chance to relax his exhausted body.

"So it's you that Vladimir Semyonovich spoke about." The doctor smiled. "He asked me to take care of you. I owe him a lot. Can you strip down for me?"

Trofimov stripped off everything but his underpants and approached the doctor. The doctor examined him. At length he gave a sigh.

"Well, Trofimov, your condition is far from good. You have dystrophy, aggravated by scurvy and pneumonia. I can't even take you in right now. The hospital's overcrowded, and we've a long waiting list."

It was something Trofimov could have foreseen. He had no hope of being hospitalized.

"What was your occupation before you were arrested?" the doctor inquired.

"I was in the army, an infantry captain," Trofimov answered.

"What did you do before the war?"

"I finished my first year at an automobile construction college in Moscow."

"And do you have any profession besides that?"

"Well, after high school I worked for half a year as a truck driver."

"But maybe you have some other hobby?" the doctor's face clearly showed his disappointment.

"Yes, doctor. I was in a radio engineering group at school and also in college."

"Oh, excellent." The doctor's face lit up in a bright smile. "Are you good at that sort of thing?"

"I guess so." Trofimov slowly grasped what the doctor was hinting at.

"Could you fix my radio receiver? It's an old thing and it hasn't worked for almost a year."

So the greedy bastard wants me to work for him first. His first inclination was to explode and curse the doctor, but his common sense pulled him up sharp: he couldn't afford to throw away this one chance of survival.

"Can't you find a specialist to repair it, doc?" Trofimov faked a smile.

"No, the fitters work only for the authorities. So I'm asking you: could you do me this favour? I'll provide you with all the materials."

"I think I can do it. Can you give me at least one day's leave, say Saturday?"

"Sure," the doctor smiled. "Now take this." The doctor handed him a bottle of cod-liver oil. "One spoon after each meal. And this …" He produced a bottle containing a solution. "This is for your ulcers and boils."

"Thanks," Trofimov responded.

Next morning, as they sat on their bunks together with Vaskov, the barracks orderly, Bondarenko asked about his visit to the doctor. "So, Captain, he told you to revive his corpse of a radio set first?"

"That's right. And he said he'd take me in whenever there's a free bed. Which means when I finish his work."

"What a bastard." Timoshkin blazed with indignation. "Can't he see you're only half alive? Now you've gotta work extra hours after your day down the mine?"

"Well," Trofimov said, "he promised me a day's leave on Saturday, so I work for him both Saturday and Sunday. What could I do?"

"It's a good deal," Vaskov said, "and the doc's quite generous. He figured this guy had nothing to offer as a gift, so he asked for a small service instead, and even gave him a day off. And you, old chap," he turned to Timoshkin, "cut the bullshit. You're in a labour camp, not back in your native village."

"Exactly," Bondarenko put in. "And, Captain, if you collapse before you finish his radio, he'll take you in anyway and let you finish the job later, when you get better. Alas, I can't help you. I'm a simple village guy."

"I could help Sasha," Goldberg intervened. "I know quite a bit about radios."

"Thanks, Yakov. You're a good friend."

"How could I be anything else after you saved me from those thieves in Vanino jail?"

"Fourth barracks! Time for breakfast! Line up!"

6

The cell in Vanino transit jail was packed. The lucky ones got a place on the three-storey bunks. The not-so-lucky ones stood in the narrow gangway between the bunks. The totally unlucky remainder sat under the lower row of bunks on the damp, dirty floor.

Trofimov was among those who stood by the bunks. He and Timoshkin, his pal from the same cattle car that brought them to the transit camp, had one place on the bunk between the two of them, so that while one enjoyed sleeping in a sitting position, the other stood alongside him. It was Timoshkin's turn to sleep, so Trofimov stood and observed the thieves on the upper bunks playing cards. He and Timoshkin had been there for two weeks, waiting to be transported to Magadan, capital of the "land of Kolyma." They were full of anxiety. They had heard a lot already about Kolyma, from where, according to the song, there was no return. They had also heard that convicts were forced to fulfill impossibly high production quotas, working in mines and at logging sites. Those who failed to cope received a "penal" half-ration of food and quickly died.

Trofimov and Timoshkin became friends. They were fellow war veterans, and it hardly mattered that Timoshkin had been just a private, while Trofimov was captain of a battalion. They were common prisoners, and Trofimov's epaulettes had been torn off by the SMERSH back in Latvia. Although Timoshkin showed deference, addressing his mate as "Captain," it was just habit. They were both from the Urals, Trofimov from a small industrial town, Timoshkin from a village about a hundred and fifty kilometres away. Although Timoshkin was imprisoned for having been in German captivity, while Trofimov had served with the troops that took Berlin and reached the River Elbe, both men's sentences included charges of treason.

Feeling drowsy and barely able to keep his eyes open, Trofimov noticed a ray of sun struggling through the small dusty window beneath the ceiling. It looked as if morning had come, and with it his turn to sleep sitting on the bunk.

"Hey, Timoshkin," Trofimov called.

Timoshkin continued snoring. Trofimov called him once more, with no result. Only when he shook him did his friend open his eyes.

"That you, Captain? Is it already time?"

"Yeah. Come on, sleepyhead," Trofimov barked. "It's morning. High time I got some sleep."

"Really?" Timoshkin yawned. "Shit. I feel like I slept just a quarter of an hour. Got anythin' to smoke, Captain? I can't move 'nless I've got some smoke in my lungs."

"Where the hell would I get tobacco?" Trofimov shrugged. "Don't you remember, we finished my twist yesterday?"

"Too bad," Timoshkin complained. "Even on the Leningrad front, and in spite of the blockade, we had tobacco. The food, I grant you, was poor, but we always had somethin' to smoke."

"That's because we were soldiers of the glorious Red Army, Stalin's eagles," their neighbour on the bunk interrupted. "We had bread, canned pork, and plenty of tobacco because otherwise the Nazis would've taken Moscow and the Volga and the Urals and the whole of Mother Russia. They'd have strung the Great Leader up by his balls. But now? We're prisoners, camp fodder, garbage and manure for Stalin's great projects. We're enemies of the people, 'subject to liquidation.' Don't you understand that, man?"

"Right," Trofimov agreed. "So anyway, Zakharych, get up and let your comrade-in-arms have a snooze."

Trofimov noticed Andreyev, their neighbour on the right, lighting a home-rolled cigar.

"Andreyev," he called, "leave the butt, just a tab-end, for this glorious defender of heroic Leningrad."

"Shit. Again?" Andreyev cursed. "Well … Let me smoke my half first."

"Here's your saviour, Timoshkin," Trofimov grinned as his friend leaped down from the bunk to let him take his place. "I'll have a couple of drags myself."

"No problem, Captain," Timoshkin answered, watching Andreyev smoke. Trofimov also waited patiently for him to finish, and at the same time took in what was happening around them. On the top bunks thieves lay stripped to the waist, their bellies covered in garish tattoos. They had been playing cards since the previous morning, but now there was some disturbance among them: two of them had nothing more to bid with and watched their neighbours for a decent item of clothing to seize. Trofimov had seen lots of professional thieves during the last few months, and he knew their way of randomly extorting anything of value from their "civilian" neighbours: a good jacket, a decent pair of shoes or glasses, sometimes even a gold tooth. Together with Timoshkin and a few other war veterans, he had been involved in the occasional punch-up with them. Just then he noticed one of the thieves catch sight of a dark-haired man wearing a jacket of fairly good quality.

"Hey Yid! Gimme your jacket."

"What's that?" The man turned his head.

"You fuckin' deaf? Peel that jacket off."

"Why?"

"'Cos I'm telling you, you filthy Yiddish asshole," the thief yelled. "Take off your fuckin' lapserdak or I'll cut your guts out and hang 'em on the bunk."

Trofimov watched the scene. His moral principles required that he intervene, but the laws of the Gulag maintained that in order to survive, you never got involved in other people's quarrels. He had already witnessed at least a dozen such episodes: had he intervened in every case, he would be dead by now. But Trofimov sensed that their new victim was another war veteran. If the man resisted and the thieves tried to kill him, Trofimov decided he would have to intervene.

"Didn't you hear what I said?" the thief asked, getting down from the bunk and grabbing the man by the shoulder.

"Go to hell," the man reacted, throwing the thief's hand off.

A knife appeared in the thief's hand.

"Look, Captain," Timoshkin said. "Our thieves are playing around again."

"C'mon, Zakharych, we've got to help the guy," said Trofimov.

"I don't know. It ain't our—"

Trofimov rushed forward and Timoshkin followed. Without

warning, Trofimov clouted the thief hard, and he crumpled to the muddy floor. He dropped his knife, and Timoshkin picked it up. The other thieves leapt down from their bunks and a brawl broke out. Trofimov, Timoshkin and the man they had defended were joined by a few others wearing dirty soldiers' uniforms.

"Cut it out, you bastards." The order rang through the cell, followed by a gunshot fired into the ceiling. "Cut it out or the next shot goes right into your fuckin' bellies."

The fighters broke off and turned towards the speaker, a tall, fat-faced MGB sergeant.

"Who started this brawl? Speak up, you scum."

"It's them," one of the thieves pointed a finger at Trofimov. "These filthy fascist traitors."

"They started it," Trofimov retorted. "They tried to rob this guy." He pointed at the Jewish prisoner. "They pulled their knives on him."

"That's a fuckin' lie, citizen Guard," another thief bawled, and pointed at Trofimov. "This fascist attacked Skull for no reason. He pulled the knife."

"You lying sleaze," Timoshkin shouted but crumpled as the butt of the sergeant's submachine gun struck him in the stomach.

"Well, now you can have a rest in the Black Hole," the sergeant said with a smirk.

The Black Hole was a small cell with no bunks. There was an inch of muddy water on the floor. It was there that the three newcomers got acquainted. The man Trofimov and Timoshkin had defended was Yakov Goldberg, an engineer from Leningrad. He was a war veteran and a victim of the post-war purge campaign against alleged Zionists, Soviet Jews who had allegedly expressed sympathy for the cause of their Jewish homeland in Palestine. Any Jew was a suitable scapegoat or victim. As the MGB saying went, "Give us the man, and we'll find the charge." Rumour had it that some MGB officer had boasted he could beat Karl Marx himself into confessing that he worked for Bismarck's gendarmerie.

Yakov Goldberg never had any Zionist dreams about Palestine, not that he had any special patriotic feelings towards Soviet Russia either. He had settled down and had a wife and three kids whom he could not afford to put at risk. In any case, there was no legal way of emigrating from the Soviet Union, and he was not one of the tough smart guys who tried to flee abroad illegally. He thus had no choice but to get on with life in Russia, to try and survive and avoid falling victim to the next round of purges. So far the Goldberg family seemed to have managed this. They were not swept up in the terror of 1937 and 1938, and were alive and well. None of their relatives were purged, their children were growing up, and they had their room in a Leningrad communal apartment.

The War was the first major upheaval for the Goldbergs, especially since it became known that if the Germans won, they would wipe out the Jews. Yakov was drafted and sent to the front as an artillery platoon commander and later promoted to command his own battery. He was as good a soldier as most others, and certainly no coward. Throughout the war he clung to the hope that this was a temporary upheaval, and that as soon as the war ended, everything would resume the way it was before. That is, if he did not get killed, or his family did not fall into Nazi hands. The latter was highly improbable, since they were evacuated to Central Asia, where German troops were hardly likely to reach. Nor were the Germans in a position to win the war: there were too many countries united against them. The only calamity for the Goldbergs would be Yakov's death in action. But every soldier's life depended on chance. All he could do was hope for the best. He did hope, and his hope was rewarded: he was not killed but only wounded, and when the war ended, he was still alive in Danzig. He came back home, to the joy of his wife Roza and his children, and no one imagined that any further terrors could strike them.

It all began while the war was still on. The *Red Star* newspaper published a few stories about various cowardly elements among the population. Allegedly, some of them dodged serving on the battle front and remained in the rear, while others emerged as miserable cowards in battle, for which they were executed or sent to a penal battalion. Such stories became common in the press. The strange thing was that the cowards had surnames like Rabinovich, Zilberman or Ratsker. It could of course be mere coincidence, but, again strangely, among the main villains of these stories those with typical Jewish surnames were an absolute majority. Goldberg noticed all this, and deep inside worries gnawed at him. However, at the moment all of this was sufficiently remote for him not to dwell on the issue. After all, he was an honest combat officer. He could never be charged with cowardice, nor was he affected by the increasingly touted saying that "a Jew usually fights in Tashkent." He himself was never in Tashkent, but had fought on the front line, as everyone could see. He could hardly believe that the Soviet government could launch a full-scale official anti-Semitic campaign, if only to avoid comparisons with their Nazi archenemies. But by the last few months of the war, he learned that some Jewish survivors of the German occupation were purged for allegedly intending, or even merely desiring, to emigrate to Palestine. All of this was quite ominous, because every survivor of 1937 knew perfectly well how dangerous such charges could be. They were, of course, impossible to prove, but they were equally impossible to refute.

Goldberg was not a Communist Party member. He was a Jew who occasionally practised his faith. He attended the synagogue on major festivals. If he were caught up in a purge, he would have little chance of proving his innocence. But such cases involved only civilians who had survived Nazi occupation, and at the time nothing happened to him. He ended the war serving in the victorious Soviet Army and returned home safely, but very soon the clouds began gathering. One Jew after another was purged for alleged Zionism. Party meetings condemning Zionism as a tool of foreign imperialism took place here and there. Then Zhdanov's speech against Jewish nationalism was published everywhere in the press, followed by yet another series of local Party meetings. Popular sentiment echoed the official line. Increasingly the Goldbergs heard words like "filthy Yids" from their Russian neighbours or strangers in the streetcar. Rumour spread about Jews literally being thrown off trains. The Goldberg family's Russian neighbours in their apartment barely disguised their disdain and hostility.

Finally the thunderbolt struck. Yakov Goldberg was summoned to a Party meeting at his factory. He was openly accused of Zionism and of wanting to emigrate. One colleague after another made speeches, accusing him of not knowing recent Soviet literature and of reading instead foreign writers like Dickens or Balzac, of never humming Russian folk songs, but arias from operas, of praising the role of the former Allies in the war, and even of sabotaging the factory's production plan. The latter charge might have been pinned on any factory employee, as the official production quotas were so high that suppliers could never satisfy demand, and the factory directors only survived by sending in bogus reports. Toward the end of the meeting, Goldberg was made to answer the charges. He was sufficiently versed in Soviet life to realize that any attempt to refute the charges would complicate his position, and the most he could do was to express repentance as sincerely as he could. He did that, but his fate had evidently been decided at some higher level. He was fired from his job and then, as usual, after a further month of terrifying waiting, he was arrested in the night.

Then followed a spell in the dungeons of the Leningrad MGB's "Big House," where he was beaten and charged with Zionist activities, as well as threatened that his wife would also be charged. After that he was sentenced, and then came the usual routine of deportation in a cattle van, transit jails, and finally Vanino, where he came across Trofimov and Timoshkin.

His woollen jacket, sent by Roza, was the only valuable item he still owned. It could be exchanged for bread or tobacco, or as a bribe for the work assigners. That was why Goldberg refused to hand it over to the thief. The incident could easily have cost him his life, and he was lucky that the other veterans took his side. Now these men became his mates in their life together in the camp.

For the next few nights, Goldberg and Trofimov sat up in the attic of the Medical Section and worked at repairing the doctor's radio.

7

The population of the fourth barracks stood in a column for the morning roll call and shivered in the bitter cold. Out-voicing the gusting wind, the guard sergeants shouted the surnames, and the convicts answered as usual, calling out their names, articles and terms of sentence. Trofimov did not hear his surname called, and responded only when Bondarenko jabbed him slightly in the ribs. He felt very unwell after several sleepless nights of working on the radio set. His frostbitten hands and feet ached, and his head was reeling. Every movement was an effort. He could not imagine how he would manage to work for a whole day.

"Hold on, man," Bondarenko whispered. "You must at least get to the workplace. Donna fall on the way, for Chrissake. Yakimov's escorting us, and he's no better than Makarov."

"I know," Trofimov whispered.

"If you stumble, that's as good as being sloppy, or refusing to work, and it's fatal. Hey. What's going on over there?"

"What the heck are you doing?" A guard's fist slammed into a prisoner's face. "Back to the brigade, you scum."

"I'm sick … I'm very sick, citizen Officer," the man muttered. "I can hardly stand on my feet."

"What's that? What's going on?" Lieutenant Yakimov, commander of the guard escort approached. "Another malingerer?"

"Yes, comrade Lieutenant."

"Try this one for size." Yakimov's face broke into a leering smile. He grabbed the goner by the collar and hit him hard in the face. With his face covered in blood, the man moaned and sagged to his knees. Yakimov gave the guard a sign, and the screw kicked the prisoner in the stomach with his heavy boot. The man fell on the snow.

"Okay," Yakimov smiled. "Fill in the form and say he refused to work, then take him to the Black Hole. We'll open a case against him."

Trofimov and his pals exchanged glances. They well knew what that meant. A refusal to work officially qualified as "sabotage" under article 58/14. The man would stand trial, either here or in Orotukan. He could be executed for sabotage or given a new term.

"Attention, prisoners. Get into line. One step to the right or left counts as an escape attempt. The guards will shoot without warning."

One, two, one, two, one, two … Trofimov had been cleaving the rock for several hours. Each time he raised his pickaxe, he felt sure he would drop it. Surprisingly, he kept on hacking and remained on his feet. He finally dropped the tool just when Bondarenko's voice sounded.

"Watch out, guys, one of them's coming this way."

God Almighty. Once again he had to summon up his nonexistent strength and appear to be working enthusiastically. Trofimov tried to bend, but sensed that at any moment he might fall and never manage to rise. Instead he knelt, lifted his pickaxe and tried to raise himself. Bondarenko tried to help him.

"Faster! Speed it up, you lazy loafers." A sergeant carrying a stick emerged from around a turn in the gallery. His eyes came to rest on Bondarenko, who worked away vigorously with his spade, trying to hide Trofimov from view. If the screw saw Trofimov's sluggish movements, he would beat him, after which he might never get up again. The sergeant could shoot him on the spot. Suddenly the sergeant turned and left. Trofimov raised his pickaxe, but it fell from his grip with a clang, and Trofimov's body collapsed beside it like a felled tree.

"Here he is." Bondarenko's voice came from somewhere far above, as if from the sky.

"How's it going?" The foreman Gusev appeared.

"Trofimov's finished," replied Bondarenko.

"Dead?"

"Not yet, but soon."

Gusev glanced at Trofimov's body, then took his wrist and checked the pulse:

"Still breathing." He turned to Bondarenko. "You, Mikhail and Sinitsyn take him to the watch-post. And don't forget to say that he's not just slacking or those suckers may shoot him."

"Surely." Bondarenko and the other man raised Trofimov's body and moved with him along the gangway toward the cage elevator. Haulers with empty barrows made way for them, enjoying the chance of a few seconds' rest.

"What's that? Another corpse?" A tall blond lieutenant emerged in front of them.

"No, Chief, he's still alive. He's sick," Bondarenko said.

"Sure he isn't shirking?" The lieutenant looked into Trofimov's face. "Certainly looks like a dead duck."

"Can we go, citizen Chief Lieutenant?" Bondarenko asked.

"Yeah. C'mon, get back to it." The lieutenant looked at Bondarenko, then again at Trofimov. "Take your corpse to the third drift on the right and leave it there. He'll soon croak."

Bondarenko shuddered. The drift was a small gallery in an old section of the mine where the gold seam was exhausted, and no one ever went there. Trofimov might languish for two or three days before dying, a common fate for labourers who fell while working.

"No, citizen Lieutenant. The law requires that he be taken to the Medical Section."

"What law? I'm the law here," the lieutenant snapped. "Do as I tell you."

"No, for Chrissake." Bondarenko's voice seemed to come from somewhere far away. "He's a war veteran and an old comrade of mine. I ain't gonna do that."

"Are you contradicting me?" The lieutenant's face showed his astonishment. "I'll shoot you on the spot if you disobey." The lieutenant's hand reached for his holster.

The blood rushed to Bondarenko's head. He knew that this was no empty threat. What was he to do, defy an all-powerful camp officer for … for the sake of a dying man? Yes! Yes, he had to. Trofimov was his pal since the war. But those were different times. Now it was "You die today, and me tomorrow." No, never! He, Mikhail Bondarenko, was not a piece of scum. He was an old partisan and would always stand up for a comrade-in-arms. He had long ago lost all fear of death. He was a Christian—maybe not a very good one, but still—No, he couldn't do something so despicable, no matter what the consequences.

"So," the lieutenant took his pistol. "Do what I tell you, or I shoot you here and now."

"C'mon then, Chief. Show us how you shoot an unarmed man." Bondarenko taunted.

"I'll count three." snapped the lieutenant. "One …"

God bless us! The bastard's really gonna shoot me like a dog, thought Bondarenko. And without any last confession. I've gotta pray. Maybe the Lord can hear me.

"Two." The lieutenant's voice barked right by his ear.

God have mercy, I forget all my prayers. I can't remember a single one. Forgive me, Lord, sinner that I am. Give me your salvation. Let my death for a friend's sake be a redemption for all my sins.

"Three." The lieutenant raised his pistol.

Forgive me, Lord. Bondarenko waited for the next second,

when his life would end. How many times had he looked death in the face? But at those times he could fight for his life. Not now.

"Mikhailov, why the hell d'you want to shoot the guy?" A short, stocky captain emerged in front of them.

"This scum refuses to obey, comrade Captain. I told him to take this corpse to the empty drift, and he …"

"That's not true, Captain," Bondarenko interrupted, with a sudden feeling that this may be his and Trofimov's last chance. "The guy's still alive. Us two were taking him to the Medical Section."

"Hmm, alive you say?" The captain seized Trofimov by the wrist and checked the pulse. "You're right. You want to take him to the doctor?"

"Yes, Chief."

"Who are you?"

"Prisoner Bondarenko, Mikhail Savelyevich, 58/2 and 58/4, twenty-five years."

"You're a tough guy, Bondarenko. You realize that?" The captain smiled. "And you're a good friend. You were a soldier, right?"

"A partisan."

"Even better. I like tough men like you. Take this." The captain produced a nearly full pack of Herzegovina-Flor cigarettes and handed it to Bondarenko.

"Thank you, Chief." Bondarenko put the pack in a pocket of his pea jacket.

"Now take your buddy to the doctor. By the way, what job are you doing?"

"A face worker."

"Do you know carpentry?"

"Sure, citizen Chief. I'm from a village. All the men do carpentry."

"Excellent. You'll work on timber from tomorrow. My name's Poletayev. When you come tomorrow morning, tell the supervisor to send you straight to me."

"Thank you, citizen Chief." This was a lucky day. Except for what happened to poor Trofimov, but that was all too common in the camps.

Bondarenko and Sinitsyn lifted Trofimov and moved toward the cage.

"God bless, Mikhail." Sinitsyn crossed himself. "I thought he was going to shoot us like dogs."

"He could have done," replied Bondarenko. "Even so, I couldn't betray Trofimov. I'd have felt a real bastard if I did."

Sinitsyn asked Bondarenko to give him half a dozen of the cigarettes.

"Sure," Bondarenko smiled. "You deserve it. You stood up for Trofimov with me."

He handed six cigarettes to Sinitsyn, and lit one for himself. It was the only one he could afford to enjoy. He intended to barter the rest with the senior trusty for a good load of twist, so that he and his pals were provided for quite a while.

8

Late on Saturday evening Bondarenko, Timoshkin and Goldberg sat on their bunks and smoked the shag that Bondarenko had bartered in exchange for the Herzegovina-Flor. Tomorrow's day of rest had not been cancelled—not yet at least—and they had enough twist to last them for a while.

"That's one more week over, guys," said Goldberg, inhaling deeply. "If I wasn't so damned hungry, I'd feel almost happy. Maybe our whole term will pass like this, day after day."

"Donna place your hopes on that," Timoshkin said. "There's fifteen years to go."

"Will they keep us here that long?" Goldberg wondered. "I bet there'll be some kind of amnesty eventually."

"Oh, you mean a special plane will be sent from Moscow to fetch you, Yakov?" Bondarenko grinned. "With a personal invitation from Stalin? No way. That Cockroach with his whiskers knew what he was doing putting us here. He always did. During the collectivization he sent a quarter of the peasants to croak in the far north. Later he took all the grain from the collective farms and starved thousands and thousands of peasants to death. Now he proclaims that all those who were in captivity during the war were traitors. What makes you think he's gonna change his mind?"

"I simply can't believe there's no hope for us."

"That's just how it is," Bondarenko answered. "Sooner rather than later we'll all be done for."

"How's Sasha doing?" Goldberg changed the topic.

Bondarenko shrugged. "He was unconscious for a week. Now he's a bit better, even smiles sometimes."

"What does the doc say?" Timoshkin asked.

"He says he's got pnew ... pew ..."

"Pneumonia?" Goldberg prompted.

"Right, and his feet are inflamed. If he survives, he'll have to have them amputated. But he's not likely to pull through. It's too late. Although ... there is one slim hope: Yatta is taking care of him."

"Yatta?" asked Timoshkin.

"Our famous medicine man. He's a Yakut or a Chukchi or somethin', and he can perform miracles."

The door of the barracks hut opened, letting in a stream of cold air. A guard entered.

"Fourth barracks! Evening roll call. Line up!"

The population of the hut rushed toward the doors.

The inside of the hospital looked just a little cleaner than an ordinary barracks. It was just as crowded and had the same double bunks. Here, however, there were mattresses, pillows and blankets. There was an electric lamp, and the window had real glass in it. All the patients looked to be in terrible condition, with frostbitten faces, swollen scorbutic mouths and bandaged limbs. These were the lucky ones. Twice as many inmates lay dying without medical help, either in their own barracks or in the so-called "dead men's barracks." The luckiest went to the hospital in Orotukan, but to obtain a transfer there required a considerable bribe.

Trofimov was among the hopeless cases. For days he had lain in a delirium. At one point he saw himself back at the battlefront under enemy attack. The next instant the scene changed, and he was in Razzhivin's torture chamber. His mother's face appeared in the corner of the sky, calling him home for dinner. During this time he saw nothing and no one around him, totally oblivious even when the hospital staff poured medication into his mouth.

But now he had regained his senses, and he could see the ward and the rows of bunks, though it was dim and blurred, and he hardly realized where he was.

The door opened and two figures emerged. They headed towards him. Who were they? SMERSH officers come to take him to his execution? Work managers intent on sending him back to the mines? No, the newcomers were dressed in white. Medical staff perhaps? Or maybe they were angels come to bear him away to heaven? His grandmother used to say that angels always wore white garments. The next moment he recognized the taller figure. It was the doctor. Trofimov nursed a vague grudge against him but could not remember why. It hardly mattered.

"Here he is, Yatta," the doctor told his companion. He pointed to Trofimov. "Try and get him back into a state where he'll qualify for the weaklings' brigade. Although frankly, I reckon there's little hope. He'll most likely die within a week or so."

"Who knows, Chief? Who can know though?" The second man spoke Russian with an odd accent and peppered his speech with superfluous phrases and conjunctions. "But our great shamans, you know, managed to kick the spirit of illness out of many folks. And Qergina, my woman, taught me many of her skills, you know."

"And that, you old son of a bitch, is why you're here and not in the mines," the doctor grinned. "You're meant to help with cases where Soviet medicine has proved powerless."

It occurred to Trofimov that the doctor must trust this man a lot. To suggest that Soviet medicine was at all powerless was enough to earn him another sentence for anti-Soviet propaganda. "As for this guy," the doctor continued, "Vladimir Semyonovich himself asked me to try and help him."

"Old Vladimir?"

"The same. Your old friend and benefactor and mine. I hope you're not ungrateful. You won't refuse the old boy?"

" 'Course not, Chief. We Chukchi people return good for good, you know."

"Fine. Treat him as if he were no less a person than, say, the managing director of the Dalstroy Construction Project. Understand?"

"I'll treat him even better than that 'cos he's old Vladimir's friend."

"And remember, if he dies," a mocking note sounded in the

doctor's voice, "you'll go back to the mines." He grinned. "I'm joking of course," he said.

The doctor left the ward, leaving the man standing by Trofimov's bunk. The man came closer so Trofimov could see him. He was one of the Siberian native peoples, short, stout and of uncertain age. Most of his long black hair had turned grey, and his copper-bronze face was wrinkled. His back was straight and his step was firm. He bent down over the bunk and looked closely at Trofimov.

"Hi, chap," he said in his accented and slightly eccentric Russian. "I'm Yatta. I've come to kick the demons of disease from out of your body, you know."

"Hi there, old guy," Trofimov muttered indifferently.

All he wanted was to die here in the hospital ward, but this man called Yatta raised Trofimov's body slightly and stripped him down to his underpants. The flesh seemed to be rotting on his bones. Especially bad were his calves and feet, which were a mass of festering ulcers.

"Hey, chap." Yatta's face broke into a benign smile. "You look really bad, you know. The devils have taken most of your flesh, but not quite all of it though. Your bones are still in place, and so is your head. And since that's the case, we can restore the whole of you, through the art of the Great Shamans. First, I gonna treat you with the grass of the Sun Being."

Yatta produced a flask containing a dark liquid. He poured a little onto a piece of cloth and rubbed Trofimov's body.

"This may cause you some pain," he continued, "but it's just to make you feel better, you know."

"So are you the famous native healer that people talk about?" Trofimov muttered. "They say you're good."

"I donna know whether I'm good or not," Yatta smiled. "I met many folks, some good, some bad. I was forced to fight with a few of them too. But the Merciful Beings are witnesses. I always tried to be honest. Now your flesh is taken over by Evil Spirits that want to devour it. But I gonna wrest it back from them. And if I succeed, your body and soul will remain together for many years to come."

Yatta's voice sounded soothing. It was firm and confident, the voice of a sorcerer who knew the mysteries of life and death. Trofimov dozed, overcome by a sense of comfort and reassurance.

"He's asleep," Yatta observed to himself as he continued anointing and massaging Trofimov's body. "It's proper sleep, though, not another deadly coma. Yeah, Yatta, son of Orokei of the Telqap clan, you ain't lost your touch. C'mon, old man, do your job. The Merciful Beings are on your side."

The door of the ward swung open and Bondarenko, Timoshkin and Goldberg entered. Bondarenko had met the native healer before.

"Remember me?" he asked Yatta. "I'm Mikhail, and this is Yakov and Zakharych. We came to ask about Trofimov."

"Hush, he's sleeping," said Yatta, "for the first time in many days. It's in a man's sleep that his flesh fights off the Scurvy Spirit."

"Really?" Bondarenko walked over to Trofimov's bunk. "He's asleep all right."

Goldberg and Timoshkin stepped closer.

"Well, ain't that somethin'!" Bondarenko exclaimed. "Here, Yatta, somethin' for you." He produced a loaf of bread, a sizeable hunk of dried reindeer meat and a bottle of Moskovskaya vodka.

"The vodka is for you, Yatta." He handed over the bottle. "The meat and bread are for our guy."

"Thanks," Yatta smiled.

"No problem," grinned Bondarenko. "A good job deserves good pay. Now we gotta go."

"Where on earth did you get that vodka, Mikhail?" asked Goldberg on their way back to the barracks.

"Well, a guy has to know his way around here. A week ago the screws had a boozing party. I waited till they fell asleep. There was one bottle left on the table, so I, well—"

"You stole it?" There was a note of surprise and reproach in Goldberg's voice.

"What the fuck d'you mean I stole it?" Bondarenko flared up. "Stealing is when you take things from ordinary people. Those men are screws. Back in my partisan days we took loot and trophies from the Nazis, and whenever we made a successful raid, it was counted a lucky day. Otherwise we gotta get supplies from our fellow Russians, and we hated doing that. What you got from the enemy was a trophy. Anyway, our Chukchi guy is saving Trofimov's life."

"I'm afraid there's not much that can save him," Timoshkin sighed. "He looks terribly sick."

"I agree, he looks really bad," Goldberg echoed. "But there are cases when even the hopelessly sick recover. I rather like this guy Yatta. I watched his face when he was treating Sasha."

What about his face?" Timoshkin asked.

"Well," Goldberg said, "he has the face of a zealot, the face of a real healer. He's not a quack. I've heard folk medicine works miracles. Siberian shamans are famous for that. Was he one of them?"

"Either that or the son of a shaman."

Bondarenko caught the sound of footsteps ahead. He hissed and dragged his two companions in among the bushes. Three camp guards armed with submachine guns emerged on the path ahead of them. Although prisoners were not formally banned from walking around the camp, it was not formally allowed either. In the camps if something was not specifically permitted, it meant you did it at your own risk, so any meeting with a camp guard was dangerous. You could easily be beaten for supposedly breaking the rules, or charged with attempting to escape. And no one wanted that.

9

The door to the ward opened and a thuggish hospital orderly called Parnov came in, followed by three patients who were able to walk. They brought swabs and floor cloths and a bucket of water.

"Stay on your bunks," Parnov ordered in a shrill voice. "And you," he turned to his assistants, "get on with your jobs, and be quick 'bout it, you bastards."

The men swabbed down the floor. This job was meant to be done by the orderlies, but the latter regarded such work as beneath their dignity as trusties, and they exploited convalescing patients for this purpose.

The population of the ward observed all this with curiosity. The ward was never cleaned without some special reason. This sudden cleaning operation meant that something was about to happen, and whatever it was, this "something" probably boded more harm than benefit for the inmates.

"Citizen Orderly," asked one of the patients, "is someone coming from Orotukan?"

"None of your fuckin' business," snapped the orderly. "You'll see soon enough."

The cleaning operation continued.

"What do you reckon it means, guys?"

"It means top brass are coming. What else can it mean?"

"I can guess that much, but who?"

"You ask who?" someone speculated. "It's probably our very own Major Avdeyev. Is that good enough for you? He'll come and inspect and see who's loafing, and then he'll send us back to the mines."

"You're kidding," another voice chimed in. "Who needs goners like us in the mines?"

"Well, he'll definitely send you, you idiot, because of your long tongue."

"Quit it," someone interrupted. "Why try and scare folk? Don't listen to him. I swear it isn't Avdeyev. It's someone from higher up. They wouldn't scrub the floors like that just for Avdeyev."

"It may be some medical inspector," someone else chimed in. "He may ask us about our complaints, and we can ask for larger food rations. Then he might discharge us from the camp on health grounds."

"Discharge us?" another patient spluttered with laughter. "And give you a personal amnesty while they're at it?"

The door swung open and in came Major Avdeyev with the doctor and another man in civilian clothing.

"Here you are, comrades," the doctor said. "This is the ward for serious cases."

"I can see that for myself," Avdeyev barked. "Actually it doesn't look too bad, does it?"

"Well, at least they took the trouble to polish it for the visitors," the civilian grinned. Together with Avdeyev he walked along the rows of the bunks, looking at each patient and occasionally muttering something.

Suddenly Avdeyev gave a yelp. "Ponomarev, come over here," he shouted.

"Yes, citizen Major?" The doctor approached Avdeyev.

"What's that?" Avdeyev pointed at Trofimov.

"That's patient Trofimov, citizen Major. He's got pneumonia, scurvy and general dystrophy," he said.

"Patient Trofimov? Did you say 'patient'?" Avdeyev grinned. "He looks more like a corpse. Hey, you," he screamed at Trofimov. "Up on your feet. Can't you see who's standing here in front of you?"

Trofimov showed no response. Avdeyev grabbed him by the shoulder.

"Fuck off, Razzhivin," Trofimov cried out in his sleep. "You won't get anything out of me, you scum."

"So, you call this rotting corpse a patient? Can't you smell it?" Avdeyev pinched his nose and turned away from Trofimov. "Nine out of ten of your so-called patients are like this. Will you ever get this trash back on their feet?"

"Probably not, citizen Major. I'm not at all sure," the doctor muttered, trying to find some way out of this calamity. The authorities' fury could mean his dismissal from medical work and return to hard labour. But what a hypocrite Avdeyev was. As if he hadn't himself strictly limited the number of patients admitted to hospital so only the hopelessly sick were allowed here, while all others had to work. It stood to reason that the hopeless cases were never likely to recover, but now Avdeyev had turned on him; this meant that a new scapegoat was required, and he, Ponomarev, was the chosen victim.

"Not at all sure?" Avdeyev's voice roared into his ear. "If you're not at all sure, why are you keeping this trash here instead of using the beds for those that can be got back to rejoin the workforce?"

"Exactly," the civilian concurred. "The production management always want to know why there are constant workforce shortages."

"So, Ponomarev," Avdeyev turned to the doctor again, "Do what you have to do and be quick about it."

"And what do I 'have to do,' citizen Major?" Ponomarev realized Avdeyev meant he was to eject the patients from the hospital, and he was not in a position to argue with the commandant, but his conscience protested. A clear order from Avdeyev would shift the burden of guilt from himself onto the camp commandant.

"You don't know? Are you stupid? Clear the hospital beds of this garbage. For instance, get rid of this one." He pointed at Trofimov. "And this one, and that one." Avdeyev singled out a good half of the ward's population. "We don't even need 'em back in the compound. Take 'em out and dump 'em in the woods. The wolves can have a nice dinner, unless they're fussy about eating this rotten meat." Avdeyev giggled. "And write out the official death statements."

"Maybe I'd do better to have them taken back to the barracks, citizen Major."

"You and your rotten humanitarian feelings again. Fine, have 'em taken back to the barracks if you want, but I warn you: not a single one of them is going to stay here."

"Yes, citizen Major."

"Get on with it." Avdeyev's voice sounded calmer. "And don't forget that I can send you back to the mines at any time, like I did Ganin before you."

With that Avdeyev and the civilian left the ward. The doctor sighed. The storm had passed. He had at least managed to prevent the cold-blooded murder of his patients. He looked out into the corridor and saw hospital orderly Kozlenko there.

"Kozlenko," he called.

"Yes, Chief?"

"Bring your buddies over here."

Kozlenko disappeared and in a few minutes reappeared with four other orderlies, including Yatta.

"Now listen. All these patients (he pointed out the ones selected by Avdeyev) have to be moved back to the barracks by tonight. Take some of the ambulant patients to help you."

The four orderlies went away. Only Yatta did not move.

"What's the matter, Yatta?" the doctor asked.

"Chief, you wanna take these poor sick men out of the hospital?" asked Yatta in a trembling voice.

"Yes. Didn't you hear? Orders from Avdeyev."

"But the poor guys will die."

"Shut up. Don't preach at me. Do you know what Avdeyev told me to do? He told me to have them dumped in the woods and let them die." Yatta's face shivered. "I had a hard enough time persuading him to let me take them back to the barracks, so please don't make a fuss. Just do what I tell you."

The orderlies returned to the ward with a group of ambulatory patients, and the offloading of the hospital's unwanted population began. The poor goners hardly reacted. Half of them were unconscious anyway. Even those not yet at that stage seemed to care little about this new turn of fate. Nor was there any protest from those who stayed on in the ward. Nothing disturbed the evacuation process. It was just another clearing away of human refuse that happened regularly in the camps.

10

Alexander Trofimov, or what was left of him, lay on a bunk, halfway between the stove in the centre of the barracks and the outside wall. He was covered over with rags, the remnants of his padded jacket. Nothing of the former soldier could be recognized in his emaciated body, and certainly no one would have recognized the army captain who once led his unit into battle, who lay in the trenches under a German artillery barrage, crossed the front line, shot three rapists in Berlin and confronted a SMERSH officer to save a young soldier from the firing squad. Trofimov himself remembered those events only vaguely, no longer sure whether they had happened to him or to someone else.

He realized that he would soon die. No one bothered him anymore. No one expected anything of him, no one demanded hard work. He was left to lie on his bunk in peace. He saw everything around him as if through a kind of frosted glass. He hardly recognized the figures around him, their voices did not bother him. He was quite content to lie there, except for the constant pain in his frostbitten feet. He was too feeble to concentrate on anything. It was better this way: lie still and wait till you depart to what people call the afterlife, or merely disappear into nothingness.

But who was this, dragging at his shoulder, offering him a warm bowl of broth, muttering?

"Here, Sasha. Somethin' to eat."

Trofimov slowly opened his eyes and stared. He could see a man but did not realize who it was. Was he a screw come to escort him off to the penal colony? The foreman come to drag him back to the mine?

"No, Sashok, that ain't gonna work." The man's voice resembled that of a nanny persuading a small child. "C'mon now, eat this up. It's Pyotr Timoshkin, your buddy." The man stroked Trofimov's cheek, at the same time slowly and delicately turning his head. Timoshkin … he once knew that name. It seemed it was the name of a friend, not an enemy … not Razzhivin, not Avdeyev and not Belyayev or Makarov.

"Yeah," the man continued, "it's me. Nobody else. Come on, eat some skilly. It's nice and warm."

Trofimov had no desire to eat. That took effort. All he wanted was to lie and doze.

"What? Why, Timoshkin?" he murmured. "Leave me alone. I want to sleep."

"No, my dear chap," Timoshkin replied. "That ain't gonna work. Eat your skilly and then you can sleep."

"But what for?"

"If you stop eating and you die," Timoshkin sounded almost like a preacher, "that will be the same as suicide, and suicide is a mortal sin. Our life comes to us from the Lord, and only He has the right to take it away. If you kill yourself, your wretched soul will be lost for all eternity. So eat. Eat for the Lord's sake. Do it for me."

"And for me as well," added Goldberg. "I'm your friend too, Sasha. I owe you my life, and I want you to eat."

"Me too," said Bondarenko, "your old comrade-in-arms. For the days we spent together in the war."

All three of them looked into Trofimov's face imploringly. At last he recognized them, the ones who had stood by him in this hell, all the time he had been here.

"All right," Trofimov sighed, "I'll eat it if you want me to."

"Good," Timoshkin responded joyfully. "Eat!" He gave Trofimov spoon after spoon and Trofimov obediently swallowed, but the sweat on his forehead showed how much effort it cost him.

"Well at least he ate the skilly." Timoshkin sighed.

"I'm afraid he's not going to last very long," Goldberg said.

"No, he won't live," Timoshkin affirmed. "Maybe a couple weeks at most. I'm amazed he's still alive."

"Well," added Bondarenko, "that's the way it is here in the camps."

"How could they throw him out of the hospital in such a state?" Goldberg's voice quavered.

"They do that sort of thing all the time," Bondarenko said. "The doc isn't a bad guy. This was Avdeyev's orders."

"Still, after Sasha did him a good turn," Goldberg protested.

"He had no choice," replied Bondarenko.

"So, how's our guy getting on?" Vaskov suddenly emerged in front of them. "Still ticking?"

"Yeah," Bondarenko said, "but I dunno for how long."

"I just got a parcel," said the barracks orderly. "I'm going to pick it up right now, and I'll share some of it with him."

"Thanks, Yefimych."

It would be wrong to say that Vaskov pitied Trofimov. During his two years in the camps he had seen dozens and dozens of men die: young and old, sad and cheerful, good and bad. As barracks orderly, it was his responsibility to deal with each death that occurred in the fourth barracks. He had long ago developed a special immunity to grief, the kind found among professional morticians and undertakers. Frankly, this guy Trofimov was not likely to survive for long in the camps anyway. He hopelessly lacked the essential traits of character for that. He was proud and recalcitrant, and you couldn't afford to be like that here. Here you had to bend before the authorities who had total power over your life and death. You had to be flexible enough for them to recognize your obedience and submission, so they had no cause to get angry with you. But this poor guy had a look in his eye such that any camp commandant or officer could sense his outrage and protest, even if he said nothing and seemed to obey. Apart from which, he reacted far too personally to the camp regulations, and to the viciousness of officers and guards, whereas a sensible prisoner developed an indifference to such things. You had to learn to live your everyday life in spite of it all if you wanted to survive for even a short while.

Vaskov reflected that this guy Trofimov was quite lucky to be dying in the barracks with his friends taking care of him. With his character he might very well have been shot or beaten to death by some officer or screw at his workplace. He could have been framed for some alleged "escape attempt" or executed as a "saboteur," or he could have ended up in a penal compound where they worked you seventeen hours a day without a dinner break on a food ration of 400 grams a day. Or something else. There were many deadly places in the Gulag.

But Trofimov was a close friend of Mikhail Bondarenko, who for two years had been Vaskov's reliable bodyguard and had shielded him against many enemies. Therefore Bondarenko's pals were always included whenever Vaskov granted personal favours. For that reason he was prepared to sacrifice half the bacon he recently received in order to help Trofimov, although even this was hardly likely to save the guy.

11

"Beketov."

"Died this afternoon, citizen Lieutenant."

"Bondarenko."

"Mikhail Savelyevich, 58/2, 58/4 and 58/10: twenty-five years."

"Vaschenko."

"Dmitry Vassilyevich, 58/10: fifteen years."

"Goldberg."

"Yakov Moiseyevich, 58/6, 58/10: fifteen years."

"Dodonov."

"Mikhail Ivanovich, 58/1, 58/10: twenty years."

The evening roll call went on as usual. Trofimov's name was not mentioned, which meant he had been taken off the lists. Towards the end, the prisoners sighed with relief, anticipating the conclusion of this ritual, eager to climb into their bunks and sink into the welcoming gulf of sleep and forgetfulness.

Suddenly Belyayev's baritone rang out again through the frozen winter air. "Attention all prisoners." Everyone stood where they were, ready to absorb any fresh news, even though they fully realized it would most likely be bad.

"Listen to the following announcement from the Judicial Board of the Seimchan Camps Administration. The following convicts (there followed a list of four prisoners) have faced the Judicial Board on charges of sabotage, wrecking and anti-Soviet propaganda. The Judicial Board of the Seimchan Camps has found all four guilty on all charges and sentenced them to the supreme penalty of execution. The sentence has been carried out."

Belyayev paused and then continued: "Once again I have to remind a number of convicts who are not taking their duties towards the Soviet motherland seriously that the Soviet State will not tolerate a negligent attitude toward the performance of duties. Those of you who show no sign of reforming will be isolated as anti-social elements and will be regarded as beyond redemption." He paused again. "Remember this. All of you. At ease. Dismiss."

Belyayev ended his proclamation and then looked at his watch. It was already one o'clock. He wondered whether this was a good time to visit Liza Gnatyuk, his mistress. Why not? She wasn't an official, just an ex-convict. He walked over to the stables. As he rode his horse out of the compound gates, it occurred to him that that new girl—Lyudmila or whatever her name was—who recently came to work in the Seimchan Administration, was also quite attractive. Should he try and date her? It wouldn't interfere with keeping Liza as his mistress: a former prisoner was not really a person, so he wouldn't be violating the Soviet moral code.

"Yet another s'rprise for the night," Timoshkin spat angrily as he, Bondarenko and Goldberg walked back toward the barracks. "Not a single month goes by without some new executions."

As the three men reached their bunks, they were surprised to find Yatta engaged in a whispered conversation with Trofimov.

"Yatta?" Bondarenko asked.

"Yeah, it's me," replied the Chukchi. "I promised old Vladimir to take care of Sasha, you know. And I also promised you as well." He turned to Bondarenko. "It was you who presented me that bottle of vodka, right?"

"Yeah."

"You wanted me to take care of your friend. And we Chukchi always return favours."

"God bless you, Yatta, and give you luck!" Timoshkin made the sign of the cross over him.

Trofimov lay on his bunk with Yatta seated at his side. It was the middle of the working day, and the barracks was empty except for a few goners. Trofimov was almost naked as Yatta massaged his body with herbal ointment, all the while muttering in his native language. Had there been someone there who knew the Chukchi tongue, they would have heard the following:

"O you, Great Lord of the Midday Sun, and you Merciful Beings, I call on you to assist me to help this poor guy. Come to my aid as I try to extract his poor frail flesh from the grip of these powerful Evil Spirits. These Spirits are as mighty and powerful as they are bloodthirsty and hungry for human flesh. They hold his flesh in their claws as a hawk holds his prey. They're eager to devour this poor boy bit by bit, driving his poor soul from its body, leaving it lost and lonely, wandering in the dark of those deserted passages between the Upper and the Lower Worlds. So you, Great Lord, and you Beings who help us men, don't turn a deaf ear to my call! Render me the help I need to overcome the bloodthirsty Evil Spirits and to tear this man's flesh from the Evil Spirits' sharp claws, and to reunite his soul and flesh once and for all. Help me, oh Omnipotent Beings. I offer my prayers to you, and I place all my hope in you."

These improvised incantations were similar to what Yatta had heard long ago from the shamans of his tribe and from Qergina, who had been his woman for several years. As he chanted, he was carried away by the words and felt as if he really was a powerful shaman, able to conquer illness and triumph over calamities. He had never been a shaman, though. He was a reindeer breeder and a small-time trader. It was the woman Qergina to whom he owed his knowledge of traditional native medicine. Nevertheless, these folk remedies usually worked better than anything the scanty and sporadic Soviet medical service had to offer, and it was this arcane medical knowledge that gave Yatta his special position in the Fifth Compound.

Officially Yatta was one of five hospital orderlies, but in reality he ranked alongside the official physician in the camp's Medical Section. Folk medicine was banned as quackery by Soviet laws, even regarded as a criminal offence, but in practice, if a man had an official position in the hospital, it was up to the doctor to decide how to use him. The staff officer in charge of the Medical Section could of course veto any candidate for a hospital job. Like most officers holding this position, Lieutenant Mashin was an idle loafer and he hardly ever interfered in anything, unless it threatened his own position. So when Ganin, who was doctor at that time, expressed a desire to take on this stocky native, whom he commended as an extremely honest man (a rare virtue among camp trusties), Mashin saw no reason to block the appointment.

From then on Yatta's special position continued. He treated his patients with herbal remedies and was regularly allowed to go to the woods to pick herbs and berries. Soon Avdeyev and other camp officers discovered that he was also an excellent hunter and trapper. So, in addition to his medical duties, Yatta was detailed to set snares for foxes and to hunt wild game for the officers' meals. In this way all parties were satisfied: the medical authorities, the camp officers and the sick prisoners whose chances of survival were thus improved. After Yatta helped treat Major Avdeyev for a stomach ulcer, he became a special favourite, and the major lifted all prohibitions on the practice of "quack medicine" in his camp.

"Hey, friend!" Yatta called one of the goners who was still capable of walking.

"Yeah?"

"Can you go and look whether the water's boiling, and if it's ready, bring it here."

"Sure."

"That you, Yatta?" Trofimov opened his eyes as the ambulatory patient brought the hot water and Yatta mixed it with his brew.

"That's me, my boy." Yatta smiled kindly. "Your tea's ready. Drink it up."

"What kind of tea?" Trofimov enquired feebly.

"It's made from last year's berries: foxberry, bilberry and blackberry, the ones preserved under the snow and ice from last summer."

"You're kidding," Trofimov's voice conveyed disbelief. "Can berries survive the Kolyma winter?"

"Yeah," replied Yatta, "some can, and those that can are even juicier as a result, you know. Their juice is good for fighting off illnesses and bringing back your vital forces. Especially if it's mixed with some herbs." He inspected the tea. "It's ready now, drink it up." He poured it into a mug and handed it to Trofimov.

"Nice tea. Much better than that stuff from the canteen."

"Sure it is," Yatta smiled. "It's 'cos it's absorbed some of the vital forces that the berries soaked up under the snow, and it passes on those forces to you."

"Tell me, Yatta," Trofimov asked, "Why are you taking such good care of me? I'm going to die anyway, along with at least half of those that came with our transit contingent."

"No." There was a commanding note in Yatta's voice. "You ain't gotta think like that. When your soul feels like that, it's easier for the Evil Spirits to take over your body. You must think about life, though, and wanna live. Then I'll manage to fight off those Evil Spirits."

"But what sense does it make?" Trofimov insisted. "It'll only make me more upset when the time comes to die."

"No," Yatta was emphatic. "Donna say that. You cannot know. Maybe our camp commandant gonna kick the bucket before you do. Maybe even the Big Chief with his moustache gonna die first."

"Ha." Trofimov grinned. "You must be joking. That pockmarked bastard? He'll survive us all."

"No," Yatta shrugged, "not necessarily. Everything is in the hands of fate. I wasn't taught to read fate by the stars, but I can see that his filthy soul is imprisoned by Evil Spirits. But sooner or later they'll seize his flesh too. When that happens, he won't be able though to call on the Creator, or the Merciful Beings. They never help evil men, you know. And the Evil Spirits will devour his flesh and his soul, and there'll be no room for his evil soul in the Upper World."

"Why are we talking about this?" Trofimov said. "We could find ourselves before a firing squad for such conversations. How come you trust me so much? What if I'm a stooge?"

"Oh no. I know you ain't a stooge," Yatta said. "You're a real man. I can see that. And a real man can never be a stooge."

Trofimov insisted. "How can you know that?"

"Well, you know, you've got scars all over your body," replied Yatta. "I know they're the result of torture."

"That's right," Trofimov confirmed. "Whacked with crowbars."

"There you are. The Big Moustache's underlings tortured you, but they wouldn't need to do that to a weakling. They'd only do that to a strong man in order to break him. But they ain't broken you. Old Vladimir told me you defended an old man who you didn't. even know at all, and you got two weeks in the Black Hole for that. Would a stooge do that? But now you need to sleep, your body wants to sleep," said Yatta as Trofimov finished his tea. "And you gotta respond to the demands of your flesh."

"Yes," Trofimov yawned.

"Sleep," Yatta insisted. "When you rest, the Evil Spirits loosen their grip on your body."

Yatta left the fourth barracks hut and walked toward the Medical Section. On the way he came across an orderly dragging out the corpse of a deceased patient. Yatta greeted him and went on his way. After a few paces, however, he met another orderly from another barracks. He too carried a corpse.

"That's not a good omen," Yatta said to himself. "I wonder what the hell it can mean? Does it mean that guy's gonna die despite all my efforts?"

As he reached the hospital he was met by one of the ambulatory patients who worked as a janitor. "Yatta, you're just in time."

"What's the matter?" Yatta could not conceal a sudden disquiet.

"Your fellow orderlies are here, they're anxious to see you. They threatened to break my bones if I didn't reach you within half an hour."

"Fine, I'll go and see them," sighed Yatta.

On entering the Medical Section he went straight to the basement, where the orderlies usually lounged. Kozlenko, Chernyayev, Parnov and Azizbekov sat on wooden crates playing blackjack.

"So here you are, old man," Parnov wore a crooked smile. "We've been waiting a long time."

"I was treating a guy who's dying," Yatta explained. "One of those who were thrown out of the hospital."

"Were you now?" Kozlenko smiled mockingly. "And that's precisely what we need to talk to you about. Take a seat." He pointed to a free crate. Yatta sat down, and Kozlenko handed him a shag cigar.

"So some freak was kicked out of the hospital, was he? In that case, why the fuck are you spending precious medicine treating a corpse?"

"Sorry, guys." Yatta tried to conceal his mounting anxiety. "I'm bound, though, by the pledge I gave to his friends and to old Vladimir."

"Pledge? What pledge?" Azizbekov burst out laughing. "Here we are in Kolyma, and he talks 'bout pledges. Pledges to whom? To this half-dead trash?"

"No, Mahmud, you're wrong." Yatta's voice was quiet but firm. "That guy is anythin' but trash. He's a real man. You too would look far worse than you do if you'd spent a season down the mines."

"And so you donna owe us anything more, is that what you wanna say?" Chernyayev asked. "Ain't you remember the agreement? And now here you are, contributing less than one third of your assets to the general fund. If you gave as much as we agreed, we'd have vodka and shag for the whole year. Apart from that, we already promised the chief geologist we'd supply him with your drugs and with reindeer meat. How are we gonna look him in the eye now?"

Yatta's thoughts raced as he figured out how to extricate himself. During the two years he'd worked in the hospital, he had been forced to surrender a considerable part of his medicines, pelts and game to these other four orderlies. He had no choice. They were a close-knit group of thugs, and he was out there on his own. No one could protect him against their sort. His contributions were part of a black market operation that flourished in the woodlands, run by the trusties, members of the local population and various geological prospecting teams. The geologists were their regular trade partners and constantly needed venison and medications. This trade brought in a steady profit, and the four orderlies were eager to keep everything for themselves, except for what they had to give the camp officers to keep them sweet. It had been increasingly difficult for Yatta to save the medications he needed for treating sick prisoners from their grasping hands.

"Well, Yatta," Kozlenko broke the silence. "You say he's a goner 'cos he worked in the mines. Fair enough. He'll die soon anyway. So what exactly do you owe him? The five of us have our own little cosy corner here. We're guaranteed to survive and we'll be a force to reckon with for a good long time. You, supposedly, are still one of us, so your obligations to us should take precedence over any others. And now," he added, "come and have some vodka with us."

12

After a few weeks, Yatta's treatment began to work. Trofimov stopped coughing, his ulcers healed, his gums were no longer swollen, and the inflammation in his limbs subsided. Moreover he slept well and had a good appetite.

By contrast, Goldberg was not at all well. His hands were frostbitten, and his feet were bloated because they were permanently wet from the water swilling in the mine, and he had no proper boots. Trofimov spoke about him to Ganin when the latter came to see him, and Ganin promised to talk to the doctor. As for Bondarenko and Timoshkin, unlike Goldberg, they were doing quite well. Bondarenko worked as a carpenter and managed to place Timoshkin as his assistant. The two of them spent their days in a warm workshop. In addition, they were granted permission to receive parcels, and had already got supplies from relatives.

One evening Trofimov sat on his bunk with Yatta, eating reindeer meat provided by the Chukchi huntsman.

"Tell me, Yatta," Trofimov asked, "do all Chukchi practise folk medicine?"

"No," replied Yatta. "Only the shamans, you know. But I learned it from my woman, Qergina. She was the daughter of a powerful shaman. He was killed by the Reds—the Bolshevik Russians."

"Yeah, I know," Trofimov said. "The Soviets practically wiped out the shamans. Is it because of your contact with them that you're in the camps?"

"No," answered Yatta. "I bet they know nothing about it. It's because I was a runaway and lived on my own in the woods for years before they caught me."

"What were you running away from?" inquired Trofimov.

"From exile. They herded all our people into collective farms, and all my family and I were … I forgot the word for it."

"Dispossessed? Dekulakized?"

"Yeah, just that. We owned a herd of three hundred reindeer. They thought we were rich. So they took all our possessions and sent the family into exile in the forest areas. Me, my wife and kids, my old mother, and another dozen aunts, uncles and cousins. But you know, we had to walk all the way, escorted by soldiers. My mother, the kids and the old folk died on the way. My wife died later, when we were felling trees. And then I fled. I wandered in the woods, hunting, trapping and selling furs in return for a rifle and bullets. But three years ago they caught me. At first they beat the hell out of me. They wanted me to confess that … I ain't remember what exactly. Then they left me alone. And then, you know, they said that I must go to prison for fifteen years, and they sent me here."

"Did you have to do hard labour?" asked Trofimov.

"Yeah, I was logging for a few months. Then that old doc, Vladimir, spoke to me when I was in the hospital. Because of him I'm here now."

"So Vladimir Semyonovich Ganin is your benefactor as well?"

"Oh yeah, he's a great old man."

"Indeed," said Trofimov. "Where are you from originally, Yatta?"

"From the Anadyr plateau, a few score verst west of the Bering Strait. I've seen the Strait too, though. You can get from there to Alaska."

"So you roamed all the way between the Bering Strait and here?" asked Trofimov.

"Yeah, I went to the Strait with the traders twice. Then I wandered all over the Anadyr Plateau with my kinfolk. Then I was deported to the woodlands. And I roamed from there all the way to the banks of the Kolyma River, where I was caught."

"Listen, Yatta," said Trofimov, a sense of excitement welling up deep inside him, "if you needed to, could you find your way from here to the Bering Strait?"

"Yeah, I know the way, especially in the east, where the plateau is. I don't quite remember mountain crossings, though, but I got friends nearby who know the way."

13

For the next couple of weeks Trofimov could not help recalling his conversation with Yatta. As it emerged, Yatta knew practically the whole route to the Bering Strait: across the Strait lay America, a land beyond Stalin's rule. All of which meant that if they escaped from the camp together, they might have a chance to flee from this terror and misery and reach a safe haven. Therefore … therefore … but how to persuade Yatta to flee with him?

With Yatta's hunting skills they would not starve. This was a unique opportunity, there would never be another. It would be crazy not to take it. But how would they get out of the camp compound? Both the inner and outer zones were surrounded by three rows of barbed wire several metres high. There were four watchtowers, and a screw with a machine gun on each of them, watching round the clock. If they managed to get out of the compound and camp enclosure, they would have to go deep into the forest, beyond the reach of pursuers. To live by hunting, they would need weapons, at least one rifle. But they could think of something, maybe, when the time came. After all, they were experienced war dogs.

With whom should he escape? Just himself and Yatta? A larger company would be much better, stronger. They could fight off pursuers and wild beasts. So who should they choose? Certainly Bondarenko. He was tough and an excellent fighter, he had lived in the woods and Trofimov trusted him. The same with Timoshkin, and Yakov too. He could discuss the idea with them without fear of betrayal. The question was whether all of them would agree. Mikhail would: he was capable of taking risks. The other two less so. They might have reservations. Leaving a familiar form of misery for a new one was scary. Yakov was getting sicker, although Ganin had some influence with the present doctor. In any case, it was only fair to suggest it to them. If they refused, he and Yatta could escape on their own.

Trofimov thought about this day after day, and for the first time since his arrest a year and a half ago, life acquired new meaning. Before, he realized he was doomed, and his only concern was to steal one more day before the inevitable end. Now it looked as if he might be granted a new lease on life.

A few weeks later Trofimov was walking.

"Well," Vaskov told him one morning, "it looks like in a week or so you'll be sent back to work. But before that happens, d'you feel like spending a bit of time here as my official aide?"

"Sure, no question."

"Fine," Vaskov smiled. "It's almost an official position. It's an accepted custom that the barracks orderly can have a goner who's still on his feet as assistant. So, after the roll call each day I'll send you to chop firewood and bring water. Try to avoid meeting the bosses. If you do meet someone, just say you're the assistant to Vaskov, the fourth barracks orderly."

"Thank you, Yefimych," replied Trofimov. "I'm truly grateful."

"You're Mikhail's buddy, and he's been my pal for two years. To be frank, though," he added, " I never thought Yatta would manage to get you on your feet. You were in a real bad way."

"I know," Trofimov said. "I was ready to die. Yatta gave me back the will to live."

"Good," said Vaskov. "Course, you realize you won't survive all twenty-five years of your sentence, but you can live for quite a while with your advantageous position."

"Advantageous? Are you joking, Yefimych."

"Not at all. You're Mikhail's pal, and he's my crony. I'm a trusty and I have connections with other influential trusties. Although Mikhail is just a labourer, he's no ordinary convict. He's a tough guy, the petty bosses are afraid of him. You're also old Ganin's favourite, and he's quite influential too. Yatta treats you as a friend, and he's an important man. So there you are."

"But I can't keep bugging you and them all the time," Trofimov argued. "And I'm on the black list: I'm to be used only for hard labour, nothing else."

"On the black list?" Vaskov looked sympathetic. "That's no good. But often the bosses ignore the black list. They know that if you give a guy a better job, he'll never get lax, let alone turn to thieving. By the way, old Ganin has been appointed storekeeper, so his position as tool grinder is going to be vacant. I'll talk to the guy in charge of work assignment, and so can Mikhail. He won't refuse if we both tackle him, especially if Ganin asks him as well. Ganin cured the guy of TB after all."

"Thank you again, Yefimych." Trofimov spoke from the depth of his heart.

"Actually," Vaskov opened the door and looked outside, "the compound's already empty. C'mon, bring us some water."

Trofimov took the bucket and went out.

Spring had begun in earnest. The snow had melted away, fresh needles grew on the larches and birdsong could be heard overhead. Trofimov's return to the world of the living coincided with nature's own resurrection. He smiled as he walked towards the well, enjoying the freshness in the air and the sunshine.

"Stop. Where are you from?" A red-haired guard emerged in front of him.

"Fourth barracks, citizen Guard. Assistant to barracks orderly Vaskov."

"You sick?" inquired the guard, staring hard at Trofimov.

"Recovering from pneumonia."

"Fine." The man glanced at Trofimov's bucket. "You're back at work now?"

"Yes, citizen Guard."

"Okay, off you go."

Trofimov sighed. He reached the well, threw the pail down the shaft and started hauling it up, sensing the weight of it. When the water arrived, he splashed some into his mouth and set off back. His hands and arms were still sore, but to his delight he found that the bucket did not weigh too heavily. The life seemed to be returning to his limbs. It was wonderful to feel strong again, especially with his recent ideas in mind.

I'll talk to Mikhail tonight, he thought.

The day was a busy one, chopping firewood, lighting the stove, bringing and boiling water. In the evening the prisoners returned from their labour to the barracks.

"Well, Captain," smiled Bondarenko, "How was your first day back on your feet?"

"Fine," replied Trofimov. "Yefimych took me on as his assistant, and he's promised to help get me a new job grinding tools."

"He's a good guy, Yefimych," said Bondarenko, "not a scumbag like so many trusties."

"He is, yes," Trofimov answered. Out of the corner of his eye he watched as Timoshkin and Goldberg went to the stove to dry their foot bindings. "Mikhail, I've something to talk to you about in private."

Bondarenko's face expressed curiosity. "Just the two of us?" he asked

"For now, yes."

"Okay, wait until retreat. I know a place behind the latrine. The screws hardly ever go there—the stench is too bad."

Trofimov could hardly wait till the barracks population finally tumbled into their bunks after supper and the evening roll call. He lay down and waited a few minutes, then cautiously sat up and glanced at Bondarenko who seemed to be sound asleep. The moment Trofimov's eyes fell on his face, he came to life and whispered, "C'mon, Captain, let's go."

The two of them crept towards the door and quietly opened it, then stepped out and closed it behind them. Looking around to make sure no one was watching, they made their way to the camp latrine, a small shed with six toilet pits, used by more than a thousand inmates. It was rarely cleaned, and the stench was appalling. Behind the latrine was a log storage warehouse, and between the two structures was a narrow gap where several people could hide if need be, especially after dark. Trofimov and Bondarenko edged their way into this gap and leaned against the wall of the storage shed.

"So what d'you wanna tell me, Captain?" Bondarenko asked.

"I want to talk about our future, Mikhail," Trofimov replied. "Sooner or later we'll all be lying under the hill with nametags on our feet. We've got to do something about it, otherwise our position's goddamned hopeless."

"What are you trying to say?"

"I'm trying to say that we've got to escape."

For half a minute Bondarenko said nothing, then broke the silence.

"I've thought about it myself. What's more, I spoke to Zakharych about it, when you were still bad. We didn't wanna leave you on your own, so we decided to wait till either you died or, with God's help, Yatta got you on your feet. I guess now is a good time to talk. What about Zakharych?"

"Sure, and Yakov as well."

"Fine," Bondarenko said. "Yakov's a bit soft, but he's reliable, a real soldier. It won't be easy, but I guess we can manage." He paused. "Where d'you think we should head? Not towards western Russia, we'd never get there, and what would we do there without money or passports?"

"I wasn't thinking of European Russia," Trofimov said.

"Ah, so that's it. You mean to go into the forest. That's an idea. I lived in the Byelorussian forests for three years in my partisan days, so I'm used to that life. It's possible."

"No, I mean something quite different," Trofimov said.

"What then?" Bondarenko looked surprised.

"I want to go to the Bering Strait, and across to Alaska."

"Cross over to the other shore? To America?"

"Yes. We can ask for political asylum there."

"Hmm," Bondarenko twirled his moustache. "That really is something. Can we find the way without a guide? Who would agree to help us? Everyone's scared to death. It's a capital offence to assist fugitives. Besides, guides have to be paid. Where do we get the money?"

"There is one man who could be our guide," replied Trofimov. "For years Yatta roamed Kolyma and Chukotka, and he knows the route."

"Are you nuts, Captain?" Bondarenko's voice sounded disappointed. "You mean we'd rely on Yatta, a trusty?"

"He's no ordinary trusty," replied Trofimov. "He holds that position because of his skills in folk medicine and hunting. He was a reindeer breeder."

"It ain't matter," Bondarenko retorted. "He's found a nice cosy spot for himself in here. Why would he risk all the danger and uncertainty? Mark my words: never trust a trusty!"

Trofimov had not thought of this. He took it for granted that Yatta could be trusted. The stocky bronze-skinned Chukchi was anything but a traitor, so it came as a surprise that he now had to persuade Bondarenko, his own most trusted companion.

"Don't you remember how he nursed me back to life?" he exclaimed. "Why would he do a thing like that? He had no obligation. Would a trusty do it?"

"You're a shithead, Captain," Bondarenko frowned, "not to see any difference. Do I have to spell it out to you? Yatta's a nice guy, I donna deny it. And he's generous. I presented him with a bottle of vodka, and that was enough to make him take on the responsibility for you. But that's a different matter from what you're suggesting."

"A different matter?"

"Yeah, for Chrissake. You can rely on him here in the zone, but escaping is a completely different thing. Why for God's sake does he need to escape anyway? You, me, Zakharych, Yakov—we have no hope here. Eventually we're gonna kick the bucket. But he's found his cosy niche, he has his trusty's ration, and he can even eat game and fish. He's under no threat of being assigned to ordinary hard labour 'cos they'd never find another medicine man like him. So why does he need to take such a risk?"

"Maybe you're right. He might refuse," Trofimov hesitated. "I won't be surprised if he does. But still we can ask him. He's no rat."

"Holy shit," was Bondarenko's response. "I agree, he'll not report on us here in the zone, but escaping is an entirely different kettle of fish, understand? If he knew about such plans and didn't report them, he'd face the firing squad. You think he'd risk that? Your own self comes first, doesn't it? And that goes for everyone, abso-bloody-lutely everyone. So let's escape just the four of us. We'll never make it to the coast, but they'll never track us down, the forests are too vast. We could live free for a dozen years. But never put our lives at stake by trusting a trusty. Never."

A pause followed, and for some time the two of them contemplated one another. Then Trofimov grabbed Bondarenko's hand.

"Listen, Mikhail," he implored. "For Christ's sake, listen. Do you want to bury all hope of getting out of this frozen hell? Do you want to get out of the camp just to spend years on the run, hiding from the authorities, in a constant state of tension? Is that what you want?" Trofimov's voice became rough. "D'you want to bury your last chance of real freedom just because you distrust a native medicine man?" Trofimov sighed. "God help us. Our rulers really did achieve their goal, didn't they? No one trusts anyone, so nobody can ever agree on a joint plan of action. There's no doubt about it: at this rate the Soviets will stay in power for another two hundred years."

"Damn." Bondarenko flushed. "If you mean to entrust our fate to a Chukchi, I ain't gonna have any business with you, d'you hear?"

"Calm down," Trofimov said. He placed his hand on Bondarenko's arm. "Listen, there's no way I'll talk to Yatta about this without your consent. Or Yakov's or Timoshkin's. But I'm pleading with you to look at things from a broader perspective. On my honour, I'd never do this unless we all agreed. Do you trust me?"

"I do, so far," replied Bondarenko after a pause. "At least I ain't got no reason not to trust you."

14

The workday was in full swing with the crash and clatter of pickaxes and crowbars inside the mine and the rumble of wheelbarrows as they emerged from the galleries. It was late spring, the peak of the gold mining season, which lasted only four months. The authorities were anxious to get as much out of the labour force as they could.

Goldberg was in very bad shape and only managed to work because of the foreman Gusev, who was lenient on him, and because he was Bondarenko's pal.

Goldberg wearily trundled his wheelbarrow. Every step was torture, and the pain in his swollen feet was searing. He felt as if his body had no muscles left, no energy, just ribs protruding from beneath his skin. The decking led uphill for a certain way, and his barrow grew heavier and heavier. It took all his effort to prevent it from slithering off the runway. To spill the broken rock meant a savage beating. Only on the return run with an empty barrow could he relax and move more slowly, since the screws never watched the downside of the gallery. At last he was close to the dumping point. One more effort, and the contents of the barrow cascaded down the chute into the railcars standing at the bottom. As Goldberg turned off to the side, his feet stepped into a swill of ice-cold water, but it was good to be able to move at a slower pace.

Of the four friends, he was the only one unlucky enough to still work in a mining brigade. Bondarenko and Timoshkin were employed as carpenters, and Trofimov helped Vaskov in the barracks. Trofimov had promised to talk to Ganin about transferring Goldberg to the hospital. Evidently Ganin was doing something, and now all he could do was wait. Hell, how his feet hurt!

"There you are, Goldberg," smiled Gusev. "Drop your barrow, it's dinner time."

What luck. At last his body could rest. The work teams moved towards the elevator cage, and the gallery was packed like the streets of Moscow on May Day. Among the dozens of heads in front of him he spotted Bondarenko and Timoshkin. Lucky guys. How fortunate to be a peasant and able to do carpentry.

The door of the cage opened and the crowd of men rushed forward, pushing and jostling one another. Goldberg got almost to the entrance, but the door closed, and the cage went up without him. Someone tapped him on the shoulder. He turned and saw … Bondarenko. Hell, how could he still be here? He had been so far ahead just a short while ago.

"Tonight behind the warehouse," Bondarenko whispered in Goldberg's ear. "Me and Zakharych will be there, and the captain as well."

Once the inhabitants of the barracks were sound asleep, Bondarenko touched Goldberg on the shoulder. Quietly he got off his bunk and joined the others. Without a word, the four of them made their way out, and proceeded to their secret meeting place. Not until they were deep inside the gap between latrine and warehouse, invisible from the well-lit path, did anyone open his mouth.

"Well," Trofimov broke the silence, "do we all know why we're here?"

"I told Zakharych," replied Bondarenko, "But not Yakov yet."

"All right," said Trofimov. "Yakov, listen."

As Trofimov talked, Goldberg's eyes opened wider and wider. He had expected anything: news of a new transit, a new case opened against him by the Godfather—anything but this. To escape from this prison compound, guarded by screws with submachine guns and dogs, where an inmate's every step was under surveillance, seemed like something crazy, a fantasy, certainly not for real. He had heard professional thieves tell stories of daring escapes, concealed in the back of a truck or wearing camp officers' uniforms and carrying false documents. Those were fairy tales and nothing more. But Trofimov was serious.

"So," whispered Bondarenko, as Trofimov ended his speech, "what d'you think, Yakov?"

"Well …" Goldberg did not know what to say. "It's a daring plan. Are you serious?"

"Abso-fuckin'-lutely!" replied Bondarenko.

"Where will we go once we're out?"

"That's something we haven't yet settled," Trofimov said. "Mikhail and I disagree about it."

"We'll talk about that later," Bondarenko interrupted. "But the first steps are clear enough. We've gotta break out from the camp and get far away into the woods, where they'll never find us. That alone is worth trying."

"Looks like you're right," Goldberg muttered, feeling the pain in his feet. "But … how will we survive in the wilds? Won't we die of cold and hunger in the first few days?"

"No, not if we have weapons—knives, or even guns," Trofimov said. "That's crucial. Then we'll be able to hunt. Mikhail and Timoshkin have hunted before, they'll teach the two of us how."

"How are we gonna get guns?" Timoshkin asked.

"A good question, Zakharych," Bondarenko replied. "I say we can get a couple from the screws, then we ambush a few more and get guns for each of us."

"Too many killings," muttered Goldberg, whose brain was still processing these new ideas.

"How the hell can we manage without that?" snapped Bondarenko. "D'you think they'll give us their guns of their own free will? Or d'you want to go without guns and croak within a week?"

"I don't know," answered Goldberg, "but it looks like we'll leave a pile of corpses behind us, wherever we go."

"Just look at him," snarled Bondarenko.

"Well, Yakov," Trofimov said, "there's no other way. Either we kill them, or they kill us. This is war, Yakov, a war of destruction that the state launched against us. They are the enemy. We can't expect mercy from the men in blue epaulettes. We've got to fight them like we fought the Germans."

"So, you mean *à la guerre comme à la guerre?*" asked Goldberg.

"And what does that mean?" inquired Timoshkin.

"It means that in war things will be on a warlike footing," replied Trofimov. "Yeah, that's roughly how it's got to be, Yakov. There's no other way."

"May I think it over for a while?" Goldberg's voice conveyed his hesitation.

"Well," Bondarenko grinned, "if you were talking to a set of thieves, they'd say no, either you're with us, or we finish you off. But we ain't thieves, so you can make your choice—seize your chance to be free or die a slave. Right, Captain?"

"Yes," Trofimov said. "It's up to you, Yakov."

Bondarenko added, "We don't know yet when we're gonna escape. It could be in a couple of months, maybe in a month. So next time we ask you, Yakov, you've gotta have an answer. Agreed?"

"Yes."

"Fine," Trofimov smiled. "Then it's agreed."

"And what about the second question?" inquired Timoshkin, "The one you and Mikhail disagree about?"

"Well," Trofimov looked at Bondarenko. "You don't mind, do you, Mikhail, if I tell them?"

"Go ahead," Bondarenko said. "They've got to know."

"All right," Trofimov said, and told the others about their argument over including Yatta.

"I think it'd be great to get to America," said Timoshkin after a pause. "Americans are good guys. Not like the English. They didn't send anyone back to the Soviet Union by force. I wouldn't be here now if I'd been in the American zone when the war ended."

"But how do you know Yatta won't rat on us if we tell him?" Bondarenko interrupted.

"Oh no," Timoshkin shook his head. "He's not one to do that."

"Of course he ain't," said Bondarenko, "but if he knows about our plans and donna rat, he'll be shot. However good a guy he is, self comes first. Remember that."

"Listen, Mikhail," said Timoshkin. "I can read people. I know a scumbag when I see one. Yatta isn't like that."

"How the hell can you know for sure?" Bondarenko objected.

"There are ways of knowing, Mikhail," responded Timoshkin. "I watched Yatta when he treated our captain. He did it like it was his own son or younger brother. He had nothin' to gain by doing that. Would a scumbag do that?"

"Oh, shit," Bondarenko said. "You're talking about utterly different things. I didn't say that Yatta's a bad guy and a snitch. It's just that if he hears about our plans and doesn't report on us, he may face a firing squad. And who wanna die, after all?"

"No," Trofimov objected. "There have to be reasonable limits to one's distrust."

"I agree with the captain," Timoshkin said.

"Do you?" grinned Bondarenko. "And what about you, Yakov? Do you agree with them?"

"I think I do," replied Goldberg. "I've watched Yatta for several months. He's a noble figure. I think if we told him, there wouldn't be much risk. After all, we trust each other. Theoretically we can't know for sure that none of us is a snitch. We trust Vaskov too. We talk with him about a lot of things."

"You're all crazy," snapped Bondarenko. "I can tell you one thing: it's either him or me. If you wanna trust him, count me out of the game, d'you hear?"

"You're not right, Mikhail," said Timoshkin in a calm voice.

"You'll understand I was right when you end up freezing in the Orotukan tent!"

15

On a Saturday night the barracks building that housed the Culture and Education Section was full of people. One group sat at a table, looking through the newspapers *Magadanskaya Pravda*, *Soviet Kolyma*, and the *Far Eastern Komsomol*, while another group sat around a man with a guitar singing prison songs. Yet another group stood by the wall chatting in low voices. Trofimov sat at the far end of the room, talking with Ganin.

"Well, Alexander Ivanovich," Ganin smiled, "My congratulations on your recovery. I honestly didn't expect it. You were in a really desperate state."

"Thank you, Vladimir Semyonovich. Was it you who sent Yatta to treat me?"

"In a manner of speaking. I talked to him after you were thrown out of the hospital. He was uncomfortable with the idea that you and the other folk had been kicked out and faced certain death. I told him it would be good if he could take care of you in the barracks. At first Sergey, the doctor, was unwilling to let him, but I spoke to him, and he agreed. He never refuses me. He needs my advice."

"Sure he does," Trofimov grinned. "He was a mere fourth-year student when he was arrested. Thank you for everything, Vladimir Semyonovich. And how are you?"

"More or less okay, my dear fellow. More or less," smiled Ganin. "I'm in charge of the camp depot. My predecessor Smorchkov was caught embezzling. Lots of people didn't get their summer boots and ended up with incurably swollen feet. Monsieur Avdeyev found himself in an awkward position. To request a further reinforcement of his workforce would have been too much to ask even in the Gulag, so Smorchkov is in a penal camp, and I've taken his place. Avdeyev needed an honest man to take care of the supplies, and who is more honest then an ex-field surgeon of the Imperial Army?"

"True enough," laughed Trofimov.

"So," Ganin smiled, "I have the good fortune to spend my last few days in a cosy corner."

"But it's too early for you to be thinking of death," Trofimov said. "You're not that old, after all."

"Oh please, Alexander Ivanovich. I'm a physician. I can give an appraisal of anyone's health including my own. I've got TB, and it can't be cured at my age. I've got another year, maybe two."

"That's sad," sighed Trofimov. "You twice saved my life. I don't know how to thank you."

"Never mind, my dear man. You showed your own nobility when you stood up for poor old Gilman, God bless his soul. As for my own death, there's nothing tragic about it. I'm seventy-three. Most people live less long. Most of my friends are long dead, and I'd have done better to die before 1945. But maybe all this is a divine punishment for my sins."

"Sins? What sins?"

"Well, I participated in the Russian Civil War, and the anti-Bolshevik Volunteer Army were no more angels than the Reds were. There were the same shootings, hangings, tortures and anti-Jewish pogroms. I didn't take part in them personally, but on the other hand I did nothing to save the victims. I believed in the White cause and I closed my eyes to the evil that they did, so I'm an accomplice."

"There's hardly anybody in our times who's not in that position," Trofimov said. "I dealt harshly with men at the front. I passed three death sentences on deserters. I believed then that I was doing the right thing, and it's only now that I begin to doubt it."

"Oh? And what are your thoughts on the subject now?" inquired Ganin.

"I think it's a moral perversion to force someone into acts of courage through fear. A deserter is a coward, or a weakling, it's true, but that's hardly a reason to put him to death. There are always enough brave men."

"Yes, you're right," Ganin agreed. "There were times when Russia was saved by volunteers alone. During the Napoleonic invasion, or Minin and Pozharsky for instance."

"True. But to change the subject, Vladimir Semyonovich, I have a request to make of you."

"What kind of request?"

"My friend Yakov Goldberg is in a very poor state. Not as bad as I was, but very bad. Would it be possible to talk to Doctor Ponomarev about him?"

"I can certainly do that. As I said, Sergey doesn't refuse me. As soon as there's a place there." Ganin paused. "Actually, I have a request for you too."

"I'll do my best. What is it?"

"It's very confidential. I need to talk to you tête-à-tête."

"Certainly," Trofimov replied. "I know a secret place where we could talk. Let's go there."

"I want to talk about Yatta," said Ganin as they stood in the narrow gap between the storage warehouse and the latrine.

"Does he have problems?"

"Yes. He's somewhat in danger."

"From whom?" Trofimov was surprised.

"Well," Ganin looked worried, "there are men who have a grudge against him. They could become a real threat. They're quite powerful here, and most prisoners wouldn't want to confront them."

"Who are they?" Trofimov asked.

"It's the hospital orderlies. Yatta needs help against them. I'm too old and sick to put up any fight, but you and your friends are real men. I know you could do that."

"Of course. Yatta saved my life after all."

"I thought you'd say that, Alexander Ivanovich." Ganin shook him by the hand. "I also hope that in a while you'll have a chance to take my place as tool grinder in your brigade."

I wonder what it could be, Trofimov thought as he lay on his bunk. Those orderlies look an unpleasant set of guys, yet what grudge could they have against Yatta? Strange. Anyway, I'd be a cowardly bastard if I didn't come to his aid. Should I tell the guys about it now, or is it better to wait? I still have another problem: how am I going to persuade Mikhail about Yatta? He's so obstinate. "Me or him" indeed! God help us! If that's Mikhail's position, does it mean we should turn down the whole idea of including Yatta?

16

Yatta stood in front of his fellow orderlies Kozlenko, Parnov, Azizbekov and Chernyayev, who sat on empty crates in the basement of the hospital.

"C'mon. Have a seat, Yatta." Kozlenko broke the silence and pointed to a crate. Yatta sat down.

"So, let's have a little chat." Parnov's voice sounded almost friendly. "You remember, Yatta, what we talked about some time ago?"

"Yeah," Yatta replied.

"That's fine," said Azizbekov. "And you realize that you broke your promise?"

"No," replied Yatta. "We've got enough of everythin' to supply the prospectors, you know."

"No, buddy," Kozlenko smiled. "I counted the supplies yesterday. All your stuff together amounts to between 150 and 200 grams short of one litre."

"But you know, I'm gonna make some more within a few days though," said Yatta.

"Possibly," Kozlenko continued smiling. "But it takes a few months before it becomes workable, doesn't it? And we promised Stepanov to have some stuff ready within a month. So what do we do?"

"Guys," Yatta began, "I—

"Enough!" Parnov exploded. "Are you trying to make fools of us? What about that fuckin' dirty Yid that was brought here yesterday? I hope you're not gonna waste your stuff on him, are you?"

"But I must," responded Yatta. "Yakov's my friend, and the old medicine man asked on his behalf."

"He must," snarled Parnov. "Just look at him. Still trying to fool us and peddling his drugs hell knows where. Fuck, no. That ain't gonna wash. You lousy savage, you're gonna be very sorry for this."

"Anyway," Kozlenko added, "we're giving you yet another final warning, Yatta. But if … if you don't cooperate, we'll talk to you in quite a different way. Remember that."

"Yeah, Nikolay," Yatta tried to put on a smile. "But you know, I do understand what you're saying."

"I hope so," Kozlenko smiled slyly. "It's in your interests after all. If push comes to shove, we can always manage without you."

Yatta sat in his room, smoking one home-rolled cigar after another. Every fibre of his body was filled with a sense of approaching danger. He had known this feeling before, goodness knows how often, and so far his forest dweller's keen eyes and ears had responded in good time to enable him to react. They had only once failed him, on that summer night when he was caught. He had visited the old trapper Nikiforov, who supplied him with bullets. Who knows, though, whether it was Nikiforov who betrayed him? Or one of his own family? Or one of the neighbours? Anyway, soon after Yatta left Nikiforov, a unit of soldiers arrived together with tracker dogs. They tracked Yatta back to his tent and seized him. He ran for it, but the dogs were quicker. He was savagely beaten and forced to march back to Nikiforov's cabin for identification, after which he was force-marched for three days to the jail in the nearest town centre. Then followed months of detention in various jails, interrogation and beatings, broken ribs and teeth. Officers in blue epaulettes tried to get him to confess to spying for the Americans. He spent a long period of detention in an overcrowded regional jail before receiving a sentence with various tricky articles from some local judicial board, then another transit, and eventually he turned up here in the Fifth Compound.

Yatta was forced to live with his fellow orderlies Vassily Parnov, a thief from Shakhty, and Viktor Chernyayev, who was either a burglar or a German collaborator, or both. A year later they were joined by Nikolay Kozlenko, a gangster from the notorious Moscow "Black Cat" gang, and later by Makhmud Azizbekov, a gloomy Central Asian who had served as bodyguard to some local party boss, and who for some reason had fallen out of favour. These four formed a powerful little group and were feared by most of the camp population. How many wretched patients' lives could have been saved by all the medicines and fresh meat that Yatta was forced to hand over to them? But what could he do? He could not confront and take on all four of them. Who would support him in such a conflict?

Yatta had to yield to their demands. Problems had recently arisen after Ganin requested him to take care of Trofimov. Certainly Ganin was a decent man. He had tried to stand up for an obvious goner, and Trofimov really deserved to be saved from death. Yatta could not refuse the old doctor, but in order to save Trofimov he had to withhold some of his medicines. Yatta hoped that his companions would not notice, but they did, and they responded with threats that became increasingly vicious. Now Ganin had asked Yatta to help yet another man, Trofimov's friend Yakov. There was no doubt that the gang of four were on the verge of carrying out their threats. So what could he do? Neither the old doctor nor the recently appointed junior one could give him any protection.

And Trofimov? The more Yatta thought about it, the more likely it seemed to him that Trofimov might be the man to help him. If he stood up for someone whom he did not even know, he would be unlikely to refuse the man who had saved his life.

Yatta remembered the question Trofimov once asked him about finding his way back to the Bering Strait. Surely that wasn't just idle curiosity. He must be thinking of escaping, and wondering whether Yatta might serve as a guide. He must value Yatta's life highly, and would surely come to his defence. Trofimov also had those three pals. If Trofimov came to his defence, they might well join in the fight to help him. This seemed almost too much to hope for.

Great as his fears were, Yatta was a man of his word. From his early years in a nomad camp in the tundra, he had come to believe that there were certain things anyone with a sense of self-respect had to do, even if it put his life in danger. One of those things was to keep promises, especially to someone to whom you owed your very life and wellbeing. He had promised Ganin to respect any of his requests and would have felt terrible if he ever refused his one-time saviour. The more so since the man for whom Ganin put in his request was Trofimov's friend. If this man too owed Yatta his life and health, then he, Yatta, would likely gain not just one but two friends willing to defend him. And three against four was not such a bad match. No matter what the odds, Yatta decided to treat Goldberg, trying at the same time to avoid an open clash with the orderlies, at least until Goldberg was back on his feet.

17

Yatta stood beside Goldberg and rubbed his swollen feet with an ointment. Goldberg's face betrayed the pain he was in, but he said nothing and merely gritted his teeth.

"Patience, old man." Yatta's voice had its usual reassuring sound. "Donna move your feet, keep them still. That's fine." He watched as Goldberg strove to hold his feet in one position.

"Okay, Yatta," Goldberg smiled through the pain. "It's just bearable."

"But you know, you're in a good state, man," Yatta said, "compared to what your pal was in."

"Sure," Goldberg responded. "I thought Sasha was going to die."

"I didn't think so," Yatta disagreed. "It's true, those Evil Spirits had him in a tight grip, but a medicine man mustn't ever think that this is the end. Nor should the patient think so. You know, bad thoughts make your soul weaker, though, and the Evil Spirits stronger. And you ..." Yatta added after a pause, "you ain't in no danger. So, just enjoy your rest."

"Yeah, it's a real vacation." Goldberg smiled. "I never thought I'd ever enjoy another one before I died."

"You wouldn't have either, but for old Vladimir," Yatta said.

"I know."

"Now listen, man," Yatta said as he finished the treatment. "You keep this flask with you and smear your feet four times a day. My other orderly mates don't wanna me to treat you. They threatened me. So I can't keep visiting you. But this is something you can do yourself." He dipped his finger into the flask and took a bit of the stuff from it. "You see, this is how much you have to rub on. No more, no less. Four times a day. There's enough for a week here. Then I'll come again."

"Fine."

On the way out of the hospital, Yatta met Paramonov, one of the ambulant patients. He glanced at Yatta but said nothing. Lucky he didn't see me in the ward, Yatta thought. Will they try and settle scores with me tonight? They can hardly kill me though: that would be too big a profit for them to lose, but they can certainly "degrade" me, or do some other nasty things.

As night came, Yatta lay on his cot deep in his thoughts. He shared a room in the trusties' barracks with Parnov and Chernyayev. It was a tiny room with three iron cots, one small table and a couple of chairs. Would they set on him right now, or wait? They were particularly displeased at the special attention he paid to this new patient. Hopefully Goldberg would be smart enough not to show his ointment to anyone. After all he was a regular hospital patient, so treating him was Yatta's direct responsibility.

O Creator and Merciful Heavenly Beings, how Yatta of the Telqap wants not to die. Or, more exactly, it was not death that he feared, it was the pain they would inflict on his poor vulnerable flesh. He had seen them beat other patients, and by the time they had finished, blood gushed from the poor guys' mouths. He had also seen them do what in thieves' slang was referred to as "degrading": it meant gang raping their victim. This was something that no one with an ounce of self-respect could ever tolerate, especially in the camps, where it turned the "fag" victim into the worst of pariahs.

Yatta had closed his eyes, but he was on the alert. While living in the forests he had learned to relax in such a state, somewhere between wakefulness and sleep. You hung in a state of sweet drowsiness, but with all your senses responsive to any alarm signal. It was an essential ability living in the wilds, and he again found a use for it. A few hours passed. Parnov and Chernyayev seemed to be snoring in their cots.

But listen! The door opened ever so slightly. Yatta jumped off his bed and rushed to the window. Parnov and Chernyayev leaped from their cots and blocked his way. All four had knives in their hands.

"Well, Yatta," Kozlenko's voice was calm as usual, "we warned you, didn't we?"

"I ain't understand, guys, though," Yatta played for time. He'd make a run for it when the chance came. He had to get to the fourth barracks, where someone might come to his aid.

"Ha," Parnov laughed. "Look at him. He ain't understand. So maybe you understand this?" He brandished his knife.

"But what's this for?"

"Look," Kozlenko said. "We spoke to you, but still you went and gave that filthy Yid a flask of your ointment. How many times do we have to warn you, eh?" He turned to his cronies. "So what do we do with him?"

"To start with, I guess we've gotta degrade him," said Azizbekov. "And then we'll see."

All four of them slowly closed in on him. When Parnov was within a few inches of him, Yatta leaped at him, kicked him in the groin and pushed him over toward Chernyayev. He rushed for the window, kicked out the pane, and still wearing only his underwear jumped out and sprinted off towards the fourth barracks. His assailants followed, but he was the better runner. Would Trofimov and his pals defend him? They were his only hope.

At last he reached the fourth barracks. Yatta ran in, found Trofimov and shook him awake.

"You, Yatta?"

"It's me, Sasha. Please help me. They're after me."

Trofimov realized immediately and woke up Timoshkin and Bondarenko.

"What the fuck's the matter, Captain?" Bondarenko sounded angry.

"It's Yatta, Mikhail. He's pleading for help."

"Hmm," Bondarenko grabbed three knives from a secret hiding place in a cache by the wall and handed one to Trofimov and another to Timoshkin.

"Go on, guys, I'll be with you in a minute," he whispered.

"C'mon, Timoshkin, let's go," Trofimov urged.

The four orderlies burst into the barracks.

"Didn't manage to run far, did you?" smiled Kozlenko. He froze as he saw Trofimov and Timoshkin at Yatta's side, holding knives.

"Leave Yatta alone and get out of here, now." Trofimov's voice was calm and firm, and he stressed each word.

For a moment the orderlies assessed this unexpected challenge.

"What the fuck?" Parnov broke the silence. "This is our problem. Stay out of it, or you'll regret it."

"We'll see who the hell regrets it." Bondarenko emerged and stepped forward with a crowbar in his hand. "Touch Yatta, and I'll break all your fuckin' ribs."

"Yatta's our friend," Trofimov added. "You're not going to touch him."

The orderlies exchanged glances.

"Well, guys," muttered Parnov, "I guess we can't argue with a crowbar."

"Right, Fyodor," said Azizbekov.

"Let's go," Kozlenko said, and the orderlies retreated.

"You'll pay for this, you scum," threatened Azizbekov as he left.

"We'll see," Trofimov said. "Remember: if a single hair falls from Yatta's head, you're finished."

"Thank you." Yatta turned to the three men. "From now on you're my brothers."

"You saved my life," smiled Trofimov. "What is it they want of you?"

"You know, it's a long story," Yatta replied hesitantly. "They wanted me not to treat anyone. They need my medicines for themselves."

"For themselves?" Timoshkin's voice expressed surprise. "What do they need them for? They're healthy and strong as bulls."

"Donna be stupid, Zakharych," Bondarenko said. "They're selling them somewhere. Right, Yatta?"

"Yeah, to the geologists."

"Well, Yatta," Bondarenko turned to him with a smile, "now you owe us something too."

18

Trofimov, Timoshkin and Bondarenko lay on their bunks, talking in whispers.

"Well, Mikhail, do you trust Yatta now, after this incident?" Trofimov asked.

"I reckon so," Bondarenko replied. "I bet he's thinking about the same idea himself, 'cos it's hardly safe for him to stay here. Sooner or later those bastards'll get him. So, who's gonna talk to him? I guess you should, Captain. You know him best."

"Yes," replied Trofimov. "He trusts me too."

"Better sooner than later," Timoshkin added, "or he may take off by himself any day."

Trofimov and Yatta stood in the hiding place between the latrines and the warehouse and took turns smoking a shag cigar.

"Look, Yatta," Trofimov began, "you remember we told you we might need you to do something for us soon? Well, the time's come."

"Yeah, brother," Yatta nodded. "I'm ready to do anything. Just tell me what."

"Those bandits are after you," Trofimov said. "What do you plan to do? They won't leave you alone now."

"I can tell you though, I trust you," Yatta responded. "You know, I shall be gone from here soon, as soon as the winter comes. I have places to go, and there are folks that I know."

"That's what I want to talk to you about."

"You mean—" Yatta looked Trofimov in the eye with deep interest.

"Exactly. I'm proposing that we all—all four of us—go with you. It'll be better for you in our company. We're strong and we're good fighters. If we can get guns, we can fight off pursuers."

"When did you think of this idea, Sasha?" Yatta asked.

"You remember when I was sick, you told me the story of your wanderings. I asked you whether you'd be able to find your way to the Bering Strait, and you said yes."

Yatta inhaled deeply. "And where are you thinking of going? My plan was to reach the Anadyr forests where Qergina my woman lives. I hope she's still alive. We parted about a dozen years ago, but it was a mistake, we were mad at one another. I'd be happy to see her again and be with her at least once more in my life."

"You know, Yatta, I had something different in mind," Trofimov interrupted. Yatta looked puzzled. Trofimov continued: "It's hopeless to settle anywhere on Soviet territory. Sooner or later they're bound to track us down. I want to go to the Bering Strait and cross to Alaska."

"The land on the opposite shore?"

"Exactly. Alaska is America, and the Americans are at odds with the Soviets, so I guess they wouldn't hand us back to them. Over there we could live in peace and freedom. You told me once that some of your kinsmen are over there. You could join them."

"Yeah," Yatta confirmed, "about one third of our Telqap tribe moved there. There were no border guards on the Strait at that time, and you could travel freely to the opposite shore and back."

"So what d'you think of the idea?" Trofimov asked.

"Maybe you're right," Yatta's voice expressed hesitation. "But you know, it'll be very tough going. Half the route is through tundra, and it's hard to hide there. The other half is over hills and rocks, although I know some of the passes. Our kinfolk roamed a lot in that area." Yatta fell silent, then continued, "But you know, if we wanna cross the tundra though, we gotta go in winter. It's tough then, there are blizzards all the time. A good deerskin yaranga—that's a Chukchi tent—is good protection, though. And it's the polar night there in winter. It'll prevent the Big Moustache's men from tracking us down. But we gotta get guns though."

"Yes, we thought of that. We'll have to kill a few screws and get their submachine guns, but we've still not decided how to do it."

"We can find a way," Yatta nodded. "We could use some trick and outsmart them. You know, the great warriors of olden times knew many tricks, and they often won even against superior forces."

"Right," Trofimov confirmed. "But are you really sure, Yatta, that you know the whole way?"

"Almost, although there are parts of the route that I donna know well. Some of my friends live there, and I have links and bonds with them. They'll help us."

"That's encouraging," Trofimov smiled. "So you want to go in winter? Are you sure we'll survive?"

"Yeah, if we have guns. We can raid a collective farm. They will have a couple of reindeer, a sled, a tent and other things. Then we can survive the winter."

19

It was dinner break in the mine and no one was around. The wheelbarrows stood idle, and tools lay scattered. Bondarenko and Trofimov, who now worked as a tool grinder, sat together in an empty gallery entrance.

"Everythin's fine except there's not a goddamned thing to smoke," Bondarenko broke the silence. "You say Yatta agreed?

Why does he think we should wait till winter?"

"He says it's less risky. First, because the guard dogs can't track us so easily, and secondly, the water we have to cross will be frozen. Besides, in winter we'll have the cover of the polar night."

"How the hell will we survive the cold?" Bondarenko interrupted.

"Yatta claims that proper clothes and a good Chukchi tent will protect us from any cold or blizzard."

"Well," Bondarenko thought for a while, "maybe. But to get them we'll need guns."

"That's a problem we have to solve."

After supper, Trofimov, Timoshkin and Bondarenko walked towards their barracks.

"How's Yakov?" Timoshkin inquired.

"Not too bad," Trofimov smiled. "He's resting and feeding on reindeer meat."

"Lucky guy," Bondarenko exclaimed. "Real smart to fix himself a sick leave and vacation without croaking."

Suddenly three figures emerged from behind the office building, disguised by the dusk of the approaching summer night. They moved cautiously, but the friends felt their approach from the rear with a sixth sense innate to experienced soldiers and scouts. With a single movement they wheeled to face their attackers. One of the assailants tried to rush Trofimov with a knife, but his reward was a sharp kick in the crotch. He screamed and fell to his knees, dropping his knife. Another attacker struggled with Timoshkin, who grabbed the hand that held the knife. Meanwhile Bondarenko picked up a piece of metal tube from the grass and moved in on the third man. At that point, seeing their chance of success was slim, the attackers turned tail and retreated.

"Did you recognize them, Mikhail?" asked Timoshkin, when the friends reached their barracks hut.

"Sure, it were those damn hospital orderlies. Who else?"

"So they're after us already," concluded Trofimov.

"What did you expect?" Bondarenko said. "We took Yatta's part against them. Obviously they're gunning for us now."

"Then we've got to do something," Trofimov said.

"Carry knives. All the time." Bondarenko said. "Tuck 'em under your breeches."

"D'you still have your crowbar, Mikhail?" asked Trofimov.

"Abso-bloody-lutely. I keep it in a very safe place."

"How did you manage to get it, by the way?" asked Timoshkin.

"Easy. They're building a new dorm for the screws. The construction workers went off to help with the mine and they forgot to take some of their tools, and so …"

"What a guy." Trofimov laughed. "It's certainly an advantage, but they can get one the same way."

Suddenly the door opened and two figures appeared in silhouette, Vaskov and Yatta.

"From now on Yatta's going to stay here with you guys," Vaskov announced. "It's safer for him here."

"Have they been onto you again, Yatta?" Trofimov asked.

"Look at my shoulder." Yatta removed his jacket and showed them a tightly bound soiled bandage.

"Holy shit," Bondarenko exclaimed.

"When did this happen, Yatta?" asked Trofimov.

"You know, a couple days ago. I was on the way back from my traps. The screw who escorted me left me at the checkpoint, and two of 'em appeared. Nikolay and Makhmud. They stabbed me with a knife, but I ran for it. All last week they were after me."

"Why didn't you tell us?" Trofimov inquired.

"You know, I was too shy to bother you," Yatta replied.

"You should've told us," Trofimov insisted.

"They attacked us too," Bondarenko said, "as we were coming back here from the canteen."

"Well, you're in real trouble," Vaskov sighed. "Those men are cutthroats."

"We've got to think," Trofimov said firmly. "If we let things trail on, they're going to whack us sooner or later."

"Maybe complain to the authorities and report that they tried to kill Yatta," Timoshkin suggested.

"What, rat on them to the bosses?" Bondarenko spat in disgust. "No, never, that stinks. And besides, Avdeyev might remove Yatta, not them. Yatta can hunt and trap for the bosses anywhere. If they remove him, how the hell will we get in touch with him?"

"Yeah, that's a question," Timoshkin shook his head.

"What do you think, Captain?" Bondarenko turned to Trofimov.

"I think we have to get rid of them for good, but a direct attack won't work. We'll just get into trouble with the authorities."

"So?" Timoshkin threw Trofimov a questioning glance.

"So we have to outsmart them. Make it look as if they, not we, attacked. For instance, if they go for Yatta again, we can ambush them and come to his aid. Even better, if Yatta were not alone but with me. I remember very well the karate lessons I had in Vanino from a Japanese corporal called Fujimoto."

"Okay," Bondarenko outlined the plan, "this Sunday you sit and chat with Yatta on the grass in front of the bathhouse. Those bastards won't miss a chance like that. Take your knives with you. Zakharych and I will wait behind the bathhouse."

"And you, Mikhail, take your crowbar," Trofimov reminded him.

"Sure thing. As soon as they show up, out we come and break their bones for them."

"Then," Trofimov continued, "we'll go to the doc and tell him they attacked Yatta and we defended him. Yatta can tell him the whole saga about their conflicts. What d'you think, Yatta?"

"Sounds good," Yatta nodded.

"And you," Trofimov turned to Vaskov, "don't breathe a word to anyone."

20

The following Sunday the Fifth Compound was allowed to rest, and the prisoners enjoyed a long-awaited break from their labours. Trofimov and Yatta sat on the grass, chatting as planned.

"So you were born in the Anadyr region?" asked Trofimov.

"Not quite," Yatta replied, "I was born in the foothills of the Pekulney Mountains. It was what we call Imlirilin, the month of melting snows and spring waters. My father and brothers were at the pastures with the herd because the cows were calving."

"How many reindeer did your father have?" Trofimov inquired.

"Let me count. About fifteen score, three hundred."

"Not bad," Trofimov nodded.

"At that time, though, it wasn't that many," Yatta said. "It was just an average herd. Some owned two hundred score. That's several thousand head."

"Incredible," Trofimov said. "So your people didn't live all that badly under the tsar."

"Well, the Sun Chief left us largely to ourselves. He ain't take our pelts and never touched our herds. But you know, the Soviet bosses took all our furs and more than half of our cattle."

"They didn't fleece and strip the hide off you, did they?" The snarling voice was that of Kozlenko, who suddenly appeared with his three buddies. "That's what we're gonna do to you now, my friends."

Trofimov and Yatta jumped to their feet and pulled their knives. Azizbekov and Kozlenko attempted to rush Trofimov, but the latter was too quick. He delivered Kozlenko a kick in the groin and countered Azizbekov's knife with his own. At the same time Yatta dodged Chernyayev's knife and kicked his assailant in the shins. Azizbekov made another attempt, but was now confronted by Bondarenko who emerged from the bushes with his crowbar and smashed it into the bandit's ribs. Kozlenko recovered from Trofimov's kick and sprang to his feet, but Bondarenko's crowbar landed across his head, and he fell unconscious. With knife in hand, Timoshkin moved in on Chernyayev and Parnov from behind, diverting their attention from Yatta and Bondarenko. The two orderlies hurled themselves at Timoshkin and found themselves caught between him, Trofimov and Bondarenko. They tried to flee, but Trofimov, Yatta, Timoshkin and Bondarenko blocked their escape.

"Throw down your knives. On your knees, hands behind your heads," Trofimov ordered calmly. "And be quick about it, you bastards."

Chernyayev and Parnov saw their position was hopeless and obeyed. Kozlenko lay unconscious, while Azizbekov sat on the ground bawling in his native language.

"Well," Bondarenko smiled victoriously, "we warned you not to touch Yatta, didn't we? But you took no notice. So what the fuck are we gonna do with you now?"

"Forgive us, buddies," Parnov suddenly broke down and sobbed.

"Have mercy on us."

"Mercy? On shit like you?" Trofimov looked him straight in the eye. "When did you ever have mercy on anyone?"

The other two orderlies sobbed and pleaded for mercy.

"So that's what you are, fuckin' cowards." Bondarenko spat in disgust and turned to Trofimov. "So, Captain, what are we to do with 'em?"

"Well," Trofimov paused, "they have to be rendered harmless. But don't smash them up completely. Then we'll hand them over to the bosses."

"Good idea," Bondarenko nodded. He took his crowbar and approached each one in turn and dealt him a blow, breaking one man's arm, dislocating another man's elbow, and crushing the third man's knee.

"Now let's tell the doc the whole story," Trofimov said. "He's a good type. He'll understand."

"What the hell happened?" the doctor asked. "Do I understand correctly that they tried to attack Yatta?"

"Precisely, doc," Trofimov confirmed. "On three separate occasions."

"What did they want from you, Yatta?" the doctor asked.

"Well, they wanted most of my medicines for a long time," Yatta explained. "They threatened me. Then, you know, about a month ago, they decided to degrade me. But these guys—Sasha, Mikhail and Pyotr—the three of them came to my defence. Then, today they caught me and Sasha sitting and chatting and tried a knife attack on us again. Pyotr and Mikhail came to our assistance, and we fought them off."

"Did you injure them?"

"Well, somewhat." Trofimov was serious. "We were attacked and there was nothing for it but to fight back. They had knives, so we had to hit them hard before they could stab us."

"Okay." The doctor nodded. "I understand. But, Yatta, what did they want your medications for? Had they found some market for them?"

"Yeah, boss," Yatta said. "You know, they sold them to those people who are looking for gold in the woods."

"The geologists?"

"Yeah, that's it. They sell my medicines to them."

"Damn," the doctor snarled. "I suspected as much, but what could I do? They're tough guys."

"Not any more, they aren't." Bondarenko grinned. "And I'll guarantee, they ain't gonna be tough for a very long time."

The doctor thought for a moment then said, "You understand that I'll have to report this to Avdeyev? I'll stress that they were after Yatta. I bet he'll be mighty angry at them. Where are they now?"

"Have a seat." Major Avdeyev showed Doctor Ponomarev a chair under Stalin's portrait. The doctor always felt uncomfortable in this office. One word from this powerful man, a mere silent gesture, could send him straight back to the mines. The very thought made him shudder, and he prayed to God (of whose existence he was uncertain) that he might avoid this fate.

"What's the matter?" asked Avdeyev.

"There's been a serious incident, citizen Major." The doctor forced himself to look the camp chief straight in the eye. He knew Avdeyev could not stand his subordinates lowering their eyes. "It's our hospital orderlies, Kozlenko, Chernyayev, Parnov and Azizbekov. They tried to kill Yatta."

"Holy shit," Avdeyev frowned. "When?"

"Actually, they tried several times, citizen Major. The first time was about a month ago. He had to run away and hide in one of the convicts' barracks. He didn't even sleep in his own room, just wandered from one barracks to another. Finally they attacked him again this morning."

"What did they want from him?" Avdeyev's voice was angry, but the doctor felt relieved: he had evidently managed to channel the commandant's anger in the right direction.

"It's a long story, citizen Major. For a few years they've been stealing from the hospital, especially drugs, and have sold them to the geologists. They sold pelts as well. But more than that they wanted Yatta's herbal medicines, and they thought he wasn't giving them enough."

"Scum, bastards." Avdeyev produced a stream of curses. "Here I went and gave them a nice cosy corner, the sort of place that other cons would go to hell and back to get, and they aren't satisfied. Well, I'll deal with them."

"Actually, they've already been dealt with, citizen Major."

"What do you mean?"

"When they attacked Yatta this morning," the doctor explained, "a crowd of labourers rushed to his rescue and made mincemeat of them. The four of them are in the hospital with fractures."

"Well, well." Avdeyev grinned. "I would never have thought those folk were capable of that. They all look so shit scared. But evidently they're really fond of Yatta. He saved the lives of so many, didn't he? But as for those stinking scumbags," he added after a pause, "you say they already got their due?"

"Yes, citizen Major. I examined them myself. They're in a bad state."

"And d'you know who did it?"

"Hard to say, citizen Major. There were too many of them, a crowd. Some from the fourth barracks, some from the fifth."

"Well," Avdeyev lit another cigarette, "strictly speaking it's a breach of the law, but if there were so many involved, we'll just leave things the way they are. After all, the bastards got what they deserved." He paused. "At least, they got what they deserved from 'the people.' Now they're going to get something from the authorities as well." He laughed. "Get 'em out of the hospital and take 'em somewhere a good long way into the woods. I guess the wolves will appreciate a bite of their fat asses. Draw up a formal death certificate for each of them. After that you can pick a new team of more trustworthy men. You can even take some from among the 58-ers, to start with, at least. Whatever else, they don't steal."

In the evening the three friends sat on their bunks enjoying the tobacco from Timoshkin's parcel. Their meditative mood was suddenly broken by a loud voice.

"Are Trofimov, Bondarenko and Timoshkin here?"

"Here," Trofimov answered. "What's the matter?"

"Doctor Ponomarev wants to see you straightaway."

"We're on our way."

They rose, cursing under their breath at the unexpected interruption, and walked towards the hospital.

"It's bound to be something to do with our little dust-up," Timoshkin broke the silence.

"I don't think so," Trofimov said. "In that case we'd be summoned to the Godfather himself. It's something else."

"Who the fuck can tell?" Bondarenko cursed. "Maybe the Godfather's waiting for us with a regiment of screws."

"Maybe the doc wants to warn us," Trofimov guessed. "Or give us some advice before we're questioned."

Trofimov knocked at the door of the doctor's office.

"Come in," they heard the doctor's voice. The doctor was seated at his desk.

"Have a seat," the doctor's face wore a shining smile. "I have a surprise for you."

"Like what, doc?" asked Trofimov.

"Well, you've gone and crippled my hospital orderlies, so I need to replace them. Avdeyev was so mad at the poor bastards that he didn't even ask who did them in. He gave orders to have them carted off into the woods. I'm taking the three of you, and Goldberg as well, as soon as he can walk."

"You kidding, doc?" Bondarenko was first to emerge from his stupor.

"Why would I joke about something like this?" the doctor's voice was serious. "You start tomorrow. I can't promise you'll stay on the job for long, though. You've got bad articles in your files. But you'll be here until the next inspection from Orotukan at least. The hospital needs orderlies who do the job well and don't steal. Avdeyev specially stressed that I get a reliable team. To tell you the truth, I'm really glad to have you guys instead of that lot. They were bandits. They robbed the hospital and threatened everyone, including me. So there we are. Let's have a cig to celebrate."

As the three friends left the hospital, they heard loud screams and curses. A group of camp guards dragged Kozlenko, Parnov, Chernyayev and Azezbekov towards the camp gates.

"Citizen Guard! For Chrissake!" wept Kozlenko. "We aren't guilty. Not guilty at all." He burst into sobs.

"There's not a fuckin' thing I can do," the head guard replied. "It's the chief's orders."

"Look at them," sighed Timoshkin. "This morning they were so strong and scary, and now they're helpless wretches. But it's a cruel punishment sending them out to freeze to death in the woods."

"Ha," Bondarenko laughed. "So you pity them, Zakharych? They wouldn't pity you."

"Anyway," said Trofimov, "it's not we who are sending them to their death. We merely 'rendered them harmless.' The rest is fate. It's better for us all that they're not here any more."

21

Within a month Trofimov, Bondarenko, Goldberg and Timoshkin were unrecognizable. Wearing white gowns and caps with red crosses, they looked well fed and strong. They sat in the corridor, taking in Yatta's instructions.

"Look, Mikhail," Yatta handed Bondarenko a glass jar containing a jam-like substance. "This is red whortleberry. Make a whortleberry tea for those fellas. Can you manage?"

"No problem, Yatta, I know how to make tea."

"Be careful though," Yatta warned. "Not more than the width of your third finger."

"Sure." Bondarenko walked off towards the ward.

"And you, Sasha," Yatta turned to Trofimov, "come with me. Give a spoonful of dogrose potion to each of the patients then come back and help me with a needle leaf footbath. And you, Pyotr, the doc wants you for somethin'."

Trofimov and Yatta entered the ward. It was filled with so many cots that they overflowed into the corridor.

"Sergey Ivanov," called Trofimov. "Is there someone of that name here?"

"Here he is," a voice answered from the middle of the ward, "but he's been unconscious since last night." The man pointed out a neighbouring cot.

The man lying in it had the usual appearance of a goner, with a dark frostbitten face, deep-sunken eyes and protruding teeth—just like Trofimov a few months before.

"Ivanov," Trofimov addressed him. "Hi, buddy, have something to drink."

The man did not respond. His eyes were half closed, his mouth slightly open, muttering. Trofimov opened his mouth with one hand and tried to pour in a spoonful of medicine. The patient clamped his jaw shut.

"Mikhail," Trofimov called loudly.

"Yeah, Captain?" Bondarenko replied from the other end of the ward.

"Come over here and help me give this guy his medication."

"One moment." Bondarenko stepped over and opened the patient's mouth and held it, while Trofimov poured in the medication. Trofimov sighed. How much suffering he saw each day. He was accustomed to scenes of human misery; after all, he had seen plenty of blood and terrible injuries at the front. But those were fresh wounds with fresh blood from the fighting, and however horrifying, there was a certain tragic glory about them. Here, on the other hand, men literally rotted alive.

A patient on a neighbouring cot opened his eyes and stared at Trofimov. "Are you one of the new orderlies?"

"Sure am. Only just noticed me?" Trofimov grinned.

"Where are the old ones?" the man asked. "We've not seen them for a long time."

"They're gone for good, old man."

"For good?" The man opened his eyes wide. "Were they sent back to the mines or the logging site?"

"Even better than that. Avdeyev ordered them carted out to the woods. By now they've probably been gobbled up by wild animals."

"Really? That's fantastic." The man seemed genuinely delighted.

"Yes, they tried to whack Yatta, so—"

"They went after Yatta? I hope the bastards fry in hell."

"I've no doubt they will," Trofimov agreed.

"But you look familiar. Don't I know you, comrade?" the man asked.

"Quite possibly." Trofimov shrugged.

"Yeah, I know you. You were the neighbour of my pal Petrukhin. He told me about you. You were just a corpse then, but Petrukhin said you were a captain at the front and that you were even decorated by Zhukov himself."

"Vassilevsky, actually," Trofimov corrected him.

"Comes to the same thing. So it's really you?"

"Looks like that," Trofimov nodded. "And what happened to Petrukhin?"

"Kicked the bucket. And now," he added after a pause, "it looks like I'm next in line. But you, you were half dead, and now you're alive and well. What a change of fortune."

"It's thanks to Yatta," Trofimov said. "He raised me from the dead. And you shouldn't be talking about croaking either. You know that Yatta can work miracles. I'll ask him to get you some fresh reindeer meat. He usually feeds it to the bad cases. It helps a lot, I swear."

"Real venison?" The man opened his eyes wide. "If only I could get a taste of that before I croak. I haven't had decent food for almost two years."

"Hey, Captain." Bondarenko called from the next rows of cots. "Two more corpses here. Help me."

Trofimov approached. "You take him, and I'll take the other one," said Bondarenko, nodding toward a body. The dead man's eyes were dull and glassy. Trofimov recalled that his name was Sadovnikov and that he was a shoemaker. No doubt he had a wife and kids somewhere, waiting for him, not realizing he was dead and gone, just one more victim among the thousands claimed by the great Soviet construction projects.

Trofimov picked up the body under the arms while Bondarenko did the same with another corpse a few rows away. They moved them out into the corridor and laid them on the floor beside the entrance to await Doctor Ponomarev, who would make out the death certificates.

"I'm gonna visit Yefimych tonight," Bondarenko said. "D'you want to join me?"

"Sure," Trofimov agreed. "We haven't seen the old chap for quite a while. How's he doing?"

"So far he's alive and well. What else would you expect of

someone in his cosy position?"

Trofimov, Bondarenko and Vaskov sat smoking their home-rolled shag cigars and toasting bread over the stove. It was early evening, and the barracks was empty, so the three of them could smoke and eat openly, without fear of someone coming to beg.

"Well, how do you enjoy being trusties?" asked Vaskov.

"Huh," Bondarenko grunted, "it's a real vacation, and a chance to fill my belly at last. When I wake up in the morning and hear them banging on that rail, I just can't believe I don't have to go and break my back for the next fourteen hours. I can go anywhere in the camp, I can smoke and relax, and even gloat over the others. What a change."

"But folks are dying all the time," Trofimov observed.

"Yeah," Vaskov sighed, "That's the norm in Kolyma, but you ain't seen the penal camp at Polar Creek. Up there two dozen cons die every day."

Trofimov sighed. "You can't afford to take every death to heart, otherwise you'd be driven crazy."

"Exactly," Vaskov nodded. "You've gotta cling to your place in the warmth if you want to survive. And you four better find a way to grease the authorities' palms, or you won't stay on as orderlies for very long. With your sentences under article 58 you shouldn't even be orderlies. It's against regulations. Once an inspection team comes from Orotukan, you'll be sent back to the labour gang. But even before that happens, the doc will expect some token of your gratitude. And so will Lieutenant Samsonov. He didn't block your appointments, and that was a great favour, but he expects you to show your appreciation. And so does Belyayev. He's in charge of all in-camp affairs."

"My God," Trofimov exclaimed. "The doc, Samsonov, Belyayev?" Where the hell can we find bribes—sorry, *gifts*—for all of them?"

"That's for you to figure out." Vaskov's voice turned harsh. "There are various ways. For instance, you've got dozens and dozens of patients. Many of 'em would grease your palm with quite nice things from the parcels they get: sweaters, boots, real food, like bacon, or even vodka. Keep whatever you collect and hand it over to the bosses."

"Hell, no," Trofimov snapped. "I'm never going to take bribes. That's lousy."

"Just as lousy as all the rest of this damned camp life," Bondarenko grinned. "Yefimych is right. We've got no other way. We could also ask Yatta to give up some of his pelts."

"What a life," Timoshkin groaned. "First those thugs, Kozlenko and co., and now we're gonna do the same thing. But at least we won't grab his medications."

"At the front, I never dreamed I could fall this low," Trofimov said. "But somehow in the camps a man has to change his ways. What a load of shit."

22

"So, guys," said Goldberg, joining in the conversation, "Do you still think we should go on with our escape plan? Life's not at all bad here now."

"Don't be naïve, Yakov," Trofimov said. "We won't be in the hospital for long. Anyway, we're still slaves and slavery is lousy no matter how you look at it. We have to take full advantage of our present position to get ourselves ready."

"We still have to commit all those murders, don't we?" Goldberg said.

"Of course. How the hell can we get out of here otherwise?" Bondarenko answered with a grin.

"My point is," Goldberg continued, "that when we were down the mine, we could justify killing them because we would die otherwise. But now we're not going to die. It's true, we want our freedom, but do we have the right to take other men's lives for that?"

"You're talking shit again, Yakov," snapped Bondarenko. "The same old song. 'Take other men's lives' indeed. What 'bout during the war? You were in charge of a gun battery. What the hell were you doing, other than shelling the Fritzes and killing them off by the score? Did you have all these scruples then?"

"That was … different." Goldberg sounded hesitant.

"What was different about it? Because they were Germans, while this lot are, so to speak, our fellow Russians? Well, what are these so-called fellow Russians doing to us? Haven't you seen 'em beat the shit out of scores of convicts every day? Haven't you seen those goners in the medical section? It was your fellow Russians that turned them into physical wrecks."

"Keep your voice down, Mikhail," Timoshkin tugged him by the sleeve.

"Okay," Bondarenko lowered his voice. "Anyway, Yakov, you've gotta give us your answer. Are you with us or not? Yes or no? If not, just fuck off right now and leave us alone."

"You needn't talk like that to Yakov," Trofimov interrupted. "He's one of us. But Yakov, you have to make a decision. Mikhail is right, we can't get away without putting up a fight. They are the enemy. They'll kill us if we don't kill them. They started this war of extermination, not us."

"Well, Sasha," Goldberg said shyly, "probably you're right. That's just the way I feel."

"I understand you." Trofimov put his hand on Goldberg's shoulder. "I had feelings like that when I killed my first Germans. It came as a real shock, but it was my duty—a savage duty—and one I couldn't avoid. These bastards here, I know them all too well, beating and shooting, dragging men off to the Black Hole and God knows what else. Anyway, it's up to you, Yakov. I need you to make a decision soon."

"Yakov, it'll be very dangerous f'you to stay here if the four of us run for it," Timoshkin said. "The bosses know you're our pal, and they won't spare you. They'll beat the shit out of you."

A deep silence followed.

"Still, can I think it over?" asked Goldberg.

Goldberg spent the next few days in painful hesitation. He immersed himself in his work at the hospital and tried not to think about anything. At night as he lay on the straw mattress in his cot, in comfort compared to the bare wooden bunks of the fourth barracks, he turned the idea over again and again, and again and again he failed to make a decision. Logically he agreed that his friends were right, but his soul revolted against bloodshed. His background was that of a traditional East European Jew, not that he or his parents followed the kosher laws—out of sight of other Jews they ate pork and non-kosher food. But in other respects they were typical Jews from the Pale of Settlement, peaceful, non-violent and faithful to the Talmudic commandments. Although periodically abused, they were reluctant to fight back and kill. Some of the younger ones resented this attitude and became either die-hard communists or they embraced Zionism and went to Palestine. But Goldberg was neither a communist nor a Zionist. He lived mostly according to the centuries' old tradition of the Ashkenazi Jews, and instinctively rather than consciously he had inherited most of their ways and attitudes.

He was barely four years old when the White Volunteer Army launched a pogrom in which almost half of his extended family was massacred. Hardly any of his relatives even thought of fighting back. They hid and hoped that the Red Army would come and save them. He was in his late twenties, already married with two children, when the Germans invaded Russia and began implementing their "Final Solution" to the Jewish question. This time he was called up and fought at the front, and never thought of dodging the draft. He had to contribute to the defeat of Nazism and save his fellow Jews from annihilation. But the war for him was a temporary aberration, in which the rules of normal life were suspended for a time. It was not he who declared war, and all he could do was live by the rules of war until the hostilities ended, after which he could go home and continue life as before.

Finally the war came to an end, and Goldberg returned to his wife and children, only to fall victim to a wave of anti-Semitic purges when the regime suddenly chose Soviet Jewry as its new target. This was something no one could have predicted. Up until the postwar years, the regime had turned against various groups— former Whites, children of the old elite, *petite bourgeoisie* and peasants—but never openly against the Jews. Goldberg had no plan of action for such a situation. All he could do was try to survive one way or another, although for him at no point did it ever mean taking up arms against the regime. Now his friends Sasha Trofimov, Bondarenko and even softhearted Timoshkin proposed that he do exactly that. For them, unlike him, it was easy to transfer their former attitude to the Germans to the guards and officers and all representatives of authority in the camps. For his friends it was quite natural to declare war. Was it cruelty on their part, or simply sound reason and common sense? Or was it that, having grown used to killing during the war, they could resume doing so at any time? Not that he felt inclined to condemn them. After all, they were true friends and fine human beings, probably the noblest figures in the whole of this goddamned Fifth Compound. And Goldberg personally owed his life to Trofimov and Timoshkin. The only thing was that he could not think the same way they did. For them these boys with submachine guns were an enemy to be eliminated at all costs. For Yakov, vicious and rude as they were, these youngsters were fellow human beings who happened to be drafted into the home army and assigned to camp guard duty. Much of their cruelty was due to brainwashing by their political officers. For Trofimov, Bondarenko and Timoshkin, and certainly for Yatta as a traditional tribesman, it was natural to dismiss them as enemies for slaughter. This seemed anything but fair to Yakov Goldberg as a Jewish husband and father, and one of a nation that had shed no blood for almost two thousand years. Therefore let the others do whatever they planned, Yakov Goldberg was unable to join them.

On the other hand, Timoshkin was right: if they fled and Yakov stayed behind, the authorities would round on him and beat him into confessing that he knew of their planned escape but failed to report it. That in itself was enough to get him executed or, even worse, sent to one of those vicious penal camps. Goldberg remembered the pain he had been subjected to during his interrogation in the Lubyanka, and only in his worst nightmares could he imagine going through that again. If he stayed, that would be his fate, the ultimate cost of retaining a clear conscience. Was it perhaps too high a price to pay? After all, he was no saint, just an ordinary human being. Moreover, whether or not he joined them, his friends would proceed with their plan, and those youngsters in uniform who happened to stand in their way on that day would die anyway. There was no way to prevent that. More precisely, there was only one way to do so, and that was to report them to the authorities. But that was unthinkable.

With or without him, Trofimov and the others would carry out their plan and kill the camp guards, and there was nothing he could do to stop them. It would thus be unreasonable not to take the chance to escape. And what a prospect! Surely they would never reach Alaska, but even so it would be wonderful to spend a year in freedom, feeding on fresh game, free of constant fear, far from officers and screws, and all in the company of men he liked and trusted.

But when he thought like that, he found it hypocritical to abjure responsibility for the lives of those men that his friends were going to kill. Thus, hour after hour, day after day, he found himself unable to make a decision. As time wore on, he more and more often noticed that questioning look in the eyes of his friends.

23

One evening in the barracks, Trofimov, Bondarenko and Yatta talked over some urgent questions without Goldberg, who had not yet given his answer.

"So, Yatta," Trofimov began, "you think we should wait three more months, until winter? Maybe we should go now, while we're free of escorts?"

"Yatta, I realize that you know better," Bondarenko joined in. "But I ain't sure we'll survive the winter. No one ever fled in winter before."

"Yeah, I understand you guys," Yatta replied, "but in summer there are too many obstacles, all those rivers, creeks, lakes and swamps. We'd have to make big detours to get round them. That would waste a lot of time."

"But are you sure we ain't gonna freeze to death?" Bondarenko interrupted.

"No," Yatta was quite firm. "Not with good clothes and a tent. If need be, our Chukchi men can sleep right on the snow, if they're properly dressed with their belts tightened."

"So," Bondarenko continued, "when do you think we should go?"

"Not before the twentieth day of Githa-elhin, the second winter month, when the rivers freeze."

"That's October," said Bondarenko. "So we've gotta try and stay on as orderlies until then."

A loud rumbling noise outside drew the three men to the window. The compound lights blazed, and groups of guards, fully armed and carrying lanterns, ran past the barracks window, shouting commands as they ran.

"What the hell's going on?" Bondarenko wondered.

"Who knows?" Trofimov said. "Maybe a knifing? Or some stooge has been knocked off."

"Could be," Yatta agreed. "Last summer, before you came, a couple of stooges were strangled in one of the barracks. That caused an almighty uproar. The entire camp population were stripped naked and kept standing outdoors for several hours, feeding the mosquitoes … Or maybe," he added after a pause, "maybe someone's escaped?"

"Let's go have a look," said Trofimov.

The three of them stepped outside.

"Back off, you filthy scum." the sergeant roared. "Stay where you are."

"What's the matter, Sergeant?" Trofimov asked.

"None of your fuckin' business," snapped the sergeant.

It was some time before Trofimov and his friends made their way to the staff building, where they saw a group of convicts and trusties talking.

"Hey, folks, what's going on?" Trofimov asked them.

"Three guys escaped," came the answer.

"Any idea who?" Bondarenko asked.

"Not the faintest," the man shrugged. "Somebody from the fourth barracks," he said.

"From our old barracks?" Trofimov was surprised. "I wonder who it could be?"

"I guess Yefimych knows," Bondarenko said.

"So, Yefimych, got any idea who they are?" inquired Trofimov.

"Sure," Vaskov nodded. "It's Sorokin, Losev, and Zakharov from one of the logging teams."

"Such quiet types. Who would imagine?" Bondarenko gaped.

Losev was a collective farmer from Yaroslavl region, serving his sentence either for stealing a few ears of rye from the field, or for being an Old Believer. His teammate Sorokin was a former university student from Leningrad, and Zakharov, the third of them, was a locksmith from Moscow. They belonged to the same work team, one that almost always managed to meet its production quotas. All three men had seemed somewhat withdrawn. Whenever there was talk about some risky subject, they always shied away. Now it turned out they had been the boldest of the bunch, and had made a daring escape attempt.

"How'd they manage it, Yefimych?" Bondarenko asked.

"They were very smart. The night before last was the birthday of one of the screws, a Sergeant Kovalyov. This guy had earned an official favour for somethin' or other, and he decided to throw a drinking party. Nearly a third of the screws got roaring drunk and had vicious hangovers next day. These guys picked their moment and hit their guard over the head with the butt of an axe while he was pissing."

"There'll be a mighty row upstairs," Trofimov grinned. Some of the screws will face court martial."

"I donna think so," Vaskov said. "I bet Avdeyev will hush the incident up. The scandal could threaten his career. He may pick on a small bunch of scapegoats, two or three, but hardly more than that."

"But those guys were dickheads to flee on such a clear night as yesterday," Bondarenko commented. "They gonna be caught in a few days at most."

"Maybe. But it was too good a chance to miss with the escort so lax," said Vaskov. "From now on I bet the screws will never be allowed to go for a leak," he added. "They'll have to piss right there on the spot."

"More than likely," Trofimov agreed.

"That's it," Vaskov nodded. "So if they were thinking of escaping, how could they miss a chance like that? But," he added, "you're right, I doubt they'll get very far."

24

"Here you are, buddy. Have a drink." Trofimov poured a spoonful of medicine into the patient's mouth. The man swallowed the liquid and then addressed him: "Comrade Trofimov?"

"Yes? What is it?"

"What's with those … those guys that fled? Are they still on the run?"

"Yes," Trofimov said, "looks like it. If they were caught, we'd know."

"How long since they fled?"

"A week or so."

"Then they made it." Varlamenko's eyes shone with delight. "Way to go, guys!"

"Hush, man," Trofimov cautioned him. "There may be stooges around. And even if they aren't caught," he added, "where the hell can they go?"

Suddenly there was a rasp from the ward's loudspeaker:

"Attention! Attention! All inmates and administrative personnel of Fifth Compound to gather immediately in front of the Staff Headquarters for an extraordinary roll call. This concerns every person in the compound at the present moment."

"What the hell's that for?" Trofimov wondered. "Do the patients have to go as well?"

The loudspeaker repeated the message over and over again. At that point one of the guards entered the ward.

"Everybody out to attend roll call." He nodded towards Trofimov. "You too."

Trofimov walked along the main path toward the staff building. Numerous other groups of prisoners headed the same way. On the square in front of the building, a large crowd had assembled, lined up in columns. Major Avdeyev stepped up in front of the company, followed by Belyayev and other officers.

"Greetings, prisoners," Avdeyev addressed them. There was a muttered chorus of half-hearted greetings from the crowd. "Do you have any idea why I've summoned you?" Avdeyev asked with a vicious leer on his face.

"No, citizen Major," a few voices responded.

"Well," Avdeyev grinned with satisfaction, "I will inform you. A week ago three convicts fled from our compound. Belyayev, announce the names."

"Sorokin, Pyotr Vassilyevich: 58/2 and 58/4: twenty-five years; Losev, Nikifor Stepanovich: 58/1 and 58/4: twenty years; and Zakharov, Vladimir Petrovich: 58/10: ten years," Belyayev rapped out the information.

"A week ago," Avdeyev continued, "these convicts committed the offence of attempting to escape, badly injuring one of the camp guards." The crowd remained silent. "Well, they didn't get far." Avdeyev turned to the guards standing by. "Bring them here."

Three guards marched over to the exit that led to the outer zone and returned pushing the three runaways in front of them. The men were handcuffed, their faces a bloody mess and their jackets soaked with blood and mud. One of them couldn't walk and was dragged by the guards.

"Here they are," Avdeyev proclaimed. "Here are the scum, this dirty rabble who thought they could outsmart the MGB and the Soviet people. See what's happened to them. And that's what happens to anyone who tries to sabotage the process of lawful punishment, and to anyone who dares to launch terror against our servicemen on duty. We shall show no pity for any offender. That's the way it is, and that's the way it always will be." He turned to Belyayev. "Read the sentences."

Unlike Avdeyev, Belyayev's voice sounded calm and indifferent.

"The Judicial Board of the Fifth Camp Compound of the Seimchan Camp Administration, having considered the case of the following convicts: Sorokin, Pyotr Vassilyevich, 58/2 and 58/4; Losev, Nikifor Stepanovich, 58/1 and 58/4 and Zakharov, Vladimir Petrovich, 58/10, has found the above-mentioned persons guilty under Articles 58/7, sabotage, and 58/8, terrorism, and sentenced them to capital punishment. This sentence is final and not subject to appeal."

An anguished silence fell over the crowd. It lasted for a few minutes, uninterrupted.

"And now you can all go and think." Avdeyev finally broke the silence. "At ease. Dismiss."

The crowd of prisoners dispersed.

"Poor guys," sighed Timoshkin.

"Poor ain't the word for it," said Bondarenko. "You know, I honestly hoped they'd made a getaway. At first I thought they'd be caught the very next day, but when the days passed and they were still on the run, I thought they'd made it. I had that gloating feeling towards the bosses: 'There you are, you scum, swallow that. You can't do a fuckin' thing.' But now Avdeyev and his crew are celebrating, as if to say, 'Here you are back in camp and no one can get beyond our reach. These bastards tried it, and now, you load of shit, look what happened to them.' " Bondarenko paused and turned to Goldberg: "And you, Yakov, still can't decide whether it's a good thing to whack one of the screws?"

The next day the doctor ordered Trofimov and Goldberg to go to the Seimchan central drugstore to fetch medications. Although the four of them, as trusties, went without escort, their freedom of movement was limited. They had to seek permission from Belyayev to leave the compound. They had to stand through the roll call like ordinary labourers, waiting till they could speak to him. Finally the roll call ended, and the two of them approached Belyayev.

Belyayev stared at them. "You're new hospital orderlies, aren't you?"

"Yes, citizen Lieutenant," Trofimov replied.

"What do you want?"

"We've been charged by Doctor Ponomarev to fetch some new medications from Seimchan," answered Trofimov.

"Medications? Hmm. How much time do you need?"

"I guess until six o'clock," Trofimov said.

"Six o'clock?" Belyayev raised his eyebrows. "Why so long? So you can go for a drink? Or go after the wenches?" He stared at Trofimov. "What are your names?"

"Trofimov, Alexander Ivanovich."

"Goldberg, Yakov Moiseevich," Goldberg added.

"A Yid?" Belyayev stared at him.

"Yes, I'm a Jew."

"A Yid here in Kolyma," Belyayev smirked. "This is a good place for all of you rootless cosmopolitans. Being a smart Yid you've found a nice warm corner for yourself even here. Article?" he inquired.

"58/6 and 58/10, fifteen years," Goldberg responded.

"And yours?" he turned to Trofimov.

"58/1b, 58/6 and 58/11: twenty-five years."

"And with sentences like that, under those articles, you've been appointed orderlies?" Belyayev gave both men a long, searching glance. The two of them remained silent.

"All right," Belyayev said. "It's six thirty now. Be back by one. If you come a minute later, I'll send you straight to the mines, clear?"

"Yes, citizen Lieutenant."

"Off you go."

"Thank you, citizen Lieutenant."

Trofimov and Goldberg approached the exit. The guards on the gate first ordered them to stop then recognized them as orderlies and let them pass. The two men walked along the forest trail, enjoying the fresh air filled with woodland aromas.

"God," exclaimed Goldberg, "I haven't walked in the woods for almost two years."

Trofimov smiled. "I feel almost free."

"Do you know the road well?" Goldberg asked.

"I checked the map," Trofimov reassured him, "and I've a good memory for locations. We go all the way along this path and then take the right fork."

"Then you lead," said Goldberg. "D'you think that bastard Belyayev has seriously taken against us?"

"C'mon," Trofimov smiled, "he just puts on the swagger to show us who's boss. The local authorities love to do that. But I guess we should buy a bottle of vodka for him in Seimchan."

It was midsummer and the woods looked beautiful. The larches were covered in fresh needles and looked much thicker than in winter. Under the trees glowed the bright spots of ripening berries.

The men stopped from time to time to pick and eat them. The sun shed the generous warmth of the brief northern summer, when nature revives for a short while before relapsing into the icy lethargy of a seven-month winter.

Amazing, thought Trofimov, it's such a different feeling to be on your own, with no screws and dogs following you. Then his thoughts turned to Yakov who had still not given his answer. Trofimov knew they had to ask him some time soon. But not just now.

The path they followed intersected with another. Trofimov recalled from the map that this new path led straight to the Seimchan highway in one direction and in the other down the slope toward the Kolyma River, where logging teams were busy felling trees. The highway in turn ran from north to south. Towards the south it led to the regional centre of Seimchan, a small town of a few thousand with several camp compounds, a gold mine and a military air base. Northwards the highway led to the top of a small mountain range, towards the dreaded penal camps.

"Here we are, Yakov," Trofimov smiled. "We round this curve, and in a hundred metres we come to the fork."

As they rounded the curve, they stopped, rooted to the spot. On the left side of the road were three human silhouettes, which with some difficulty they recognized as the three runaways who were recently caught. They were stripped to their underpants and tied to the trees with metal wire. Their bodies were covered from head to toe by a dense black cloud of gnats. Their faces, like the rest of their bodies, were swollen and bruised, almost purple in colour. Their half-closed eyes were dull and glassy, and their lower jaws hung loose. For a few minutes Trofimov and Goldberg stood quite still, unable to move or say a word.

"Let's bring them water from the spring," Trofimov at last broke the silence.

"Maybe we can untie them," Goldberg suggested.

"It won't work," Trofimov said. "We don't have wire cutters, and we'll never untie the wire with our bare hands. Even if we managed to do that, they won't live long. I'm sure the screws broke their legs to make sure they couldn't run away." He approached the bodies and examined them. "Yeah, their legs and arms are broken."

"Can't we do anything for them?"

"All we can do is smash their skulls and put them out of their misery. Before that let's give them some water. Go and fill a flask from the spring. I'll look for a stone."

Goldberg bent over the spring and filled his flask. Trofimov looked for something hard and heavy, but there was nothing. Goldberg walked over to the three men with his flask. At that moment a screw emerged as if from nowhere.

"Clear off," he snarled. "What the fuck are you doing here?"

"We're hospital orderlies," Trofimov said. "We're going to Seimchan to fetch medications."

"Get on your way then," the guard's voice grew calmer. "Don't try and approach those three. It's forbidden."

"C'mon, Corporal," Trofimov looked him straight in the eye, "you mean to say these poor guys have no right even to a sip of water?"

"That's the major's orders." the guard shrugged. "Anyway, as far as they're concerned, the sooner they croak the better it'll be for them."

Trofimov looked at the guard. He had the ordinary face of a youngster from some village or small town. Most likely he had been sent here by the regional military commissariat, was fed up with the service and dreamed of going home. But however benign he looked, he refused to let them give any water to the suffering prisoners. If they disobeyed him, he would have quite willingly gunned them down on the spot.

Trofimov and Goldberg were silent as they got to the divide in the paths, and they set off along the right fork still unable to speak. Even Trofimov, who had seen many horrors and knew the authorities were capable of almost any atrocity, was shocked and numbed by what they had seen, the more so when he imagined himself in place of one of those prisoners. Indeed, there was no hope of mercy. The only thing was to fight and to die fighting rather than allow oneself to be captured.

When they reached the highway, Goldberg finally broke the silence. "You know, that's something … something beyond any limits," he exclaimed. "Such … barbarity."

"Yeah, buddy," Trofimov replied, "that's what they're like. For them we aren't human beings. We're worse than cattle, just raw material for their fascist experiments. They'll do everything they can to scare us and discourage the slightest resistance. Even the threat of death isn't enough because our life is no better than death. So they resort to something more horrible than death." He paused. "Now you've seen what they're like. Maybe now you're ready to join us."

"Yes!" Goldberg exclaimed passionately. "Against men that brutal I'll happily fight to the death."

"Is that your final word?" Trofimov asked.

"Yes."

25

Late in the evening Trofimov and Ganin were sitting on the bunks next to one another in Trofimov's room.

"You look really well, Alexander Ivanovich," Ganin said with a smile. "Not like when I first met you. In fact you look better even than a couple of months ago."

"Well, that's what it is to be in a warm place, Vladimir Semyonovich," Trofimov grinned, "although being here has its own problems. Do you think I could ever have imagined that I'd have to appropriate dead men's parcels and trade them for vodka to give to the authorities? You can understand how incompatible that is with an officer's honour."

"Well, dear friend, life is complicated," sighed Ganin. "Sometimes it forces a man to revise his beliefs. Previously I'd rather have shot myself than do a good number of the things I do here, but I can't live by those rules any more. In the first place, I've nothing to shoot myself with. And if you lose your job, those who replace you will take things not just from the dead but from those who are alive and capable of surviving. Try to stay on here until the next inspection dismisses you. Or else ..." Ganin's voiced sounded suddenly mysterious.

"Or else what?" Trofimov pricked up his ears.

"Or else until you can make your way out of this hell."

"I don't understand what you mean, Vladimir Semyonovich."

"Well," Ganin sighed, "of course you have more than enough reasons not to trust me, just like everybody else here. If you feel uncomfortable, there's no need to say anything, but, *entre nous*, it's my guess that the five of you are planning to escape. I'd be surprised if you weren't, now that Yatta has joined your company."

"How do you know that?" Trofimov asked after a pause.

"Well," Ganin smiled, "I'm an old stager in this camp, so I pick up many things at a glance. As I said, you're more than entitled to suspect me, though I know perfectly well that I'm not one to double-cross anyone." He paused for half a minute. "If and when you actually set off on your way, you'll know that for sure."

"If it really is so, what then?"

"Then I can only offer you my blessing and wish the five of you good fortune. I'd be happy to go with you, but I'm old and sick and feeble. I can't even dream of such a thing. Although," he added, "it would be wonderful to spend one last month as a free man and die in the wilds, lying by a campfire. The fire would burn, a wall of trees would surround me, and I would lie there and watch the stars and say my last prayers to the Almighty. That alone would be worth an escape attempt, just to avoid croaking as a wretched slave of the Soviets. But I couldn't be a burden to you, it would be dishonest on my part."

"But maybe you'd consider it, Vladimir Semyonovich?" Trofimov suggested.

"No." The old man's voice was firm. "You're young men. I'm an old ruin. I've no right to put your lives at risk. I wouldn't be able to keep up, I'd need long rests, and that would give the men in blue epaulettes all the time in the world to get you." He stopped for a moment. "There is just one thing that I'll ask you to do."

"What's that, Vladimir Semyonovich?"

"You know, Alexander Ivanovich, that I shall soon die. That doesn't trouble me. All I want is to die a Christian, having made my last confession to the priest. Here in the Fifth Compound there is only one ordained priest, but he's a stooge, so I don't regard him as having any authority to be the Lord's representative. If you make your way, you may eventually reach some inhabited land with real churches and real priests. When you're there, if it's not too difficult, please go to a church and pray to the icon of Saint Vladimir for the peace of my sinful soul. Maybe you can ask a holy father to say a short prayer for me. Promise me you'll do that, dear Alexander Ivanovich, and then I can die in peace."

"I promise you, Vladimir Semyonovich, on my honour as a human being and as an officer. I'll even arrange a proper requiem for you."

"Alexander Ivanovich, I can't express how grateful I am to you." Tears came to the old man's eyes, and his face shone with a smile. He took Trofimov's hand and shook it. "I don't know whether I'll be alive or dead by then, but I hope the Lord will hear your prayers and forgive me my sins."

For Christ's sake, thought Trofimov, as he walked towards the hospital, I don't believe that old man's a stooge, though it's quite reasonable to suspect that he could be. Hell no. He felt ashamed of his thoughts. Wasn't it Ganin who got him into the hospital? Wasn't it because of him that Yatta took such care of him? I can't believe any stooge would ever do that. Maybe I should tell the guys about our conversation. But not Mikhail. Mikhail may get suspicious and decide to whack him. He's too quick to act. Who should I talk to? To Yatta first of all.

At the hospital Trofimov waited until he and Yatta were free then he took him down to the basement and told him about his conversation with Ganin.

"What do you think, Yatta?" Trofimov asked as he ended his story. "Is there any chance of his being an informer?"

"No, never. For the sake of the Creator and the Merciful Beings." Yatta's voice was firm and confident. "You know, Ganin is one of the best men I ever knew, as much a man of honour as you are, Sasha."

"I feel the same way," Trofimov agreed. "Let's keep this a secret from Mikhail for a while. Mikhail's hot-headed and might decide to do away with the old man."

"No," Yatta's voice sounded harsh. "That old man is my saviour and benefactor. Anyone who tries to harm him will have to deal with me. I'm still a good fighter."

"No, Yatta," Trofimov shook his head. "That's overreacting again. We just won't tell Mikhail that Ganin guessed about our plans until we actually break free."

"And," Yatta continued, "you know something, Sasha? You said he'd like to die a free man."

"Yes, but he refused to go with us because he thinks he'd be a burden."

"We've gotta take him with us, you know," said Yatta firmly.

"I agree, but he said definitely not. He thinks it's dishonest on his part, because of his age and poor health."

"I gotta talk to him myself," Yatta insisted. "It's to him that I owe my place in the hospital. But for him I'd have croaked down in the mines long ago. We can get a sled with a couple of reindeer specially for him to ride in."

"Well, try and talk to him," Trofimov said.

"I will. He has every right to be with us, you know. He'd like to die out in the woods. For us Telqap people, the wishes of an old man are sacred. It's our ancestral law. If Mikhail doesn't wanna him with us, I ain't gonna go with you either."

"No, Yatta," he exclaimed, "you can't do that."

"Oh, yes I can, you know," Yatta replied in a calm voice. "I know I am in your debt, but I have a debt to him as well. And so do you. I beg you not to reject him."

"I'm telling you, I've got nothing against his going with us. It's him, not me, who refuses. Persuade him if you can."

"I will persuade him."

The rest of the day Trofimov could not help thinking about this perplexing new situation. It would be hard to persuade Bondarenko to take Ganin with them. Years in the camps had made Bondarenko harsh and pragmatic. He would reject the idea of taking a sick old man with them. He would claim that there was no room for charity, and maybe he was right. The only objection to that attitude was Yatta and Trofimov's personal feelings about the old man. What if Yatta refused to escape without Ganin? What would be the result? A fatal collision of opposing wills. Mikhail and Yatta were obstinate as mules, it was next to impossible to persuade either of them to give in.

Trofimov sided with Yatta. He felt most uncomfortable leaving the old man in this hell. Yet it was true, a sick old man would be a considerable burden, though less so with a sled. If things went as planned, and they got submachine guns, they could raid a collective farm and take sleds and pack reindeer. Old Ganin could ride in the sled. Even if he was right and he died soon, by that time they would be deep in the woods, beyond reach of their pursuers. He had to find a way to present this to Mikhail.

In the evening Trofimov took Bondarenko to their room in the trusties' barracks and recounted the substance of his conversation with Yatta, without telling him that Ganin had figured out they were planning to escape. He said that Yatta had previously talked with Ganin about escaping, and it was then that Ganin had expressed his desire and his reservations.

"So Yatta maintains there's no way he'll go without the old man?"

"That's what he says," Trofimov confirmed, "and we can't do it without a guide."

"But it's crazy to take someone that old," said Bondarenko. "He won't hold up."

"If we get sleds, he won't be a problem. He could be quite useful, being a doctor."

"Well, maybe you're right," Bondarenko said. "If we get guns, we can take as many sleds as we want. Zakharych and I are good carpenters, we could make another sled for ourselves. But let's wait and see. He may refuse to go."

26

Trofimov was giving medications to the patients when one of the ambulant patients approached him.

"Comrade Trofimov."

"Yes, what is it?"

"Comrade Yatta wants to see you as soon as you're finished. He'll be in the basement."

Trofimov finished distributing the remaining medicine and went down to join Yatta.

"Yes, Yatta?"

"Ganin refuses." Yatta's face expressed disappointment. "He stubbornly refuses."

"I told you so," Trofimov responded. "He was firm about it when he talked to me, and he's not a man to change his mind. Maybe it's better for him to stay. The hardships of such a trip are likely to be too much for him."

"But," Yatta turned to face Trofimov, "I'm afraid he's gonna pay for what we're about to do. He was with us all this time. Everyone knows I owe my place in the hospital to him. The bosses may think he helped us, and in that case he's finished."

"Comrade Trofimov," the same patient called.

"What d'you want?" asked Trofimov.

"Doctor Ponomarev wants to see you both right now."

"Okay," Trofimov sighed. "Let's go, Yatta."

When they entered the doctor's office, they saw Bondarenko, Goldberg and Timoshkin already there.

"You called us, doc?"

"Yes, guys." The doctor looked embarrassed. "I'm afraid I have some unpleasant news for you."

"You're going to dismiss us?" Trofimov guessed.

"I'm forced to." The doctor avoided looking them in the face. "You four, that is. Not Yatta," he said.

"Ain't you satisfied with our work?" Bondarenko inquired.

"It's not that. You're doing a good job." The doctor forced a smile. "If it depended on me, I'd keep you all on. But we have an inspection team coming from Orotukan."

"I get it," Trofimov said with a grin.

"Avdeyev summoned me," the doctor continued, "and told me quite bluntly to put things in order before September. That means dismissing all the Article 58-ers from hospital jobs."

Bondarenko tugged on his moustache, "Is there no way to—?"

"I'm afraid not." The doctor sounded apologetic. "I'm forced to do this, for the time being anyway."

"For the time being?" Trofimov looked him in the eye.

"Some time towards the New Year," the doctor sighed heavily, "I'll most likely catch the new team embezzling or doing something they shouldn't, and then I'll be in a good position to claim that you were the only honest guys, and I'll recall you."

"By the New Year, you say, doc?" chuckled Bondarenko. "I bet we'll all have kicked the bucket by then."

"Well, I've done what I could, believe me."

"I'm quite willing to believe you," said Trofimov, "and I don't blame you. Are we dismissed from this moment?"

"No, not until the end of the week."

"Thanks, doc."

In the evening the four men sat in their room in the trusties' barracks.

"Well, guys," Trofimov drew deeply on his home-rolled cigar, "our last days in this luxury. From Monday it's back to our fourth barracks and back to the grind."

"And," Bondarenko added, "we've gotta think what to do next. First of all, we have to try our damnedest to avoid getting sent back to the mines. That'll put paid to all our plans. The mine heads are all barbed wired with screws and dogs everywhere. There'd be no damned way of breaking out of there."

"Can't we try running from the compound?" suggested Goldberg.

"That won't work now," Trofimov said. "After those three guys escaped, they tightened up security."

"And it ain't gonna get better for a long time," Timoshkin added.

"We can't wait too long, though," Trofimov said. "We can't afford to spend another winter here."

Timoshkin agreed. "In that case, we've gotta get some place other than the mine, like a logging team. There's no barbed wire there. The small teams are usually guarded by just one screw. That could be the best place to make a break for it."

"Good thinking. We'll try getting into a logging team," said Trofimov. "All four of us have to be together."

"Well," Bondarenko suggested, "that's not too difficult to fix. We just grease the palm of the senior work assigner with something of real value."

"Which is not easy," Goldberg commented. "I've had no parcels for a month. What about you?"

"I ain't either," Bondarenko said. "My wife's not doing too well.

I wrote her some time ago not to send me anything."

"The same with my woman," Timoshkin said. "These are bad days for us collective farmers."

"I haven't had a letter from my wife for a long time either," said Goldberg. "I'm afraid she might be in the jug. The kids have probably been sent to an orphanage."

"Never mind," Trofimov concluded. "No matter what, we'll get some gift for Matveyev."

"It has to be within a couple days, before the assigner makes up the lists," Bondarenko said. "Trusties hate rewriting their work lists. But I've got another idea."

"What's that, Mikhail?" Trofimov asked.

"Well, I was a partisan scout after all. A good scout is always good at swiping things. I could lift something nice from one of the officers—a pack of real good cigarettes, for instance."

"That's too risky," Goldberg said. "They might search the camp high and low. Anyway, Matveyev may refuse such a gift."

"Yeah," Timoshkin agreed. "That would only work if we hid it somewhere and presented it to Matveyev a bit later. But we need something that Matveyev can take on the spot before he finishes his list."

"What a hopeless goddamned conundrum." Trofimov raised his hands in despair.

"Look," said Bondarenko, "I'll go to Seimchan tomorrow and swipe something like a pack of cigarettes, or a good watch."

"That might work," Trofimov agreed. "Mikhail, go see the doc right away and invent some pretext for a trip into town."

"Sure," Bondarenko agreed. "Just let me finish my cig."

"Hullo, guys, what are you up to?" Yatta entered the room, smiling as usual.

"Well, Yatta," Trofimov turned to him, "our luck seems to have run out."

"Why so?" Yatta seemed surprised.

"An inspection team's coming from Orotukan," Trofimov explained, "and Avdeyev told the doc to fire us. We're thinking up ways to avoid being sent back to the mines. If we get sent back there, we'll never escape."

"We need a gift for the senior work assigner," Bondarenko resumed.

"Oh, donna worry about that," said Yatta. "You know, I've got several ermine skins stashed away. You can take them."

"Oh, Yatta," Trofimov exclaimed, "you somehow save us every time."

"The same way you saved me," Yatta said. "If you want, I can go to Stepan myself and present a skin to him."

So Yatta did as he proposed: he presented two ermine skins to Matveyev, the senior work assigner, and Matveyev organized a separate logging team consisting of Bondarenko, Goldberg and Timoshkin, with Trofimov as foreman. As Matveyev said, it was the best he could do for the 58-ers in anticipation of the camp inspection. He also promised to move them to some warmer spot around the New Year, but they hardly cared about that, since they did not expect to be in the camp that long.

From then on the four of them spent day after day slaving on the logging site. Every morning they walked four kilometres to the site, escorted by a single corporal armed with a Kalashnikov. Their route followed the same path to the fork leading to the Seimchan highway. At that point they turned left instead of right and headed down the gentle wooded slope towards the bank of the Kolyma River. Every day they saw the remains of Losev and his fellow runaways, still bound to the larches. Morning after morning and night after night, they saw that terrible sight. By the end of August only their skeletons remained, but the authorities did not remove them, so there they stayed as a macabre warning to Trofimov and his friends. Contrary to expectations on the part of the authorities, this did not change their minds. They were just waiting for winter.

The short Arctic summer came to an end. The larches lost their needles and stood bare and gloomy. The last flocks of birds had flown south, the first snow fell and the woodland creeks iced over. The days with their endless toil dragged on. Morning after morning, escorted by the same screw, the four men walked four kilometres to the logging site. Each day the screw had them make a fire for him so that he did not freeze as he guarded them. Then they divided into pairs: Trofimov worked with Timoshkin, Bondarenko with Goldberg. They hewed notches in the tree from both sides, then felled it with a saw, taking care to avoid being hit by the falling trunk. With their axes, they cut off the branches and finally dragged the trunk onto the pile. So it went: tree after tree, hour after hour, day after day.

The screw was by no means a pleasant customer, but he was not especially nasty either. He watched closely as they worked, without even a break for a smoke. After the first seven hours, it was dinnertime and a mobile kitchen arrived bringing them standard portions of skilly and bread. After dinner came seven more hours of labour. One day the guard gave Goldberg a good beating for failing to move away smartly from the falling trunk: he suspected him of trying to get hit in order to be released from work. Apart from that he rarely touched them, and merely cursed. Unlike many other screws, he hardly ever hurried them at their work, since checking the production quota was not his responsibility but that of the foreman. In fact, their guard was bored rather than anything else and usually sat dreaming of his next week's leave. He was thus completely unaware of the fate that these four seemingly quiet and obedient labourers were preparing for him.

PART II: ESCAPE

1

Trofimov and Ganin sat on the cot in Ganin's room in the trusties' barracks. It was late at night, and in the dim natural light the two men's faces were hardly visible.

"Well, Vladimir Semyonovich," Trofimov broke the silence. "It's time to say goodbye. We're moving off in a few days' time."

"Oh, another transit?" Ganin threw him an understanding smile.

"Sort of," Trofimov said and smiled back.

"How soon?"

"As soon as the rivers ice over."

"Well," the old man smiled again, "I wish you luck, Alexander Ivanovich. I wish for all of you to reach your destination safely. You're the sort of men who can manage it." He paused. "It would be unfair if all of us were to die here one by one. Someone has to break out, and you're the ones to do it. God bless you."

"Are you sure you won't join us, Vladimir Semyonovich?" Trofimov looked the old man straight in the eye. "We'll get a sled and a couple of deer, and you can ride in the sled."

"No," Ganin replied. "All I want of you is that you remember to go to church and say some prayers for my soul. That's all. You aren't a believer, are you?"

The question plunged Trofimov into thought. "To be honest, I don't know," he said. "In our Soviet schools they taught us that there was no God and could be none. On the other hand, they told us so much bullshit that now I'm not sure what or whom to believe. So I'd not be too surprised if God existed. On the other hand, if he does exist, why does he allow so much filth and violence in our lives?"

"Well, be that as it may. But you will do that for me, won't you?"

"Absolutely, Vladimir Semyonovich. If only we can make our way to a free land where there are churches. On my honour."

"Then I can live what's left of my life in peace. God bless you, Alexander Ivanovich."

"You too, Vladimir Semyonovich. We'll never see each other

again," sighed Trofimov.

"Not in this life. But maybe … maybe in the next."

"I don't know anything about that, but it would be nice."

"Farewell and God bless you." The old man hugged Trofimov and made the sign of the cross over him.

"Farewell, Vladimir Semyonovich. I hope things won't turn out too badly for you here."

As he walked out, Trofimov looked back for one final glance at the old man's face with its sad but proud expression.

A couple of days later, just as Yatta had forecast, in the early morning it began to snow. It was not a blizzard that could quickly bury a man, but a moderately heavy fall, steady and continuous. Yatta predicted it would continue for another couple of days. It was therefore a perfect time for them to make a start, and it would be unreasonable to miss the opportunity.

In the interval between reveille and breakfast, Trofimov, Bondarenko, Goldberg and Timoshkin went to the latrine to meet and discuss their final arrangements. Immediately after breakfast, they had a brief meeting with Yatta, and Bondarenko reminded him of the location of their logging site.

The workday went on as usual. They laboured without pause. They could not carry out their plan until after the lunch break, otherwise their absence and the screw's body would be discovered in the middle of the day. The best time was soon after the lunch break, after which they would have the remaining six hours of the workday and another hour for the journey back in which to make their getaway. Since many foremen kept their teams working after normal hours in order to complete the day's work plan, they would have a further hour before any search was mounted, plus another three quarters of an hour at least before anyone reached their work site and established that they had escaped. The five of them thus had at least eight hours and forty-five minutes at their disposal.

Corporal Vassily Panteleyev slowly stumped around on his skis, keeping an eye on the men at work and smoking yet another in his endless chain of shag cigars. It was ten to four in the afternoon according to his watch, which meant six hours more—an eternity—before he could lead the prisoners back to the compound and himself return to the warmth of his barracks, to a game of cards and his evening drink. For all those hours he would sit shivering in the biting wind and even envy the convicts who were kept warm by their hard work. How sick and tired he was of this Arctic region with its short cold summers and long frozen winters. Why, even in the fall your spittle froze as you spat! Then there was the constant canned beef for breakfast, dinner and supper, his only pleasure the nocturnal masturbation on his cot, while he dreamed of some girl with a nice pair of tits and a nice round bum. He had more than a year to go before he could return to his native town in central Russia. On the other hand, what sort of life awaited him there? Slaving away in the local ore mine, lining up for hours outside the food stores, and an endless series of trade union, Young Communist League and other goddamned meetings. Meanwhile he would be forced to see the girl he had hankered after but who had chosen another. He had gone off to do his military service without even having been kissed!

Timoshkin raised his axe and struck Trofimov on the shoulder. Cursing, Trofimov dropped his axe, launched himself at Timoshkin and punched him in the face.

"Hey!" Panteleyev yelled, "What the fuck's going on? Back to work, you filthy shitasses. Settle your scores in the evening, not now."

Trofimov and Timoshkin took no notice and continued struggling.

"You scumbags," Panteleyev shouted angrily. "I'll teach you a lesson." He removed the Kalashnikov from his shoulder, rushed at the fighting men and beat both of them with the butt of his gun. As he did so, Bondarenko leapt behind him with his axe. He brought the blade down on the screw's head and his skull shattered. His lifeless body fell onto Trofimov and Timoshkin, pushing them into the snow.

"Captain. Zakharych." Bondarenko urged. "Get up. He's finished."

Trofimov and Timoshkin scrambled to their feet. Goldberg

turned away and raised his eyes to heaven.

"There we are, guys." Timoshkin glanced at his friends and at Panteleyev's dead body. "We're free!" He hugged Trofimov and Bondarenko. "We're really free." He walked around ecstatically, his nose bleeding and his right eye starting to bruise.

"Don't tempt fate, Zakharych," Trofimov said quietly. "That's only the first step." He looked around. "Mikhail, get into his uniform. Luckily there's no blood on it."

Bondarenko dragged Panteleyev's body towards the fire and stripped off his clothes.

"Poor bastard," Goldberg sighed. "He's so young, twenty at most. And now …"

"I don't know how many more we'll have to kill," Trofimov said. "But we'll definitely have to, perhaps even today. If Yatta comes along with an escort, then … What time is it now?"

Bondarenko, who had finished putting on Panteleyev's uniform with a warm sweater underneath, looked at the dead man's watch. "Four o'clock," he said.

"Yatta's due here within half an hour," Trofimov reminded them. He looked at Bondarenko. "Why, Mikhail," he said, "You look like a real soldier."

"Not a bad trophy," Timoshkin agreed.

"Will you hear when they come, Mikhail?" Trofimov asked.

"Sure."

"Then give us the signal." Trofimov turned to the others. "The rest of us will hide."

Bondarenko searched the pockets of his new army greatcoat and produced a flask. "Look, liquor."

Trofimov looked in his direction. "Have a sip and give us some."

"To our liberation." Bondarenko raised the flask and drank.

Trofimov echoed. "To our long-awaited freedom."

Bondarenko's low whistle sent all four scurrying into the bushes. Bondarenko seized the Kalashnikov. A minute later, Yatta appeared escorted by a single guard. Bondarenko took aim and fired a single shot at the man's head. The screw fell dead. Trofimov, Goldberg and Timoshkin emerged from behind the trees.

"Yatta," Trofimov cried and hugged him.

"You were just in time, though," said Yatta. "He was getting suspicious why I put my traps so near the logging site."

"Anyway," Trofimov grinned, "everything worked out, and here you are. And we've got another set of warm clothes. Who's getting these?" He looked at the body and coat of the second guard. "Looks like your size, Yakov." He turned to Timoshkin. "You don't mind, Zakharych?"

"No way," Timoshkin said.

Goldberg moved closer to the fire and changed. When finished, he turned to face the others, hardly recognizable in his new uniform.

"Looks great, Yakov." Bondarenko gave him the thumbs up. "A perfect fighting man."

"Let's go," Trofimov interrupted. "Put the fire out."

Bondarenko and Goldberg strapped on the skis left by the two guards and took up their Kalashnikovs. Timoshkin and Yatta stamped out the fire, then the group set off through the falling snow.

Now came the second, crucial stage of their operation. The logging sector, which included their site, was several kilometres wide. The boundary of the sector was marked by a narrow strip of open ground with a ski track patrolled by three groups of guards, each consisting of five men. Each team oversaw one third of the ski track, a length of about three kilometres. If a would-be runaway managed to escape the screw guarding him, he had to cross this track, leaving footprints that would be discovered by one of the patrols within a quarter of an hour. But there was a loophole in this system which Trofimov had detected long ago: if the runaways had guns and ambushed one patrol group, the neighbouring patrol would hardly know anything about it, since they were not expected to cross the borderline of their own sector. Nor would they be alarmed by a short burst of submachine gun fire: they would assume that their neighbours had shot either at an escaping convict or at a wild reindeer or moose. It was this flaw that Trofimov intended to exploit.

As the five men reached the ski track, they took up a position among the trees. Bondarenko and Goldberg held their Kalashnikovs ready for action.

"It's great luck we've already got two submachines," Trofimov whispered.

"Yeah," Bondarenko agreed. "And you know what? Be prepared in case they have dogs with them. They hardly ever do, but still …"

"Fire as quickly as possible, and don't waste half a second," said Trofimov. "Now dig deep into the snow." They dug quickly and hollowed out a small trench.

"Yakov," Trofimov called, as they finished digging in, "would you feel more comfortable if I shot instead of you?"

"Thanks, Sasha." Goldberg replied.

"It's no problem for now," Trofimov smiled, "but later, when we all have guns, everyone's going to have to use them." He raised himself slightly, moved toward Goldberg and took his Kalashnikov.

"Hush. They're coming," Bondarenko warned. They heard the hissing of skis and then sighted a group of five soldiers moving along with an Alsatian dog.

"Hell." Trofimov whispered. "They've got a dog with them after all."

The patrol approached, and as they got closer, the dog barked and strained at the leash in their direction. Trofimov and Bondarenko's guns exploded simultaneously and fired two or three salvoes. The soldiers had no time to respond.

"Looks like they're finished," Timoshkin muttered.

Trofimov whispered. "Yakov, Yatta and Timoshkin, take 'em away. Mikhail and I will watch and make sure no one's left alive."

Goldberg, Timoshkin and Yatta moved toward the bodies. None of them stirred. Once the corpses of the men and the dog had been removed, they reassembled among the trees.

"Take their weapons," Trofimov said.

They took five Kalashnikovs from the dead men, and also their cartridge pouches and bayonets.

"How many magazines do we have?" Trofimov asked.

"I got twenty in each of the two pouches," Bondarenko said.

"Twenty in one and eighteen in the other," Timoshkin echoed.

"Twenty-one," said Goldberg.

"I have twenty-three," said Yatta.

"That makes a hundred and twenty-three altogether," Trofimov calculated. "Not bad."

"Yeah," Bondarenko agreed. "It won't be easy for those scumbags to get us now."

"And look here," Timoshkin called. "Three more flasks of liquor. And some twist."

As they ransacked the dead men's backpacks, they discovered cans of meat.

Goldberg grinned. "I already feel hungry as hell."

"We've no time for grazing now." Bondarenko retorted. "Not till we make a halt. Right, Captain?"

"Precisely," Trofimov agreed. "We'll go as far as possible before nightfall. Now change into their clothes, quick."

Trofimov and Timoshkin began changing. Without the warmth of a bonfire, the cold wind chilled them to the marrow as they stripped. They took off their convicts' pea jackets and donned the soldiers' sweaters and jackets, then their deerskin overcoats. Eventually all of them but Yatta were dressed in military uniform, complete with boots and fur caps sporting the red star badge. Finally they strapped on their skis.

"We're all set," Trofimov concluded. "Let's go."

With Yatta leading, the group crossed the ski track and moved down the slope toward the Kolyma River, where they crossed over the ice and moved into the forest.

2

They had been moving for several hours, five heavily armed men in uniform with kitbags on their backs and submachine guns on their shoulders.

"All quiet behind, is it? No pursuers?" Trofimov broke the silence.

"None so far, Captain," Bondarenko said.

"Things are going as planned," Timoshkin observed, "unless someone by chance ..."

"No one should be following," Trofimov said. "Hardly anyone comes out to the logging sites during the workday, and that section of ski track where we crossed is covered by that one patrol and nobody else. If they were Germans, someone might double check, but in this shithouse they'd hardly be likely to do that. Not many would be willing to do anything beyond their direct responsibility."

"Someone could have heard the shooting from the road," Goldberg said.

"Quite likely," Bondarenko said. "They probably thought the patrol team was fooling around. Otherwise they'd have been after us long ago."

"Even if they found we were missing, they can't know which direction we're heading," Trofimov said. "We've got to put at least twenty kilometres behind us by midnight. Then we can afford a short rest." He paused and turned to Yatta. "Are you sure you can see the way in this darkness and snow?"

"Oh, yeah," Yatta assured him. "I've strolled all over these parts many times. And you know, this snow is no obstacle to us Chukchi reindeer men."

"Good." Trofimov smiled and looked round at his colleagues. "Are you tired, Yakov?"

"Somewhat," Goldberg put on a smile, "but not too much."

"At-a-guy," Trofimov grinned. "Keep going. Another four hours." He turned to Timoshkin. "Zakharych, give him your flask. Have a sip, Yakov, to fortify yourself."

Timoshkin held out the flask to Goldberg.

"And have a cig as well," Trofimov continued. "It's a good energy booster. I wouldn't mind one myself."

"Me too," said Bondarenko.

The party halted and leaned against the trees, sheltering from the snow and wind beneath the branches.

"Wow," Bondarenko announced as they lit up, "our first smoke as free men."

"It is indeed," Timoshkin said.

"Incidentally," Trofimov pointed out, "we have a decision to make. We need a leader. After all, we're like a raiding party in enemy territory. Someone has to be in charge. Any ideas?"

"No question in my mind," Bondarenko answered. "You, Captain.

Who else?"

"I agree," Timoshkin said. "You have the highest rank."

"Yakov was a captain too," Trofimov commented.

"Still, you ..." Bondarenko stopped short. "How to put it? You're more distinguished, you got a decoration from Vassilevsky himself, and ..."

"Mikhail's right," Goldberg supported Bondarenko. "I was an artillery captain, but I never fought hand to hand. How many battles were you in, Sasha?"

"I can't remember," Trofimov answered. "Lots of them. I lost count somewhere around 1943."

"That's what I'm saying," Bondarenko exclaimed. "Who could be better than you?"

"Well," Trofimov said, "I guess we can make a final decision tonight, when we stop. We'll have more time then." He looked at the others. "Let's move on."

They moved along a path that evidently only Yatta recognized. It was still snowing, and pitch dark. They badly needed food and rest, but they could afford only a short halt. They had to reach the collective farm Yatta was leading them to in order to pick up vital supplies. After that they had to move on further. Only when they'd gone a few dozen kilometers did Trofimov plan for them to have a first night's sleep. Now they would break for an hour to rest and have a meal. They gathered brushwood, made a tiny fire, opened the cans of meat and then rested.

"Good God," Goldberg exclaimed. "We haven't relaxed like this since we worked in the hospital."

"Well," Timoshkin said, "many guys never had a rest at all."

"You know," Trofimov said, "if we hadn't had that period in the hospital to recuperate, we wouldn't have had the energy to escape."

"I remember how worried I was when we attacked those orderlies," Timoshkin recollected. "We could have ended up in a penal camp."

Bondarenko grinned. "That's Kolyma for you, Zakharych. As the proverb goes, out here 'the taiga is law, and the bear is district attorney.' If you dare to do anything, then either you're lucky and win, or you're finished. Losev and his friends had bad luck and ended up tied to the larches. I hope we're luckier. At least we've got this far."

"Don't tempt fate by boasting, Mikhail," Goldberg interrupted.

"Donna be modest, Yakov," Bondarenko grinned. "We're already beyond their reach, ain't we, Yatta?"

"Yeah," Yatta agreed. "They'll hardly be able to find us here. You know, I'm not leading you along human trails, we're following wild animal paths."

"That's good, Yatta," said Trofimov. "They'll soon cordon off the roads." He looked at the watch he had inherited from Corporal Panteleyev. "It's quarter past twelve now. We were supposed to get back to the compound about three quarters of an hour ago. I guess they'll wait about forty minutes more, maybe an hour, then they'll realize something's wrong. It'll take them another thirty minutes to get out to the logging site. That means we've around three hours before the pursuit begins. Now, how about our leader?"

"You know my choice," said Bondarenko. "You."

"Any other suggestions?" Trofimov glanced at Timoshkin. "What do you think?"

"Same as Mikhail," said Timoshkin. "You're the best man for the job."

"You, Yakov?"

"You, Sasha, no doubt. You're the most experienced commander."

"And you?" Trofimov turned to Yatta.

"For every reason, you're the best. And you know, you've been marked for this by the Creator and the Merciful Beings. They've preserved you from the claws of evil specially for this."

"Well," Trofimov glanced around his comrades, "if you're sure you want me, so be it. Now there's something I want to say to you.

"First of all, congratulations on achieving your freedom. How long we've dreamed and planned, without ever being sure of success. Now it's happened: we're free men again. But this is only the beginning. We have a long way ahead of us. I don't need to tell you how tough it's going to be. We're just a small bunch of brave guys pitted against an enormous power." Trofimov paused and then continued in a more buoyant tone. "But we have certain advantages. We have these boundless forests and the tundra, which they'll never be able to comb through. For us they'll be a refuge from our pursuers and a reliable route to our destination. We have an expert guide, who's also an excellent hunter and traveler." Everyone turned to look at Yatta. "Yes," Trofimov said, "I mean you, Yatta. And we're armed to the teeth in the way other fugitives could only have dreamed about. Furthermore, all of us are real fighting men, much better than any of those screws. Hardly any of them have ever been in combat. And all that counts for something." Trofimov was no public speaker, but he found himself carried away by his own rhetoric.

"We've a long, tough journey ahead of us, but who is better suited to undertake it than we are? Far ahead lies a land of life and freedom. To get there we shall have to be tough and stick together to the last. Each for all, and all for each. I can't guarantee that every one of us will make it to Alaska, but ..."

"We understand that, Captain," Bondarenko nodded.

"Okay," Trofimov continued, "but I'll do my best to see us through. Let's hope we make it safely to Alaska, but there's always the chance we could die on the way. In camp we faced death in slavery. To die out here, free men and fighters, is much better than rotting in the camps.

"This afternoon we were Soviet slaves. Now we're soldiers, fighters, rebels, ready to fight to the death. We can't afford to pity them. The cost of pity will be too high." He looked briefly at Goldberg. "Accept that this is war, but remember: we're soldiers, not thugs and cutthroats, not bandits. Those chasing us are our enemies, but no one else, not the ordinary people. They're not responsible for the crimes of our rulers. These poor people could still betray us of course, out of fear."

"Not always out of fear," Bondarenko disagreed. "There are real scumbags among them."

"Right," agreed Trofimov. "But you can never know for sure who are the scum. Nor can you take it out on the innocent just because there are one or two bastards among them. Otherwise we'd cease to be soldiers and become mere bandits. Now, when we get to this collective farm, we're going to take some tools, a sled and a few reindeer. With them we can survive on our own in the wilds without bothering the locals. Yatta says he has friends around here whom he trusts. We will rely on them and no one else. In a word, we shall neither plunder nor kill any innocent folk. Only the screws are our enemies." He paused.

"I don't even want to mention that any of us might commit rape. I gunned down three rapists on the spot in Berlin in May 1945, and I don't have a single regret about it. Men who do that sort of thing are scum, not soldiers."

"Dead right. That's what they are," Timoshkin agreed.

"And finally," Trofimov continued, "let's decide how we make decisions. I suggest that when there's no emergency and enough time to consider, we should discuss things together. In case of emergency, I take command. I don't need privileges, like an officer's ration. We'll all eat the same food from the same pot, and we'll all take turns as night watchman, me included. What do you prefer: just one of us on patrol for the whole night, or do we change every two hours?"

"Well," Bondarenko said, "I can keep watch all night long."

"Me too," said Timoshkin.

"To my mind, a two-hour shift would be better," Goldberg said.

"I can manage either way," said Yatta.

"Fine," Trofimov concluded. "I myself prefer two-hour shifts. Remember, we're not going to be sleeping tonight. But tomorrow night I'll take the first watch duty, then Yatta, then Mikhail, then Timoshkin and finally Yakov. And for that first night we'll sleep for at least ten hours. We'll need a long sleep by that time."

"Agreed, Captain."

Trofimov looked at Yatta. "Tell me, are you sure there's no wireless in the village?"

"Wireless? What's that?" asked Yatta.

"Those boxes with metal rods, antennas. You can talk to someone far away."

"Oh yeah," Yatta smiled. "I know what you're talking about. No, there are none, not there."

"And how long does it take to get from this village to the nearest village office?"

"Oh, maybe, about a day's hard ride on a fresh deer."

"Well, that's okay then. It means the authorities won't know anything till tomorrow night. So, come on, let's move."

"Yeah, it's time," Bondarenko agreed.

3

The village had one main street. Small log houses lined it on each side, their backyards facing the forest. Not a light penetrated the darkness, and not a star shone through the snow clouds. Trofimov, Timoshkin and Goldberg hid in the thickets near the village outskirts and waited for Yatta and Bondarenko to return from reconnoitering. Their hearts raced as they strained their eyes for any danger. What if the warehouse and reindeer corral turned out to be guarded, and they had to shoot and wake up the whole village? There was no sign of movement, however, and eventually the two scouts returned.

"There's no one there except for one old chap," Bondarenko assured them.

"Okay," Trofimov said, "then we make straight for the warehouse and surround it. Mikhail and Yatta, make a loop around the edge of the forest to cut off his retreat. We three will go the direct route."

"Understood, Captain."

"Let's go."

Bondarenko and Yatta disappeared among the thickets while the others moved along the snow-covered street.

"Here's hoping no one wakes up," Timoshkin whispered.

Trofimov nodded. "I don't want any shooting."

In a few minutes they reached a small square with a relatively large log warehouse to one side. In front of it a watchman walked to and fro. He wore a warm winter fur coat and cap and carried a rifle. Trofimov, Timoshkin and Goldberg held their submachine guns at the ready.

"Hey! Who's there?" the watchman suddenly yelled and raised his gun. "Who are you?"

"Don't do anything stupid, old man," Trofimov announced. "We've all got submachine guns."

Bondarenko and Yatta emerged from behind the warehouse. The watchman looked round and saw them, and his knees began to shake.

"Drop your gun," Trofimov ordered the man, and he dropped it into the snow. "Now get down on your knees, hands behind your head."

The watchman obeyed instantly, fear radiating from his eyes.

"Don't be afraid," Trofimov said quietly. "We won't harm you, so long as you don't do anything silly."

"If you were a screw," Bondarenko grinned, "I'd surely knock you off with my own hand. But you're a collective farmer, right? Got any kids?"

"Yeah," said the watchman. "I got three. The elder one's serving in the army right now. There was another one, older than the rest, but he got killed in 1943."

"We've been at the front," Trofimov told the watchman. "Now open the door for us."

The watchman took the keys from his pocket and unlocked the warehouse door.

"You got a lantern?" Bondarenko asked.

"Yeah." The watchman produced a small lantern and lit up the dark entrance.

"Go in," Trofimov ordered. The watchman and all the others stepped inside.

The watchman's lantern lit up the shelves along the walls. Methodically the four men selected the supplies they needed: sacks, a crowbar, fishing gear, cooking utensils, matchboxes, bottles of oil, kerosene jars and knives. Trofimov glanced around, and sighted four medium-sized sleds.

"Are those the only sleds you've got?" he asked.

"Yeah," the watchman said. "Some of the households have them, and there's a big one near the stable, but we ain't got many. Most of 'em were taken from us during the war."

"Well," Trofimov said, "we'll take all four, a reindeer for each sled and one more for meat. Yatta and Mikhail, go get the deer." He turned to the watchman. "How many have you got?"

"About a thousand head," the watchman replied. "Our manager guards those deer like the apple of his eye. They're the only ones left from the wartime."

"Do you have a lasso?" asked Yatta.

"Sure," the watchman searched the shelves and produced a long lasso.

"Take us to the corral," Bondarenko tugged the watchman by the sleeve. The old man led him and Yatta along a small sideroad to a large fenced area. The watchman opened the gate and they stepped inside.

"Oh, these are good, really good. They're Yakut reindeer," Yatta observed appreciatively.

Yatta selected five animals, adjusted the reins round the head of each of them and led them out toward the warehouse. Meanwhile Trofimov and Timoshkin prepared the sleds, loading one of them with large skin bags.

"Everything's ready," Trofimov reported. "The only problem is the tent."

"Is there no good yaranga?" Yatta enquired.

"No. There are two tents, but they're both very old and the poles are rotten."

"Let me have a look." Yatta gave Trofimov the reins and walked into the warehouse where he found the parts for two movable tents, skins and poles, lying on the floor. Yatta examined them.

"You're right, Sasha, these are bad. But there are good skins here, you know, although the poles are bad. They ain't gonna stand up to a bad blizzard. Take some reindeer skins, and I'll make some new poles myself."

Timoshkin and Bondarenko packed away the reindeer skins. "Okay," Trofimov announced, "everything's ready. Let's move."

"But ... my dear ... comrades," the night watchman stammered.

"What's wrong, old man?" Trofimov asked.

"They're gonna ... they're gonna hold me responsible. They'll charge me with all this."

"Ah, I see." Trofimov turned to his friends. "The old guy's right. He'll be accused of helping us, and that means ten years for him at least. What shall we do?"

"Tie him up," Timoshkin suggested.

"Yes, please. Do that." The watchman welcomed the suggestion enthusiastically. "And give me a good beating into the bargain. Then maybe the bosses won't suspect ..."

"A very good idea, Captain," Bondarenko observed.

Trofimov agreed. "Zakharych, bring us some rope and something to gag him."

Timoshkin went back into the warehouse and reappeared with coils of rope and rags. He and Trofimov tied up the watchman. Bondarenko clouted the man expertly in the face, so as to cause a heavy nosebleed and a crushed lip, but without hurting him too badly. The old man ended up lying in the snow, tied hand and foot, his mouth gagged and spurts of blood all over his coat and the surrounding snow.

"Looks natural enough," Trofimov examined the results. "Now off we go."

Trofimov looked at his watch.

"It's four thirty. In about an hour the village will wake up. We've got to keep moving for the next eighteen hours. One of us can rest on the deer's back in turns, say, every three hours." He looked at Goldberg. "You look tired, Yakov. You go first."

"Actually," Goldberg smiled. "I'm quite capable of moving under my own steam."

"That's an order," Trofimov insisted.

"Oh, well, if that's the case." Goldberg climbed on the back of the fifth deer. With that their company moved through the outskirts of the village and back into the forest.

4

The chief of the Seimchan Camp Administration played host at a banquet. The tables were filled with every kind of dish, from fried reindeer meat to salmon caviar, as well as bottles of vodka and wine. Above it all, hanging on the wall like a Communist icon, a huge portrait of Stalin, smiling and smoking a pipe, presided. Around the table sat more than a dozen men and women, most of them MGB officers and their wives. The hero of the occasion was Major Avdeyev, who sat with his faithful Lieutenant Belyayev at his side. Two female convicts served at the table, taking away dirty dishes and bringing clean ones.

The banquet had been in progress for a few hours and everyone was tipsy. There were bursts of loud conversation. Suddenly Lieutenant Belyayev interrupted his tête-à-tête with the young woman in civilian dress who sat next to him. He refilled his glass with vodka and rose to his feet.

"Dear comrades," he began, "I want to raise one more toast

in honour of our gathering." The public seemed not to notice his appeal and continued chattering loudly. Belyayev began again, trying to shout them down. "Comrades, I'd like to—" This time he got the support of Colonel Serov, chief of the Seimchan Camp Administration.

"Attention, comrades!" Serov's roaring bass echoed through the room. "Our young lieutenant wants to say something. Go on, Lieutenant."

"Comrades." Belyayev raised his voice. "I want to propose one more toast to our dear Pavel Egorovich. For the past several years, he has been much more than a superior officer to all of us, his subordinates. He has been just … just like a father, who has helped wholeheartedly, advised and guided all of us in our onerous duties. At no time has he ever behaved towards us—how should I put it—like a formal, indifferent superior authority. On the contrary, although firm and demanding, he has always been most caring and cordial. He has been of immense help to all of us. At any time one could knock on the door of his office and ask his advice. You appreciate, therefore, comrades, how delighted we are now that Pavel Egorovich has received such handsome recognition from our government, which … which never forsakes those who honestly and valiantly serve our motherland. Pavel Egorovich, here's to your new honour and distinction." Belyayev concluded by raising his glass.

"Well," Colonel Serov added, "I am glad to join in this toast. For my part, I want to say that to my mind Major Avdeyev long ago deserved this new decoration. For more than twenty years he has served our Soviet motherland. He has devoted all his time, all his energy, to our tough and demanding service. Indeed to my mind he deserves to be a colonel by now. Yes, comrades, it still happens that a good and reliable officer serves our country for years and years, dedicating his whole heart and soul and all his energy to our demanding service, but because of some red tape he fails to be promoted or decorated the way he deserves. Sooner or later, our leaders remember everyone who serves our motherland. Yes indeed, as we now see in the case of our own Major Avdeyev. The directive awarding him the Order of the Red Banner has been signed by no less than Comrade Stalin himself. Within a month we shall see our Pavel Egorovich with this decoration emblazoned on his chest. So let us toast him once again. Your health, Pavel Egorovich."

There was a cheerful clinking of glasses.

"Thank you, comrade Colonel." Avdeyev responded. "And thank you, Leonid. Thank you from the bottom of my heart, you bastard." Avdeyev's eyes were watering. "How nice it is when the young … and I wasn't all that soft on you. I got angry, I shouted and cursed you all. So it's nice of you young people to forget all that and remember only the good. Now I want to raise a toast to our young generation. To you, Leonid. And to our newcomer here." He turned to one of the young women. "To our charming Lyudmila, who has come to adorn and enhance our rude male collective."

"Thank you, Pavel Egorovich," said the young woman with a rapid smile.

"My pleasure, Lyuda." Avdeyev's face beamed like the sun. "And where are you going to be working?"

"In Srednikan Camp Administration."

"Oh, quite close to us. I hope that we'll see each other. Cheers, comrades."

There was another clinking of glasses. Someone switched on a gramophone, and the room echoed to the sound of a tango.

"Anyone feel like dancing, comrades?" one of the officers proposed.

"Of course," Belyayev turned to Lyudmila. "Lyuda, may I have the honour?"

"With pleasure, Leonid." They rose and walked to the next room followed by a handful of others.

A junior lieutenant dashed into the banqueting room, puffing and panting.

"Comrade Colonel, I need to talk to Major Avdeyev. It's an emergency!"

"What the hell can it be?" Colonel Serov sounded surprised. "Pavel Egorovich, go and sort it out."

Avdeyev rose from the table and walked over to the messenger. "Yes, Aristov? What's the matter?"

"I have to talk to you privately, comrade Major."

"What the hell's this all about?"

"An emergency, comrade Major."

"Oh well," Avdeyev sighed. "Nothing for it, an emergency is an emergency." He motioned towards the door, and he and the junior lieutenant walked out.

"Well," said Colonel Serov, "such things happen. In our line of service a man never belongs to himself."

"I don't think it can be anything specially serious," his wife added. "He'll be back soon."

At that point Belyayev and Lyudmila reappeared, chatting in low voices and smiling at one another. They rejoined the company at the table.

"How long have you been here?" Lyudmila threw Belyayev a radiant smile.

"Six years. I was sent here in 1942."

"And aren't you bored to death," she asked, "so far from civilization?"

"I'm ready to serve wherever our country needs me," Belyayev said proudly. "But actually, it's not really that bad here. Oh no, by no means. At first, it's true, you miss your hometown and friends. But eventually you start to appreciate the exotic side of living out in the taiga, riding the deer, hunting and so on. It's rather romantic, isn't it? You make new friends, and then lots of things out here are much easier than back home."

"Easier?" Lyudmila sounded surprised.

"Exactly. For instance, if you're an executive of any rank, you don't waste your time on mundane drudgery. There are convicts to do it for you. What about another dance? Would you mind?"

When Avdeyev reappeared in the banqueting room, instead of taking his seat, he stood by the door.

"I'm sorry, comrades, I need to leave immediately. Belyayev, come with me."

"Oh, what a pity, Pavel Egorovich," the colonel's wife lamented. "You're the hero of our celebration."

"There's nothing to be done, Maria," her husband interrupted. "Duty calls." Then, turning to Avdeyev: "I hope, Pavel Egorovich, that when you actually get the decoration, we'll have another big celebration."

"Thank you, comrade Colonel." Avdeyev forced a smile. "Belyayev and Aristov, hurry up."

"Which work team was it?" Avdeyev turned to Lieutenant Solovyov.

"The fourteenth logging team, comrade Major. The foreman was convict Trofimov, and the other members were convicts Bondarenko, Goldberg and Timoshkin."

"And who was the guard?"

"Corporal Panteleyev, first squad of the third guard platoon."

"How the fuck did they kill him?"

"He was hacked to death with a logging axe."

"Shit!" Avdeyev yelled. "I bet the dickhead went for a piss, didn't he?"

"No, comrade Major. There's no urine stains anywhere. Our team examined the site thoroughly."

"Fuck it all." Avdeyev snapped. "I don't understand how the hell it happened."

"The fugitives obviously distracted him."

"Haven't we told them God knows how many times to be on the alert every single moment?"

"We'll find out everything once we catch them," muttered Solovyov. "And there's also—"

"What else?"

"Another of our soldiers is dead."

"Another?" Avdeyev felt the muscle in his cheek quiver.

"Yes, comrade Major. Private Belenko from the second platoon."

"Also whacked with an axe, was he?"

"No, comrade Major. Shot in the head, looks like with Panteleyev's gun. Belenko usually escorts Yatta on his trips into the forest."

"Yatta?" Avdeyev's eyes opened wide. "You mean—"

"Yes, comrade Major. For some reason Belenko came to the fourteenth logging team's site and was shot dead, evidently by the fugitives. I checked on Yatta, and he hasn't been seen since yesterday morning, when he left with Belenko. So—"

"Yatta's escaped with those bastards? I don't believe it! He had no fuckin' reason to run away. His position here was good."

"They could have threatened him," Belyayev observed. "But for whatever reason, he's gone with them."

"Comrade Major, may I come in?" Lieutenant Makarov appeared

at the door.

"Any news?" Avdeyev asked, cherishing a hope that Makarov would announce the fugitives had been caught.

"Yes, comrade Major. Patrol A, five soldiers from third platoon under Sergeant Bagirov, have been found in the woods at the side of their patrol area, all shot dead and stripped of their clothing, guns and ammunition."

"Shit and sand!" Avdeyev was on the brink of losing all self-control as the bad news showered on him like an avalanche. "No doubt those bloody scumbags again. Who else? Any tracks? Clues?"

"No, comrade Major," replied Makarov. "Everything's covered with snow. It's been snowing heavily since yesterday."

Avdeyev groaned and lost all trace of his usual bravado.

"What shall we do now?" He tried hard to concentrate and make some decision.

"Makarov, were the bullets in the bodies checked?"

"The results are not known yet, comrade Major, but most likely they're from Panteleyev and Belenko's guns."

Avdeyev took in the information then ordered, "Get every last camp officer in here. We're holding an emergency meeting."

"Yes, comrade Major."

"Fuck it all," Avdeyev unleashed a train of curses, forgetting the presence of subordinates. "Who would imagine this could happen now? After Losev and the others were caught I was sure no one would dare try again." He turned to Belyayev again: "Are you sure Yatta's with them?"

"Yes, comrade Major, absolutely. I think their plan is to use him as a guide."

"Traitor. Scum. Bastard!" Avdeyev exploded again. "I'll get him. And he won't get away with being shot. Hell, no. I'll ... I'll have him fried over a slow fire. Or buried alive. I'll chop off his hands and feet and throw his body out to freeze in the bush! I'll ... And you, Belyayev, why are you sitting here? Get search parties after them."

"I've done that, comrade Major. I sent Lebedev, Grinkov and Anikin with their platoons."

"Good. Now connect me with the chief of the neighbouring compound, Major Filimonov."

Belyayev got on the line and called up Filimonov, then handed the receiver to Avdeyev.

"Major Avdeyev speaking. Major Filimonov, please ... He's away in Seimchan? All right, when he gets back, tell him to call me ... Yes, it's an emergency ... This is the Fifth Compound calling." Avdeyev handed the phone back to Belyayev. "Contact Captain Garshin for me."

Within a minute Avdeyev was speaking to Garshin.

"Mikhail? Avdeyev here ... Yes, I've got a major screw-up ... Yes, an escape ... Five of them, armed. They killed two guards, and a five-man patrol ... I've no idea where they've gone to ... Yes, you can. Summon a couple of platoons and get them to search the area ... Thanks, Mikhail."

Yatta led the first deer by the reins, and the others followed, Trofimov, Timoshkin and Bondarenko on skis, and Goldberg riding a deer. It was late morning. The snowfall had stopped, and the woods were filled with the dusk of an arctic winter day. The disc of the sun glowed none too brightly, accompanied by three false suns, like a sovereign and his retinue.

"How's it going, Yatta?" Trofimov asked, bringing the group to a halt. "I'm sorry I can't relieve you, but I need you to take us in the right direction."

"It's okay, I'm fine," Yatta smiled back. "A reindeer man can go for days without sleep."

"Will you manage until tonight?" Trofimov asked.

"Sure."

Trofimov walked over to where Goldberg sat drowsing on the back of a reindeer.

"Yakov."

"Is it time already?" Goldberg yawned.

"It sure is. You've been riding for four hours."

Goldberg looked at the sky overhead.

"God, it's getting late." He jumped off the deer and landed in the deep snow.

"Zakharych, you are next in turn to ride. Let's take a short rest now for a smoke and a sip of liquor. To rouse our spirits, so to speak."

They rolled shag cigars and passed the flask from man to man.

"It's eleven thirty," Trofimov said, checking his watch. "They know everything by now."

"My God, I bet there's an almighty row going on," Timoshkin said with a frown.

"That's not our problem now," Trofimov smiled. "We're at least fifty kilometres away, and we've made so many changes of direction. Yatta, you seem to know all the paths."

"Sure I do." Yatta shrugged. "I spent a year in this area hunting. Anyone would know it by now."

"No way," Timoshkin said. "I ain't got the faintest idea where we are. I just remember one turning after another, and one path leading into another. I'd have lost my way long ago."

"I hope the screws looking for us have a hard time of it." Goldberg grinned.

"By eleven tonight," Trofimov said, "we should be about a hundred kilometres away, far beyond their reach. Then we can afford to stop for the night, have a good meal and a proper rest."

"For the whole night?" Bondarenko looked at Yatta. "How? We've no shelter, and the tent is—"

"We Chukchi are used to spending nights in the open," said Yatta. "You know, you just gotta be dressed warmly enough, and girdle yourself tightly with thongs. I've spent dozens of nights in the open like that."

Trofimov shrugged. "Maybe you Chukchi are men of iron, but the rest of us will end up frozen. Is there no way of making a quick shelter?"

"Well, I know how to build an Aiwan igloo," Yatta said. "The Aiwans build them when they're hunting or traveling. We Chukchi don't do that, but I lived for some time with the Aiwans on the coast, and I know how to make a snow igloo. It's as warm inside as in a yaranga tent."

"I read about these Eskimo igloos," Trofimov recollected. "I still can't imagine sleeping in one and not freezing to death."

"Igloo making is an old art, you know," Yatta explained. "I'm gonna show you how."

"Well," Bondarenko grinned, "I spent three years in dugouts, and cattle cars and camp barracks. Why not try this? And talking of food, let's slaughter the gray reindeer and have a feast. How about it?"

"We must make a sacrifice to the Lord of the Woods, though," said Yatta.

Bondarenko frowned. "You intend to present it to someone else? What are we gonna eat?"

"We can eat the deer's meat," Yatta explained, "but first we must perform the ritual sacrifice, though. We're in the realm of the Lord of the Woods, so we can make our way only if he helps us."

"Oh, well," Bondarenko sounded relieved, "if you don't mean to give all the meat away to your Lord, then let's do it."

"Yeah, let Yatta do whatever he thinks is right," Trofimov looked at his watch. "It's time to go."

Bondarenko and Trofimov mounted the reindeer, Yatta took the front animal by the reins, and they were on their way.

5

Lieutenant Belyayev operated the wireless transmitter. "Come in Crane. Come in Crane. This is Falcon calling. What's new? Over."

"Hello Falcon," came a voice from the transmitter. "Crane reporting. The search continues. No results so far. Over."

"Falcon calling. This is Falcon. If you find anything, report immediately. Over and out." Belyayev switched to another wavelength. "Calling Daisy, calling Daisy. This is Falcon. Please report results. Over."

A crackling sound came from the transmitter, then another voice. "Calling Falcon. Daisy calling Falcon. Nothing has been found so far in our sector. Over."

"Fucking shit," Belyayev cursed, then suddenly realized he was on the air and changed his voice. "Falcon calling Daisy. Continue searching."

The door opened and Avdeyev appeared.

"Anything to report?"

"Nothing, Pavel Egorovich. Frankly speaking, I don't think we're going to find them near the camp now. They've had enough time to get a long way away, and after the snowfall there are no tracks to follow."

"They're smart, those scumbags," Avdeyev cursed. "They chose a perfect time. Did you contact compounds six and seven? And number thirteen?"

"I did all that, Pavel Egorovich."

"Well," Avdeyev sighed, "I hope we catch them before the authorities in Magadan find out or several heads will be on the block."

"D'you think so, comrade Major?" Belyayev asked.

"And what do you think?" Avdeyev snapped. "You expect to get a decoration? Five of those scum escaped, and seven servicemen killed on duty."

"I don't think it will be all that serious," Belyayev said, although his voice lacked any confidence. "They'll be caught on the way to Magadan. No one's ever got there without being caught."

"I just pray that they do something stupid," said Avdeyev, "like trying to hijack a plane. You remember how it was four years ago? Or at least move in the direction of Magadan. In that case they'll be caught for sure, and our heads will be spared."

"Where else could they go?" Belyayev asked.

"Where else?" Avdeyev yelped. "You ask me that? Why do you think they took Yatta with them? He spent ten years in the forests out east. It's very likely they'll head there, rather than going south or west on the usual escape routes."

"But what will they do in the East? There's just taiga, and hardly a single village around. They can't survive there."

"But they can," Avdeyev retorted. "They can hunt, trap and a whole lot of other things. For Yatta that's a way of life. It'll be next to impossible to fetch them back once they get out to those areas. The troops can't comb the whole taiga from here to upper Anadyr. Our only hope is if they move towards Magadan."

It was late in the evening before the fugitives stopped for the night. In a small clearing Timoshkin and Yatta started a fire, while the others tethered the reindeer.

"At last we can enjoy a nice meal," Bondarenko mused. "I'm hungry as a bear."

"Me too," said Timoshkin, "and dog tired as well."

"First we make a sacrifice," Yatta reminded them.

"As in the Gospel," Goldberg reflected. "Render unto Caesar that which is Caesar's and unto God that which is God's."

"Right," Bondarenko chuckled. "And unto runaway convicts that which is theirs. And the same to the screws—a bullet in the head or a knife in the ribs."

When the campfire burned steadily and the deer had been tethered, Trofimov said, "It's time. Will we take this fat gray one?"

"Right," Yatta agreed. "I need someone to help. I'll hold the deer with the lasso round its neck, and the other will take it by the antlers and stab it."

"Fine," Trofimov agreed. "Mikhail?"

"Sure," Bondarenko nodded. "I can do that. I've been slaughtering cows and pigs for years."

"But," Yatta said, "donna do it in a cruel way, like some of you Russians do. The reindeer is a noble animal, a gift of the Creator."

"Don't you worry." Bondarenko tested the knife. "It needs sharpening."

Bondarenko sharpened the knife on a boulder, while Yatta made incantations in his own language. When Bondarenko was ready with the knife, Yatta took the lasso, and threw it over the reindeer's neck. He pulled it closer to them.

"Go ahead, Mikhail," Yatta said.

Bondarenko grabbed the deer by the antlers and with one quick movement cut the animal's throat. The deer fell on its side, writhing. Yatta yelled then grabbed the knife from Bondarenko, pushed him aside and stabbed the deer through its heart. The animal's convulsions ceased.

"What's wrong, what's the matter with you, Yatta?" Bondarenko protested.

"Oh oh," Yatta lamented. "You hurt the reindeer. You gave him a painful death. Now it can't be sacrificed."

"Damn," Bondarenko cursed. "You're off your head. What did I do wrong?"

"You brought pain and disgrace upon the deer," Yatta wailed. "You can't kill a deer like that. Only filthy scum, men who kill their own mothers, or an enemy warrior who has no mercy on old folks or kids—only people like that can be killed in such a way. But not a reindeer, a gift to man from the Creator and from the Lord of the Woods. We can slay them for meat, but never should we cause them pain."

"Yatta, I ain't a kid. I've slaughtered a hell of a lot of cattle in my time."

"I donna know about your Russian cattle," Yatta answered. "But the reindeer is a gift of the Heavenly Beings. It has to be slain without causing it pain."

"For Christ's sake, shut your trap," Bondarenko yelled, "or I'll come and get you."

"Mikhail, you talk that way to me, to someone older than yourself?" Yatta's voice was calm but filled with contempt. "Come on. Let's fight it out." He squared up to Bondarenko.

"Are you crazy?" Trofimov came between them. "Starting a brawl at a time like this! We five have nobody in the world except one another, and the whole Soviet state against us. We've not been free for two days and you're already fighting." He paused and sighed deeply. "If this is the way we're going to carry on, we might as well shoot one another and have done with it. If we can't stick together like brothers and comrades-in-arms, there's no hope for us. No goddamned hope whatever." He paused again. "As your commander, I order you to stop right now and shake hands."

"It's okay by me, Captain," Bondarenko shrugged his shoulders. "It's Yatta who's making all the fuss."

"Listen to me though, Sasha," Yatta pleaded. "Just listen to me. I've got something to say."

"You see?" Bondarenko snapped, "He's hopeless."

"Shut up, Mikhail." Trofimov cut him off. "Go on, Yatta, tell us what you want to say."

"I just wanna say that we are in the domains of the Lord of the Woods," Yatta explained emotionally. "We've to respect his rules, and only then will he give us his help. These rules say that we've to make a fair sacrifice to him, and to the Creator and other Heavenly Beings. The only way to do that is to slay the deer painlessly, so that the deer's soul departs comfortably into the dwelling of the Lord of the Woods. If you hurt the deer, its soul will go there filled with pain and will beg the Lord of the Woods for vengeance. Any man who is not on good terms with the Lord of the Woods will never get out of the forest alive."

"I get it. I understand you, Yatta," Trofimov said. "Now what can we do to make a proper sacrifice? Can we still sacrifice this deer? After all, he didn't suffer too much, you stabbed him right away in the heart."

"Yeah," Yatta agreed. "I did that, and hopefully that may calm the Lord. But we can't make a sacrifice of this deer now, it's sullied by pain. We've got to sacrifice some other deer."

"Maybe we can catch a wild deer and sacrifice it?" Trofimov suggested.

"No," said Yatta, "a wild deer already belongs to the Lord of the Woods. Domestic reindeer are man's property and only they can be sacrificed. We can take sometime another reindeer for food, so when the time comes, we will make a proper sacrifice of that one."

"Agreed." Trofimov nodded. "We'll do as you say."

"That will be the right thing to do, you know," Yatta agreed. "Hopefully the Lord will forgive us this misdeed, 'cause Mikhail is new to the woods, and he ain't know the rules."

"I'm sure the Lord of the Woods will forgive us," Trofimov said, then after a pause, "I hope we can still eat this deer."

"Yeah," Yatta agreed. "We can do that. In fact it's better to eat it, so it wasn't slaughtered for no purpose. Killing without purpose is an even worse misdeed."

"Very sensible, Yatta," said Bondarenko. "I was afraid you wanted us to leave it for the wolves."

A couple of hours later, after Yatta, Bondarenko, and Timoshkin had finished dealing with the reindeer's carcass, the supper was ready, and the five men sat around the bonfire eating with great gusto.

"Well," Trofimov said happily, "our first proper meal as free men! Six months ago we could never have imagined that in a short time we'd be free, armed, beyond the reach of the screws, enjoying such a meal."

"Thank the Lord." Timoshkin crossed himself. "Thank you, Lord, that we've lived to see this day."

"Indeed," Bondarenko exclaimed. "Even if we get whacked in the end, at least we shall die free."

"And now," Trofimov's voice became solemn, "I want to swear

an oath to you. By my honour as a combat officer, I pledge to you that I'll do everything in my power to get you all to Alaska. It's possible we might die in a fight, but we'll meet an honourable death, in battle, not in the hands of Stalin's underlings. If I break this oath … if I can't save you from that fate—"

"Then you'll die on the larch," Bondarenko grinned. "Or in the death tent, like the rest of us."

"Possibly. But I'm confident that'll never happen. Now you must pledge to obey me."

"Yes, I vow to obey you," Bondarenko announced.

"By my parents' last refuge," Yatta proclaimed.

"Yes, I swear. I pledge to obey." Goldberg and Timoshkin echoed their oaths.

"This deserves a toast," Bondarenko announced and raised his flask. "To our freedom and success."

"Let's settle yet another matter," Trofimov continued. "It may happen that one of us gets wounded or sick—seriously, I mean, very seriously. The others will have to face the choice of abandoning him or—"

"Never!" exclaimed Bondarenko. "We'll care for the wounded right to the end. Either we all get better or all die. If the wounded one dies, then the rest can move on."

"Spoken like a true soldier," Trofimov said. "Let's also vow to care for the sick and wounded right to the end."

"We reindeer folk," Yatta said, "we have a custom that someone who's mortally sick, or too old, asks his friends to kill him. And his friends do that, they don't refuse, never."

"Can you force a man to be killed?" Goldberg asked.

"Only if the man desires it," Yatta replied.

"I once killed a guy in our partisan unit for that reason," Bondarenko said. "The poor guy's stomach was ripped open by a grenade. He begged us to finish him off. I did it."

"I've seen that too," Timoshkin added. "A guy got a dum-dum bullet in his lung, and his friend finished him off."

"Yeah," Trofimov agreed, "I guess that if someone's in terrible pain and wants to die, then it can be done. Otherwise, if it's not a fatal wound, we take care of him to the end. Unless, God spare us, we're encircled, and then—well, we'll kill ourselves and the wounded. Can we agree on that?"

"Agreed," all four men responded without hesitation.

"Why are we talking about such sad things?" Timoshkin interrupted. "I reckon none of us is going to die right now. Let's have another drink and more meat."

"Sure, but don't drink too much," Trofimov warned. "We still have to build a shelter for the night. What do you think, Yatta?"

"Just for now, you know, we'll make an igloo," Yatta said. "We can make it in a couple of hours. And we've got to make the poles for a yaranga as soon as possible."

"I want to keep moving for the next three days," Trofimov said. "Get as far away as possible."

"I would rather make the poles first," Yatta insisted. "This is the blizzard season."

"I'd rather risk getting caught by a blizzard than by the screws," Trofimov said. "We'll do another seventy kilometres and then make the poles."

"I agree with the captain," Bondarenko said. "Better to die under the snow than in the hands of the MGB."

"Well," Yatta shrugged, "as you wish. You know, I myself have spent many nights in the open air."

"And one last thing," Trofimov concluded, "concerning watch duty at night. I propose that we release Yatta from that duty, since he's our guide and provider. He has too many responsibilities already."

"Of course," Timoshkin agreed. "Yatta more than deserves a full night's sleep."

"No," Yatta objected. "I donna want to do that. I'm one of you, and I'll be the best on guard at night. I know the sounds of the forest. Don't relieve me of that."

"No," Trofimov insisted. "That's my order. We can't afford to have you going underslept. We need you well rested, alert and able to be a guide at any time."

"I don't see no reason for that," Yatta argued, "especially when it comes to being on guard. I should spend time on guard with each of you. I can teach you the meaning of the sounds in the woods at night."

"Okay," Trofimov laughed and relented. "If you're so opposed, have it your way." He looked at his watch. "Almost twelve o'clock. Time to make our igloo."

The night was dark and cold. The snowfall continued lazily, and only occasional stars could be glimpsed in the sky. The igloo stood in the middle of a clearing with the sleds standing side by side next to it. The four reindeer were tethered to trees by long ropes and continued trying to dig themselves down into the snow. Trofimov walked around the clearing, feeling with pleasure the weight of the Kalashnikov and bayonet on his shoulder. The wood was filled with the small sounds of nocturnal life, the crackling of branches and twigs in the frosty air, the sighing of the wind and the occasional thump of a snow plug falling from a tree.

Trofimov summed up the events of the last few days. The enterprise they had waited for with a mixture of enthusiasm and concern had at last begun. There was no turning back. They had crossed their Rubicon. "Farewell, mainland, forever." In that song the "mainland" represented home and freedom and past happiness. Now they had another chance for freedom, but this was a new and very special form of liberty. It would not bring them home. On the contrary, it separated them forever from their homes and families and from everything in their past lives. Trofimov's native Urals were thousands of kilometres beyond the sunset, along with his family and his mother who had lost two of her sons in the war and recently lost her husband. Now he, Alexander Trofimov, her last surviving son, was also lost to her. From now on, his path could lead only forward, to the East, through wild woodland and tundra, toward the rising sun and the safe haven of Alaska. Or to his death. What did tomorrow hold?

It all looked so strange, yet there was nothing unusual in what was happening to him. It was just another struggle, and he was used to every kind of battle. They were a small group, pitted against a powerful enemy, but the woods, the winter and the boundless space were their allies, and powerful allies they were, to those able to take advantage of their gifts.

All around him stood the age-old forest. These larches might have seen the first Cossack explorers, Dezhnev and Poyarkov. How many mysteries this forest concealed in its depths: thousands upon thousands of Russians and native Siberians had died here of wounds or starvation, killed by wild beasts, or killed by one another in skirmishes. Some of them, pursuing their mysterious paths, had maybe stopped in this very spot, made their bonfires, rested for the night and vanished in the morning in the depths of the forest and of time.

He heard a loud rustling in the thickets. God damn! Had they already tracked them down? Was everything to end just when it was beginning? Trofimov rushed toward the trees and cocked the trigger on his gun. A fox emerged from behind the trees and slunk towards their sled, eager to collect the remains of the slaughtered deer. Trofimov dashed forward and the animal made off.

6

For the next four days they moved constantly, stopping only to eat and sleep at night. Each night they built an igloo, only to destroy it the following morning to cover their tracks. Yatta wanted to make a major stop in order to make poles for the tent, but Trofimov insisted on moving still further.

Once in the early morning on a perfectly ordinary stretch of path, Yatta stopped suddenly and looked up into the sky.

"Something wrong, Yatta?" Trofimov asked.

"A blizzard's coming," Yatta replied. "A heavy one, you know. We have to build an igloo right now, or we'll be buried in snow."

"Are you sure?"

"Yeah."

Trofimov looked upwards. The sky was covered with low clouds. Small birds flitted nervously. The sound of the wind was peculiar, as if somewhere a large unknown creature moaned. Trofimov recollected having read somewhere that low flying birds were the sign of an impending storm.

"If we're really in for a blizzard, let's not waste time. Yatta, can an igloo withstand a heavy blizzard?"

"Yeah, for sure, if it's built properly."

"Right, come on, let's get started," Trofimov urged.

As they worked on the igloo, the wind grew stronger and stronger. Gusting along the ground, it sent snow whirling like serpents from a fairy tale, and as the wind gathered strength, thick snow fell from the sky. Soon the men could hardly stand on their feet. At one point Goldberg's fur cap was torn off by a gust. He rushed to retrieve it but could hardly see it.

"Sasha! Mikhail! Help me catch my cap!"

Trofimov and Bondarenko leapt forward and with great effort retrieved their friend's headgear.

By the time the entrance to the igloo was complete, the blizzard raged at full strength.

"Now," Trofimov said, "bring our stuff inside. We need food for the next few days."

"We'll never get the reindeer carcass through the entrance," Goldberg pointed out.

"No," said Yatta, "but we can cut the legs off, and that should be enough."

"Be quick about it," Trofimov urged.

Bondarenko and Trofimov hacked off the two hind legs while Timoshkin and Goldberg collected their belongings and stuffed them through the entrance. Yatta set about organizing things inside.

Timoshkin said, "I'll get snow for drinking water." He collected two full buckets and passed them inside.

"Looks like we're all set," said Trofimov.

"Tether the reindeer more tightly," Yatta's voice came from inside the igloo, and Timoshkin took care of this final task.

At last, utterly exhausted, the men crawled inside the snow house on their stomachs. Yatta had spread the reindeer skins on the snow floor, everyone lay down and within a few moments the five of them were sound asleep.

When Trofimov opened his eyes, it took him a moment to figure out where he was. All around was pitch dark, without a spot of light. Outside the snow walls the blizzard roared. He felt around with one hand and ran up against a body lying on the floor.

"Who's that?" the body yelped with Bondarenko's voice.

"There you are, Mikhail," Trofimov said.

"That you, Captain?"

"Who else could it be?"

"Turn on the lamp. I can't see a bloody thing," said Bondarenko.

He raked blindly through their belongings.

"What's the matter?" It was Yatta's voice.

"Yatta, can you see in this dark?"

"Sure."

"Find the lamp," Bondarenko said.

Yatta retrieved their "kolymka," which they had made from a meat can. Trofimov produced his lighter and the kolymka glowed in the darkness, waking up Timoshkin and Goldberg.

"I've got to eat something," Bondarenko said. "I'm hungry as a horse."

"What do we have?" Goldberg's voice sounded drowsy.

"You forgot, Yakov? We worked hard to hack off those two deer legs and get them in here." Bondarenko reminded him. "We'll have to eat it raw, though."

"Shave off the meat and eat it like that," Yatta said. He took a knife and cut thin shavings from the reindeer leg. In a few minutes they were all enjoying the frozen meat shavings, seasoned with salt.

"Well, we managed it," Trofimov said with satisfaction. "The blizzard's blowing, but we're alive and well, and properly sheltered. How long could this go on, Yatta?"

"Who knows?" Yatta said. "It could end tomorrow, or it could last several days."

"Do we have to stay in here all that time?" asked Goldberg.

"Of course, Yakov, what else can we do?" Bondarenko grinned. "Are you unhappy? This igloo's gonna protect us from that bloody blizzard, and that's all we need for now. Or would you rather be on the run with a set of screws on your heels?"

"Even screws couldn't chase us through a storm like this," Timoshkin said. "Probably they're sitting in their tents, shivering."

"Sure they are," Trofimov agreed. "This blizzard is a good thing. It'll wipe out our tracks. How far are we from the camp now?"

"About eight score kilometres," Yatta replied.

"A hundred and sixty. We're getting on well."

"Yeah, we're still in the lowlands though," Yatta explained. "Soon we'll get to the hills, and it'll be slow going then."

"I wonder what's going on in the camp?" Timoshkin mused.

"What's going on? An almighty crazy hubbub, that's what." Bondarenko chortled.

"I worry they'll take it out on those who stayed," said Goldberg. "Vaskov might suffer, and Ganin."

"I'm afraid you're right," Trofimov heaved a deep sigh. "Ganin's very vulnerable. Vaskov slightly less so. He's buddy-buddy with everyone. But as for Ganin …"

"Yeah," said Yatta. "I'm very sad about that, you know. I begged him: 'Come with us, old Vladimir. Come with us.' I promised to let him ride on a sled. But he wouldn't agree. What's gonna happen to that poor old man?"

"Well," Timoshkin sighed, "I hope the good Lord will take care of him."

"And to think I wasn't sure about him right to the last," Trofimov said. "I had my doubts, and was afraid he might betray us. What a noble man. I feel terribly guilty."

"There's no reason for that," Bondarenko broke in. "You'd be a shithead to trust anyone there. All we can do is try and keep his memory bright. You offered him a chance to come with us, and he was clever enough to refuse."

"Maybe you're right, Mikhail," Trofimov agreed. "But he could still suffer because of us."

"He certainly could. What do you expect of our glorious secret police?" Bondarenko said. "They spare no one. And whatever we do or don't do, they usually finish us off."

"How I'd love to settle scores with them," Trofimov exclaimed. "To be moving not toward Alaska, but in the opposite direction, to Moscow. I wish there were not five, but five hundred thousand of us. Then those scum would get what they deserve, and the Big Moustache would end up hanging by his neck under the red stars on the Kremlin towers."

"I understand what you're saying," Bondarenko said. "But this ain't the right moment for a revolt. The people behave like sheep."

"I know. But why? Why?" Trofimov groaned. "The Russian people were always ready to revolt to defend themselves. They overthrew the tsar and took the land for themselves. Why do they put up with these butchers for decades on end?"

"Because the people are weary, worn out," Bondarenko said. "Remember what they've been through. The Civil War set brother against brother, father against son. The Reds, Whites and Greens raided the villages, people died of hunger everywhere. Then there was the famine in 1921, and more people died, then the collectivization and everythin' turned upside down again, and more hundreds of thousands of people starved to death. Then in 1933, the fuckin' commissars seized the entire harvest right down to the last grain, and people ate cats, dogs, horse skins, even their neighbours. And what do we want, after all? Just bread. We'll do anythin' for a loaf of bread."

"You're dead right," Timoshkin agreed. "I felt exactly like that after the 1933 famine. I hardly wanted anything but a hunk of bread."

"This situation could last for another half century," Trofimov said. "What an awful time we live in." He paused. "Remember 1945, right after V-Day? A dozen million soldiers, all armed and hardened in battle. If only we could have reached some agreement, we'd have made mincemeat of that Party and MGB scum."

"Yeah," Bondarenko said. "If only we could have agreed. But how really could we? You couldn't even talk about it. I spoke to one single guy, my good friend, and said that maybe they'll disband the collective farms and return the land to us. As a result, here I am. The thing is, hardly anyone wanted another upheaval. We should think ourselves fuckin' lucky that we at least agreed upon an action. We have a chance."

That night Trofimov lay on the reindeer skin, unable to sleep, turning his conversation with Bondarenko and Timoshkin over and over in his mind. He wondered whether the situation in the country at large was really so hopeless. Had the Russian people really got so discouraged about protesting? Had they really reverted to their attitude of endless patience, humility and readiness to tolerate an inhuman existence for ages to come? Or maybe the problem lay in a lack of leadership? Stalin and his clique had succeeded in wiping out any potential alternative leaders, the would-be modern-day Sten'ka Razins and the Pugachevs, as well as any potential Decembrist plotters among the military, together with millions of other people.

On the other hand, take the convicts in the labour camps. Technically speaking they could not rebel, under tight surveillance day and night, with screws, guard dogs, and submachine guns. Yet what if they suddenly had a chance to rebel and turn against their tormentors? The five of them, for instance, had managed to find one another and act against all the odds, and there were thousands of other war veterans. Certainly they were weakened by hunger and drudgery, and many of them were on their last legs, "goners." But a few weeks of good food could restore most of them to life. It was hard to believe that they too did not dream of turning against their oppressors.

Trofimov rolled himself a cigar and smoked for a while as he listened to the roaring blizzard. What would it need to start a similar storm among the labour camp population? If, for instance, he and his comrades had changed their minds and decided not to escape, but to stay and fight? It might seem ridiculous at first glance: a small bunch of men pitted against a great power. Yet even a small group, as heavily armed as they were, could do a lot. They could ambush and attack prisoner escort parties on foot. Properly executed, the operation could successfully wipe out the entire escort, including the guard dogs. The liberated convicts would surely join them, especially with the prospect of fresh reindeer meat for the next few weeks. If they could repeat that operation and get away with it, they could raise their number to that of a battalion. Then they could attack camp compounds: the watchtowers were primitive constructions, good for watching and shooting at unarmed prisoners, but totally unfortified against a siege from outside. They could easily be set on fire and destroyed. Then it would be a military problem to capture the entire camp zone. So many more arms and men. And if a dozen compounds could be captured and liberated, then rebellions could start in further camps, and the blaze of rebellion would flare. Could he—should he—try and persuade his friends to embark on such a scheme?

Numerous problems would arise. Where would they get supplies to feed the rebels? Hunting and fishing could not provide for thousands, but there were hundreds upon hundreds of reindeer and cattle at the state-owned cattle procurement bases. The Gulag authorities owned cattle and pigs. Canned food was brought in to feed the screws, and with thousands of the latter killed in the rebellion, there would be food enough to feed all the fighters, at least for a while.

What about weapons? They could obtain submachine guns,

the stationary type, but not artillery or tanks, or an air force, and without them the rebels would be no match for the government troops. That was a problem indeed. They would have to avoid full-scale battle operations and adopt hit and run tactics. But after all, the partisans in wartime occupied Russian territory had done just that—also Yugoslav, Polish and other partisans. And there were the so-called forest brethren in Latvia. One could also arrange to smuggle in supplies of arms, say from America. A lot of gold was mined in the Kolyma region, and if that were seized, it would pay for weapons and food. Unless, of course, the Soviet troops severed the supply lines. Yet that too could be prevented. In the end they might be able to proclaim a new Far Eastern Republic as a homeland and safe haven for all refugees from the Kremlin tyrants.

If such a thing happened—if—then would he, Trofimov, be capable of leading such a rebellion? He was only twenty-six, but during the Civil War people of that age, Reds and Whites, commanded regiments, divisions and armies. And he, after all, was a combat officer with years of war experience, a good reputation and decorations. Soviet propaganda could hardly represent him as a traitor, because hundreds of men throughout Russia knew him. Also, he was a commoner. The White generals Denikin and Kolchak were noblemen, aristocrats, and that was their crucial weakness, because serfdom and its cruelty were still fresh in the Russian people's collective memory. To put their trust in "white bones" and "blue blood" was out of the question. But he, Trofimov, was the descendant of generations of workmen from the Ural factories and of Orenburg Cossacks. He was truly one of the Russian people.

Trofimov almost burned with excitement. In his imagination he saw thousands of armed rebels under his command, liberated labour camp compounds, burning watchtowers, broken fences of barbed wire, hundreds of slaughtered camp guards. With all the passion of a former Young Communist, he envisioned himself as the Garibaldi of Kolyma, a harsh but fair leader. He imagined the rage and fear that would grip the Kolyma authorities as they heard the news of spreading rebellion, and of rebel fighters coming closer and closer to their own residences to demand retribution for their evil deeds. Soon they would take the Fifth Camp compound and capture Avdeyev. And what would they do to Avdeyev, he wondered? Nothing but justice. He would face a firing squad, but only if Avdeyev had done nothing to harm Vladimir Semyonovich Ganin. In the event he had done something to the old man, then he himself would be to blame. Trofimov would deal with the scumbag the way he deserved. He would hand him over to the compound prisoners, and it would depend on their anger and their fantasy what sort of death he would die—beaten to death, decapitated with a saw, strung up by his balls, drowned in the crapper, or fed to the wild animals.

A terrible thought entered Trofimov's mind: the authorities would stop short of nothing to crush rebellion. There was one thing they could do when they realized the gravity of the situation. They would kill off the convict population of Kolyma. There were thousands, maybe millions, of convicts in the Northeast. The authorities only need gather them in the centre of their compounds and rake them with machinegun fire from the watchtowers. It would be so quick and easy. That would deprive the rebel forces of reinforcements, and they would dwindle day by day, until the last few dozen of them were killed or captured. It was such a rapid and easy solution.

Tsar Nicholas II would probably have stopped short of perpetrating such carnage. So would Kolchak, Denikin and maybe even Lenin. But not Stalin, or Beria! And he, Alexander Trofimov, would then be responsible for all that.

That was something he would never be ready to do. He was no pacifist, and had always despised that Christian and Tolstoyan belief in non-violence; he firmly believed that fighting inevitably demanded sacrifice. But the lives of millions of innocent people? That was too much.

Another thought struck him: his aging mother and other surviving relatives were in Russia, at the mercy of the enemy. As long as he was a fugitive, the Kolyma authorities would be unwilling to spread news of his escape outside their own domains. His mother was still relatively safe, at least as safe as anyone could be during that reign of terror. But if he were the leader of a major rebellion, and Stalin and other supreme authorities got to know of him, they surely would not spare his relatives. They would wipe out his kin, up to his cousins five times removed. And as for his poor mother, her death would be terrible.

Alternatively, if they were smart enough, they might imprison his mother and blackmail him: "Come on, Trofimov, surrender, or we'll skin your mother alive." His poor, kind and completely innocent mother.

Trofimov shivered at the thought. No, there was no way to undertake any such ambitious schemes. So, Trofimov, lay these crazy plans aside and concentrate on getting yourself and your comrades to safe haven in the Far East, where the sun rises. That's the best thing you can do, so do it successfully.

7

Trofimov and his friends sat around the fire in front of their snow house, eating and smoking. Newly made tent poles, tools and wood shavings lay scattered around them. It was midday, and the red globe of the sun hung in a dark blue sky.

"Mikhail," Timoshkin asked, "can we finish the job by tonight?"

"If they were ordinary tent poles," Bondarenko shrugged, "then we'd finish by then. But Yatta says we need more than two dozen of them. Yatta, why do we need so many of the damned things for one tent?"

"But it's a yaranga, you know," Yatta insisted. "We need three foundation poles, twenty-four support poles, eight crossbars, a dozen *uttamit* and three poles as stretchers to tighten the skin."

"That's a hell of a bloody lot," Trofimov exclaimed.

"But, Sasha," Yatta retorted, "that's the least we need to make a good firm yaranga. A light one will never stand up against a blizzard, never. In the open tundra there can be half a dozen blizzards every month, and out there they're much more fierce. Only a good, a firm yaranga can stand up in those blizzards, believe me."

"Well, you know better than I, Yatta." Trofimov shrugged the matter off.

"Yeah, Captain," Bondarenko gave a slightly mocking grin, "you always take Yatta's side."

"Don't talk bullshit, Mikhail," Trofimov shot back. "Yatta knows best what to do. On other matters you or Timoshkin know better, and there it's your word that counts."

"Donna get pissed off, Captain," Bondarenko laughed. "I'm only joking. After all, you're in command, and I never argue with my commander. Never ever."

"Stop it, you guys," Timoshkin said. "Let's talk about somethin' more pleasant."

"Like what?"

"About women," Bondarenko proposed.

"Yes, we could do that," Goldberg agreed.

"Let's each of us talk about his experience with women," said Bondarenko. "I guess there are no virgins among us?"

"You must be joking," Timoshkin grinned. "We're all old soldiers."

"Right, Captain, you start."

"What can I say?" Trofimov began. "There's nothing special to tell. I had several women during the war. 'Field wives' they were called. Before the war I had only one love, but it was unrequited."

"Oh, the classroom beauty, was she?" Goldberg put in.

"Exactly," Trofimov said. "Of course she paid no attention to me."

"Ah, it's always like that, " Bondarenko observed. "So you had to get to the battlefront to lose your virginity?"

"Right. Exactly a year later. Three months after I arrived at the front."

"First baptism by fire and then by fucking." Bondarenko chuckled.

"You got it. She was a nurse in a field hospital. I got a piece of shrapnel in my shoulder. I fancied her but I was too shy to approach her. In the end she asked me directly why I didn't go in for 'it.' The two of us remained together all the while I was in hospital. After her was Lena Korobova, our battalion wireless operator. That affair lasted until my next injury. Then I was hospitalized in Saratov for three months, and I had an affair with Natasha, one of the nurses. I liked her very much, and even corresponded with her for a while afterwards. For the rest of the war and for half a year when I was stationed on the River Elbe, I was with Olga, a physician. When I got to Latvia, I met Laima, a Latvian widow. She was wonderful, though, to be honest, she only slept with me for the sake of my officer's ration. But I took advantage of that too. I felt frustrated and homesick. I just wanted some warmth, and maybe some fun too."

"That's not too good. But many officers were in that position," Timoshkin remarked. "Whoever was in command of our unit, no matter whether they were good guys or scumbags, they all did it."

"Of course they did," Bondarenko laughed. "They weren't saints after all."

"Of course not," Timoshkin said, "Lord forgive them."

"I never did any of that," Goldberg objected.

"You didn't? How come? In that case it's your turn, Yakov," said Bondarenko.

"Oh, it's not at all an interesting story," Goldberg smiled. "I was just a nice, shy Jewish boy. I couldn't imagine being with any woman until I was married, and I wasn't a success at dating. My aunt Rebecca, a born matchmaker, found me a nice girl and soon after we were married. I was so shy on that first night."

"Is that right?" Timoshkin sounded surprised. "So how is it people say that Jews are such big fuckers?"

"People say God knows what about us Jews. We're scrooges, we're filthy, we're traitors—and now we're great fuckers too. In fact, most of us are very modest folk. I didn't have a single affair during my married life."

"What 'bout at the front?" Bondarenko asked.

"No, not me." Goldberg shrugged.

"I donna believe it," Bondarenko exclaimed.

"It's the truth."

"Which means, you're the only one of us," Trofimov said, "who's chaste. And what about you, Zakharych?"

"Nothin' to match your achievements," Timoshkin said with a shy smile. "My father married me off when I was fifteen. Since then Vera and I were together all the time. We had three kids. The eldest, Dmitry, turned eighteen this summer and is about to be drafted. I never was any great stud, though I did have one affair in Germany, in that English camp just after the war."

"I also married my first girl," Bondarenko said. "But that wasn't the start of things. The two of us had been together for a whole year before that. Until she got pregnant."

"A familiar story," Timoshkin nodded.

"Right. Even then I didn't want to get married. I wanted to play around. One day her dad and four brothers caught me outside the village and gave me a beating. Fuck it all, what they did to me! I never experienced nothin' like that again until I was in the jug. They broke my nose and a couple of ribs and …"

"It's hard to imagine, Mikhail, that someone as smart as you got himself into such a mess," Trofimov commented.

"That's precisely what it was. One hell of a mess." Bondarenko grinned. "They told me, 'Either you marry Anyuta, you fucking shithead, or we'll cut your balls off and string them up on a birch!'"

"So you married her?"

"Of course. What the hell else could I do? Leave the village? This was already 1934, and you couldn't go nowhere without a passport. But despite all that, I'm glad I married her. My Anyuta's a real beauty, and smart too, and in bed she's—wow! No words to describe it. We lived together happily until the war. We had two kids. It was a great life we had, those seven years. After that, in the partisan unit, I got friendly with our nurse. She was nice too, but no match for Anyuta. I used to sneak back to our village from time to time, just to make love to her. If I'd been caught, the Fritzes would have skinned me alive. Anyway, after the war, we were together again for seven months, and then I got jugged. You know, guys, the only thing I'm really sorry about now is that I'll never see my Anyuta again."

"Yeah," said Trofimov, "All ties with our past lives are broken. All we've got to hope for is a new life beyond the Bering Strait."

"If we ever get there," Bondarenko said. "But if I'm gonna get whacked, the one thing I'd like before that is a good screw with a nice girl. I'm afraid that's somethin' I'm not gonna get either."

"I'm sorry, but that's something I can't promise. Maybe only some time in Alaska." Trofimov laughed.

"I realize that, Captain," Bondarenko sighed and turned to Yatta. "And what about you, Yatta? I bet you've got a story to tell."

"Well, I started with my cousin, you know, the daughter of my uncle."

"Isn't that incest?" Goldberg asked.

"It's common among our people, though. Many boys and girls start like that," said Yatta.

"How old were you?" asked Trofimov.

"Fifteen. After that I fell for one girl. Her father was rich and had five hundred head of deer. But I wasn't rich, you know, I had only a hundred head. So I had to live in her father's household and work as his herdsman for three years."

"As a labourer?" Timoshkin asked.

"Something like that. It's a custom among the Chukchi. We call it 'naund'o'urgin,' which means 'serving for your wife.' After that you can marry your bride and be co-owner of her herd. During those first three years you can't screw your bride. But we started making love in the second year, and once her father caught us at it."

"Did he beat the shit out of you?" Bondarenko asked.

"Not really," Yatta said. "But he roared like an angry bear and told me to get out."

"But eventually you ended up marrying her?" Trofimov guessed.

"Yeah, thanks to his elder wife, Omrina, my mother-in-law. She persuaded him and pointed out that the girl's honour would suffer. So, he ordered his sons to give me fifty lashes. They did that, and I took my beating. But still by the end of the term we got married. We lived a good life together for about nine years, until the collectivization. By that time we had a herd of three hundred head and four kids. There was no adultery, just wife companionship."

"Wife companionship? What the heck does that mean?" Bondarenko's eyebrows shot up.

"It's a very old custom. Almost every Telqap man has at least half a dozen sworn brothers that are not actual blood relatives," Yatta explained. "It's just as tight a bond as blood, sometimes even stronger. A man can sleep with the wives of his sworn brothers."

"Wow! That's not bad." Trofimov chuckled. "So how many wives of your sworn brothers did you manage to screw?"

"Eight."

"That means you're the screwing champion among our company," Bondarenko exclaimed. "Who would've thought it? You look such a reserved kind of guy."

"It's one of our most important bonds though," Yatta explained. "Life is tough out in the tundra, and you've got to have many relatives and friends. If you have plenty, you're a respected man among your tribesmen and neighbours, but if you haven't any, you'll be miserable."

"Well, there's somethin' to be said for that," Bondarenko

agreed.

"And do you know where they all are now?" Trofimov asked.

"No." Yatta shook his head. "When we were dispossessed of our property, the Soviet commissars sent us all in different directions. We haven't heard nothin' more of one another. Although I did hear that three of my wife-companions moved to the East, to Alaska along with many of the Telqap people. I hope to meet them there."

"And who is this other woman, the one you hope to see along the way?" Trofimov asked.

"That's Qergina," Yatta explained. "I met her out in the taiga, after I fled. My wife and kids were all dead by then. Qergina's from our Upper Anuy kinfolk. Her father was a powerful shaman. But when the Soviets came, they froze him alive in an ice hole in the Anuy River. She fled to the woods in the foothills, and we met in the second year of my wanderings. She taught me the art of the medicine man. She is a shaman and a medicine woman for the local folk. I spent four years with Qergina, but we had a stupid quarrel and I took off. I hope she'll accept me back."

"Well, guys," Trofimov looked at his watch, "we'd better get back to work. We have to finish these poles. We can't stay too long in one place."

All five of them resumed their work.

8

Lieutenant Belyayev and the manager of the Stalin Collective Farm sat at table in the manager's log house, drinking vodka and eating dried carp.

"So you understand what I'm saying?" Belyayev asked.

"Of course, comrade Chief," the manager reassured him. "We'll do everything we can to capture these scumbags."

"And remember," Belyayev's voice grew harsh. "It's your responsibility. Soviet law obliges all local authorities to render every possible assistance to the security organs in searching for enemies of the state. And be careful: they're armed. One man was inattentive at his post, and they hacked him to death. They took his machine gun and shot six more of our guards, so that now we've got an armed gang of anti-Soviet marauders on the loose."

"Donna worry, comrade Chief," the manager assured him again. "I can provide a couple of dozen good tough guys from the village. Some of them are trappers and know the neighbourhood well."

"That's fine then," Belyayev smiled. "Let's have another drink."

"To our success, comrade Chief." The manager took the bottle and poured another glassful for Belyayev and himself.

Belyayev raised his glass. "To our great leader, Comrade Stalin."

"To Comrade Stalin."

"So what are the results?" Avdeyev inquired, when Belyayev returned from his two-day trip.

"I've been to all the collective farms in the area, Pavel Egorovich," Belyayev reported. "I spoke to all the managers, and each of them promised to raise men and comb the woods in their neighbourhood."

"Did you tell them about the reward?"

"Certainly. A boxful of tobacco, two bottles of Stolichnaya vodka, and a dozen sets of cartridges."

"Well," Avdeyev wore a gloomy expression, "we'll see whether the fuck that'll work or not."

"It must work, Pavel Egorovich. All the men are trappers in these villages, which means they're good pathfinders and trackers."

"You did well. But I wonder whether we can rely on all that village trash. They don't care a fuck about anything, and they'll only help us in return for a reward. Trofimov and his cronies are excellent fighters. They need only shoot down a couple of those guys, and the other shitheads will piss themselves and run away." He paused. "Now, tell me, did those five bastards have any close friends here in the camp?"

"Of course, Pavel Egorovich, First of all there's the elderly convict Ganin. You must remember him."

"Sure I remember. The old White Guards officer. It was he who first persuaded me to promote that cursed Yatta. If I hadn't listened to all that bullshit about native miracle cures, that stinking little Chukchi would have croaked long ago, and the bastards would have had no guide. Trofimov was a living corpse before Yatta treated him and got him on his feet."

"Yes," agreed Belyayev. "And he did it specially at Ganin's request. Ganin has been a friend of Trofimov's for almost a year. My informers saw them together regularly."

"Did they meet a lot in the last few days?" Avdeyev asked.

"They did," Belyayev confirmed. "It was also Ganin who asked Ponomarev to take them on as hospital orderlies."

"Ponomarev," Avdeyev exclaimed. "Right, I'll get him too. Anybody else?"

"Well, there was Vaskov, the orderly in the Fourth," Belyayev said. "He was a long-term crony of Bondarenko's. But it looked like a friendship of convenience only. They could hardly have confided in him."

"Anyway," Avdeyev said, "I'll deal with them later on. Right now I want you to bring me the old geezer."

"Yes sir." Belyayev saluted, turned and made his way out, closing the door behind him

Avdeyev leaned back in his chair and took another cigar. He tried to recollect the appearance of the elderly convict Ganin. It was probably more than a year since he last laid eyes on him. At that time Ganin was a physician in the Medical Section. Later he had been put in charge of the warehouse by Belyayev; Avdeyev merely put his signature to the appointment. It seemed a sensible decision at the time. The old White Guards officer was one of the very few who did not steal.

"Comrade Major, may I come in?"

"Yes, come in." Avdeyev raised his head.

A guard entered and escorted Ganin into the office. Avdeyev looked into the old man's face. There was nothing special about it, the usual wrinkled face of an old convict, with a half-bald head and bluish marks of frostbite on his cheeks. A perfectly ordinary veteran of the camps. Obviously he would deny everything.

"Ah, Ganin, here you are," Avdeyev put a smile on his face. "Remind me, what's your full name?"

"Vladimir Semyonovich."

Hell. How proudly he said that, in a manner suggesting he was no camp trash but an equal, if not a superior.

"Right. Have a seat, Vladimir Semyonovich."

Ganin lowered himself into the chair where previously Belyayev had sat. Hmm, and the way Ganin sat down, in a manner that Avdeyev could not recall among any other convicts, or, for that matter, among his fellow MGB officers, even those of higher rank. The only people who moved like that were old imperial officers or English lords of the sort he had seen in movies.

"A cigarette?"

"Thank you, citizen Avdeyev." Ganin took the proffered cigarette. Even his manner of lighting it was unusual for the camp, with none of the rapacious eagerness of your average convict.

"Well," Avdeyev continued smiling, "I'd like to talk to you about your friend."

"Which friend, monsieur?"

"A man called Alexander Trofimov, who happens to be one of the group of five recent runaways."

"What about him, monsieur?"

"Everything about him." Avdeyev was getting annoyed. "You must know him quite well. You were buddies after all."

"Monsieur," Ganin's face took on a sudden arrogant look, "first of all, we could not be 'buddies' as you put it, if only because in age he could well be my youngest son."

"Never mind." Avdeyev suppressed his irritation. "I hope, though, that you are not claiming that you don't know him?"

"Certainly not." Ganin smiled as though recollecting something pleasant. "I saw him on occasion, and we had a number of good chats about this and that."

"And it's about those chats that I want to hear. Did he ever mention his plans to escape?"

"No. Never."

"Are you absolutely sure, Vladimir Semyonovich?"

"Absolutely." Ganin wore a firm expression.

"Maybe there was some vague reference?" Avdeyev insisted. "Some faint hint?"

"Absolutely not."

"Then what did you talk about?"

"The usual camp topics of conversation," Ganin shrugged his shoulders. "I told him my life story, and he told me his."

"Really? And he didn't ever curse the Soviet state, Comrade Stalin, or me personally, for instance?"

"No more than anyone else."

"So you're saying that he did do that. Is that so?"

Ganin grinned. "Do you think, monsieur, that he'd praise the Soviets after what they did to him? After the torture he endured when he was interrogated? After you turned him into little more than a living corpse?"

"So there you are," Avdeyev eagerly grasped this line of pursuit. "He indulged in anti-Soviet talk. So what exactly did you hear from him?"

"I don't remember," Ganin's voice continued calm as before. "I've heard so many things here in the camps, I can't remember everything."

"Is your memory really that short?" There was a threatening overtone in Avdeyev's voice.

"It is. I'm an old man, after all, a very old man. When you get to be my age, your memory might start playing you up too."

"Nonsense." Avdeyev snapped. "Don't try and hoodwink me—me, a representative of the Soviet state."

"I am not," Ganin's expression remained calm and impassive. "All I mean to say is that I don't retain a mental record of the details of every conversation that I've had. But I can swear that there was absolutely no mention of any escape. Be logical. Why on earth would Trofimov talk to me about that? Me, a frail old man with TB and asthma? They couldn't take me with them. And after the executions in August, who would confide in a stranger if he was thinking of escaping?"

"Enough of this crap. I know you were Trofimov's crony. It was you that sent that Chukchi to him. It was you who persuaded Ponomarev to take him on as a hospital orderly." Avdeyev's voice calmed slightly as he continued: "Now, either you tell me all you heard from Trofimov, or else …"

"There's nothing I can tell you."

"You don't remember, is that it?" Avdeyev grinned. "Well, I have means of refreshing your memory." He rang a bell on his desk. Two guards entered the room and looked at Avdeyev for directions.

"This venerable old gentleman," Avdeyev grinned, "has problems with his memory. Can we refresh it for him?"

"Yes, comrade Major. Right here?"

"Yeah, right here. Try the 'fifth corner' between the two of you."

"Yessir."

One of the guards faced Ganin, grabbed him by the collar and held him, while the other stood back some distance. The first screw dealt Ganin a heavy punch straight in the face, sending him reeling back towards his colleague. The latter pitched him forward again towards the first guard who clouted him again. Ganin was thrown back and forth, each time suffering terrible blows to the face, chest and stomach. His face convulsed with pain, but he remained silent. Soon he was unable to stand and collapsed on the floor.

"Hold on a moment," Avdeyev ordered, and turned to Ganin. "Well," he said, "maybe now your memory's recovered?"

Ganin lay on the floor and remained silent.

"Oh, not yet, I see?" Avdeyev yelled. "You rotten old carcass, speak up when your superiors talk to you."

"I've nothing to tell you." Ganin's voice was firm. "You won't achieve anything by beating up an old man, Monsieur Avdeyev."

"Okay, carry on!"

The two screws resumed their job. The old man clenched his broken teeth and felt the taste of blood in his mouth. Then his eyesight clouded over with a grayish-red veil, and vague figures emerged from it … his old Second Caucasian Regiment, racing forward to the north in the direction of Moscow. He looked for his grey stallion to join in the chase, but could not find him. Shock waves crashed against his forehead, almost shattering his skull; he tried to run, but a powerful explosion knocked him to the ground. He saw darkness in front of his eyes and felt the ground by his cheek.

"What's the matter?" Avdeyev looked at the two guards standing over the old man's body. "Carry on!"

One of the guards tried to raise Ganin's limp body.

"Looks like he's finished, comrade Major."

"So soon? Let's have a look." Avdeyev stepped over to the body and felt Ganin's pulse. "Shit. The old bastard has croaked. Take him away."

The two guards dragged the lifeless body towards the door.

"Wait a moment." Avdeyev said. "Call Belyayev. And get someone to clean up the blood."

"Yes, Pavel Egorovich?" Belyayev appeared in the doorway.

"Come over here and have a seat," Avdeyev said.

Belyayev settled in the chair and looked at the pool of blood on the floor.

"I want to deal with the others," Avdeyev began. "Start with Ponomarev."

"Do you want to open a case against him?"

"Hmm," Avdeyev became thoughtful, then, "No, fuck him. I don't want to mess with that bastard. Just send him to the mines. Give him a nice hard job, digging and hauling. Understand? And that other bastard from the Fourth, what's his name?"

"Vaskov?"

"Yeah, send them both to the mines. They can both croak there. But first give 'em a spell in the Black Hole."

"For how long?" Belyayev asked.

"A month. When they get out they'll still be good enough for two months' gold digging."

9

Trofimov and his men finally reached the foothills of a mountain. To their right was a wooded slope, with a rocky descent on their left. At the bottom was a narrow valley with a small ice-covered river, and beyond that a range of craggy mountains stretching to the horizon.

"The famous Konginsky Range," Trofimov said, gazing at the distant mountains.

"Yeah," Yatta confirmed.

"And your friend Stepan lives where?"

"In a village a few kilometres from the range," Yatta said.

"Are you sure we can trust him?" Bondarenko asked.

"Abso-bloody-lutely, Mikhail," said Yatta firmly, at the same time teasing his friend. "In the past I helped defend his house and his family against bandits. We fought side by side. He's a good man, you know."

"Well," Bondarenko sounded unconvinced. "There're very few folk that haven't turned rotten amid all this Soviet shit. I bet the locals have been bribed with vodka, shag and ammunition, so they catch us and turn us in. I'd rather try and cross these mountains on our own."

"But I donna remember all the good passes," Yatta argued.

"In that case," Trofimov said, "we have to risk it. In the good old days of the tsar, the locals always helped runaway convicts. Remember in the song: 'the women fed us bread, and the men gave us shag.' Those days are gone for good, of course."

"That's right," Timoshkin agreed. "Now folks are scared to death, and it's not surprising. You can get ten years for not informing on someone."

"Anyway," Trofimov interrupted him, "Yatta should see his friend on his own first. Yatta's his buddy, after all, and he'd be least likely to betray him. If we all turn up at his place together, he might get scared and do something unpredictable."

"Good thinking, Captain," Bondarenko commented.

"Yeah," said Yatta, "that's the best idea. But, you know, the rest of you should stay well clear while I go and see Stepan. If somethin' happens, they won't find the rest of you."

"Where should we go?" Trofimov asked.

"To Sable Creek, a dozen kilometres 'way," said Yatta. "They won't find you there, at least not for a while."

"Right, that's where we'll go." Trofimov ordered.

Two hours later, their party reached a small clearing on the banks of a frozen creek. They halted, unharnessed the reindeer for a longish stopover, and made a bonfire.

"How long d'you think it'll take you?" Trofimov asked.

"'Bout two days," said Yatta. "But don't wait more than three days."

"That's until Saturday," Trofimov calculated.

"Right. If I'm not back by then, take off and get as far away as you can."

"What about you, Yatta?" Timoshkin asked.

"If I'm not back by then," Yatta said, "it means I got caught. They're bound to torture me. I'm a tough guy, and I can hold out for some time. But sooner or later, though, they're gonna break me. Nobody can stand up to them indefinitely."

"You're serious?" Trofimov turned and looked at him hard.

"Yeah," Yatta nodded. "I mean what I say. If you stay here longer, you'll get caught as well. You have to move on. Do you have that special kind of a clock that helps you to find the way?"

"You mean a compass?" Trofimov reminded him.

"Yeah, you know, you'll need that to find your way."

The clearing was silent as the four men took in what Yatta had said.

"It's not a good plan," Goldberg protested. "We can't leave Yatta to be slaughtered."

"Doesn't matter, Yakov," Yatta retorted. "There's no better way, though. Otherwise, you know, we all perish."

"Yatta's right," Bondarenko agreed. "I know what torture is. No one can stand it for ever."

"Are you sure, Yatta, that you have to go?" Trofimov asked him. "Maybe we could find the way ourselves?"

"I think so too," Timoshkin said. "After all, we vowed not to hand no one of us over to the screws."

"No, Pyotr," Yatta said firmly. "I've got to try. We could lose our way."

"Okay, then," Trofimov sighed. "Thank you, Yatta, for … for taking the risk. Good luck."

"I'm off, then," Yatta said. "I should be there by late night, I s'ppose."

Yatta rose to his feet, shook hands with each of them and hugged Trofimov.

"Goodbye, Yatta, God bless you." Timoshkin made the sign of the cross.

"Good luck." Bondarenko nodded. "I hope all goes well. Take your submachine gun just in case."

"No, Mikhail, that's not a good idea, you know. I'll attract too much attention. Nobody carries them around here. Anyway, 'bye, guys."

Yatta put on his skis, took his hunting rifle, and vanished into the groves.

It was late at night when Yatta finally reached a small log cottage in the woods. As he came closer, he heard a dog barking. He cautiously approached and knocked gently on the door. At first there was no response, then a movement behind the door.

"Who the hell is it at this time of night?" an angry male voice called. Yatta recognized the voice immediately.

"It's me, Stepan, Yatta. Let me in. It's not good for me outside here. They mustn't see me."

The door opened, and the stout figure of his friend appeared framed in the entrance.

"God bless us." The host crossed himself. "Is it really you, Yatta? Or is it a ghost? Come in."

"No, it ain't a ghost. Not yet." Yatta grinned and followed Stepan into the log house. In the centre of the large room was a huge Russian brick stove, with a bedding niche on top of it. The furniture consisted of a table and chairs and several shelves. Household articles, hunting rifles, clothing and utensils hung on the walls. In the far corner an oil lamp glimmered in front of an icon.

"Don't worry. I'm here on my own," said Stepan. "Glafira's visiting her sister-in-law, and the kids are at boarding school in Seimchan. Come, Yatta, have a seat and let's drink to our meeting."

"Thank you," Yatta said. "D'you have some of your famous moonshine?"

"Oh yes, it's always here for guests."

Stepan opened a small hatch in the floor and took out a bottle half full of liquid. He took two glasses from a shelf and poured for Yatta and himself.

"Cheers, Yatta." Stepan raised his glass.

"Cheers, Stepan."

"So, Yatta, tell me how you're doing, and what brings you here?"

"Well," Yatta heaved a sigh. "Things ain't been going too well until recently. I was caught four years ago and sent to one of the camps near Seimchan."

"Really?" Stepan raised his eyebrows.

"Really, Stepan. I'm on the run, and I've got four friends with me."

"God bless us!" Stepan crossed himself. "So you're one of those … The commissioner from the district centre dropped by the other day and told us about five runaways. The authorities promised vodka and shag and cartridges for help in tracking them down."

"Yeah," Yatta confirmed, "that's us right enough. And I came here to ask for help. You know the passes across the Konginsky Range, and we need a guide to get across."

"And where … where have you got to get to?" Stepan sounded worried.

"That ain't matter, Stepan," Yatta replied. "We've just got to cross the range. We can pay you ten fox skins."

"No." Stepan shook his head. "I can't. If they find out, they'll … they'll shoot me and do God knows what to Glafira and the kids." He paused. "And you … you should go now, before someone sees you."

"You're refusing?" Yatta looked him straight in the eye.

"Yeah. I'm sorry, Yatta."

After a long pause Yatta gripped Stepan by the shoulder. "Have you forgotten our friendship? Forgotten how we fought together against those bandits from Omsukchan? Have you forgotten that?" Yatta spat and moved towards the door.

"Yatta," Stepan rose with tears in his eyes.

Yatta stopped and looked at him.

"Forgive me, Yatta, forgive me for Christ's sake." Stepan burst into tears. "I've got four little kids, and they won't spare even them. Forgive me, Yatta, it's only because of the kids." His face expressed such misery that Yatta felt sorry for him.

"Can I at least hope that you won't rat on me? You won't tell no one, will you?"

"No, of course you can rely on me," Stepan said. "Strike me down with leprosy, let me rot alive, let me fry in hell!"

"In that case," Yatta sighed, "farewell, Stepan. And may the blessing of your Christian God rest on you and your home and family. I donna blame you. I can see that they've scared you to death, and you ain't the only one. Farewell, Stepan. I wish you luck."

"Farewell, Yatta." Stepan wiped his tears with the back of his hand. "God bless you and save you from any awful fate."

As Yatta moved away through the forest, he felt no grudge against Stepan. He understood him. His family and children really would be in danger if he helped him and his friends. Stepan was only human, and that overwhelming dark force was always there, ready to destroy him and whoever else stood in its way.

10

"So who was here yesterday night?" Stepan's wife asked, looking him straight in the eyes.

"It was Prokhor," Stepan said. "He was on his way to check his traps."

"You're lying," she said. "Why should Prokhor leave by our back yard? I know it was some runaway convict. Who was it?"

"You remember Yatta?"

"That Chukchi tramp?"

"He ain't a tramp," Stepan retorted angrily. "He's a good guy, and he once helped us fight off those bandits."

"I remember that, but what did he want?"

"He needed a guide to cross the mountains. He's escaped from a camp with a few other guys."

"O my God!" She crossed herself. "I hope you didn't agree?"

"No."

"That's fine." She turned to face him. "Let's go."

"Go? Where to?"

"You know where, to the collective farm manager."

"You mean—"

"You know what I mean," her voice grated. "We gotta report it, then we'll get some hunting ammunition and other things. Otherwise they'll purge and do away with us too."

"Shut your trap, woman." Stepan exploded. "You expect me to rat on my good old friend?"

"You wanna risk everythin' just because of your Chukchi?" she retorted.

"Hell, no!" Stepan hit the table with his fist. "Never in my life. You hear? If ever I hear that again—"

"You're really nuts," she shook her head. "How d'you think I'm going to survive without you? And what about the children? You know how they treat kids in those orphanages. How will they survive there?"

"Shut your trap, for Christ's sake," Stepan snapped. "I will never, ever, rat on Yatta. Do you hear? And if you go and report on him, I'll break every fuckin' bone in your body. I'd rather freeze to death in an ice hole than betray him. Now no more about it. No more, d'you hear?"

"Well, I'm not going to risk everythin' just 'cause of your goddamned Chukchi," she retorted. "I'll go to the manager myself. I gotta think about the children."

Stepan grabbed her by the arms and swung her round to face him. "So you'd rat on me too? They'll charge me with aiding a runaway, understand? And you'll be left alone with the kids. Do you understand that?" He paused. "I'd rather kill you now and be charged with murder than face a political offence. I'm a straight and honest Siberian. I won't allow treachery in my household."

"You're a crazy idiot." She shrugged helplessly. "Now calm down. I'm not going nowhere without your consent, of course. All I want is to keep misery from our home."

Trofimov, Bondarenko, Goldberg and Timoshkin sat beside their tent at Sable Creek.

"I don't know when he'll arrive, tomorrow morning or earlier," Trofimov said. "He said to wait till the day after tomorrow."

"If Yatta's safe," Bondarenko said, "he'll be here by tomorrow night. And if he isn't here by then, it'll be risky staying on till the next night."

"He told us to wait, and that's what we're going to do," Trofimov insisted.

"You're the leader," Bondarenko conceded. "And your word's final. Only I don't understand why he told us to wait till Saturday. I realize he's got to try and cover his tracks. But that would take only a day at the most."

"If he said Saturday, then he knows best," said Timoshkin. "You've already seen what an ace he is at surviving in the taiga. And it ain't all that risky to stay here till Saturday. Even so, if he gets caught, they have to take him to the nearest militia station. That'll take another two days. Any interrogation could start only on Sunday morning. So there's no reason for us to leave before

Saturday night."

"I don't like it," Goldberg said. "I don't like this whole arrangement. Yatta's our comrade, the one who made our escape possible, and if he's caught and tortured and we go away so as to save our own skins—"

"What the hell could we do 'bout it?" Bondarenko interrupted. "Launch an attack on a militia station? They've got a couple of dozen men and a machine gun, and the militia headquarters will be right in the middle of the village. Yatta himself told us to wait only until Saturday night."

Suddenly a heavy snowfall began, and the wind increased.

"Another blizzard, for Chrissake." Timoshkin crossed himself.

"Put some stones up against the poles, and make it fast," Trofimov ordered. "Then get inside the tent."

They rushed to haul stones and plant them round the base of the tent poles then they crawled inside.

"We should bring in some firewood, or we'll freeze to death," Timoshkin said.

"You're right," Trofimov agreed.

The two of them went outside to collect branches. The wind howled. Once back inside, they closed the entrance flap and lay on the deerskins.

"What luck," Timoshkin exclaimed. "How d'we know how long to wait for Yatta?"

"You're right," Trofimov agreed. "He may stay at his friend's homestead till the blizzard ends."

"If that man can be trusted," Bondarenko said. "Otherwise, he'll need another shelter."

"He knows how to manage," Trofimov said, "and he's survived so far, hasn't he?"

"Well, Captain," said Timoshkin, "I only know that even in the Urals where I come from you must never get caught in a snowstorm. Whole carts can get buried under the snow. And our little snowstorms are no match for this sort of blizzard."

"But we're no match for a man like Yatta either," Trofimov smiled. "He's a native Siberian, and he's lived with these blizzards since he was born. I'm sure he'll find shelter."

11

Yatta moved along on his skis through the raging blizzard. Sometimes it was a tremendous effort to stay on his feet, and he was almost carried away, but he forged on. He had experienced blizzards before, and each time he had found shelter—the den of some animal, a cave or a trapper's abandoned cabin. Once he had been swept off his feet by the wind and hurled into a crevasse where he was found unconscious by Qergina, the best and last woman in his life.

What a fearful wind. Maybe it was better to head back to Stepan's. No, that was too risky. Of course, in a blizzard like this, Stepan couldn't go anywhere either, and neither could his wife Glafira if she had returned. Still, it was better not to return there. Stepan was too scared, and you never knew what to expect of a man once he'd lost his nerve. Furthermore, someone else might turn up at Stepan's place to sit out the blizzard, and the faces of all five of the runaways had by now surely been printed on paper through that machine.

On and on he went, looking at the snow-covered ground ahead in search of some natural shelter. He could not remember how long he had been going when his sharp eye caught sight of the entrance to a bear's den. What luck! Yatta took the rifle from his shoulder, checked it was loaded, then fired a shot into the almost invisible recess in the ground. A moment later a black bear's head appeared from the hole with a roar. A second shot hit the bear square between the eyes. The animal fell silent and rolled over. Its eyes slowly faded and finally closed altogether. Yatta loaded one more cartridge and put another shot directly into the creature's eye, then approached the hole, half blocked by the carcass. He pushed the bear's body back into the den and crawled inside. He knelt over the bear's dead body and whispered, "O Lord of the Woods, forgive me, bastard that I am, for having killed you in your own home. There was nothing else I could do. I fired the first shot just to knock at your door, but you came out and were about to attack me, so all I could do was defend myself. But I would never have poked my nose into your blessed den but for this blizzard that threatened to bury me alive. I cannot die now, because I have vowed to lead four other folks into the Land of the Rising Sun. They will perish without me. In order to save them, I violated your home by breaking in like a burglar. Forgive me for this. I pledge that I will try to bring you one grey spotted reindeer buck as a sacrifice in recompense. And now let your own flesh turn into our flesh, let your heart refresh our own hearts, and may your spirit strengthen the spirits of five of us on our long and dangerous journey."

Another figure moved through the forest, struggling against the blizzard. Glafira, the wife of Stepan, had left the house when her husband went to check his traps, and set off in the direction of the militia department in the local district centre. The wind gusted hard, and clouds of snow blinded her eyes, but she had to go just a few more kilometres, to Demyan's cabin, where she could wait out the blizzard. Then, as a reward, her family would collect a sackful of flour, a good box of twist tobacco and a big package of cartridges.

Certainly Stepan would be angry with her, and might even beat her for doing this, but he would realize that there was no other way. Those runaways were bandits and outlaws. Why should she put her own and her children's lives at risk?

The wind howled, and she could see very little, but that didn't matter: she knew the path to Demyan's cabin well enough to find her way blindfolded. Come on, come on! It wasn't so very far. Suddenly an almighty gust of wind lifted her off the ground and carried her away. Save me, Lord! She grabbed the trunk of a larch tree, but the next moment her grip loosened, and another gust threw her into the snow and bowled her along like a plaything. She tried to rise to her feet, but the wind and snow pinned her to the ground.

"Help me! Help me!" Glafira screamed, although she knew nobody was there in that Siberian woodland, probably not a living soul within twenty kilometres. The next moment she found she could cry no more as a wad of snow plugged her mouth. She saw only darkness in front of her. Another gust of wind carried her off again and sent her rolling over and over. Then her head hit the trunk of a great larch tree, and everything went black.

Yatta sat on the floor of the bear's den in the darkness and ate raw bear's meat. The animal's body lay beside him with one paw cut off. He felt quite safe and sound, eating the still warm, fresh meat and saying his prayer of thanks to the Creator and the Merciful Beings for providing him with such a good shelter and such divine food. He thought about how to take the carcass with him. It would be a good source of provision for quite a while. Apart from which, to slay this honourable beast and not consume all its flesh would be a disgraceful sin for which the Lord of the Woods would certainly punish him.

The blizzard lasted for three more days. On the fourth day they emerged from their tent, dug out their belongings, made a bonfire and sat in the open air.

"Well," Trofimov looked at his watch, "I guess Yatta will probably be back some time tonight."

"Hopefully nothin' hinders him now," Timoshkin said.

At that very moment, Yatta emerged from the trees, dragging half of the bear's carcass behind him, towing it with several leather thongs. All four of them jumped up and rushed to greet him.

"Old man, at last you're here." Trofimov hugged him.

"Here you are indeed." Bondarenko greeted him with a happy chuckle. "I knew Yatta would find his way."

"Where did you spend the blizzard, Yatta?" Goldberg asked.

"In a bear's den," Yatta replied. "I shot the bear and took his den. But that's a sin though. We gotta make a sacrifice to redeem ourselves."

"Surely," Timoshkin agreed, looking at the carcass. "Now we'll have more than enough to eat."

"All right," Trofimov interrupted, "back to business. Did you see your friend, Yatta?"

"Yeah, I did. Stepan refused," Yatta sighed. "He's afraid for his family."

"Well, I suspected that might be the case," Bondarenko said. "People everywhere are so fuckin' scared. I hope he won't rat on us."

"He won't do that," Yatta said confidently. "He's a good guy. But still, we best take off as soon as possible and try to find a way through the pass ourselves."

"D'you remember the way at all?" Bondarenko asked.

"Not very well. The one way I know is very steep. There's a roundabout way from the south side. It leads over the lower slopes. I think I can find it."

"You say from the south?" Trofimov queried.

"Yeah, that's the one I remember."

"If we go too far south, we get into a populated area," Trofimov observed. "I bet they're combing the forests in all the neighbourhoods. We'll have to be constantly on the alert."

"I know, Sasha," Yatta agreed. "There are two villages there, but they're several kilometres from the path leading to the pass."

"Then we can take the risk," Bondarenko said.

"Okay. We'll eat now, and then off we go." Trofimov ordered. "We've no time to lose."

12

A knock on the door distracted Major Avdeyev from his thoughts.

"Come in."

"A telegram for you, comrade Major." A soldier handed him a telegram.

"Where from?" Avdeyev felt a slight flutter in his chest.

"Magadan."

Avdeyev grabbed the telegram. As he read it, he felt the ground give way beneath his feet.

"Damn it all!" he muttered. "The time has come …"

"May I go, comrade Major?" Avdeyev heard the messenger's voice as if from outer space.

"Yeah, go. And tell Lieutenant Belyayev to come here."

"Yes, comrade Major."

Avdeyev lit a cigarette as his thoughts wandered chaotically. He could not tear his eyes from the telegram text. A commission was due to arrive from Magadan to investigate the recent incident in the Fifth Compound. Avdeyev was too experienced a serviceman not to realize that such investigations usually had fatal consequences for those who were investigated. The rules were harsh in the MGB. Those who failed to prevent an incident of such gravity would pay with their career, their freedom and possibly their life.

"You called, Pavel Egorovich?" Belyayev stood in front of Avdeyev's desk.

"So, Leonid." Avdeyev forced a smile. "Have a seat. We have news: a commission arrives from Magadan the day after tomorrow. Looks like our goose is cooked. Here's the telegram."

Belyayev took the telegram and read it.

"It doesn't necessarily mean that," he began, though his voice lacked confidence. "We did all we could. I don't think they can charge us."

"I don't think they'll charge you personally," Avdeyev smiled grimly. "As for me, that's a different kettle of fish. Anyway, go and get everything in order before this commission arrives."

"Yes, Pavel Egorovich."

Belyayev turned and was about to go when Avdeyev called him back. "Hold on a minute, Leonid. What's the most recent news of the search?"

"It's continuing," Belyayev reported. "All roads have been cordoned off, and all the woods and forests are being combed."

"How far?"

"About a hundred and fifty kilometres radius."

"Only a hundred and fifty?" Avdeyev demanded. "By now those bastards will be at least two hundred and fifty kilometres away. How I wonder are they ever going to catch them?"

Belyayev's face turned red.

"Petrov and myself personally visited all the rural Soviet Councils all the way to Gydan. The authorities have been warned. And there are locals who know their own area like the back of their hand. So there is still hope."

"Hope?" snapped Avdeyev. "After a month of searching, you talk about hope? Go and do the job I asked you to do."

As Belyayev left, Avdeyev reclined in his armchair, smoking one cigarette after another. He realized he should not take it out on Belyayev. He was a good guy and seemed very devoted, though any devotion was automatically suspect. Would it survive Avdeyev's fall? Avdeyev realized all too well that it probably wouldn't. If he were ever caught up in a purge, Belyayev would surely try to forget the very name Avdeyev, just as he himself had done with Edward Berzin, the legendary Cheka officer and founder of the Soviet Kolyma camp system.

The only thing that could improve Avdeyev's situation was the capture of those scumbags, and that was too much to hope for. Especially since the fucking idiots were searching near the Kolyma highway, towards Magadan and northwest to Khandyga. Obviously those bastards weren't so stupid as to go that way. Most likely they had headed eastwards through the forests, and it was no coincidence they took that goddamned Chukchi with them. It could take years to track them down. That old fart Ganin might well have known their plans, and if they had had his testimony, they might have known where to begin searching. But the senile fucking jerk had gone and snuffed it, preferred to die rather than help Avdeyev. Fucking shitbag! Avdeyev's rage grew all the more since he realized how fruitless it was: no one could raise Ganin from the grave.

Avdeyev felt a pain in his chest and took a few drops of his heart medication. Then he ordered his batman to prepare the sled to take him home.

Back at his home, a spacious log house in the nearby military settlement, he lay down on the sofa beneath a large portrait of Stalin and lit another cigarette. He called Agafya, the female convict who worked for them as housekeeper, and told her to bring him a bottle of vodka.

"Pavlusha, you're drinking again? It's bad for your heart."

Avdeyev turned his head. His wife Maria Gavrilovna stood by the sofa.

"Bad for my heart? What the hell difference does it make? They're going to take me away anyway. They arrive the day after tomorrow."

"Who arrives?"

"A commission from the Magadan administration."

"Is it about those runaways?"

"Of course. What the hell else can it be about? Those bastards are the primary agenda for the whole Kolyma Region. And there's nothing anyone can do about it. Nothing. The main highway is being patrolled all the way from Magadan to Ust'-Nera, and so are the minor highways and country roads, but that won't produce a single real result. Those bloody scumdogs aren't total idiots, they aren't gonna go by the roads. That's why they took that Chukchi bastard with them, to lead them along the wolf and deer trails."

"Please, Pavlusha, don't curse and swear," his wife pleaded. "You know I don't like it. And why for heaven's sake should they charge you? You're not guilty. It was just that guard who slipped up in his duties."

"Just that guard, you say. Are you crazy? Don't you remember that in the Soviet state all authorities are one hundred percent responsible for what their subordinates do? One damned stupid shithead got caught off his guard, and look what's happened: an armed gang roaming the forests, and seven soldiers killed. The Party and government have more than enough reason to put me inside. And that's exactly what's going to happen."

"Still, I don't think they'll arrest you," Maria Gavrilovna protested. "You're a distinguished security officer, with twenty-five years in the service and immense experience. You've been decorated, and Nikishev himself knows and appreciates you. At the very worst, they might force you to retire. But I don't think that will happen either."

"You don't think so, eh?" Avdeyev snapped. "I see you don't understand a thing about how the system works. Not a thing. In our system, nobody who makes a slip is shown mercy! Don't you remember what happened to Berzin? And Garanin? Both excellent Cheka officers, two of Stalin's so-called 'eagles.' And where are they now? Who the hell knows even where their graves are?"

"But that was back in 1937 or '38," said Maria Gavrilovna. "Times are quieter now. I'll have a talk with my father, and he'll contact Nikishev personally. Everything will turn out fine, believe me."

She sat down on the sofa beside her husband and stroked his head. Under the caress of her tender warm palms he quietened down, and even began to feel that maybe everything would turn out all right.

13

Their group had been on the move for several hours, and it was getting dark.

"Are we near the path you talked about, Yatta?" Trofimov asked.

"I hope so," Yatta said. "I remember there's a boulder with a picture of a black bear on it."

"A black bear? We should remember that." Trofimov looked at his compass. "But we're still going south."

"That's right," said Yatta, "but then the wolf trail turns eastward."

"Maybe it's time to make a halt," Timoshkin said. "I'm real tired, and Yakov is too."

"Not yet," Trofimov ordered. "First of all we have to figure out which way we're heading."

The group moved on. The path led up a gentle slope, and then down into a hollow, then uphill again. In the twilight it was very hard to pick out any rocks or boulders. Suddenly Yatta stopped and smelled the air.

"What is it, Yatta?" Trofimov asked.

"I smell human dwellings," Yatta said.

"Damn," cursed Bondarenko. "That's too much."

"Turn back," Trofimov ordered.

"We'll take one of the side paths towards the east," Yatta said. "I donna remember them well, but I guess they'll eventually bring us to the mountain range."

The party retraced their steps and reached a path that turned east, with a boulder lying at the fork.

"Here's a boulder, Yatta," Timoshkin exclaimed. "Maybe this is the one."

Trofimov shone his flashlight on the boulder. All five of them examined it, looking for the bear.

"No picture, no bear," Bondarenko said.

"Right," said Trofimov. "But we'll turn off this way. We must get away from any human dwelling, and get nearer to the rocks and mountains."

"Yeah, better than going anywhere near that cursed village," Bondarenko said. "I bet there's an ambush waiting for us. Maybe more than one."

They followed the path, which curved to the left and then to the right, skirting rocks and small ravines. By now it had become completely dark.

"We've gotta stop for the night, though," said Yatta. "We may lose our way."

"Right, and we're too tired to go on," said Trofimov looking at his comrades.

"At last," Goldberg exclaimed. He sat down on a stump and slumped forward.

"Get up, Yakov," Yatta said and gave him a friendly shove. "You'll fall asleep right there, and we'll never wake you." Yatta and Trofimov helped Goldberg to his feet.

"Thanks," said Goldberg. "I was drowsing already."

"Have a cig, Yakov," Trofimov rolled a shag cigar and handed it to Goldberg.

"Yatta, can you find us some wood?" asked Trofimov. "Mikhail and Zakharych, help us put up the tent."

Everyone went about their chores, and eventually the tent was up, the campfire lit and the reindeer unharnessed and tethered to the trees. Trofimov looked at the weary faces of his comrades.

"I think we should sleep now. Are you hungry?"

"Not really," Bondarenko yawned, "just sleepy as hell."

"Me too," said Goldberg.

"So's me," Timoshkin added.

"Then let's sleep without supper," Trofimov proposed. "Do you mind, Yatta?"

"No, you know, I'm used to going for days without food or sleep."

"Then you keep watch, Yatta."

Inside the tent the four men collapsed onto the skins and immediately fell asleep. Yatta stayed outside on guard, and prayed to the Merciful Beings that nobody from the nearby dwelling would come into the woods and see their tracks.

"Now," said Trofimov the next morning over breakfast, "let's decide which direction to take. Either we go on searching for another pass, or we try to go along this one. Here it's steep and rocky, and Yatta says there's a danger of avalanches. If we make it, there are vast forests on the other side, and Yatta knows that area. Apart from which, nobody will be tracking us over there. If we go on searching for other ways across, we may get too near the Zolotogorskaya gold mines. There'll be scores of screws and soldiers looking for us. So what do you think?"

"I say cross here," Bondarenko proposed.

"Can we manage it, hauling the sleds?" Timoshkin wondered and shook his head. "How will the deer get over a steep pass?"

"That's easy," Yatta assured him. "We help them, you know, and give the sleds the odd push from the back."

"Then it's no problem, Zakharych," said Bondarenko. "Better to fall down a precipice than get caught."

"At least," Trofimov said, "it's worth trying. We can always turn back if we absolutely have to." He paused and then added in a firm, commanding voice, "Let's do it."

Within half an hour they were on their way, and by evening had reached the base of the rocks.

They spent the night just beneath the rocks and the following morning began the way uphill. They moved along the shoulder of a steep slope, and progress was painfully slow. They had to push the sleds from behind to help the reindeer. Each hour they made a short halt for a quick smoke and a sip of liquor. The night before, Yatta had explained that halfway toward the summit was a small cave, and they planned to stop there for the night. The way to the cave was not easy. As they neared it, they had to cross a mountain gorge filled with snow. By late afternoon they were close to the place of crossing. From where they stood they could see the entrance to the cave. The distance was not great, only a few hundred meters, but the way to the other side was across an ocean of snow filling the fissure. And the moment they came up to the crossing place, they were hit by a forceful wind raising small clouds of snow.

Yatta looked upwards and shook his head.

"Sasha, you know, we must be very careful here. The crossing is dangerous 'cause there is much snow and it looks heavy."

Everyone stopped.

"Dangerous? But what the hell can we do? We canna stop here for the night!" Bondarenko looked around. "It's just a bare slope, we can't even make fire here, not to speak of lying down."

Trofimov looked at the other side of the white plane. To him it looked sturdy and even not too wide. But he believed Yatta's judgement.

"Yatta," he asked "do you think it's impossible to get to the cave and we should not even risk it?"

"You know, Sasha, we must go, though. There is no way back and we cannot stay here for the night anyway." Yatta sighed unhappily. "It's the only route to the top. But we must be very careful, and very slow. Or we could break the snow loose".

"So what, guys?" Trofimov looked at his friends. "Ready for another challenge?"

"Yatta says, doesn't he, that there is no other way around. So, Sasha, it looks like we really have no choice. Just be careful." Goldberg looked upwards and shrugged. The slope was so steep, it looked as if it was overhanging the path. It was impossible even to think of climbing it from here.

"Yatta, you go ahead with the first sled, it will mark the way for us," Trofimov commanded. "Mikhail, take the second one and be careful, it's heavy. Just follow Yatta and I will help you from behind. Timoshkin, you lead the third sled and follow my steps. And you, Yakov, take care of the sled with our meat and supplies. It's not heavy and it will not be too difficult to handle."

They moved carefully. In the gorge the wind howled, ready to push them off the narrow path beaten by Yatta's sled. Small whirlwinds of snow bit mercilessly into their faces and blinded them. They could hear nothing but the roaring of the mountains. It felt like the crossing was endless. But they moved on and on, one step after another.

At last they sighted the cave entrance. Yatta and Bondarenko with their deer and sleds made it inside. Trofimov stayed at the entrance and watched Timoshkin and Goldberg slowly approaching him.

Just as Timoshkin was about to enter the cave, Trofimov was deafened by a strange, ear-breaking noise, as if heavy artillery was directly shooting at them. The next moment a wave of snow emerged from above, and within a fraction of a second the two men, with their sleds and reindeer, disappeared under an enormous cloud of white.

"What's going on, Captain?" Bondarenko leaped out of the cave, and looked around in disbelief. "Where are Zakharych and Yakov?"

"A snow slide." Yatta blurted, rushing out of the cave.

"Snow slide!" exclaimed Trofimov. "Does it mean the poor guys were swept away?"

It was already dusk, and difficult to see anything. There was not a living soul anywhere to be seen.

"God, looks like they were swept away by this fuckin' snow slide." Bondarenko sounded nervous and angry. "What—"

"Do not curse, Mikhail. You can make Spirits of the Snow angry with us!"

"You know, Sasha", Yatta looked down the gorge, "they may still be alive. Let's call them."

"Zakharych! Yakov!" they shouted at the top of their lungs.

A moment later they heard a faint response. "We're here. Help!"

"Down there." Trofimov stared down the precipice and saw two silhouettes clinging to a rock.

Yatta grabbed the lasso, hanging around his shoulder and waist, and hurled the noose down toward the two men. Timoshkin grabbed it first.

Trofimov and Bondarenko grabbed the end of the lasso, and the three of them hauled Timoshkin up into the cave. After that Yatta threw the lasso to Goldberg and they hauled him to safety.

"Thanks!" Goldberg whispered, stroking his cheek covered with bleeding scratches.

"Thank Yatta, Yakov," said Trofimov. "Without him and his lasso we'd have had no way to save you."

"A lasso's a basic tool for any reindeer man," Yatta said. "Without it no one can survive in the forest, or in the mountains or tundra."

"You must teach us all how to use it."

"Sure, Sasha. If the guys want to learn."

"They have to. It's an order."

"I'd be glad to learn another survival skill," Bondarenko grinned, happy to see his friends safe.

"Me too," Goldberg smiled timidly. "But I'm afraid I might be too clumsy."

"Well, you've still gotta give it a shot," Bondarenko insisted. "This ain't city life; out here you gotta be smart and able."

They returned to the cave. The cave was not large, but was high and wide, at least near the entrance. All five men with their remaining deer and sleds had more than enough space to settle comfortably.

For a few minutes they relaxed, leaning against the walls, and had a smoke. Then they took the brushwood gathered that morning at the foot of the mountain and made a bonfire. They spread pieces of reindeer skin around it, and settled down to enjoy rest and the warmth.

"Well, our meat's all gone. What are we gonna do?" Timoshkin was his practical self.

"Yeah, gone. Two deer, two sleds, including the one with food," confirmed Trofimov. "But we're all alive, comfortable and warm in this cave. And it's a miracle Yakov and Zakharych weren't injured. No broken bones at least."

"Yeah, I know, we are lucky." Bondarenko agreed. "But still, I'm hungry as hell again."

"Well," Trofimov hesitated, "there must be game around, but—"

"There's lots of game," Yatta said. "Mountain sheep and birds. I'll catch us somethin'."

"The start of the hunting season," Bondarenko grinned. "What a pity. We had enough meat to last a month."

"It's not just the meat. The tent poles have gone as well."

"Well," Trofimov lifted his hands in a pacifying gesture, "we'll make new poles and new sleds to carry them. And now, let's have some rest, melt some water, and then Yatta will go with someone and hunt for game."

"Great idea to go hunting," Bondarenko sighed stretching out on the deer skin. "I'm so goddamned hungry. It's like the worst times with the partisans."

They thawed the snow in a kettle and greedily drank it all. It was warm near the fire. The cave was not drafty, cosy even, with patches of light from the fire playing on its ragged walls. Little by little energy returned to the men.

Bondarenko was the first to break the silence. "Captain, tell us some more about yourself, before we go hunting. Otherwise thinking about food will kill me!"

Trofimov shrugged, looking at joyful tongues of fire. "Well, what can I say? I'm an ordinary Soviet guy from an industrial town. I led an average life with the same average expectations. I went through high school, signed on in the Young Communist League, spent a year on a construction site then went to college in Moscow. My father was a trucker. He worked at a nickel plant."

"So you're working class and peasant stock?" Bondarenko seemed somewhat pleased.

"Yeah. My mother was from Orenburg Cossacks, but my real advantage was that by the time I was seven, they opened a new high school nearby, and it was big enough to accommodate all the kids in the district. At first I never thought of any future, except becoming a trucker like my dad, but I was fond of math and history. There was building and construction going on all around. The entire country looked like one gigantic construction site."

"And as a good Young Communist, you were keen to take part, right?" Bondarenko grinned.

"Yes. It's strange, but at that time I believed all that ideological bullshit. So did everyone else."

"Why did you work on a construction site?" Goldberg put in. "Working class children were admitted to college immediately after school. My father was an accountant, a white collar worker, so I had no other way, but you—"

"I had the true Komsomol spirit." Trofimov laughed bitterly. "I honestly believed that one should have some working class experience before going to college. I could drive, so I got my industrial training in my dad's trucking team. Later I used those skills on the building site."

"You were lucky to have some qualification," Goldberg commented. "I had none, so I was just an oddjob guy."

"And are you sure you really were a Soviet patriot, Captain?" Bondarenko gave a disparaging laugh.

"Sure. I believed the Soviet Union was the greatest and freest country in the world, a bastion of justice, so to speak. I believed we were building a new society in which everyone would have a fair life. What I saw around me seemed to confirm that. I was born and brought up in a dirty overcrowded wooden hut until I was ten.

Then mom and dad received a good large room for the five of us in one of the new areas of town. As a working class boy, I could go to high school and even look forward to college. I had no reason to doubt. There were the purges of course, but I believed they were aimed at genuine enemies. I remember how we all reacted to the trial of Bukharin and Rykov. We held weekly meetings of the Young Communist League while the trial was going on, and we wrote a collective letter to the Central Committee demanding that all the accused be executed. As teenagers, we also even made a snowman looking like Bukharin and then destroyed it with snowballs."

"What enthusiasm," Bondarenko said mockingly.

"That's not all," Trofimov continued. "There was another episode of which I now feel terribly ashamed. A boy and a girl from our class had fathers who were caught up in the purges, and we held a special meeting of the Young Communists to expel them from the organization as enemies of the people. I—"

"Made a speech calling for their expulsion from both the Young Communist League and the school?" Goldberg guessed.

"Not quite, but you're close. I said that they weren't responsible for their fathers, and probably didn't even know about their anti-Soviet activities, but if they were good members of the League and Soviet patriots, they should stand up and repudiate their fathers. Most classmates agreed with this suggestion, and so did our teacher. The whole meeting called on Mikhail and Lena to reject their fathers."

"And did they?"

"No. Mikhail said he was convinced of his father's innocence, and that the security police would re-examine his case and find him innocent. After that, being the confident idiot that I was, I voted in favour of him and Lena being expelled. And so did all the others."

"Well, I'm not surprised to hear that," Goldberg sighed. "It was such a common story."

"Were you also a true believer, Yakov?" Bondarenko asked.

"No," Yakov answered. "How can I put it? In a sense I was too remote from politics. I accepted everything that was happening as a natural part of the world I lived in, just as there are forests, fields, winter weather and thunderstorms. I assumed that all the propaganda was just the way society functioned, although I hardly believed a word of it. The Young Communist League for me was a form of social activity. I saw clearly that society wasn't fair and just, but I regarded this injustice as normal. After all, Tsarist Russia was hardly a fair place either, especially for us Jews. So I saw my goal as …" Goldberg paused. "I saw my goal as surviving in such a society and adapting to it. Nothing more."

"Well," Bondarenko said, "I didn't never think about things in the way Yakov did. I worked on a collective farm, and the work was too hard to leave any room for thinking. Besides, I had to work in my own garden too, 'cause what you earned on the farm wasn't enough to survive on. After I finished work I was so fuckin' exhausted that I wanted only to have a nice drink and chase after the girls. After I got married, I had to work even harder. Call that justice? When was there ever any of that for us peasants? At first, it's true, the Soviet authorities gave us the land. But then they took it back again and forced us all to slave away on collective farms. Then there was the year of the famine, 1933. I remember it really well. We all realized that any protests were absolutely useless, disastrous in fact: we knew they'd send in the tanks and that would be the end of us. During the war I had one single foolish hope: that Stalin would do away with the collective farms and give us our land back. And for just once expressing that hope I landed up here, in Kolyma."

"I'm here too. And d'you know why?" Trofimov volunteered. "Because I didn't want to uphold and defend Soviet rule in what they referred to as the 'newly liberated' country of Latvia."

"I'm here because I was born in the wrong time and place, and with the wrong sort of origins," Goldberg chuckled.

"Just look at us," Timoshkin sighed. "All of us with such different lives and fates, and all of us have come to the same end."

"Anyway, soon it'll be getting light." Trofimov rose. "Can we go hunting, Yatta?"

With rifles and a lasso over their shoulders, Trofimov and Yatta set off into the wilderness. They walked along the slope, then turned into a narrow rock-sided passage that brought them out onto a small ledge overlooking a precipice. There they took up position on the ice-cold rock and waited for game to appear. After some time, the vaguely shifting silhouette of a horned animal appeared close by them, and with a rapid flick of his lasso, Yatta caught the beast by its horns.

"Great stuff," Trofimov whooped.

Yatta yanked on the rope and hauled in the kicking and struggling mountain sheep.

At that moment, the silence of the night was broken by a distant roar. This time it was no avalanche, but an aircraft.

Trofimov clenched his fists and exclaimed. "This is too much for one day. At least they can't see us among these boulders."

"Pay no attention, Sasha. Grab the lasso." Yatta commanded. "Now quick, get your knife. Stab it, but donna pull your knife out. Leave it in."

The plane was directly overhead for a moment then its lights faded into the distance, along with the roar of its engines. Finally it vanished in the west.

"Well, the bastards didn't see us, and we got our meal."

14

Avdeyev did not take his normal seat at the desk. It was occupied, along with five other chairs, by a commission consisting of MGB colonels and lieutenant-colonels. The head of the commission, a young, athletic looking blond-haired colonel, sat in Avdeyev's armchair, and Avdeyev found himself wondering whether he would ever sit in that seat again.

"So, comrade Avdeyev," the colonel's voice was calm, "can you give us an accurate account of what happened?"

"Should I start from the beginning, comrade Colonel?" Avdeyev tried to appear calm and confident.

"Yes, please," the colonel nodded. "We're fully informed about the current situation, but we want to know how it started."

Doesn't sound too nasty, Avdeyev thought. Hopefully, he'll continue in the same way. Deep down, however, he realized that a polite commencement of their conversation meant nothing, and that his fate had probably already been decided. However, this realization was still obscured by vaguely blossoming hopes.

"Well, comrade Colonel, these are the facts," Avdeyev began. "Four of the five runaways, convicts Trofimov, Bondarenko,

Timoshkin and Goldberg, made up a logging team. The fifth, whose name is Yatta, he has no surname or patronymic, worked as a hospital orderly in the Medical Section. At some point before 10 October, these five evidently worked out a plan of escape. On 10 October they were escorted by Corporal Panteleyev to their usual logging site. There they diverted Panteleyev's attention and hacked him to death with a logging axe."

"Was Panteleyev armed and kitted out according to regulations?" asked one of the commission members.

"Yes, absolutely. He had a submachine gun, and an additional supply of cartridges, as well as a bayonet."

"Very strange," the colonel observed. "An armed and fully trained soldier, who could quash any resistance immediately with one burst of fire, allowed convicts to approach him from behind so close that they struck him with an axe? There's something wrong with that."

"Evidently, comrade Colonel," Avdeyev concurred. "Panteleyev must at some point have violated regulations, and that's why they managed to catch him off guard. There's no doubt, he was the one responsible."

"No point in discussing that. He's beyond reach. Go on, comrade Avdeyev. Tell us how it was that the convict Yatta, a hospital orderly, managed to join the group? Was he allowed out without escort?"

"No, comrade Colonel. On that day he had left the compound with Private Belenko as escort."

"For what reason did he leave the compound?" asked the colonel.

"In order to check some fox traps," Avdeyev stammered.

"Does that mean he was engaging in trapping for someone? For one of the compound administration?" asked a lieutenant-colonel.

Avdeyev turned pale.

"That's not relevant to the subject," the colonel interrupted him. "Go on, Pavel Egorovich."

"For some reason, Yatta brought Belenko to the logging site," Avdeyev continued, "and the four others ambushed Belenko and shot him dead using Panteleyev's weapon."

"Does that mean that this Belenko was also not on full alert?" the colonel enquired, looking Avdeyev straight in the eye.

"Yes, evidently, comrade Colonel," Avdeyev muttered.

"And then they shot dead an entire patrol group under Sergeant—?"

"Bagirov," prompted Avdeyev.

"And after that, they seized the weapons and ammunition from the patrol and disappeared in the woods, armed to the teeth?" the colonel's voice grew harsher. "And then they pillaged the Korneyevo collective farm?"

"Yes."

The colonel chuckled maliciously. "The picture becomes clear. Your subordinates carried out their duties in such a negligent fashion that five unarmed convicts equipped only with logging axes were able to gain the upper hand and seize their weapons. The result is that we have a dangerous, well-armed anti-Soviet gang on the run. You won't deny that this reveals, shall we say, a certain negligence on the part of their superiors, and yourself in the first instance."

"Yes, it does," Avdeyev muttered, "but …"

"But what, comrade Avdeyev?"

"One cannot exclude the chance that some private or corporal performed their duties in a negligent way."

"Yes, of course," the colonel agreed. "But when negligence on the part of subordinates leads to fatal consequences, as it has here, their superiors bear full responsibility. That is clearly stated in Soviet Army regulations."

Avdeyev remained silent while the colonel and other commission members stared him straight in the eyes.

"It would be less serious if Corporal Panteleyev was the only one guilty of negligence," the colonel continued. "But in this case, the same negligence was shown by Belenko, and by Bagirov, all on the same day and all independently of one another. When confronted by a group of convicted criminals, all of them failed to perform their duties properly. This means that there's something wrong with the training, the political education, and the discipline in the camp compound under your command."

"Both I and the other compound officers performed our duties in full accordance with the regulations," Avdeyev muttered, "including the required combat training, political education, and army discipline and training."

"But none of this resulted in the required level of performance by your subordinates." The colonel's voice remained calm. "The only way to verify whether training is adequate is by whether or not the staff fastidiously perform their duties." He paused. "Apart from which there is another case of negligence on your part, and I mean your personal part. We've examined the files of these fugitives, and it emerges that one of them was a seasoned combat officer with the rank of captain, and another an experienced scout in a partisan unit, while two others were also war veterans. How is it that you put so many dangerous men in a single work team escorted by a single soldier who was drafted only after the war?"

"It's not my duty to make the work assignments. There's a group of special work assigners who make up the teams."

"But they are your subordinates, and therefore your responsibility," retorted the colonel. "You must check them personally. We'll be questioning them, but your explanation suggests that you place full responsibility on them and don't even check their decisions."

"It's not quite so, comrade Colonel." Avdeyev tried to remain calm, but he was gripped by a sense of impending disaster. "I did spot checks on them, and I never found any flaws in their work."

"You mean to say," one of the lieutenant-colonels interrupted him, "that four first-class fighters with combat experience assigned to one small work team isn't a flaw?"

"But the majority of the present compound population are war veterans," Avdeyev tried to protest, "and for a logging team you need strong men. I can hardly find any inmates fit for mining or logging who haven't fought during the war at the front."

"That's true," agreed the colonel, "but still there are different types of veterans." He paused. "I have hardly anything more to ask you, Pavel Egorovich. The situation is quite clear."

Avdeyev lowered his eyes.

"I sympathize with you very much, comrade Avdeyev, believe me," the colonel emphasized. "And I even think that you performed your duties no worse than many others in your position. But this escape happened in your compound, not somewhere else. It's a serious incident, an exceptionally serious one. A group of five criminals broke loose, killed seven servicemen and seized their weapons. Now they've fled into the woods, and remain beyond our reach. We've combed the territory with hardly any result. This is a most serious case of mutiny. In many respects it's even more serious than the Yanovsky case. Yanovsky didn't have a guide and never fled into the woods. He tried to seize a plane in Seimchan, so he and his group were easy to intercept. But in this case the escapees are avoiding roads and have gone into the taiga with a guide who knows how to survive in the wild. Our whole Far Eastern garrison wouldn't be enough to comb all the taiga."

Avdeyev sat with eyes lowered.

"So," the colonel continued, "we're now dealing with a criminal gang. They're strong, battle hardened, armed to the teeth, and have a good base somewhere in the woods. What will they do now, comrade Avdeyev? They're definitely not following the usual runaways' routes toward Magadan or Yakutsk."

"Probably they'll hide in the forest," Avdeyev muttered.

"That's a possibility," the colonel agreed. "And if so, how can we prevent them from doing that? But suppose they have other plans, say, to blow up the Omolon power station?"

"There are too few of them for that," Avdeyev answered.

"But can we exclude the possibility that the gang may grow?" the colonel asked. "There are other vagrants all around the Far East." He paused. "What if they start a rebellion? They can find reinforcements, seize more weaponry. Not all collective farmers are politically reliable; they could also rebel. And this Trofimov is a high-class combat officer. He got a decoration from Vassilevsky himself."

"He's scum, an enemy of the people," said Avdeyev.

"He certainly is, and therefore a hundred times more dangerous. In a while we might be facing a rebel force of several thousands, well armed, under excellent command with bases in the woods. And all this as a result of your and your subordinates' negligence."

Avdeyev felt a heart tremor and rivulets of cold sweat streaming down his back.

"Well, comrades," the colonel turned to his colleagues, "I think we can consider our enquiry complete." He turned to Avdeyev. "Please leave the office for a couple of minutes."

Avdeyev left the room. In the corridor he collapsed into a chair, feeling weak as never before. How the hell could he feel otherwise after the system had patronized, protected, and promoted him for a quarter of a century and had now turned against him? He knew all too well what that meant. He was part of the system, he owed his career, his wellbeing and his authority to it. It had seemed that it might last forever if he didn't slip up. For years he had lived with complete confidence in himself, but the turning point had come. This time it was not others, but he himself who would face the consequences.

"Comrade Avdeyev, come in please."

Avdeyev raised his head. A major stood smiling at him. Avdeyev detached his feeble body from the chair and walked back into the office.

"Please have a seat, Pavel Egorovich," the colonel invited.

Avdeyev sat down.

"By the authority entrusted to us by the USVITL administration, we hereby dismiss you from your post on the grounds of your inadequacy for this position. All camp documents must be handed over to the commandant designate upon his arrival. By Thursday you must report in Magadan to the office of Colonel-General Nikishev, chief of the USVITL administration."

The colonel gave Avdeyev an encouraging look. "Don't worry. Pavel Egorovich, nothing bad is going to happen. Your contributions are sufficient."

15

"How did it go, Pasha?" Maria Gavrilovna asked.

"How do you think? I'm dismissed. I've got to hand over all documents and files by Thursday and report to Nikishev. Most likely I'll not be coming back here, and you'll be kicked out of this house."

"No, Pavlusha, it won't be like that." Maria tried to calm her husband. "You're a renowned officer, you worked in the security organs for a quarter of a century, and you've recently been decorated."

"Decorated?" he yelped. "Don't you know how they can rip the decorations off you? Together with your epaulettes?"

"But we have good connections," she insisted. "You forget my father is a friend of Nikishev. I'll contact my father right away."

"He'll be the first to wash his hands of me."

"No, Pavlusha. Really, this isn't 1937 all over again."

"You're dead right," he answered sharply. "In 1937 they purged the Yids from Berzin's team and promoted us good, simple Russians. Now our fucking turn has come."

"Please, Pavlusha, don't swear," she pleaded. "You'll see, everything will be fine."

"For sure it will," he said ironically. "And one day we're going to be transferred to Moscow, aren't we? You simply don't understand how the system works." He lowered his head and his eyes welled with tears.

That night as he lay in their bed, Avdeyev could not sleep. He was gripped by a sense of impending doom. The shadows on the wall and bleak silhouettes of tree branches outside seemed to close in on him. He tried to force himself to stay calm. He closed his eyes, but in a while they opened again. He saw their darkened bedroom. All these years it had seemed so cosy and reassuring. Now it felt like a trap.

A thought came to him. He got out of bed quietly and walked through into the next room. He switched on the table lamp, opened the drawer of his desk and took out his revolver. He sat back in his chair, holding the revolver and contemplating. This looked like the end. Now it was time to put the final full stop. There was no other way. It was clear what was going to happen. He would be taken straight from Nikishev's office to a cell, unless they arrested him on the way to Magadan. What would happen next was equally clear. They would set to work on him in earnest, like they had with Berzin, Garanin and others. There would be sadistic beatings and tortures, and they would fry his ass on the so-called "Frinovsky saddle." They had dozens and dozens of ways to break a man, and they would finally extract from him whatever confession they wanted—that he himself had organized the escape, and that he did it on instructions from the American or Japanese or whatever other goddamned intelligence service. He would confess, as all the others did. Then he would end up in a labour camp. The camp trash would quickly find out everything about him—the "prison telegraph" worked perfectly. They would finish him off in an extremely nasty fashion: drown him in the crapper, or saw off his head. Such things happened all the time. And even if he avoided that, with his weak heart he would not survive hacking gold ore for long.

He raised the revolver, but his hand trembled. He imagined how he would pull the trigger and everything would end. Forever. No more would he see these walls, this window … Nothing. His parents were happy to believe that they would go to heaven, but he had long ago renounced God for the sake of the Party. He would serve his Great Leader to the last. But now he was about to be annihilated. Even if there was a heaven, it was not for him. One could not expect God to be so merciful as to admit a communist, atheist and mass murderer into His heaven.

Avdeyev aimed the pistol at his temple, but could not curb an animal fear of death.

"Come on, Avdeyev, do it. Do it. You have nothing more to lose. There's no other way," he muttered.

What a goddamned stupid thing to cling to life. They wouldn't let him live anyway. They'd throw Maria out of this house, and she'd have to roam in search of a job and shelter without finding any. Or she might find work on a construction site working alongside ex-convicts. Fuck! And their children, Nikolay and Olga, would be kicked out of their colleges and forced to work somewhere as janitors or garbage collectors. That is, if they weren't also arrested. O God! Why was he being punished so? For what?

Avdeyev turned to look at Stalin's portrait on the wall.

"Comrade Stalin. Joseph Vissarionovich. What have I done to deserve this? I've served you as faithfully as I could. And this bloody mess could happen to anyone. Why me?"

The portrait remained silent and sombre. The man had always been like that, whenever someone was purged at his order, and when the victim pleaded for justice.

Suddenly a glimmer of hope flashed in Avdeyev's sick mind. It occurred to him that maybe not everything was lost. After all, his father-in-law Gavrila Petrovich really had served side by side with Nikishev for a whole decade, and he must have cronies in Moscow. Yet would he do anything to protect his son-in-law? There was hardly a case when a senior security officer did that sort of thing. Hell! Avdeyev didn't want to die. He burst into sobs, then suddenly stopped and spat angrily. Fuck you, Avdeyev. Be a man. A Soviet officer. You have to be.

He held the revolver to his temple again and felt the coldness of the metal against his skin. It was as cold as the system that entrusted the weapon to him. Like everything in this state: chill, metallic and loaded with a deadly charge.

His face twisted with pain and the pistol fell from his hand with a loud bang. With a wrenching effort he rose and remained on his feet by propping his fist on the desk. Suddenly he fell to the floor, knocking over the chair, which overturned with a loud crash. In the dim light he glimpsed the portrait of Stalin above his head. But what was that? Stalin suddenly seemed to move, stepping out of the frame and advancing towards Avdeyev.

"Seize him!" The silence of the night was broken again by the loud voice of the Great Leader with its familiar Georgian accent.

"No. No, Comrade Stalin, please." Avdeyev cried, but the expression on the Great Leader's face never changed. With horror and desperation Avdeyev saw a crowd of dark ghosts approaching him from various sides. He recognized their faces ... Losev and his two friends with awful black bruises and mosquito bites on their faces. Behind them Trofimov, Yatta, Bondarenko, Goldberg and Timoshkin, his five evil geniuses. Stalin appeared in the guise of Michael the Archangel, God's punishing right hand.

Maria Gavrilovna rushed into the room.

"God bless us, Pasha, what's wrong? Are you—?" She checked his pulse, then tried to massage his chest. "Agafya! Come here! Quick!"

"Yes, Maria Gavrilovna?" The convict maid appeared from her neighbouring bedroom.

"Run and get a doctor. Quickly. Quickly. Pavel Egorovich is very unwell."

A quarter of an hour later the maid returned accompanied by the new camp physician, Doctor Astakhov, who had replaced Ponomarev after the latter's dismissal. Astakhov bent down over Avdeyev and felt his pulse.

"I'm afraid it's too late, Maria Gavrilovna."

"What?" She swung round to face him.

"I'm afraid he's dead."

Maria Gavrilovna buried her face in her hands and sobbed.

The funeral procession slowly moved along the main street of the settlement outside the compound, and made its way towards the local cemetery. The coffin with Avdeyev's body was draped with red cloth and carried by four soldiers. His grief-stricken widow walked behind the coffin, accompanied by officers from the compound and a few other guests. A band of army musicians walked ahead of them, playing a funeral march. A group of soldiers marched ahead of the procession, and another detachment brought up the rear. On reaching the servicemen's cemetery, the procession halted by a newly dug grave. The procession broke up and grouped around the grave. A colonel stepped up in front of them.

"Dear comrades!" the colonel's voice broke the silence. "We are gathered here today on a sad occasion, to pay tribute to our fellow officer who died at his post, a Chekist with twenty-five years of service to his credit, a long-term member of the Communist Party, and a great Soviet patriot, Pavel Egorovich Avdeyev."

PART III: ON THEIR WAY

1

The path snaked its way downhill, and soon groves and thickets appeared on either side. They moved the whole of that day. The two remaining deer pulled the sleds, and the men hauled the carcass of the mountain sheep. By dusk they were in the foothills and made a stop. As they enjoyed a supper of fried meat, they discussed the recent events.

"Well, congratulations," Trofimov announced. "We've crossed this vicious mountain range."

"Except for the two other deer, two sleds, stuff for the tents, and all our meat supply." Timoshkin lamented.

"But we survived the avalanche," Bondarenko objected. "We might easily have been buried alive."

Yatta said "I gotta set traps. We might need furs to trade with."

"I'll go with you," Timoshkin offered.

Yatta and Timoshkin disappeared into the woods, and the rest of the company continued sitting around the fire enjoying a rest. Suddenly Bondarenko vigorously scratched his body under his coat, getting more and more angry.

"Damn it all. I'm itching all over. We've not had a proper wash for two months."

"I know what you mean," said Trofimov. "Where can we find a bath, or a decent Russian bathhouse? We daren't go near a village."

"I once read about hot geysers here in Siberia," said Goldberg. "Are there any around here, I wonder?"

"What's that?" Bondarenko inquired.

"They're fountains of hot water that come pouring up out of the ground."

"Hot water? You're kidding, Yakov. How the hell can hot water pour up here in winter? There's nothing but permafrost underground."

"Below the permafrost is the hot mantle of the earth. It's like hot, molten metal, and when it pours out of the ground, volcanic eruptions take place. In some places it doesn't reach the surface and only warms the ground waters, and then they spring up as hot fountains."

"Never heard of such a thing," Bondarenko declared. "What 'bout you, Captain?"

"I've heard of hot geysers. It's to do with the geological structure of the earth."

"Well, if you learned guys say so, I've gotta believe you." Bondarenko shrugged. "But who would ever think? Well water always comes up cold, and you can make ice cellars. But the priests say the flames of hell are deep down there somewhere. So it's true? And I always reckoned it was just a load of bullshit."

"Well, maybe there's some truth in that too." Trofimov laughed.

"Actually there might be a link," Goldberg reflected. "Maybe the legends about a fiery hell are connected with some ancient human experience. Early humans may have descended into volcanic craters and seen how hot it gets."

"Maybe. Anyway, if these geysers are really around, Yatta must know about them," Bondarenko concluded. "And we mustn't miss out on 'em. I can't go on living with this constant itch."

"How goes the trapping?" Trofimov greeted Yatta and Timoshkin.

"Very well, you know," said Yatta.

"Listen, Yatta," Bondarenko could barely wait to broach the subject. "The captain and Yakov said that there are—shit! what's their name?—hot water pouring up from under the ground. Have you heard about them?"

"Oh, yeah," Yatta confirmed, "those are the holy springs. There are lots of them around, you know. Our people worship them."

"And you can bathe in them?" Bondarenko exclaimed. "Like in a bath all the year round?"

"Oh, yeah. When Chukchi families move from the summer pastures to the winter pastures and back, they always stop at a holy spring and everyone bathes."

"Are there any around here?"

"No," Yatta shook his head. "Even the nearest one is far away, you know. And there's always villages around them."

"Shit," Bondarenko snapped. "So we're gonna be dirty and lousy all the way to America."

"But there's baths in some of the trappers' cabins in the forest," Yatta said.

"Is that so?" Trofimov joined the discussion. "Do you know of any around here?"

"I dunno," Yatta said. "We Chukchi go without bathing for months."

"Can't we get to the nearest cabin and have a bath?" Bondarenko asked. "And maybe wash our clothes? These bloody lice are killing me."

"It would be great," Trofimov said, "but it's too dangerous. We could run into an ambush."

"You're right, it's too risky," Goldberg concurred.

"But we can reconnoiter and explore," Bondarenko argued. "I can detect an ambush ahead. I've done it before."

"Well, maybe we can try," Trofimov said.

2

Timoshkin had been on guard for nearly an hour. He was desperate for a cigarette, but remembered the agreement to be economical and waited for another half hour. Suddenly there was a wild screech from the reindeer. Timoshkin wheeled round at the sound and saw wolves. He fired a short burst, and his companions rushed from the tent. The wolves were ready to attack. There were many of them and they looked aggressive. The men fired a few shots, but were afraid of hitting the reindeer.

"We've gotta stop shooting!" Yatta shouted. "Let the wolves turn on us, then we can zap them. And I'll try to protect the deer."

As Yatta predicted, the wolves rushed the men and were met with a wall of machinegun fire, which mowed down every single one of them.

"What a mess." Bondarenko shook his head. "They might well have finished off the deer."

"Yeah," said Trofimov. "Let's check the deer. They might be hurt."

Trofimov and Yatta went to the animals, which were trembling. One bled heavily in the neck. Yatta examined the creatures. "And look, one of them has a bite in the collar, and a bullet wound in the hind leg."

"Poor thing." Bondarenko examined the wounds. "Is he gonna survive?"

"Oh, yeah," Yatta said. "If we let him rest and graze here for a while."

"You mean we've got to stay here?" Trofimov asked.

"Yes, if we don't want to lose the reindeer," Yatta said.

"If we do lose it, we'll have to pull one of the sleds ourselves," Bondarenko pointed out.

"How long, Yatta?"

"A couple of weeks maybe, Sasha."

"Then we'll stay," Trofimov said. "Without the deer we'd move much more slowly anyway."

"Yeah," Timoshkin agreed. "and we need new tent poles anyway."

"But in the meantime, we can trap fox and wolverine to use as barter," Yatta added.

The rest of the night passed without event. In the morning Trofimov and Yatta checked the traps and to their delight discovered a black fox caught in one of them.

"What luck," said Trofimov.

"Yeah, indeed. But, you know, we gotta catch another three times three, and that'll be enough to pay our next guide, if we need one."

The fox twitched in the trap as they approached. Trofimov took out his knife.

"No," Yatta warned him off. "You'll spoil the skin. Like this."

He took out a rope noose, threw it round the animal's neck and pulled hard. The fox stopped twitching and lay still.

"One good skin," Yatta explained, "is worth 'bout five times as much as a cut one."

Yatta removed the fox from the trap and stuffed it into his bag. Then he caught sight of something else, and pointed to a chain of hoof tracks in the snow.

"That's a wild reindeer," Yatta said. "Actually, two of them."

"How do you know?"

"By their steps," Yatta explained. "When they move along like this, with the tracks about two elbows from each other, it means they are going to some new pasture or a pond."

"Shall we go after them?"

"Yeah," said Yatta. "But move quietly."

They found the two wild reindeer digging into the snow in a small clearing.

"Now, you shoot the doe, and I'll catch the buck with the lasso," Yatta whispered. "But you know, we've gotta do it at the very same moment, otherwise one of them will run."

"Why take both of them? We don't need that much."

"Just do as I say. I'll explain later," Yatta whispered.

A few seconds later, at the same moment, Yatta's lasso caught the buck by his antlers, and Trofimov's bullet struck down the doe. Trofimov felt for his knife again.

"No, no! We need him alive, you know," Yatta warned.

"Why do we need him alive?" Trofimov asked.

"We'll break him in and take him with us, then have him for food later on. Or we can barter him for two good domestic ones. He's the best bloodstock, and will produce the best offspring."

"Then it's worth trying. But what shall we do with them now? Take the doe first and leave him tied up here for a while?"

"No, if we leave him, the wolves will come and eat him up."

"Then I'll go and get our guys while you guard the deer."

"Will you find your way back by our tracks?"

"No problem."

With the dead fox in his backpack, Trofimov moved along quickly on his skis and hummed a cheerful melody as he went. Without warning, something heavy struck him across the shoulders, and the next instant something hard and sharp tore into his clothing. His hand grabbed for his knife. In the same instant he looked over his shoulder. Next to his cheek was a round furry face like a cat's, but larger and with a tassel on each ear. With all his force, Trofimov rammed his knife into the furry throat and tore at the same time. The beast fell off his shoulders to the ground and lay still. It was only then that Trofimov remembered its name: lynx.

"Holy shit," he muttered to himself. "There's danger everywhere in this wilderness."

He examined the lynx's body and decided it could be of some value if he took it with him.

"Captain," Bondarenko greeted him then stopped short. "Holy shit. What happened? You're covered in blood."

"It's not mine," Trofimov said. "A lynx attacked me on the way back."

"And you neatly cut its throat." Bondarenko examined the dead animal.

"We have to hurry," Trofimov urged. "Yatta's waiting with a shot doe and a live buck."

They returned to join Yatta just in time. They saw him from a distance with rifle at the ready and several wolves lowering close by, their eyes on the carcass of the dead doe.

"Open fire. Quick." Trofimov ordered. A short burst dispatched the predators.

"What a day." Bondarenko seemed to relish the excitement. "A wolf attack, a lynx attack, and if we'd come ten minutes later, both Yatta and the deer would have been gobbled up."

"No, not me," Yatta grinned. "I'd have climbed up a larch tree."

"Anyway, we've got quite a good catch here."

"Time to go," Trofimov commanded. "Mikhail and I will drag the doe, and you take care of the buck."

"Wait, we have to make a collar to go round his neck and then lead him along," Yatta explained, taking out of his seemingly bottomless pocket a bunch of thick leather strings. He expertly braided them together into a wide band, and fixed the loose ends.

"Sasha, Mikhail, help me to keep him quiet." Yatta came up to the deer, stroked him with great caution on the cheeks and on the neck, and in one quick movement put the band around the deer's neck. With another sturdier string he pulled two ends of the band together, and added a wide loop fixing it with a big knot.

"This loop is for my hand, I will lead him myself. He must calm down. Now, let him free." The animal kicked, tried to pull in different direction, but Yatta had an iron grip on the collar.

"How will you break him in?" Trofimov asked as they reached their campsite.

"First we tie him to a tree and give him very little room to move around for several days."

"Without food and drink?"

"He can drink, but no food before the fourth day."

"And how tame will he be by then? Will he carry a load?" Bondarenko asked.

"No, he won't take a load, but he'll go wherever we lead him, though. And whoever buys him will be able to keep him with his herd for breeding."

3

They spent two more weeks at the campsite. As Yatta foresaw, the wounded reindeer began recovering. In the meantime they made a new set of tent poles and tied them together in a sheaf. One of the reindeer would haul it along. As for the killed doe, they planned to drag it themselves. The journey promised to become much harder, but there was nothing for it. They were lucky to have two healthy reindeer, so they did not have to haul the sleds themselves.

In the evenings they had a lot of time to spare, and spent hours talking about their life stories. Yatta usually remained silent, but one evening he told his friends a story of his first war experience.

Yatta was an eighteen-year-old living with his tribe and kinfolk in the tundra on the Anadyr Plateau. He helped herd his father's reindeer. The tribe lived as it had for centuries, pasturing their large herds of reindeer. Long winters alternated with short summers. The people worshiped the Merciful Beings and family spirits and followed their ancient rituals. Vague rumours reached the pastoral tundra of a ruthless war going on at some distant point in the Russian motherland.

Yatta's kinfolk did not know the term "civil war." All they knew was that there was upheaval in faraway Russia. The Sun Chief, so the rumours said, had ascended to heaven to meet the Creator, and one part of the Russian people, the Reds, fought another part, the

Whites. The Whites wanted to give power back to the kinfolk of the Sun Chief, but the Reds wanted it for someone else. The Chukchi people took scant interest in these rumours. They had problems of their own, and never thought that either the Whites or the Reds could ever affect their own lives.

One summer's day, that faraway Russian strife cast its shadow over their land. A large unit of men dressed in Cossack uniform appeared. They rode saddled Yakut reindeer, and they had rifles, sabers and heavy machine guns. At around noon, they approached the site where Yatta's kin lived. A large, stocky man with epaulettes stepped forward and cried out in Russian. Yatta knew little of the language at that time, but most of his folk did not know it at all, so nobody answered the man in epaulettes. This caused the man to break into a rage, and he screamed angrily and drew his saber. One of the Chukchi men, Ainanwat, had spent some time in a Russian fort and spoke some Russian. When the Cossack leader heard him speak, he calmed down somewhat. He announced himself as Colonel Azarov of the Bochkarev Brigade and requested food and shelter for the next few days. In the tradition of Chukchi hospitality, the tundra dwellers were more than willing to receive these unexpected guests, and their old chief, Orvo, and other elders placed several family yarangas at the Cossack troops' disposal.

But the peace did not last long. Although the Chukchi did not know it, the newcomers were the remnants of Bochkarev's expeditionary force sent by the White Maritime Government to investigate the coast of the Sea of Okhotsk. They had been defeated by the Reds and spent months wandering in the cold and thinly populated tundra. They were hungry, dirty and exhausted. Probably they hoped to find their way to Alaska, but that was a long way to go, and the colonel wanted to stop to rest and get food before moving further east.

As happens with the soldiers of all defeated armies, the newcomers were angry with the whole world, and it needed little to drive them to violence. A conflict broke out at the welcome dinner thrown for the guests. When they get hot from cooking, the Chukchi women in the yarangas wear only loincloths. The guests did not know this custom. They thought the women were available and manhandled them. The husbands were indignant. A fight broke out and quickly turned into an armed confrontation. The better-armed Cossacks won of course. They overran the camp and seized all the guns from the locals.

A reign of terror followed. The Cossacks slaughtered the reindeer and raped all the women between seven and seventy. Any resistance was brutally punished, and people were shot and hacked to death with sabers. One of the elders, old Ankjem, was lashed to death, and another, Omrilqot, was trampled to death beneath Cossack reindeer hooves.

The Cossacks enjoyed being powerful masters of these local tribe folk and did not rush to leave.

Without warning, resistance to the new rulers broke out. Rimtuwgi, the best trapper and strongest man among Yatta's kinfolk, persuaded about a score of men, including young Yatta and three of his brothers, to flee to a nearby rocky area and fight back.

Once, in the early winter, they ambushed and killed several Cossacks, took their weapons and disappeared. They settled in a narrow gorge higher up in the mountains where their enemies could not reach them and made easy targets for sniping. The Chukchi men avoided open battles, since the enemy had magic rifles, as they called their heavy machine-guns. Instead they made night raids and ambushes on small groups of Cossacks. Soon each Chukchi fighter had his own rifle. In response the Cossacks took to slaughtering both men and women, and maintained they would continue to do this until the rebels gave themselves up.

Once, as he was moving with his friends through a grove of dwarf birches in the foothills, young Yatta came across five of his kinsmen, including two women, who had been stripped to the waist and strangled. On coming closer, he saw that all the dead had had their hands chopped off. One man had clotted blood around his lips: his tongue had been cut out. Yatta recognized his maternal uncle Ainanwat. The others included his great uncle Armol, an old man named Pananto, and two kinswomen, Hiune and Titina. The young men were deeply shocked and only able to move off and return after some time.

"That ain't gotta happen no more," said Yatta's uncle Rimtuwgi when he heard the story. "You know, we have to do something before they kill everyone."

"But how are we gonna do that, Rimtuwgi?" his cousin Yynuvyje asked. "There's several score of them, and only a few dozen of us.

And they have these magic rifles."

"Yeah," agreed another man named Ainairgin. "I think we gotta surrender. We shall all die, and our deaths may be painful, but we'll save our kinfolk. Maybe the younger ones have gotta go away. But the older folks should surrender."

"No," Rimtuwgi protested. "Give myself up of my own free will? Never in my life. Rather let the Evil Spirits devour my flesh and my soul."

"But what else we gonna do?" retorted Ainairgin. "They're gonna kill them."

"No, no, no. I repeat again." Rimtuwgi countered. "We, you know, are the Telqap tribe, the bravest of all the Chukchi! But I do agree, we gotta do something to save our kinfolk."

"But what can we do?" another man asked.

Rimtuwgi became thoughtful.

"If we can seize their magic rifles, we can gain the upper hand."

"But how are we gonna do it, uncle Rituwgi?" Yatta asked.

"That's a tricky thing," replied Rimtuwgi. "I'm sure they conceal them well. However, if we can capture one of them, we can find out from him. Their overseers must know their secret ammunition store."

"Overseers?" Ainairgin asked.

"Yeah, there are some chiefs among them. Those chiefs have gilt stars, one or more, on their shoulders. We must capture one of them and force him to speak."

"Please, let me take part in the ambush, uncle Rimtuwgi," Yatta pleaded.

"Fine," Rimtuwgi agreed. "You're fit for the task. We'll wait in ambush at Raven's Hill, where the path is narrow. The Cossacks use it all the time. You, Yatta, Tangak and Nuvat, wait in ambush above that path. Even if you donna see the stars under their overcoats, you can recognize the overseers by their speech. They yell all the time. Kill everyone else, but bring the overseer back alive. Understand?"

The next two days Yatta and two of his cousins spent on top of a cliff overlooking the mountain pathway. On the third day the sharp ears of the young hunters caught the sound of reindeer on the move. The three of them pushed a large boulder towards the edge of the cliff. Soon a group of five Cossacks riding deer emerged on the pass. One of them spoke in such a commanding voice that it was easy to recognize their chief officer.

"That's the one," Yatta whispered, pointing out the man with the imperious voice.

"Good," said Nuvat, "now's the moment. Tangak and I will push the boulder and then shoot. You, Yatta, get ready with your lasso."

"Don't shoot their chief officer dead," Yatta warned.

He unbound his lasso. His cousins were ready to heave the boulder over the edge, and when the Cossacks were directly below the overhang, the young men sent it bowling down the hill. It raised a huge cloud of snow as it rolled, and it scored a direct hit on two of the Cossack horsemen. The other riders were blinded by snow. Two shots rang out, killing two more Cossacks. At the same moment Yatta swung his lasso and caught the chief officer round the elbows. The man cursed and struggled to get rid of the noose.

"Help me drag him up," Yatta called.

His companions grabbed the end of the lasso, and soon the Cossack officer was hauled up onto the overhang. They disarmed him, tied his arms behind his back, and gagged his mouth with a rag.

"Looks like we've done it," said Tangak.

"Let's see whether we've got the right man," Yatta said. He approached the captive and dragged off his army greatcoat. Epaulettes with one stripe and two stars showed up.

"Well done. Excellent fighters." Rimtuwgi praised them when they produced their captive. "After supper we'll deal with him. You, Yatta, know some of their tongue, don't you?"

Yatta nodded. "But only a very little, uncle Rimtuwgi."

"Since they killed poor Keinin, nobody knows it better than you."

"I'll try," said Yatta.

The interrogation began immediately after supper. Rimtuwgi sat by the bonfire with Yatta beside him. Two other men held the captive, and other folk stood around them.

"So, Yatta, ask him where they keep their magic rifles," Rimtuwgi began.

Yatta turned to the officer.

"Uncle Rimtuwgi is asking you, stranger, where you keep your magic rifles, you know, the ones that spit a dozen bullets every second."

"Piss off, you filthy savage," the Cossack officer snapped back.

"But you know, he doesn't want to speak, Uncle Rimtuwgi," Yatta said.

"Tell him he's going to be beaten and have his back roasted on the fire," Rimtuwgi answered.

Yatta translated. In response the officer spat in his face. Rimtuwgi shrugged.

"Well, men, you know, we've just got to force him then. Armol and Onno, start on his back."

The two young men stripped off the officer's jacket, grabbed him by the legs and armpits and held him over the bonfire, his back just above the flames.

"Ask him now, Yatta, whether he's gonna talk," Rimtuwgi urged.

Yatta translated, but the officer, though quivering with pain, remained silent.

"Hold him a bit lower," Rimtuwgi ordered.

The two men lowered the officer further, so that the flames almost licked his back. The officer screamed and his eyes were full of hate for his captors. Rimtuwgi then ordered him to be lashed across the stomach while held above the fire.

Trofimov watched Yatta's face. It wore an expression of calm and serenity despite the grisly details of his story. It was difficult to believe that the same man who did such things could have nursed Trofimov and other patients with such devotion and care.

"I see you guys did your job very seriously," Trofimov commented. "Like Razzhivin did with me. Anyway, did he crack eventually?"

"Yeah, he did. But not till two days later." Yatta's voice remained as calm as before.

"Hmm, I can imagine what you did to him before you broke him." Bondarenko chuckled.

"Yeah, his back was all charred." Yatta continued in the same calm voice. "Then we left him for the night. After that we bound a red-hot axe to his hands, but he still held firm. It wasn't until we started breaking his ribs that he broke down and talked. The next night we went to the place and seized their magic rifles."

"So," Bondarenko shrugged, "he wasn't a useless casualty. The bastard could have wiped out your whole tribe. I wouldn't have liked to be that Cossack. You guys were certainly inventive. In my unit we did things far more simply."

"And did you participate in torturing him, Yatta?" Goldberg asked.

"No, I just translated."

"I'm glad to hear that. It would be hard for me to be in the company of someone who did that."

"Then you've gotta refuse to be in the same company as me," Bondarenko said mockingly.

Goldberg stared at him. "You mean to say that you—"

"Sure. Back in my partisan days. Though we weren't so creative as Yatta's people. We just put the prisoner between three of us and beat the shit out of the bastard."

"Germans?" asked Trofimov.

"Sure. But men from the Polizei as well. What the hell else could you do, when you had to find out where they kept their stores and ammunition? And the Fritzes were no softies. They were tough guys, and they'd also sworn an oath of loyalty to their Führer. But after you've beaten a man's brains out for a couple of days, well, nobody's that tough."

"I always suspected that sort of thing was done by our troops too, and not only by the Germans." Trofimov bit his lip. "Though I never did it myself, and never saw. That was SMERSH's job. We combat troops just fought."

"If that's the case, then we're no better than the fascists," Goldberg exclaimed. "I would never have imagined."

"Once again, Yakov," said Bondarenko, "you're pitying people who don't deserve it. D'you think they'd have shown you any pity?"

"Makes no difference, Mikhail," said Goldberg. "If we do the same things as them, what's the difference between them and us?"

"C'mon, Yakov," Bondarenko snapped. "Next you'll be telling us that our partisans who shot and stabbed those Nazis were no better than the Fritzes that threw kids down the well, and other such things."

"No, I don't mean that, but—"

"But what? What, you tell me, are we supposed to do to be different? Bare our chests in front of their bayonets?"

"Certainly not. Self-defence is permitted, but torture's a different thing," Goldberg insisted.

"In that case, how were we supposed to get information about, say, SS units?" Bondarenko argued. "Or in Yatta's case, the scumdogs who were about to kill off his whole clan. You, Yakov, are a good guy, but you ain't got no clue whatsoever about some things in life. You're just like … like Jesus. He pitied everyone, including his torturers, and they nailed him to the cross and sat around drinking and playing cards. No, if I'd been there, I wouldn't have behaved like Jesus."

"What would you have done?" Goldberg asked.

"Hide in the bushes and give 'em a good burst of the machine gun. They wouldn't nail no one no more."

"There weren't machine guns then, not even ordinary guns," Trofimov retorted.

"No?" Bondarenko grinned. "Then there were other ways. I'd have rolled a couple of boulders from above."

"Well, that's you, Mikhail." Trofimov laughed. "You're never lost for an answer."

"Certainly not, Captain," Bondarenko laughed. "Nor would I ever give up without a fight, nor pity those that ain't deserve it. And I wasn't born a butcher, Yakov. Until 1941 I'd never killed nothing except cattle. I'd never even fought with a knife, only with my fists, and that's the way I intended going on in life. But when the Nazis came with their marauding, killing and burning, what the hell was I supposed to do? I took my knife and my dad's rifle, and I went off into the woods. And I fought. Why for God's sake should I pity the Fritzes?"

Bondarenko was silent for some time, but then resumed. "After the Nazis were gone, the Red Army came. I hoped to get back to my wife and kids and return to a normal life, but the Soviets got hold of me. SMERSH tortured me in a dungeon then sent me to Kolyma. What a reward! What the hell was I supposed to do? Kick the bucket in a mine or on a logging site, just so as not to kill any of those bastards? Not bloody likely. All I can do is carry on fighting, and finish off as many of those scumbags as I can. If they ever do get me, they aren't gonna get me easily." He paused again. "After all, it wasn't me that started it. I didn't ask for all this. But now that they're after me again, I'm gonna fucking give it to them hot. And I won't be sorry about it either."

"I'd rather get to the Strait without having to fight," Timoshkin said.

"Sure," Bondarenko agreed. "I only meant if we have to fight. If we ever get to America alive, I wanna live a normal life again. No more blood. But until we get there, we've gotta be ready to fight. So just forget all that bullshit about feeling sorry for those fucking screws."

"Do you remember Tolstoy's *War and Peace*?" Trofimov suddenly asked.

"I do," Goldberg answered.

"Never read it," Bondarenko admitted.

"Me neither," Timoshkin said. "I couldn't read or write till I turned thirty-five."

"Well, whatever, but it's a great novel," Trofimov continued. "There's an episode toward the end, when the war with Napoleon is over and the Russian troops are resting after a battle, and there are French prisoners there too. General Kutuzov makes a speech and he says: 'When they were strong, we had no pity for them, but now we can afford to pity them.' "

"Hardly applies to our case, though," Timoshkin observed.

"No, it doesn't," Trofimov agreed. "Ours is exactly the opposite. They—Stalin and the Soviets and their troops—are far, far stronger than us. We can't afford to pity them. Only if we were strong enough that we could beat them and march not to Alaska, but in the opposite direction, to Moscow."

"But that ain't gonna happen any time soon," Timoshkin shook his head.

"Hardly, if ever. I just wanted to make the point. We have to be tough and not fear death, either our own, or that of the enemy."

Goldberg looked Trofimov straight in the eye. "Does this mean that you are in favour of torture, Sasha?"

"Hell, no. I've been tortured myself, but I never did it to anyone else, and I won't. I guess Yatta's case was quite a special one. They had to save their kinsfolk, their mothers, wives, sisters and their kids. If we were in that position—I honestly don't know. But we're not. Our relatives are thousands of kilometres away, so we can follow the Geneva Convention."

"What's that?" Bondarenko's eyebrows rose.

"It's an international convention of representatives from all the European and American states, and it established the norms for conducting war," Trofimov explained. "It specifically banned torture and excessive cruelty."

"When did that happen?"

"I don't remember the year."

"Actually," said Goldberg, "there were two conventions, one in 1906, and another in 1929."

"What about the guys in blue epaulettes?" Bondarenko asked. "Do they treat us according to any Geneva Convention? No. They break our bones, freeze us to death, tie us up to larch trees. It's got to be mutual, ain't it? They treat us worse than dogs, so why on earth should we treat them any differently?"

"In America, where we're heading, they check against things like that," Trofimov said. "They want to know if a refugee claimant is a war criminal. If we use torture, according to international law we too will be war criminals, and that's sufficient grounds for denying political asylum. Those are the laws. If we're going to seek political asylum from the Americans, we have to stand up in front of them and be honest."

"Well," Bondarenko said thoughtfully, "maybe there's something to what you say, Captain. I just hope you don't mean we've gotta spare them all, even the worst of those bloodiest butchers?"

"Fighting is one thing," Trofimov replied. "Savagery is another."

4

The injured reindeer recovered, and the five men set off again on their journey. Four of them took turns hauling the reindeer carcass, while Yatta was responsible for the sled reindeer and the wild buck. Although all five were fit and strong, they had to rest more often, making stops during the day. Sometimes they stopped for a whole day, and it was clear that they could not make it to the Bering Strait before the end of winter. This was no longer

Trofimov's primary concern.

At present they headed for a log cabin that was a former hunting lodge. There, according to Yatta, was a small bathhouse attached to the cabin. None of them had taken a bath for almost three months, and they suffered from lice and itching. Only Yatta seemed unbothered, miraculously able to survive for months without a bath. To yield to the desire for a hot bath went against all considerations of safety, and Trofimov feared that the local authorities had set up an ambush near any cabins. Were he himself pursuing outlaws, he would have done precisely that. Even so, it was hard to give up the chance to take a bath, wash their clothes, and get rid of their lice. After long discussion, they decided to take the risk, and Trofimov sent Bondarenko ahead to reconnoiter.

It took Bondarenko half a day to reach the place, following Yatta's instructions, but he easily found the cabin. It stood in the middle of a clearing surrounded by old larches, at the foot of a tall rocky outcrop. On the other side of the clearing was a wooded slope, with a narrow pathway leading uphill. Exploring this path, he discovered that a few metres from the clearing it forked: one path ran straight to the top of the rocks, the other led deep into the woods. He explored the area for several hours. He examined the surroundings and listened to every sound, relying on the keen senses and intuition of an experienced scout, which had never failed him. He found no sign of human presence. He walked up the wooded hill and again observed all approaches to the cabin. Later in the evening he discovered nearly buried ski tracks in the snow.

"Anything to report?" Trofimov asked when Bondarenko returned early the next morning.

"Not a living soul, Captain. Someone was there several days ago, but by now the ski tracks are hardly visible."

"How many people were there?"

"One."

"Then it might be a random visitor—a hunter or a trapper."

"Might be, Captain," Bondarenko sounded hesitant. "There's a chance it could be them."

"But then it wouldn't be just one person," Goldberg said. "They know there are five of us."

"Doesn't mean nothin'." Bondarenko countered. "It could be their scout."

"Are you sure there's nobody around right now?" Trofimov enquired again.

"There was certainly nobody there during the night."

"So aren't we gonna have our hot bath after all?" Timoshkin sounded desolate.

"That's what we have to discuss," Trofimov said. "Yatta, how far's the nearest village?"

"About three days' walk."

"Is there an official village soviet, or council, there?"

"No," Yatta said confidently. "You know, the nearest village soviet is about fifty kilometres from there."

"Then it's very unlikely that someone's waiting for us there," Trofimov concluded. "Shall we risk it?"

"Yes," Timoshkin gave his vote. "There might be no other chance."

"We could still run into a trap," Bondarenko warned.

"Not likely," Trofimov said. "Although there's no guarantee. Right now there's no one there. Even if those tracks belonged to their scout or spy, he won't get back to the village till tomorrow. And he would report that there was no one there. They'll hardly send someone else out again immediately. It looks like we can risk it."

"Well, if you think so, Captain, let's give it a try," Bondarenko said with a shrug.

"We'll take off immediately to get there before dark," Trofimov ordered.

They reached the cabin by early evening.

"I can't believe it." Timoshkin looked around. "A human dwelling. I haven't seen one for months."

"And you're not gonna see another for several more months," Bondarenko commented gravely.

"Well, not till we reach Qergina's place, you know," said Yatta.

"We'll discuss that later," Trofimov interrupted them. "Now, Timoshkin, you get the cabin heated and melt snow for the bath. We'll check everything around."

An hour later, when the men entered the cabin, they felt a welcoming warmth. At last, after many days, they could take off their overcoats.

"Well done, Zakharych! It's nice and warm," Trofimov praised Timoshkin.

"Wasn't hard to do," Timoshkin smiled. "Every peasant knows how to warm the house." He gave a satisfied sigh. "I can't wait till we finally get into the bath."

"We can do that tomorrow morning," Trofimov suggested. "But for now we should have supper and—"

The door flung open and Bondarenko appeared, dragging a youth with a bleeding nose. Everyone swung round toward them.

"Take a look at this," Bondarenko said. "I caught him spying on us."

Trofimov looked at the prisoner. "Who are you? What are you doing here?"

"I … I just came, er, to check the traps," the boy muttered.

"Then why the hell were you watching us from behind the trees?" Bondarenko snapped, and dealt the boy another heavy blow in the face.

"Stop it, Mikhail," Trofimov ordered and turned to the boy. "Tell the truth," he lifted his gun, "or I'll shoot you on the spot."

The youngster burst into tears.

"Please, donna kill me," he pleaded, "I'm only seventeen."

"Then tell us everything," Trofimov demanded. "Who are you? Where are you from?"

"I'm Vassily Sinyeboyev, from the village of Shcherbakovo."

"Who ordered you to spy on us?"

"Pyotr Timofeich Konechnikov, our collective farm manager, and Zakhar Stepanych Burdakov, the Party organizer."

"So the authorities are waiting for us?" Trofimov fixed the youth with his stare.

"Yeah, comrade Chief. An officer came from the district centre two months ago and told us a dangerous gang with machine guns was in the area. Zakhar Stepanych called a meeting and mobilized thirty men from the collective farm."

"Where are they now?"

"In the village."

"Where did you spend the night on the way here?"

"In a cave."

"When do they expect you back?"

"In about four or five days from now."

Trofimov paused, then spoke: "Mikhail, take him to the cellar and lock him in. Bring him something to piss into. When our roast is ready, give him some."

"Why on earth? He spied on us, and we're gonna waste our meat on him?"

Trofimov raised his voice, "That's an order."

Bondarenko opened a hatch in the floor and shoved the boy down into the cellar. He looked around and found a small bucket, and threw that down after him.

The five of them sat and lamented their bad luck. For the first time, they would have to confront their pursuers face to face.

"Listen," Trofimov took charge. "We have to make a decision. It looks like the home guard unit won't be here for another five or six days."

"Yeah," Timoshkin said, "we've still got some time."

"Too risky, Zakharych," Bondarenko countered. "This youngster may be lying. They could be nearby." He paused and looked towards Trofimov. "Captain, if you let me, I can make him tell the truth."

"No. No force. We'll plan on a hot bath and laundry early tomorrow morning, and then we move on. Someone will be permanently on guard. The moment our guard warns of their approach, two of us—you, Mikhail, and someone else—take up position on top of the rock. It's a good place to observe all approaches to the clearing and the space around the cabin. All others remain in the cabin, and fire through the windows or the trapdoor on the roof. We'll have a good look at all the places after supper. Those who go to the cliff top, take two submachine guns with you. There has to be a storm of shooting from there. We'll signal you when to open fire: a torch in the trapdoor means 'shoot': a white rag means 'hold your fire.' "

The home guard unit was two dozen kilometres away from the cabin. The team included thirty men from three neighbouring villages and was headed by Burdakov, the Party organizer, and Konechnikov, the farm manager. The two men had guessed there was a strong chance that the fugitives might try making for the cabin, and they had organized a team of local activists and villagers armed with rifles to keep an eye on it. So as not to scare off their quarry, they camped a good distance from the cabin, but close enough to reach it within a few hours' march. They set up temporary residence in a large cave, and regularly sent out scouts to reconnoitre.

"Vassily's taking a long time to get back."

"That's no problem, Zakhar Stepanych," said Konechnikov. "It could take him a bit longer."

"He should have been back three hours ago, Pyotr Timofeich. I'm afraid something may have gone wrong."

Konechnikov looked him in the eye. "You mean—?"

"I mean just that. They're actually there, and he's been caught."

"Poor young guy if that's the case." Konechnikov shook his head. "I can imagine what those bastards will do to him."

"Well, he's a young Soviet citizen, a member of the Young Communist League. He's gotta be prepared to pay with his life if necessary."

"Surely," Konechnikov hastened to agree.

Burdakov continued, "If we head there right now, we may nab them."

"Almost too good to be true, Stepanych. That really will be something if we can catch them. We could both get promoted even to the District Party Committee."

"That isn't the point," Burdakov snapped. "We shall certainly be rewarded. But we must be ready to serve the Party and the state even without that."

"Oh, that's for sure, Stepanych," Konechnikov hastily assented. "But I can foresee how many of our guys may get killed. Remember, the bandits have Kalashnikovs."

"So what?" Burdakov retorted. "We've got to be ready to die for our motherland. There are only five of them after all. There's no doubt we can catch them."

"But if they've caught young Vassily, I bet he's told them about us. They'll be ready for us, and the commissioner told us they're very good fighters," Konechnikov argued.

"We're not that bad either," Burdakov replied. "We're all Siberians, and we know how to fight."

"Of course."

"Okay, go, Timofeich. Go and raise the men."

"Yes, Stepanych." Konechnikov got up and shouted, "Unit, get up, all of you. Quick about it."

The men moved, and Burdakov waited till they stood assembled then addressed them:

"Now listen," said Burdakov in a loud, commanding voice, "the bandits are at Fedoseyev's cabin. They've seized Vaska Sinyeboyev. We have to go right now. That way we'll get them."

"But it's at least three hours to get there," one man pointed out.

"Shut your trap," Burdakov snapped. "We leave immediately."

5

Early in the morning, the naked, happy figures of Trofimov, Bondarenko, Yatta and Goldberg enjoyed their Russian bath, splashing washtubs of water onto the hot stones, and sending up clouds of steam.

"A bit more of the birch, Captain?" Bondarenko asked Trofimov, who turned to lie face down on the bench. Bondarenko took a birch switch from the hot water and flogged him across the back.

"How does it feel, Captain?"

"Abso-bloody-lutely terrific," Trofimov exulted.

"This is a proper Russian steam bath, not like that garbage pit we had in the camp," Bondarenko announced gleefully. "I guess you've never had nothing like this, Yatta?"

"No, we don't have baths like this. But in the tundra, you know, we donna have so much firewood to heat all this water."

"Too bad. You really lost out there."

Trofimov got to his feet.

"Now, Yatta, as our guide and deliverer, you should enjoy a few lashes of the birch twig."

"Thanks, Sasha, but no, it looks to me more like a form of punishment." Yatta settled back on the bench.

An hour later, Timoshkin returned from his post on watch.

"Ah, there you are, Zakharych," Trofimov smiled. "What's going on outside?"

"All quiet," Timoshkin reported and began to undress, anticipating the forthcoming pleasure.

"Your turn on watch, Yakov," Trofimov commanded.

Goldberg dressed speedily, complaining about having to put on his dirty clothes.

"You can wash your clothes when you come back." Bondarenko grinned as Goldberg made his exit.

"Come over here, Zakharych. Come here, my dear chap," Bondarenko invited. "I'd like to give you a good twigging."

With a sigh, Timoshkin lay full length on the hot bench. He smiled blissfully. "It feels like I'm back home in my village. It's almost nine years since I had a real bath. Nothing compares with a good Russian bath."

"You know," Bondarenko recalled, "when I visited Anyuta while I was with the partisans, she usually scolded me to begin with, but then the two of us would go for a bath together and, well, that was somethin'."

"How come you were never caught?" Trofimov asked.

"Once I nearly was. I managed to run away in time, but it was a close shave."

"Did you visit her after that?" Trofimov asked.

"Not for three months, but then, yes, I went back. What else could I do? The girls in our unit had their own 'husbands.' Besides, they were all so plain you could never look at them after Anyuta."

The door flung open and Goldberg burst in.

"Alarm!" he screamed. "They're coming! I can see them from the top of the slope. About thirty men. They'll be here within half an hour."

"Get dressed," Trofimov ordered. "And put out the fire."

The men rushed for their clothes and guns, and within two minutes ran out of the bathhouse.

"Now, listen," Trofimov commanded. "Mikhail and Zakharych, get up on the rock and wait for our signal. Each of you take two submachines. Keep an eye on this cabin."

"Right, Captain," Bondarenko confirmed.

The others took up position inside the cabin. Once they were in position, Trofimov gave his orders. "Lock the door. Close the windows with the shutters. Leave a small slit for observation. Yatta, take the right-hand window. Yakov, take the left."

Trofimov scrambled up the stairs to the trapdoor on the roof. It was not long before he sighted the group of men making their way up the path toward the clearing.

"Keep watching," Trofimov commanded, "but don't fire until I give the word."

The home guard unit stopped at some distance from the cabin, no doubt expecting their quarry to shoot at any moment.

"Hey!" their leader shouted toward the cabin. "Come out and surrender."

The men remained quiet.

"Hey!" he shouted again. "Don't try and make fools of us. We've seen your tracks all around. Come out of there or you'll be shot."

The men watched in silence.

"Surround the cabin." The home guard leader ordered. "But keep your distance. They're well armed. Use the cover of the trees."

Trofimov, Goldberg and Yatta observed the enemy's movements.

"Maybe, you know, we should shoot now?" Yatta suggested in a whisper. "And give Mikhail and Zakharych the signal to fire?"

"No. Not yet." Trofimov answered in a whisper. "They're too far away, protected by the trees. If we open fire now, they'll rush back into the wood, and from there send for reinforcements. That would finish us. Instead we'll provoke them into a frontal attack, and wait till they're at point blank range. Then we open fire, and give the others the signal. If we open fire now, most of them will get away and survive."

Outside, hidden behind a thick tree trunk, Burdakov and Konechnikov kept watch on the cabin and on their men.

"No sign of life there," Konechnikov said. "No shooting either. Maybe they're out of bullets. Perhaps we should try and break in and get 'em, Stepanych?"

"I doubt it, Timofeich," Burdakov disagreed. "It's a trick. If we attack now, we may come under heavy fire and lose most of our men. Let's wait and watch."

Burdakov was uncertain what to do. It looked as if the cabin was empty, but he had a feeling that the outlaws were trying a ruse. He tried hard to figure out what it could be, but he had no inkling what to do. He realized that if the fugitives were in the cabin and if he sent his men in, they would present an easy target. The commissioner had warned them that the bastards were heavily armed with Kalashnikovs and lots of ammunition, which in itself would be more than enough to dispatch all his men.

Nervously Burdakov lit a cigar of coarse tobacco. Whenever he took responsibility on himself, he never doubted his success. What could five bandits do, even if armed, against a unit of thirty men? His main concern was that the bastards might not appear in the spot where the soldiers and home guard waited for them. The woods were vast. When he first figured out that the bandits were in Fedoseyev's Cabin, he was happy: he foresaw complete triumph, the authorities' delight and his own promotion, although, of course, it was not the promotion that mattered—a faithful servant of the Party, the Soviet state and Great Leader would do his best anyway. Still, it was pleasant to be rewarded by the Party and the state, which for him represented God and the true faith. It was pleasant to feel that your services were appreciated.

On the other hand, he had never thought what he would do if the Party and the state ordered him to lay down his own life. So far they had not done that. As a devoted Party activist he was not drafted during the war. Instead he was ordered to stay at his post and help strengthen the war effort from the rear. One of his duties had been to prepare home guard units in case of a Japanese invasion. Deep down he sometimes shivered as he recalled stories in his school textbooks about Communists who were burned alive in steam engine fireboxes during the Civil War. But in fact he remained safe: the Japanese never invaded, and the war with Germany ended in victory.

Now he saw the silent reproach in the eyes of wounded war veterans and war widows. Of course, nobody dared to say anything openly: he was an all-powerful figure in the neighbourhood. One report from him to "them" could send anyone to prison or labour camp. In his heart of hearts he realized that their reproaches were justified. He never doubted the importance of his own Party work, but he had remained safe in the rear while so many others sacrificed their lives in battle. For months he dreamed of taking part in the action that would raise his personal prestige, but at the same time he was unwilling to do anything to endanger his life. But this hunt for anti-Soviet bandits now seemed a perfect chance to prove himself. If he seized them, not only would he be rewarded, but he would be able to claim that he took part in active combat.

At the start of the operation everything went well, but now the enemy obviously had some scheme in mind, which he could not fathom. The only thing that was clear was that they might escape and deprive him of his cherished dream of victory. He had no idea what to do to prevent this.

"You know what?" Burdakov turned to Konechnikov. "I think we should open fire on the cabin. If they're in there, they're bound to fire back."

"A good idea," the manager agreed.

"Attention!" the Party organizer called to his men. "Take up positions, and fire at the cabin."

The men threw themselves down on the snow and lay prone with their rifles at the ready.

"Fire!"

A hail of gunfire began. Bullets struck the walls and shutters of the cabin and shattered the panes in the windows.

"Well," Trofimov commented, "it looks like they're attacking. Wait till they get closer before firing."

They waited for the attackers to emerge from the trees and close in, but this did not happen. After a few moments the firing stopped and some of the men outside moved toward the hill where Bondarenko and Timoshkin hid. Trofimov, Yatta and Goldberg carefully followed the movement going on outside.

"Sasha, you know, they seem to be going somewhere," said Yatta.

"I see," Trofimov said. "They've found the tracks leading up to the rock."

"Maybe we better warn Mikhail and Timoshkin?" Goldberg asked.

"No need. They can see everything and are on the alert. We'll move out and follow them from the rear. That way we'll catch them in crossfire between ourselves and Bondarenko.

Several guards closed in on the cabin.

"Do we shoot?" Goldberg asked.

"No, let Mikhail and Timoshkin start." Trofimov rushed up the steps to the roof trap, where he lit the torch and gave the signal to fire. A hail of machinegun fire exploded from up on the rock. Five of the guards who had moved toward the cabin fell into the snow. Two retreated into the woods.

"Sasha!" Yatta asked. "Why don't you want us to shoot? We could finish all of them off from here."

"But then they'd know we're here," Trofimov explained. "I want them to believe that we've gone. Then our attack from the rear will come as a complete surprise."

"There's an infantry officer for you," Goldberg exclaimed. "I could never have thought up such a scheme."

"Right, it's time to get out," Trofimov commanded. "Yatta, get your lasso."

Yatta picked up his lasso, and the men took their skis and Kalashnikovs and left the cabin, closing the door.

Up on the rocks, Bondarenko and Timoshkin lay in wait behind a boulder, trying to keep both the cabin and the curve of the path under observation.

"What's going on? What are the captain and the others doing?" Bondarenko asked. "No one's shooting from the cabin. Anyone would think they were fucking finished already."

"There's no way that could happen," Timoshkin argued. "That cabin's made of good logs, no bullets would go through those."

Suddenly Bondarenko made a warning gesture.

"What is it, Mikhail?"

Can't you hear, Zakharych? They're coming up here."

Timoshkin listened. The creaking of skis on snow could clearly be heard in the silence.

"It's them," Bondarenko said. "They've found our tracks."

"But where's the captain and the others?" Timoshkin wondered.

"Can't figure it out. But those bastards are moving up here. Let's let 'em come nearer."

Trofimov, Yatta and Goldberg moved uphill behind the home guardsmen, keeping their distance.

"When do we start shooting?" Yatta whispered.

"Not until Mikhail and Timoshkin have them in their sights and open fire," Trofimov whispered back. "Then this lot will have to retreat, and that's when we meet them with our own fire."

"Aha, a pincer movement?" asked Goldberg.

"Sort of."

A long series of gunfire bursts came from up ahead. Several guards fell in their tracks, while others hastily rushed back downhill.

"Fire!" Trofimov called in a low voice, and their machine gun salvo caught the guardsmen as they fled the gunfire from above. The crossfire was ferocious, and the home guardsmen panicked. Some tried retreating to the side in order to hide among the thickets, but there was little space between the path and the steeper ground. In any case the snow on the margin of the path was too deep, and the thickets too dense. Finally, the surviving guards, less than half of the original company, lay flat on the path.

Seeing no more resistance, Trofimov stopped shooting, and Bondarenko and Timoshkin followed suit.

"What shall we do with them?" Goldberg asked.

"Well," Trofimov said, "we can't kill them all, but we can't let them go free either." He took a deep breath and shouted to them in a loud voice. "You men. Your position is hopeless. Try and get up and we'll shoot. Surrender. You've no other choice. You hear me?"

"And who the fuck are you?" a voice yelled back, trying to sound in control.

"Infantry Captain Trofimov, First Belorussian Front. Try anything stupid, and we'll kill you all. Throw down your weapons and get on your knees, hands behind your heads."

There was no response from the home guardsmen.

Trofimov addressed the guards again, "I'll give you sixty seconds to think it over. Anyone who resists or tries to escape will get a hole in his skull."

Seconds later a guard threw down his gun and got to his knees. Right away, one guard after another threw aside their guns and knives and knelt with hands behind their heads.

"You dumb shitheads and cowards," their leader shouted at them. "What, you idiots, are you doing? Do your duty and fight."

The men ignored him.

Trofimov called out. "Follow his orders if you want, but we'll shoot you on the spot if you do. Think of yourselves."

By the time the last of the home guardsmen had surrendered, only two were left lying on their stomachs, clutching their pistols, the one who had shouted at the men and another.

"Yatta, have you got your ropes handy?"

"I always have 'em ready, Sasha."

Trofimov motioned to Yatta and Goldberg. "Tie their hands. You, Mikhail and Timoshkin, keep an eye on them. If anyone resists, shoot them."

Trofimov, Goldberg and Yatta approached each of the kneeling guards in turn and tied their hands. Yatta walked over to the two who lay on their stomachs.

"Drop your gun and get on your knees. You've no choice, you know." He prodded one man's back with the barrel of his Kalashnikov.

The two men, leapt up and rushed down the slope by the side of the path. A burst of gunfire mowed one of them down. He fell and his body rolled down the slope. The other was not hit, but collapsed and sat in the snow. Yatta's lasso snaked through the air. The man screamed but could not dislodge the noose. Yatta and Goldberg dragged him back up the path together.

Trofimov surveyed the captives.

"So, seventeen altogether."

"And ten more dead," Bondarenko added.

"Not bad. Now, what to do with their guns. We can't leave them here." Trofimov hesitated for a moment.

"Hang them on their shoulders," Timoshkin suggested.

"Not a bad idea," Trofimov agreed.

Back in the cabin, they stuffed the captives into the cellar. Timoshkin brought two bucketfuls of snow, so they had water to drink, and Goldberg brought a barrel for their "natural needs." Then they closed and bolted the hatch.

After that the five of them ate the remainder of their morning meal. They reheated the bath annex, took turns bathing, and finally, dead tired, went to sleep, leaving one man on guard as usual.

6

Next morning, Trofimov interrogated the captives. They sat on crates and barrels or sprawled on the floor at the far end of the cellar. They looked more exhausted than frightened.

"Who are you men?" Trofimov addressed them.

"Villagers from Shcherbakovo and Kuzminki," one man answered. "And this man," he pointed, "is Zakhar Stepanych Burdakov, our collective farm Party organizer."

"Really," Trofimov grinned. "So this is the man who sent you out to chase us?"

"Not just him," another man said. "It was all those commissioners from the district centre and elsewhere. The first one came about four months ago. He said five dangerous bandits had escaped from a camp. Then the chief of militia from the district centre arrived, and that day Zakhar Stepanych and Pyotr Timofeich, our manager, called a meeting. Zakhar Stepanych said that fifteen guys were needed from among us, and another fifteen from Kuzminki. He said that if we caught you, each of us would get a box of tobacco and ten bottles of vodka."

"Not a bad offer," Trofimov said. "And you agreed?"

"As if we donna know what would happen if we refused. Although … who would ever turn down tobacco?"

"Or vodka," another man chimed in. "There's never any of it in the village store, never."

"Is yours the only group or are there others?"

"I donna know about other villages," one man replied. "After all, there aren't many men left, after the war. I guess there are other groups from other places. But they're a long way away, more than seventy kilometres."

"How long have you been chasing us?"

"'Bout a month. We searched the woods around the villages, and kept watch on the cabins. This one especially. Zakhar Stepanych and Pyotr Timofeich were sure you'd make for here, 'cos it has a bath."

"Clever of them," Trofimov chuckled. "So you wanted to track us down and collect your Judas money? I'm asking you a question, you, damned idiots." he suddenly exploded. "For whose sake did you do it?"

"For our country," several voices answered. "And for the Soviet government."

"For our country. And for the Soviet government." Trofimov mocked. "Hasn't the Soviet government made mother Russia shed bloody tears for the last thirty years?" The captives hung their heads. "And what did any of you ever get from the Soviets? Slavery on a collective farm? Extortion? Labour camps? Terror?"

"Sure, chief. That's what we got," one man muttered. "But the state's always like that, ain't it?"

"So if that's what the state is like, why the fuck do you serve it so readily?"

"How d'you mean 'why'?" The man pointed at Burdakov. "What could we do? This guy, Zakhar Stepanych, came round to our houses and ordered us to pack our kits and go off to catch the bandits. That's what he said. He said they'd plundered whole villages and killed lots of folk."

"And you believed that?" Trofimov asked.

"How could we know?" another man retorted. "He said so." Then, pointing at various of his neighbours, "And he said that if I, or him, or him, refused to go we'd go straight to the camps ourselves. How could we know who you were?"

"I'll tell you who we are. We're honest soldiers, war veterans. I'm an infantry captain. I defended Moscow, I fought at Kursk, and I helped to liberate Warsaw and capture Berlin."

"Really?" The men stared at him.

"For that the Soviets rewarded me with a term in labour camp in Kolyma!" Trofimov unbuttoned his jacket and displayed the scars on his stomach from Razzhivin's torture. "Look what they did to me. Just look. That's the Soviet regime for you."

"But how could we know, for Christ's sake?" The first man pointed again at Burdakov. "He said you were bandits."

Trofimov heaved a sigh. "There aren't enough words in the

Russian language to curse you poor bastards." He paused. "And not enough tears to weep over you either."

A long pause followed.

"What are you gonna do to us, chief?" one man finally ventured.

"To you? Don't worry, we're not going to kill you. We don't need your blood. But we'll have a separate talk with your Party organizer."

"Me, comrade Captain? I'm not guilty of nothin'," he muttered.

"Not guilty, aren't you? Is that so?" Trofimov retorted. "Who gave the order to track us down?"

"The Executive Committee did. A captain from the security organs came and gave me directives."

"I see," said Trofimov and unfolded a map that they had found on Burdakov. "Show me all the places where you've set up to ambush us."

Burdakov's finger shook as he pointed out various locations.

"Here ... here ... and here ... all around the trappers' cabins."

Back up on the ground floor, Bondarenko and Timoshkin waited for Trofimov, smiling.

"Good news?"

"We found their sled," Bondarenko reported. "It was tied to a larch about a kilometre from here. And two reindeer. And cans and cans of meat and fish ... and plenty of tobacco too."

"Excellent," Trofimov exclaimed. "So, we've got one more sled and enough deer again."

"We've also got thirty guns," Goldberg said.

"We don't need that many," Trofimov said. "We'll throw most of them into an ice hole on a river. But we'll take the ammunition."

Trofimov told them about his meeting with the prisoners in the cellar and spread out the map.

"You're sure he ain't bullshitting you?" Bondarenko asked.

"Unlikely. He trembled with fear, the coward."

"What if he's lying like the boy?" said Bondarenko. "Maybe I'd better—"

"No."

"You're the boss." Bondarenko sighed.

"He also said this is the only unit within a hundred kilometres. Whatever happens from now on, we must avoid contact with anyone. We leave as soon as possible."

"But it ain't good to leave in clear weather," Yatta interrupted. "Whoever comes here later will see our tracks. Let's wait for the next snow."

"When will it snow again?"

"Soon though, in a couple of days," Yatta said.

"What are we gonna do with these bastards?" Bondarenko pointed towards the cellar.

"We must think about that," Trofimov said.

"You wanna let 'em go and rat on us?" Bondarenko said.

"We'll fix it so they don't get back too soon," Trofimov answered.

"But we can take away their skis," Yatta suggested. "Then it would take them more than a week to get back."

"Won't they starve to death?" Goldberg asked.

"They've got their canned food," Trofimov said.

"We'd do better to take those cans with us," Bondarenko objected.

Goldberg looked at him. "Do you want them to starve, Mikhail?"

"Why should I care?" Bondarenko snapped. "They were ready to turn us in. Why the hell should I care about them?"

"No, Mikhail," Trofimov said bitterly. "They're just a bunch of stupid shitheads who do what they're told without thinking. Apart from that, they're ordinary folk, hard working and oppressed by the Soviet regime." He paused. "We can't treat the entire populace as enemies."

"They are our enemies," Bondarenko protested.

"It's not their fault," insisted Trofimov. "They're poor folk, oppressed and downtrodden. If the people ever summon up the courage to rebel against this regime, it'll be them and others like them who do that. If we kill them, then everyone—villagers, trappers, fishermen—everyone will believe the authorities that we are bandits and enemies of the people. To leave them without skis and rifles will be enough to prevent anyone from tracking us down too quick."

"And what 'bout this fuckin' Party organizer? D'you want to

spare him too?" Bondarenko looked indignant.

"No. He deserves to die."

"Well, I'm glad we agree at least on one point." Bondarenko drew in a deep breath. "But as for the others, maybe you're right, we're not bloody butchers."

Goldberg listened to this exchange with keen attention.

"I don't agree. I don't think we should kill anyone."

"There you go, Yakov, the same old story," Bondarenko shot back.

"No arguing." Trofimov intervened. "As regards the Party organizer, we'll hold a trial and decide his fate by vote."

The improvised tribunal took place that evening. Goldberg brought Burdakov up from the cellar. The five members of their group sat on the bench while Burdakov was seated on the only chair.

"You are Zakhar Stepanovich Burdakov?" Trofimov began.

"Yes."

"Well, Burdakov, we've brought you here for trial."

"Yes, but, comrade Chief …"

"You organized this expedition?" Trofimov continued.

"Yes, with the help of Pyotr Timofeich Konechnikov, the collective farm manager."

"And who was the initiator?"

"None of us," Burdakov replied. "The directive came from the regional MGB administration."

"And you," Bondarenko put it, "enthusiastically took it on yourself to carry it out, didn't you?"

"You hoped for promotion as a result?" Trofimov added. "A nice warm place on the Regional Committee?"

"No, I mean …" Burdakov muttered.

"Answer the question." Trofimov ordered. "Did you hope for promotion? Yes, or no?"

"Hmm … no," muttered the defendant.

"Then why," Trofimov lowered his voice, "did you take this task upon yourself?

"Because … it was my duty."

"Did you realize what would happen to us if you succeeded?"

Trofimov asked.

"Yes, you … you would face a firing squad for … for banditry."

"Just a firing squad? Not something much worse?" Goldberg interposed.

"Yes. That's the only death penalty adopted in the Soviet Union."

"No, comrade Burdakov," Trofimov retorted, "it's not the only one. Don't you know that hanging was reintroduced in 1942. And in Kolyma, the authorities practise many different forms of vicious execution. We ourselves saw three guys crucified on trees for trying to escape from the camp."

Burdakov lowered his eyes.

"So, yes or no?" Bondarenko insisted. "Did you know about such things?"

Burdakov remained silent.

"You're not saying anythin'," Bondarenko grinned. "You knew what was going on. You hoped that we'd end up on the larches, and you on the Regional Committee, didn't you?"

"Let's hear what the witnesses have to say about this case," Trofimov suggested. "Timoshkin, bring them up."

Timoshkin went down to the cellar and let the captives up one by one.

"Over in that corner, and sit on the floor," Trofimov told the captives. He paused and waited for them to settle. "I brought you here as witnesses. Tell us how this man summoned you to take part in this expedition."

"Zakhar Stepanych and Pyotr Timofeich, the manager, went round from house to house and said this and that, and that there was a—what's the word?—a directive!" one man began. "There was this directive from the regional centre to track down these bandits. He said that you—your gang—have been on the run for several months, and that you've killed lots of people and raped womenfolk."

"I didn't wanna go," added another man. "I gotta fix the roof of my house. I told him so and said, 'Forgive me, Zakhar Stepanych, I gotta do it, or we'll freeze to death.' He got mad and yelled at me and threatened I'd be sent to the camps."

"Yeah," a third man supported him, "he told me the same about the camps. He promised that I'd freeze to death at one of their logging sites."

"That's what he told me too," said another.

"He told me they'd freeze me till I turned into an ice block."

"So, Burdakov," Trofimov concluded, "apparently you know plenty about the various methods of execution, even that people get frozen alive in the Gulag gold mines."

Burdakov avoided everyone's gaze.

"I was just doing my duty."

"Right, you fulfilled your duty to the Soviet regime. Therefore you lied to us, as you did to many others. And not for one minute did you believe in what you said. Nor did you believe the crap that you said about us, that we killed, tortured and raped dozens of people. Well," Trofimov concluded, "I think we get the picture. So what have you got to say in your defence, Burdakov?"

"It was my duty … as a Party member … as a good Soviet citizen … I …" Burdakov's voice became fainter and fainter until it finally died away.

"Okay, Timoshkin," Trofimov said, "take them back downstairs."

Timoshkin motioned to the captives.

"Your suggestions, please." Trofimov looked at his friends.

"I don't think we're entitled to try anyone, let alone sentence them," said Goldberg.

"Holy shit," Bondarenko exploded angrily. "And who is entitled? There's no other court of justice to try the likes of him."

"Yakov has the right to express his opinion," Trofimov answered. "And you, Mikhail, what punishment do you think Burdakov deserves?"

"What really can he deserve?" Bondarenko shrugged. "He deserves to be knocked off like the lousy cur he is. I wouldn't even shoot him. I'd rather hang him on a cedar tree, like we did with those Polizei collaborators."

"And you, Zakharych?" Trofimov turned to Timoshkin.

"He deserves to die. Like all of them Soviet commissioners and activists. They've sucked too much of our blood. God forgive me for such lack of mercy."

"And you, Yatta, what do you think?"

"You know, he's a mean and cowardly man, our worst enemy. He's gotta be finished off. What he deserves is to have his throat cut. That's the way our people deal with traitors, killers and child rapists."

"Well," Trofimov concluded, "everyone except one of you votes for the death sentence. It's my opinion too. An absolute majority is in favour of the death penalty. Timoshkin, bring him back up here."

"Well, Burdakov," Trofimov looked him straight in the eye. "The court has found you guilty of being a devoted henchman of a criminal regime, and responsible for the crimes of that regime. Therefore, we sentence you to death by shooting."

"But I … How's that? How can you?" Burdakov stammered.

"Quite easily," Bondarenko answered. "Just the way you and your Party did with thousands of other folk. And mark you, we ain't fascists. We won't torture you the way you and your sort do."

"You … you don't have the right." Burdakov exclaimed.

"We're outlaws," retorted Trofimov. "Soviet law doesn't apply to us."

"And in any case," Bondarenko added, "we've got nothing to lose. If we get caught, we're dead men anyway."

7

For the next few nights, Trofimov had two guards on duty, one outside and one inside the cabin to watch over the prisoners. He and Bondarenko took the first duty.

Walking slowly around the cabin in the sparse light of the moon, Trofimov listened to the silence of the winter night. He felt a sense of peace with himself and of profound satisfaction at the way he had managed the situation. Not for a moment did he doubt that the death sentence passed on Burdakov was fully justified. It was not the first time that he had condemned a man to die. There had been three other occasions during the war.

The first was in the summer of 1942, with two deserters from his unit. It was not he who passed the sentence, but the court martial. One of the deserters was a forty-year-old peasant man, the father of three children. The other was a boy of nineteen. The court martial sentenced them to death, and as usual the execution was carried out in front of the whole battalion. It was Trofimov's duty to choose the firing squad and oversee the execution. Although he was displeased that he, a combat officer, was forced to act as executioner, at the time he had no doubt that the sentence was just. Brought up with the idea that a man must be prepared to sacrifice his life for his country, he was genuinely outraged by those who wanted to hide behind other people's backs. He knew that in many cases men faced the firing squad for mere absence without leave. He had never supported that, and once confronted a SMERSH officer on one such case. But these men were real deserters. They had been found heading off back to their homes somewhere in the rear, and at the time he believed they deserved to die.

The second occasion was in the summer of 1944, in Byelorussia. It was during a raid behind enemy lines that he met Bondarenko. He had sent out his best soldiers on reconnaissance and to take hostages who might give information about enemy activity. The scouts successfully carried out their task and returned with two Polizei collaborators. These men were ready to disclose any information in exchange for their lives. After Trofimov had milked them of information, he was hesitant about what to do with them. As traitors they deserved to die, and he did not promise to spare their lives. He hoped to let them live at least until they were dealt with by a court martial. Unfortunately for them, the two men broke down and wept and pleaded for clemency. Their lack of courage outraged young captain Trofimov more than their treason. How could these goddamned traitors who had sent so many to their deaths beg for mercy? Full of rage, he took his pistol and with the words "There's no mercy for traitors," shot them both on the spot. Treason was treason, and what he did was not the worst thing that Russian soldiers did to collaborators.

Then, in 1945, after the capture of Berlin, he personally shot three Soviet soldiers caught raping a German woman. Here too he was confident that it was the right thing to do: rape and looting were a disgrace to the Soviet Army.

"Who's there?" Trofimov peered at an obscure figure emerging from the cabin.

"It's me, Sasha." He recognized Goldberg's voice.

"You, Yakov? Why aren't you asleep?"

"Oh, I've got some sort of insomnia."

Trofimov shrugged.

"I've got to talk to you, Sasha," said Goldberg.

"I can guess what it's about," replied Trofimov. "But why not talk in the morning?"

"No. Then I won't be able to talk to you alone."

"Well, as you wish. Want a cig?"

"Yeah, thanks."

Trofimov rolled two shag cigars and handed one to Goldberg.

"About this Party organizer," Goldberg began. "I don't know how to start, but I think we're taking too much on ourselves sentencing him to death."

"You think we should spare the bastard?"

"Call him whatever you like, but we don't have the legal or moral right to take his life."

"C'mon," said Trofimov, "you mean that only they have the right to shoot and freeze and beat men to death? Do only they have the right to kill?"

"No, they don't have that right either," said Goldberg.

"But they do it, and they'll carry on doing it as long as they're in power. They don't give a damn what Yakov Goldberg or Alexander Trofimov thinks about it. So why should we have mercy on them?"

"If we do the same things to them as they do to us, then what's the difference between us and them?" Goldberg insisted.

"The same things? Oh, no, we don't do the same things at all." Trofimov retorted. "We don't freeze and we don't crucify people. We aren't killing every other man among them, only those responsible for their crimes, like Burdakov."

"To begin with, we're not legally entitled to sentence anyone to death," Goldberg stated. "We're not a state, and we're not a court. If everyone went around thinking he was entitled to kill, what would happen then?"

"Legally entitled? What legality are you talking about in the Soviet Union? There's been no legality here for thirty years. Sentences passed by the secret police, three-man courts and special boards? You call that legality? Did they care about legality when they tied those three fugitives to the larches? The only legality here is the decisions of that bunch of bastards in power."

"Right. But that doesn't entitle us to take the law into our own hands."

"If we spare all the Burdakovs of this world," Trofimov snapped back, "they'll go on with their crimes."

"Well, first of all, this Burdakov isn't an actual executioner, he's just an ordinary low level Party functionary. He's hardly responsible personally for what happened to us or other people."

"Not responsible? All his life he was a devoted lackey of the Party and government. He carried out every order his bosses gave him, to dispossess and exile a quarter of his fellow villagers, draw up a black list for the next round of purges, or watch out for anyone discontented with Soviet rule, with production quotas, or with their meager wages. He didn't care what happened to these people, whether they got killed or rotted in the camps."

"But those were his routine responsibilities," Goldberg patiently insisted. "If he hadn't followed instructions, he'd have been purged himself."

"Oh, so he did all that against his will?"

"We don't know that."

"Don't know? *I* know. He did it willingly and with enthusiasm or he'd never have become Party organizer on a collective farm. The same applies to his attempts to find us. He hoped to catch us and get promoted to a higher position in the Regional Committee. And he would do the same to anyone. How can we spare him?"

"Then we have to kill all the captives," Goldberg stressed. "They all chased us, and also every local. They were all willing to track us down in return for tobacco and vodka."

"Okay, Yakov, what is it you want to tell me?" Trofimov's voice now showed irritation. "That these poor stultified people are as guilty as those who gave them their orders, and therefore everyone is guilty? But since we can't kill everyone, let's kill no one! And therefore, in your eyes, no one is responsible? Thousands and thousands are being slaughtered, and who's going to answer for these crimes?"

"You talk just like Mikhail, Sasha."

"What have you got against Mikhail?" Trofimov was on the point of losing his temper. "Whoever he is, we'd never manage our escape without him. It's unfair of you to owe your life to him and at the same time think of him as evil. Just think that one over."

"I don't think he's evil," Goldberg objected. "But you and he concentrate on revenge, and you don't see anything beyond that."

"Well, I'm no saint," said Trofimov. "I'm a soldier. That's what I am, and that's what I'll be to my dying day."

"So am I. So is each of us."

"Right, but you seem to want to play the role of an early Christian saint. You want to spare this bastard so he can go back and organize yet another team to come and chase us." Trofimov looked at his watch. "Anyway, go and get some sleep, Yakov."

"Is that your final word?"

"Yes, it's my final word. Go and sleep. That's an order."

Goldberg lay and pondered his conversation with Trofimov. He did not feel too disappointed. He never really expected to persuade Trofimov. Sasha was an exceptionally noble man, and Goldberg owed so much to him, but he was a product of that culture which glorified the killing of enemies, whether by fighting or execution. At first Sasha Trofimov had done that to the enemies of the Soviet state. Now that the state had turned against him, he was willing to slay Communists and other pillars of the system. He was something like a modern-day Bar-Kokhba, and was merciless towards his enemies. What could one expect from someone who learned to kill before he was twenty? His whole generation was, and would remain, like that.

Goldberg sighed. For a moment he felt a kind of relief. After all, he had done what he could to save that bastard Burdakov. Frankly, the guy was lucky that it was Sasha Trofimov who decided his fate. Bondarenko would probably have burned the man alive. So he, Yakov Goldberg, had done everything he could to prevent this killing, and he could do no more.

On the other hand—a thought flashed through his mind. He would be on guard in three hours' time, and if he happened to be guarding the captives in the log house, he could maybe open the hatch and set the wretched Burdakov free. The moment he thought of this, he became obsessed with the idea, and felt an impulse deep inside him to carry out his idea. But if he did, or even attempted it, would his conscience be clear? The consequences would be disastrous for himself. He could imagine how outraged Mikhail would be. And Sasha too, although Sasha would probably try and shield him from Bondarenko's rage, and maybe that of Timoshkin and Yatta too. Of course they would not kill him. Sasha would not allow that.

But if he did let him escape, Burdakov would organize a new sortie against them. No doubt that would be his idea of gratitude, and then they might all perish. He, Yakov Goldberg, would be responsible for the deaths of his comrades, and the latter, whatever their faults, were truly devoted to him and to one another. No, he could never do that.

Two hours later, when Goldberg began his watch duty inside the cabin, he looked at the hatch, which was weighted down with two heavy logs, and realized that all his plans were senseless: he could never have managed to remove those heavy logs silently on his own.

8

After breakfast, Trofimov ordered Bondarenko to bring Burdakov up from the cellar.

"Now, Burdakov," Trofimov announced, "your sentence will be carried out. Take him away, Mikhail."

"But I … don't … you have no right."

"C'mon, man." Bondarenko grinned. "You wanted to rise up to the level of the District Committee. We're gonna help you rise up even higher." He grabbed Burdakov by the elbow and led him outside. The other four followed them.

"Come on, now, comrade Party organizer," jeered Bondarenko. "Donna be such a coward."

Burdakov broke free of Bondarenko's grip and ran for it. Bondarenko caught up with him and marched him off among the trees. The four others stood waiting. Finally the stillness of the morning forest was broken by a shot.

Goldberg heaved a sigh. Yet another victim in the never-ending cycle of bloodshed. Descendants of Esau, they remained true to Esau's ways, though maybe this had little to do with Esau himself.

It was simply that, like most people, they could not resist the temptation to retaliate when they had been wronged.

Bondarenko emerged from among the trees with a smile of satisfaction on his lips.

"Well, that's that scumbag dealt with."

"I hope you didn't—" Trofimov looked him in the eye.

"God bless us, Captain. Nothing of the sort, for Chrissake. I just shot him in the head. But d'you know what? The bastard tried pleading with me to escape with him."

"The idiot."

"No shit. He told me that if I spared him, I'd be sure to get a pardon from the authorities."

"And you refused?" Trofimov teased. "I thought you'd have jumped at the opportunity." Both of them burst out laughing.

"It's not good to laugh over a man's death," Goldberg scolded.

"So you think, Yakov," Bondarenko grinned, "we should grieve? Well, I'm glad to have had a chance to finish off at least one of those bastards. They ruined my life, and I don't want to croak without having my revenge on them. It occurred to me to whack our unit's Godfather back in my partisan days, but I didn't do it. So he had me sent to the camps instead."

"Well, folks, your Party organizer has been convicted and executed," Trofimov announced to the other prisoners as he stepped down into the cellar.

"So he bought it at last, the bastard," one of them muttered.

"Does that mean, comrade Captain, that—" an elderly peasant began.

"No. We're not going to shoot you," Trofimov interrupted him. "My word of honour. No more killing."

"Then what are you gonna do with us?"

"That's what I want to tell you. In a day or two, we're leaving. After that you'll be free."

There were exclamations of surprise and disbelief.

"But," Trofimov added, "we're going to break your skis and take your sled and both reindeer. There are plenty of tools here, an axe and a saw, so you can make new ones if you want. I suppose there are some carpenters among you. We'll leave you your canned food as well."

"You're really gonna leave us the cans?" one man asked.

"Sure," Trofimov confirmed. "You don't think we'd leave you to starve to death, do you? And you'll have your knives, though not your guns, of course."

"Thank you, comrade Chief!"

"The moment we leave you'll be free."

"For Chrissake," several men pleaded, "forgive us for being such stupid fuckheads. We didn't know what we were doing. We listened to the manager and the Party organizer, and they said you were bandits. So we thought—"

"I know." Trofimov nodded. "And we don't hold any grudge against you. We know you're under the heel of the authorities. And we've shot the Party organizer, the one we regard as guilty."

"The bastard deserved it," one man exclaimed. "He had no pity on no one. He'd have ratted on us and said that we betrayed him."

"That's another thing to talk about," Trofimov observed. "When the authorities question you, don't ever tell them that you surrendered, or they'll send you to the camps. You've got to invent something. Say you were caught in a squall of machine gun fire, and that the Party organizer and others were killed on the spot. You had no choice but to lie on your stomachs until we retreated."

"Okay, we ain't that simple, Chief. We'll know what to say."

That same day, the captives' skis were burned. They would have to stay for at least another week to make new ones before they could begin their trip back home. By that time the fugitives would be far away, with no tracks left behind because of the snowfall.

In two days, when the expected snowfall began, the five men were on their way.

9

A few weeks later the travelers approached the Gydan mountain range. So far these were the highest and steepest mountains they would have to negotiate. They began the ascent toward the pass. The slope was steep and scattered with rocks and boulders. The reindeer struggled with the sleds, and the men helped the animals, pushing from behind. Progress was slow and exhausting. They made stops each hour and sometimes took longer rests. Exhausted, the men lost all sense of time. To complete their torments, a severe wind blew directly in their faces, threatening to overturn the sleds and cause them to lose their footing.

When it was dark and further progress nearly impossible, they saw the entrance to a cave. They spent the last remnants of their energy unharnessing the reindeer and starting a fire with brushwood they had brought from the foothills. After that, they collapsed onto their deerskins and within seconds fell asleep. That night, contrary to their rule, nobody stood guard.

By early the following afternoon, they stood at the top of the pass. The downward slope before them looked just as steep as yesterday's ascent.

"We'll break our necks." Trofimov seemed shocked at the sight before them.

"Where have you brought us, Yatta?" Even Bondarenko looked terrified. "How are we gonna get down that?"

"But you know, it ain't no problem. We can do it." Yatta seemed quite unperturbed.

"You're kidding, for Christ's sake." Trofimov scoffed.

"Oh donna worry, there's a special way to go down slopes like this," Yatta explained. His comrades stared at him. "We'll tie the sleds together and harness the reindeer to them from the rear. It's a common way to do it among our people."

Following Yatta's directions, the men lashed the sleds together side by side, then harnessed up the reindeer from behind.

"Will this one cope with the job?" Timoshkin pointed to the wild buck.

"Oh, sure he will. Otherwise he'll get smashed over the rocks," Yatta replied.

"Where do we go?" Bondarenko asked.

"We go on either side of the sled," Yatta explained. "Hold on firmly or you could get smashed against the rocks as well."

They lashed down all their property onto the sleds, even the guns.

"I hope no one attacks us now," Bondarenko commented. "That would be the fuckin' end of us."

Yatta yelled at the reindeer and gave the one on the right a flick of his whip.

The descent got steeper and the wind more savage. The loaded sleds skidded, shaking violently over the stony patches. It took the men enormous effort to cling to the ribs of the frame.

"Cheer up!" Trofimov shouted, trying to raise their spirits, but no one could hear him in the roaring whirl of wind and snow.

As they passed over a boulder Timoshkin was thrown to one side. He was on the point of tumbling downhill and being crushed by the sled train. Yatta snatched up his lasso and scooped him up with a quick flick, then hauled him to safety.

"Grab the sled!" yelled Yatta.

Timoshkin grabbed a rib of the fast moving sled, and their crazy descent continued.

"Well, Yatta's the hero of the day," said Trofimov that evening, in the foothills. "None of us would ever have negotiated that goddamned slope."

"Oh, it was no big thing." Yatta looked embarrassed. "I've managed things like that many times."

"Well, you saved my life." Timoshkin looked at Yatta with gratitude.

"I nearly lost my grip," said Goldberg. "I was sure it was the end of me."

"Me too," Bondarenko admitted. "I've had many things happen to me before, but nothing quite like that."

"Well, there's another baptism for us." Trofimov smiled. "Fire, blood, labour camp and now rocks."

"You're kinda right there," Bondarenko chuckled. "I wonder how many more passes we'll have to cross like that?"

"Well, we won't get no more so rough as that until we get close to the sea," said Yatta.

"If only we make it there alive," Timoshkin commented.

Their conversation was interrupted by a piercing shriek. One of the deer was down on its knees and bleeding, with a lynx on its back. Bondarenko grabbed his Kalashnikov, fired, and the cat fell dead in the snow. The deer had a gaping wound in its neck.

"Damn. Shit." Bondarenko exploded.

Timoshkin ran to the injured deer.

"Maybe he's still … I mean, can we save him?"

Yatta examined the wound.

"No, we can't, you know. His neck's bitten through, and the neck bone is damaged. All we can do is kill him." He paused. "We can make a sacrifice, and kill him with all the proper ceremonies. We've gotta thank the Master of Gydan for a safe passage. Otherwise he'll be upset and ask the Creator and the Lord of the Woods to punish us."

"Oh, yeah, I remember. Well, the poor thing's gonna die anyway. Let's make this sacrifice."

"Make a big fire, and I'll do the rest," said Yatta.

The fire blazed, and Yatta sharpened his knife on a boulder, sing-songing in his native language. When he had finished, he approached the wounded deer, grabbed him by the antlers, and quickly plunged the knife into his heart. The animal stopped moaning, and fell dead on its right side.

"Just like our kosher slaughtering," Goldberg observed.

Yatta produced a leather bag and gathered the pouring blood into it. Then he walked around, sprinkling drops of blood here and there. Finally he walked to the fire and poured a small dash of blood into it.

"Now we can cut and carve the carcass," Yatta announced.

Yatta cut off the head and laid it on the snow facing east. Then he carved flesh from various parts of the carcass and threw them into the fire. The others helped, and when they had completed this, they sat around the fire.

"Now, at last, we've made a real sacrifice," said Yatta with satisfaction.

"And lost one deer," added Bondarenko. "Lucky it ain't the only one or we'd have to carry everything ourselves. God knows when we'd get to the sea then. What month is it now?

"I don't remember," Trofimov shrugged. "The New Year's long past at least."

"Now is the end of Chachanlorgin, the second month," said Yatta.

"February," concluded Trofimov. "I don't think we can reach the

Strait earlier than June. By that time the ice cover will be gone. When does the Strait clear of ice, Yatta?"

"Around the middle of the third month," Yatta replied.

"And when do they ice up again?"

"Not till the end of the tenth month."

"We'll have to stop for the summer and set out again in the fall," Trofimov said.

"You know, we would do well to stay with my Qergina. She would be of great help," Yatta said.

10

The following month they reached the Anadyr woodlands and crossed several frozen tributaries of the Anadyr River. Soon they reached a small, hardly noticeable creek, and on seeing it Yatta gave a cry of joy and pranced around in his heavy winter clothing.

"Is this it?" Trofimov turned to him.

"Yeah. You know, this is the Kyele Creek. My Qergina lives half a dozen kilometres downstream."

"Can we get there by early evening?"

"Yeah, no problem. And we're gonna have a good long rest at last."

For months they had heard this woman's name, and in their hearts she had become a symbol of womanhood, comfort and hospitality. This mysterious woman was also to become the first true friend they were to meet on their journey.

"Maybe she's no longer there," said Bondarenko.

"No longer there?" Trofimov's eyes grew wide.

"She could have moved somewhere else, or been arrested. Some locals could have ratted on her and—"

"No." Yatta objected. "This is Chukchi territory, and Chukchi never rat."

"Who the hell knows?" retorted Bondarenko. "That was probably so years ago. Under Soviet rule many good people have turned rotten."

"Not everyone though," Goldberg disagreed. "And the natives

remain true to their customs."

"Maybe they do. But the MGB could get the poor woman anyway."

"Well, Mikhail, let's hope that she's okay, and still there."

"Yeah, Captain, let's hope," Bondarenko agreed. "And let's hope they don't know about her link with Yatta, or they could ambush us there."

"Oh no, I don't believe that," Yatta objected. "She meets only Chukchi people, and they are not traitors."

"Hell, how I hope you're right." Bondarenko sighed.

"But you know, there is another thing," Yatta went on. "I'm not sure that she's gonna welcome me. We had a terrible quarrel before I left."

Bondarenko became suspicious again. "Then she may not even let us in the house."

"No no," Yatta protested. "She'll let us stay one night anyway. The laws of hospitality, you know, are sacred among our people. But, I do hope she forgave me."

"Anyway," Trofimov changed the topic, "we'll stop here for the night. Someone should go on ahead and reconnoiter to make sure there's no ambush. Mikhail, what about you?"

"Sure, Captain."

"But, I'm going too," said Yatta. "I have to. Mikhail ain't know the area."

"Donna worry, Yatta," Bondarenko said with a grin. "I explored at least a couple of dozen new places in my partisan years, and I was smart enough, or I wouldn't be alive to tell the tale."

"But," Yatta insisted, "there are really some things around here that you donna know about. There's a gorge hidden under some rocks. You could miss it."

"It's a good idea that you go together," Trofimov intervened. "You'll make a good team."

It took Yatta and Bondarenko more than two hours to reach the spot. To their immense joy, the big tent was there, smoke rising from the vent hole. Beside it were several smaller tents. Everything indicated the place was inhabited. Bondarenko and Yatta explored the groves and thickets in the neighbourhood. They found no sign of ambush.

"You know, we've gotta see her before we go back for the guys," Yatta said. "I'll tell her there are five of us, and that we're outlaws. She can decide whether she's willing to host us, but she should know in advance."

"Okay, Yatta. Let's go."

"But I do feel uneasy, though," Yatta confessed. "We had such a bitter quarrel."

"Donna fear. Whatever happened was long ago. Now we're asking for her hospitality. You go ahead, and I'll stay on guard, just in case."

Yatta's heart was in the pit of his stomach as he moved towards the tent. What would she say? He hoped she wouldn't throw him out without even speaking. Two dogs rushed out of the tent, barking loudly. A woman's voice called them back and stopped them. The voice was hers. A woman with a rifle over her shoulder emerged from the tent. Yatta took a few steps forward.

"Yetti?" whispered the woman.

"Ii," Yatta replied.

"Yatta?"

"Yeah, it's me, Qergina."

The woman rushed towards him, and the next instant they were locked in a tight embrace. Bondarenko walked towards them.

"My pal, Mikhail." Yatta nodded towards Bondarenko.

"Hullo, Mikhail." Her Russian was as good as Yatta's but with a stronger accent. "Wait a moment. I'll bring you the snow beater."

She stepped inside the tent and returned with an engraved ivory snow beater and stood beside the men while they cleaned their fur coats.

Qergina was a tall, stately woman, middle-aged, with a beautiful bronze face and expressive narrow eyes. Her deerskin coat was covered in intricate embroidery, and her straight black hair was covered by a fur hood.

"Oh, Yatta, is it really you? Or is it a ghost?" she reverted to their native Chukchi.

"It's me. Body and soul intact and together. But I've come straight from the Land of Darkness. I've escaped from the hands of the evil demons that serve the Big Moustache. We escaped from the camp, one of those that Big Moustache's underlings have in the mining lands around Kolyma. We escaped, me and my four friends. Mikhail's one of them."

"Welcome to my yaranga," Qergina invited them in and smiled at Bondarenko. "I'll give you supper, and then you can spend the night here."

"What's she saying, Yatta?" Bondarenko asked.

"You know, she's inviting us for supper and to spend the night."

"Good evening, hostess," Bondarenko bowed to her. "Thank you for your hospitality."

"Good evening, good man. I'm glad to have you as a guest," Qergina replied.

Inside the tent it was warm, and a bright fire burned in the stone hearth in the centre. The tent was large and comfortable. Kettles and other kitchen utensils hung from nails sticking from the wooden support poles. The floor was covered with reindeer skins. Small stools made from reindeer antlers stood in the corners, some with wooden figurines on them. A large drum with drumsticks leaned against the wall.

"I have some reindeer meat to feed you now," said Qergina. "But tomorrow I'll kill a fresh reindeer."

"Thank you," Yatta smiled. "But can the other three come as well?"

"Yes, a guest in the house always brings joy."

"So she's willing to receive us?" Trofimov asked Yatta.

"Yeah, she's expecting us."

"She seems a good woman, Captain," Bondarenko added. "Quite trustworthy."

"Then let's go there now," Trofimov suggested.

11

The five men sat around the blazing hearth where Qergina cooked the reindeer meat.

"Everything will be ready, you know, in just a short while," said Qergina.

"Thank you. Thank you so much." Trofimov smiled.

Qergina smiled back. "I'm always happy to receive good guests."

Trofimov sighed and said with some hesitation, "Thank you again. Although I'm not sure that we can bring you much joy. Yatta told you that we're on the run from a labour camp. We're being pursued, and anyone who helps us may be sent to the camp too. Anyone who reports on us and turns us in will get a reward of tobacco and vodka. Maybe you'd rather have us leave straight after this meal, so you don't take such a risk?"

Qergina's face clouded over.

"And what did I do, young man, to deserve such an insult?"

"I'm sorry. Excuse me, please." Trofimov apologized. "I didn't mean to insult you. God forbid. I was thinking of your safety."

"Don't worry about that," Qergina assured him. "I know what I'm doing, really I do. For our people, guests are sacred and are always, always welcome at any time, day or night. Especially those who suffered from the Big Moustache and his henchmen. May the Creator and the Good Spirits some day destroy them. Whoever is an enemy of the Big Moustache is my friend, if only for that reason."

She took the kettle with the cooked meat and served the food in two large bowls that she placed before them.

"Sit with us, please." Trofimov invited her.

"With pleasure." Qergina sat on the deerskin beside the men and continued: "Anyone who suffered at the hands of the Big Moustache's men is a very welcome guest in my yaranga. I hate the Big Moustache. His henchmen killed my father and my mother."

"Why did they do that?" asked Goldberg.

"My father, Ranawkurgin, was a great shaman, one of the greatest in Chukotka. But when the Big Moustache's men set up the collective farms and took away the herds from honest reindeer folk, they slaughtered all the shamans and elders, and many other respectable men and women."

"I'm sorry to have asked you that," said Goldberg. "It must be painful to talk about it."

"Never mind. It happened. But it was the work of the Evil Spirits. People should know the truth, because the Big Moustache's people claim that they made us Chukchi folk free and happy."

"Well, we're all too familiar with their freedom and happiness," Trofimov replied. "Well, hostess, let's drink to the peace of your poor parents' souls." He raised his cup.

"God bless them." Timoshkin crossed himself.

"May they rest in peace," Bondarenko added.

"Amen," said Goldberg.

All six drank down a draught of the hard liquor.

"We aren't going to stay for too long," Trofimov emphasized. "Just to have a rest, get another pack reindeer, and have a bath."

"I promise you, you shall have all that." Qergina laughed.

They spent that night in Qergina's tent: Trofimov, Bondarenko, Goldberg and Timoshkin in one corner, and Yatta and Qergina together on the opposite side. For the first time in almost half a year they slept peacefully, and Qergina's dogs were perfect guards.

"And could you tell me when you plan to move on," Qergina said next morning over breakfast.

"We're not sure," Trofimov replied. "How long would it take to get to the Bering Strait?"

"Three or four months, maybe five. So you won't be there before the sixth month. But then the rivers are free of ice. You'll have to try next winter, when the sea ices over again. Until then, you know, this is the best place for you. Two hundred kilometres to the east the tundra begins. It will be hard not to get caught there. But here it's safe, and you can make preparations for your winter journey through the tundra."

"Why couldn't we leave in July or August?" Trofimov asked. "We could get to the Strait by December when it's iced over."

"But in summer it's difficult to cross the rivers, "Yatta said." And their tracker dogs can trail us."

"Yatta is right," Qergina agreed. "In winter there are frequent blizzards, and your tracks won't stay for long. It will be difficult for them to pursue you, because there's hardly any light in winter."

"Looks like you're right, hostess," Bondarenko said.

"And besides," Qergina continued, "you'll need a lot of dried meat for your trip across the tundra. There's not much game out there, lots of blizzards and no light."

"With that much food, we'll need more reindeer and sleds," said Timoshkin, practical as usual.

"I can arrange that for you. You only need to trap enough foxes and wolverines. One pack reindeer can be bought for five good skins."

"So what do you think, guys? Should we stay here for the summer?" asked Yatta.

"What else can we do?" sighed Trofimov.

"I'd rather get to America as quick as possible," Timoshkin said.

"Donna you hear what our hostess said, Zakharych?" Bondarenko asked. "D'you want to get caught?"

Timoshkin shook his head.

"Where are we to live all this time?" asked Trofimov, already making plans. "We can't abuse Qergina's hospitality for months on end."

"I'd be happy to have you here," Qergina said, "but it's not safe. Local people come to me with their ailments, or wanting me to tell their fortunes. It's better if you camp somewhere deeper in the woods. We can visit one another. Stay here for a couple of days and get some rest. Then we'll go to a spot where you can spend the summer."

"Thank you," said Trofimov. "That sounds the best arrangement."

"Yatta said you tell fortunes and cure ailments," Goldberg changed the subject. "Are you a shaman then?"

"Not quite," Qergina smiled. "My father taught me his skills, but he was killed before he passed on all his knowledge to me. I was never properly invested as a shaman, but I know quite a bit."

"Oh, you're too modest, Qergina. You really know your craft," Yatta maintained, looking at his friends. "It's she who made me into a medicine man."

"That means, Qergina, that you saved my life." Trofimov nodded in Yatta's direction. "He saved me in the camp."

"I'm glad to hear that," Qergina smiled warmly. "My people keep saying the same thing."

"Is it your main occupation?" Goldberg asked.

"Yes. The Big Moustache banned all the shamans, but the folk need someone to care for them. The hospital is far, far away and overcrowded, and they don't have enough drugs. Without me, many would die."

"And no one has betrayed you?" Bondarenko asked.

"No," said Qergina. "Chukchi are honest folk. And they need me. They swore by the souls of their ancestors not to betray me, and I vowed not to abandon them. I've been here for twenty years."

"Hell," Bondarenko exclaimed, "the Chukchi really are terrific folk, to preserve their honesty so long, despite all this goddamned Soviet filth."

In the evening, Qergina treated them to a hot bath, and the following morning they set off into the woods. Qergina gave them two of her own harness reindeer. With two reindeer to haul one sled, they did not have to stop so often to rest the animals.

"But you know," said Qergina during one of their pauses, "there are many things you've got to do."

"Like what?" Trofimov asked.

"You can't cross the tundra in winter without special coats," she said. "You'll freeze to death."

"Really?" Trofimov was shocked. "Is it that much colder out there?"

"It's not the cold. It's the wind. You can survive only in good reindeer skin overcoats."

"Where can we get clothes like that?" Trofimov asked.

"I'll get them for you in exchange for pelts, as well as sleds and reindeer," she promised.

"Well, we can trap lots of foxes—we have the time for it," Trofimov agreed.

"And, by the way, you'll need new poles for your yaranga too," she added. "The ones you have are no good for tundra blizzards."

By afternoon they had reached a small expanse of water called Otter Lake. This was where they would camp.

"For the time being, you know, you have everything you need," said Qergina. One reindeer will feed you for a couple of months. The hunting is good here, so you'll be provided for the rest of the time." She paused with a worried expression on her face. "And, I must also get some snow goggles for you. Oh dear, oh dear. You'll need them in the early spring when the sun blazes and the snow is still on the ground. You can get blinded looking at the snow then."

The men recollected the early days of spring back in the camp. In early April it still looked like winter. The snow lay everywhere and showed no sign of melting, but the sun was very bright, and the combination of snow and bright sun created an incredible kaleidoscope of colours—yellow, red, blue and violet. Many of the convicts became quite enchanted by this gorgeous display, so unusual in their dull grey lives. But woe betide anyone who admired this spectacle for too long. They ended up with inflamed eyes, and many were blinded. Goldberg and Timoshkin were warned by Bondarenko and Vaskov about this danger, and they tried their best not to look at the blazing snow. Even so, for a long time they suffered from sore eyes.

"Do these snow goggles have holes to look through?" Timoshkin asked.

"Yeah, for sure!" Yatta laughed. "They have slits, very narrow ones, but you can see through them."

"I'll bring some for you before the spring," Qergina promised. "And by the end of summer I'll make good winter garments for you. In such clothes, you know, you'll not freeze to death in the tundra."

Yatta had completed his spell of night watch duty. He beat the snow off his overcoat and entered the tent. His four comrades were asleep in one corner, and Qergina in the other. There she lay, the woman of his desire and mother of his child. How could it happen that they had that stupid quarrel and broke up all those years ago, after their son died? He walked over to the sleeping woman and looked at her face, so calm and beautiful.

"Qergina, my love," he whispered and stroked her cheek.

"Yatta?" she looked at him and threw back the reindeer skin under which she slept. She wore only a narrow loincloth, and her body was firm and stately, quite untouched by age.

"It's me, my love," he said. "I want to be together with you again. I hope … I hope you've forgiven me."

"Well," she smiled, "that was so long ago. And you know … we were both so stupid."

"How did you live here without me?" he asked in a whisper.

Qergina shrugged. "Just as before, except that I didn't have a man with me."

"Not one?"

"No. I just couldn't get close to anyone. The men from the collective farms are dreadful. And not a single fugitive appeared like you. And you? Did you have other women?"

"Not many. Occasionally some friends would offer me their daughter or other woman relative for the night, but that was all. In the camps there were no women."

"And otherwise? How did you live?"

"I wandered all over the land up to the Omolon River. I hunted, trapped and bartered pelts for ammunition, but they caught me. I guess that Mikhey, a trapper, betrayed me. I was sent to the camp, and I met these guys there. And we ran away."

"And now here you are, safe and sound." Her face shone in a smile. She stretched her arms out to him and embraced him gently. Pulling his head closer, she stroked her cheek against his. Yatta embraced her with all his strength and passion.

O Creator of us all, how I missed her. Thank you for your great mercy in giving her back to me. Yatta took off his clothes and pulled the loincloth from her thighs, and they fell on the reindeer skin in a whirlpool of bliss.

12

Qergina sat by her hearth with four young girls by her side. They came from the local collective farm a few dozen kilometres away, where reindeer were bred. There was a tight bond of mutual assistance between Qergina and the people there. Year after year they came to her for treatment for their ailments, assistance in giving birth or for advice. Despite the Soviet authorities' strict ban on shamanism and the people's fear of reprisals, they preferred Qergina to the hospital in the district centre. She never broke their trust. Now these girls had come for advice and medications for their sick relatives.

"You know, Raulena," Qergina said, "I think I can kick out the demons of disease from your uncle."

"Thank you so much, aunt Qergina."

"But as for Narginau, Notatvaal's mother," Qergina continued, "her case isn't that easy. The spirits that seized her body are strong, and there are many of them. Even I am powerless." The second girl burst into tears, and Qergina stroked her head.

"What can one do, my dear? Life is like that. Sometimes the body gets too weak, and it can't contain our soul any more, and the spirits of disease seize hold of it. But, you know, once the soul goes beyond the clouds, to the Realm of the Deceased, there it discovers its final rest and remains in a state of bliss." She paused. "Don't weep. I shall try the very best of my medicine, and I won't surrender to those demons. I'll struggle to the last."

"Thank you. Thank you, aunt Qergina." The girl wiped away her tears.

Qergina looked at her, full of sympathy. "And you know, I solemnly swear to you people, by the Creator and all the Merciful Beings, that I won't ever abandon you, if only you promise not to hand me over to the Soviets. But tell me, how are they treating patients in the district hospital? Any better than before?"

"I don't think so," replied the first girl. "But how can we get there anyway? It's almost fifty kilometres away, and it's always overcrowded. You can go all the way there, and then they'll tell you there are no beds free. You have to wait. But there are not many places to stay and wait. Mainly Russians live there, and they don't know anything about hospitality. They don't invite you to stay with them."

Qergina gave a sigh.

"Yeah, I remember all their damned talk about a new and better life, and for the sake of that better life they killed all the shamans and took away the herds from honest reindeer farmers. How much blood was shed for the sake of that better life, how much!" She paused. "But you know, all these are the woes of the past. Life goes on. You're young and you want to live, don't you, girls? It's time to think about finding men for you."

"We'd love that, aunty," one of the girls answered. "But you know, there aren't any men for us."

Qergina sighed again. She knew the perennial problems of her people. Practically all the men from the nearby settlement had been drafted during the war years. First the older men were called up. The younger ones, the girls' contemporaries, had been drafted during the last two years. Even those who were barely of age at the end of the war were enlisted and sent to the Japanese front. Only a couple of dozen men remained, and all but maybe two of them were crippled or sick, hardly capable of giving a woman a child.

"Yes, I know," she said. "But can you not find some younger boys who didn't go to the war?"

"Don't you know, aunt Qergina?" the third girl spoke up. "The young ones have all gone too, to construction sites or factories. In the cities there are too many local women."

"Yes," Qergina shook her head, "it's the same sad story all around. And one can't go anywhere without a goddamned passport."

Suddenly the dogs began to bark.

"Someone is here. I'll see who it is." Qergina put on her overcoat and went outside. Trofimov, Bondarenko and Yatta stood under the birch tree.

"Good day, Qergina." Yatta greeted her.

"Good day, hostess." Trofimov and Bondarenko bowed towards her.

"Good day," Qergina answered in a low voice. "I'm sorry, but I have visitors, girls from the neighbourhood. It would be better for you to go now and come later, towards the evening."

"All right, Qergina, then we'll see you in the evening," said Trofimov.

Inside the tent, the girls peered from the entrance and watched.

"Look, girls, men," exclaimed the first girl.

"How big and strong they are!" whispered the second. "One of them is a Chukchi, the others are Russians."

"Looks like they're geologists or something," the third girl said.

"Hmm, but why do they carry Kalashnikovs?" the first girl said in surprise. "I never saw geologists with guns."

"Maybe because there are lots of bandits around," the fourth girl guessed.

"Anyway," the first girl continued, "I don't care who they are, I'd sure like to sleep with one of them and have a kid."

"So would I," said the second. "I'm twenty-three already. Am I meant to stay here like a blossom in the wilderness forever?"

"But I'm almost twenty-five," the first girl exclaimed. "Old age isn't far away. You know, girls, I'd give up half my life just to sleep with one of those men."

"So would I," the third girl added. "Just look at them. Real men, not like our feeble youngsters."

"What's this? Spying on me, are you, you little bitches!" Qergina appeared at the rear of the tent.

"Get out of my yaranga," Qergina ordered. "Out! And never come back again, or I'll set my Spirits against you."

"Forgive us, aunt Qergina. Please, forgive us," the first girl pleaded with tears in her eyes.

"I swear by our guardian spirits, we looked only because we heard men's voices." The second girl tried to explain their misbehaviour.

"How could you dare?" Qergina gradually calmed down. "How can I trust you now? How can I know you aren't spying for the district commissioner?"

"Can't you believe us, aunty? We're good, decent reindeer girls. Do you know anyone among the reindeer folk who would work for the Soviet commissioners?" The first girl pleaded. "Please, forgive us, aunt Qergina. Punish us if you want to, but don't send us away." She fell on her knees, weeping bitterly, and the other girls followed suit, weeping and pleading. There was a minute's pause before Qergina broke the silence.

"Well," she said, "you really deserve to be flogged. You deserve a good thrashing."

She took her deerskin rawhide whip from the wall. The girls knelt down and obediently bowed their heads as a sign of submission. Qergina gave them a vigorous lashing, but the girls remained silent and patiently accepted their punishment.

"I guess that's enough." Qergina hung the whip back in its place. "But don't ever again spy on old Qergina."

"We won't, aunt Qergina. Never again."

"I hope so," Qergina's voice had now resumed its earlier calm. "Now have a seat, and I'll make you some tea."

They drank and enjoyed their tea in silence. Finally the first girl could stand it no more.

"Aunt Qergina?"

"Yes?"

"I want to ask you something."

"What is it?"

"Oh, I don't know how to start. And I'm afraid you'll get angry again. But I …"

Qergina gave a sigh. "Come on, out with it. Tell me what's on your mind, otherwise you'll never calm down and relax."

"Well, I want to ask you about …" the girl muttered, "about those men who came to see you, the men with the guns, probably they were prospectors or something."

Qergina adopted a stony expression. "You're to forget that you ever saw them. Otherwise you're never welcome at my yaranga again."

"Don't be so severe, aunty," the girl pleaded. "You have to try and understand us too."

"Understand what?"

"You are a real woman. You've had men, and a kid. But we … will anybody ever want us? Is the rest of our life going to be empty and dull?"

"Yes, aunt Qergina," the third girl put in, "if we never have children, what will happen to the spirits of our kinfolk? You know, we don't want to be the last of our line. Every woman's supposed to become a mother and bear children."

"I'm sure those prospectors would be only too glad to have us. Any men would. We're young and healthy and good-looking," the second girl pleaded.

"And you know, they look like real men. Tough and strong." the fourth girl added. "I have a feeling that the Sun and Dawn have brought us together. Don't prevent us from meeting them, aunt Qergina. For the sake of the Sun and the Dawn."

"We'll do anything for you, whatever you want," the first girl implored. "We'll come here on all the holidays to work for you. Please."

Qergina could well understand the girls. The desire for a man and for motherhood was a natural craving of their healthy young flesh. She recalled her years with Yatta, and well remembered the yearning and anguish she had felt at nights. But that was not the main thing: these girls aspired to become mothers, a sacred desire for any woman. On the other hand, it would be irresponsible. How could she put Yatta, her own man, and his comrades at such risk? But was it a risk? After all, she had lived here for twenty years, trusting her own people, and at no time had they broken that trust. They wanted her to live and help them, and they had faithfully kept her secret so that neither the Soviet authorities nor the local Party or Young Communist League had ever suspected anything. And these girls were from most reliable families, not a single Party member or Young Communist among them. Admittedly, Raulena had an older brother in the League, but he had been far away at some construction site for the last four years.

Then she thought of something else. What would Yatta's comrades themselves want? They were young men, and they had lived without women for many years. Only the Creator knew how much time they had left to them, if they were to survive at all. It was quite possible they would be upset if she prevented the girls from meeting them. Apart from which, she had to let them know that the girls had seen them.

"Well, what can I say?" she said. "You're so persistent, you little foxes. But I know your families and your kinfolk, so maybe I can trust you."

"Absolutely, aunt Qergina. Absolutely and completely. I swear it," the first girl exclaimed.

"Maybe I can ask them what they would wish."

"But you know, I can't imagine any man who would refuse," the second girl said. "And we're not at all bad looking, are we?"

"That's not the point," Qergina retorted. "And before I even talk to them, you all must swear a blood oath before me."

"Any oath you like, aunty," the first girl assured her.

"In that case," there was now an edge in Qergina's voice, "you must swear to me by your family and home, and by the spirits of your ancestors, that you'll never, never tell anyone about your meeting with these men, no matter what happens, and no matter who asks."

"I swear," said the first girl.

"We all swear," the other girls echoed solemnly.

Qergina eyed them intently. "You must remember that if you let it slip to anyone, both those men and I too may fall into the hands of the Big Moustache and his underlings."

"How come, aunt Qergina?" the second girl exclaimed in surprise. "Aren't they prospectors sent here by the authorities?"

Qergina bit her tongue. This was a delicate matter. What should she tell the girls about these men? It would be better if they knew something close to the truth, so they would be less likely to indulge in loose chatter.

"Well," Qergina sighed, "I see I have to tell you the truth. First swear again that what you hear from me now will never come to anyone else's knowledge."

"Yes, we swear, aunt Qergina," the first two girls exclaimed again. "A plague on our tongues if any of us lets slip a single word."

"Well, if that's the case, then ... But maybe first I'll talk to them, and see if they want to risk meeting you in the first place."

"I'm sure they will," the first girl insisted. "I bet they haven't had a woman for ages."

Qergina raised her hands in dismay. "Why can't you silly girls understand that that isn't the question? It's a question of their safety."

"I hope you'll tell them, aunty, that we're good girls, not Young Communists. We're really reliable," the second girl pleaded. Qergina paused. "Okay, then. Stay here, and I'll go and see them. But remember, don't you ever think of spying on me again, or you'll be kicked out of my yaranga for good."

"Never, aunty. Never." the first girl reassured her. "We'll do exactly what you tell us."

"Good. Very well." Qergina agreed. "I'll be back in a while, and tell you what the men say."

With that she whistled to one of her dogs, mounted a reindeer and rode off.

The three men rested by their bonfire after a successful hunt. They had caught a moose, a piece of great good fortune. Suddenly Bondarenko's sixth sense told him of someone's presence nearby.

"Someone's coming." He rose and walked toward the trail leading down the hill. "I can see," he called. "One person. Mounted."

"On a reindeer?" Yatta enquired.

"Yeah, I can see the antlers."

"It must be Qergina," Yatta concluded. "She's got reindeer for riding."

"I just hope it is Qergina, and not someone else," Trofimov said.

Yatta looked down at the trail again.

"Yeah, it's Qergina all right. I recognize the way she sits in the saddle."

Qergina arrived and dismounted, smiling as the men greeted her.

"Good evening."

"Good evening, Qergina," Trofimov smiled back. "Come and join us and share our meal."

"Thank you." She settled herself by their campfire and rolled a shag cigar for herself.

"Well, how are things going?" asked Yatta. "Can we come and see you?"

She turned to face them. "There's something I've to tell you," she said. Trofimov saw an expression of deep concern on her face.

"Are we in danger? Must we leave?" he asked.

"Not really," she smiled. "It's something else, much better than that, but a delicate matter."

"Then tell us, hostess." Bondarenko was impatient to hear what she had to say.

"Well, you know," she began. "the people that came to see me today were girls from the village, and they sensed that there were men around."

"Damn," Trofimov said. "In that case we have to leave immediately, right now. What do you think, Qergina? Can we stay, or is it too dangerous?"

"It's too bloody risky to stay. They could easily track us down with dogs," Bondarenko said. "We'd do better to leave, pick up Zakharych and Yakov, and move off for good."

"But, you know, wait a moment," Qergina interrupted. "Those girls are very reliable. I know their parents. I've known them since they were sucking at their mothers' breasts. I can swear that they're no threat to you."

"But you can't know everything about them and their lives," Trofimov argued. "They may be scared by the authorities, bribed or brainwashed."

"By the souls of my late parents," Qergina interrupted again, "these are none of your Young Communists. They hold on to their family charms and worship their ancestral deities. I have warned them not to say a word to anyone either."

Trofimov looked at Yatta. "What do you think, Yatta?"

"You know, Sasha, Qergina's very knowledgeable about the human soul. She can read people by their faces. You can believe her."

"Well, hostess, if you trust them so much, then ... then maybe we can take the risk and stay on," said Bondarenko.

"But, you know, they're interested in you," Qergina continued.

"Interested? What do you mean?" The men stared at her.

"Well, it's quite clear. These girls have been without men all their lives. The young men of their age never returned from the war. The girls are afraid they may never have kids of their own. They want to sleep with you."

"Are you kidding, Qergina?" Bondarenko asked.

"Not at all. They're anxious to mate with strong, healthy men like you, not with feeble youngsters."

"Hey, hey, guys! That's the kind of news I like." Bondarenko's eyes lit up.

"How many girls are there?" asked Trofimov.

"There are four."

"Just right for the four of us. I'm not counting Yatta," Bondarenko said. "Let's go back right now and tell the other guys."

"C'mon, Mikhail." Trofimov grinned. "A couple of minutes ago you were all care and caution."

"What's the problem?" Bondarenko retorted. "Our hostess trusts them, and these girls are anxious to get laid. They want us especially for that. Who could have dreamed of such good luck?"

"We've still got to talk to Yakov and Timoshkin," Trofimov reminded him.

"Then let's go right now." Bondarenko turned to Qergina.

"Shall I tell the girls to stay and wait for you?" Qergina asked.

"Tell them," said Trofimov, "but ask them to wait for a couple of days."

"All right," Qergina replied, "but no more than that. They're bound to their collective farms, and they'll have to return there before too long."

"We'll be quick." Trofimov turned to his comrades: "Let's go."

In a few hours they had returned to their camp.

"Wow," Timoshkin muttered to himself. "I ain't been with a woman for ages, not since that British DP camp."

"Well, Zakharych, now's your chance at last." Bondarenko sounded coy.

"Isn't it risky? What if they're spies sent by the local Godfather?" Goldberg wondered.

"C'mon, Yakov," said Timoshkin, "how would he know we're here?"

"They could be spying on Qergina, and just by chance saw Sasha, Mikhail and Yatta as they called in on her," Goldberg insisted. "And, if they're at all smart, they might have assumed we're the same fugitives that they're searching for all over Kolyma and Chukotka."

"Hmm," Bondarenko thought seriously all of a sudden. "There is always some risk. But Qergina claims she's known them since they were born. The chance that they're spies is one in ten at most."

"That's not so little," Goldberg commented.

"Aw, come on, Yakov" Bondarenko said. "Our chances of getting to America are only fifty-fifty, but we've not given up on that, have we? And here are women anxious to have us of their own accord. Are we gonna miss such a chance to be males again, just because we might croak tomorrow? That would be abso-bloody-lutely stupid."

"You've got a good point there." Trofimov laughed. "I think a man has to take his chances. I'm ready to take the risk," he grinned. "Just the thought makes my buddy-guy tingle."

"Mine too." Bondarenko laughed.

"Yatta, what d'you think? How big is the risk?" Trofimov asked.

"Hardly any," said Yatta. "Qergina says they're reindeer girls, and, you know, she has a lot of influence with her people. They regard her as a powerful shaman, in contact with the Spirits, and she can use that to scare them a bit, just in case they think of ratting, or even of chattering too much. These girls will keep it all a tight secret."

Goldberg smiled. "I can see, Mikhail, that once your buddy-guy gets involved, you forget about everything else. Weren't you our greatest champion of caution once upon a time?"

"Damn right," Bondarenko shot back with a laugh. "I still stand for caution, but not beyond reasonable limits. And to lose such a chance—you gotta be a complete stupid shithead to do that."

"We have to take precautions," said Trofimov.

"C'mon, Captain." Bondarenko looked him straight in the eye. "You aren't gonna tell us to turn down the offer?"

"Certainly not! We'll meet in some place that the girls don't know. Definitely not at Qergina's."

"Bringing them here is even more risky," said Goldberg.

"There are ways around that, like blindfolding them on the way."

"No. That would be too humiliating for them," Goldberg protested. "They might refuse."

"If they're really keen to have kids, they'll agree okay," Bondarenko sounded confident.

13

Qergina led the men into her tent.

"Well, girls," she said turning to the men, "here are our guests. This is Raulena," she said, introducing the first of the girls. "Next to her is Notatvaal," she nodded to the second girl. "And these two beauties are Rahtina and Gemangaut."

"But you know, aunty, they aren't going to remember our Chukchi names," said the first girl. "Why not let them call us the way all Russians do? I'm Lena, she's Natasha, and these are Tanya and Zhenya."

"Oh, yes, that's easier," Trofimov smiled and bowed to the girls. "Nice to see you. I'm Alexander. You can call me Sasha."

"Mikhail."

"Yakov."

"Pyotr Zakharych."

Qergina smiled in Yatta's direction. "And this is Yatta, my man. You've heard about him. Anyway, my dear guests, let's have breakfast. I've boiled some deer meat and made some strong tea."

The men sat in a circle. The girls helped Qergina serve the dishes then joined the men.

"Since it's the rule in good company," Bondarenko began, "I think we should drink to our acquaintance." He produced a flask of vodka from his pocket, raised it and took the first sip, then passed it to Trofimov.

"To our acquaintance." Trofimov took a goodly swig then passed the flask on.

"To our meeting," Lena announced and took a sip.

Goldberg gave a shy smile and sighed. "It's such a pleasure being in lovely female company again, after not seeing a woman for so long."

Bondarenko jabbed him in the side with his elbow. "You dickhead," he whispered in Goldberg's ear. "If you say things like that, they'll realize we're from the camps."

Qergina immediately caught Bondarenko's concern. "Don't worry. You know, I've told them already that you're being pursued by the Big Moustache's men."

Bondarenko stared at her.

"Listen to me before you say anything," Qergina cut him off before he could say a word. "I swear by the grave of my parents that these girls are reliable. Remember, they're reindeer girls from good families. They worship the Creator, the Dawn, the Noon and other Merciful Beings and their ancestral spirits. You can trust them the way you can trust me."

"I understand," Trofimov began, "but—"

Qergina cut him short. "I know what you want to say, my dear man," she interrupted. "But it's better for them to know the truth and realize the seriousness of this. Then they'll keep this secret as something sacred." She turned to the girls. "You know, not a word must pass your lips, or my curse will remain on you forever, and my spirit assistants will never leave you in peace."

"Yes, aunt Qergina, we swear by our family's protecting spirits," Lena and Natasha vowed.

Qergina smiled. "Anyway, you men, have a meal and a chat. Every person here is your friend. No Party members, Young Communists, or other Soviet hacks will ever find their way in here."

"As you say," Trofimov agreed.

"I'd like to propose a toast to our meeting with some real men at last," Lena declared, which brought a smile to all the men's lips.

"Here's to the reuniting of men and women after a long separation caused by our evil rulers," Goldberg announced, slightly tipsy, "and to our reunification in this exotic location on the edge of the world."

"You know," said Qergina, "it's worth celebrating this with a thanksgiving ceremony according to the old custom of our people."

"A thanksgiving ceremony?" Trofimov queried.

"Yeah, it's an old custom," Yatta explained.

"Who do we give thanks to?" asked Trofimov.

"To the Creator, to the Sun, to the Noon and the Stars, to the Merciful Beings, and also to our deceased ancestors," Yatta explained. "You've gotta thank them all for any luck you've had, whether in hunting, trading, building a new yaranga, or whatever."

"Then we've really got something to celebrate," Trofimov agreed, rejoicing in anticipation of the ceremony. "Tell us what to do, we don't know your customs."

"It's not difficult, not at all," Yatta assured him.

"It's great," Lena exclaimed. "And you'll see it happen. Nowadays we can only do this at aunt Qergina's. In our village we're not allowed to continue our old ceremonies. They even forbade us to use drums or family charms, and we have to hide them away from them."

"Well, those filthy scumbags are everywhere, whether in Byelorussia or out here," Bondarenko snorted angrily. "Everyone has to bow down to the Red Flag, the Red Star and the Great Leader."

Yatta stepped outside and looked up at the sky.

"You know, if we want to celebrate the thanksgiving today, we have to be quick. The sun's already high in the sky."

Qergina turned to the girls. "When have you got to be back at the collective farm?"

"In three days, aunt Qergina," Natasha replied. "The manager's away on business, and the other girls agreed to replace us till then."

"Then let's go ahead with it now," Trofimov concluded.

Qergina took her guests out to see a little herd of reindeer to select a deer for sacrifice.

"This one should be good." Qergina pointed to a fat gray buck with black patches.

Bondarenko, who had now mastered the art, threw the lasso and with Trofimov and Qergina's help hauled the animal towards the tent.

"Now, Mikhail," Trofimov jokingly picked on his friend, "do you remember how to stab it properly, so as not to offend against Chukchi custom?"

"Abso-bloody-lutely!" Bondarenko laughed. "I'll never forget that roasting from Yatta as long as I live."

"Then take your knife and go ahead."

Trofimov and Qergina held the reindeer by its antlers and turned its head towards the east. Bondarenko stabbed it through the heart, and it collapsed onto its right side.

"A good omen. That means luck," Qergina exulted.

The men butchered the carcass. Qergina collected some of its blood in a small leather pouch and sprinkled it in various directions. After that she dipped her finger in the blood and smeared everyone's forehead.

"Yatta," she called, "come and feed the Earth Spirits."

Yatta cut off several pieces of meat then walked around, burying hunks of meat in the ground. Then he cut off the antlers with a piece of the skull, walked away down the path and placed the antlers facing eastward. Meanwhile Qergina, Trofimov and Bondarenko finished the carving and carried the meat inside the tent, where Qergina cooked it. Lena and Tanya helped her, while the two other girls spread a new skin cover over the tent.

"Hey," Bondarenko cried when they covered the vent hole at the top of the tent, "why are they doing that? We'll suffocate, for Chrissake."

"Well, but that's the custom, Mikhail," Yatta explained. "You cover the vent and leave the entrance open."

"But how can we sit inside with all that smoke?" Bondarenko insisted. "It's like a Nazi gas chamber."

"Donna worry, Mikhail, there'll be enough air," Yatta assured him.

Trofimov meanwhile said in a low voice, "Mikhail, what the hell is all this? We agreed that we'd follow their native customs, so stop objecting, for Christ's sake. You want the girls, don't you? If we upset them, they might not sleep with us."

"As you say, Captain," Bondarenko agreed. "For the sake of discipline, and for the sake of the girls, I'm prepared to suffocate."

"What's the trouble, boys?" asked Qergina, approaching them.

"Hostess, is it true that for the sake of ceremony we've gotta close the vent hole and breathe in all that smoke?" Bondarenko asked with a hint of displeasure.

Qergina smiled. "That's the way our people do it, but I know that you Russians can't stand smoke. To respect your wishes, we can leave it open. Girls! Leave the vent hole open."

"But you know, aunt Qergina, that's against the custom," Tanya protested.

"Maybe, but we have Russian guests who can't stand thick smoke, and the Merciful Beings require that hospitality comes first."

"Okay, aunt Qergina." Tanya removed the cover from half of the vent hole.

After the preparations were completed, they settled around the blazing hearth. Qergina took her drum and beat it, at the same time screaming "Yo-ho! Yo-ho!"

"What's she doing?" Trofimov asked Lena in a low voice as she sat next to him.

"Scaring away the Evil Spirits."

"Are they supposed to come here today of all days?"

"Yeah, they usually try to catch people while performing the ceremony. That's what the old people say."

Bondarenko grinned. "The MGB in their blue epaulettes are also demons, but they'd only be attracted here by all this drum beating. Anyway, there don't seem to be any around."

"Where are the other two girls?" asked Trofimov.

"Spreading out sacrifices of meat and soup," Lena explained in a whisper.

"Well, maybe Yatta's right, and we ought to try and get the support of these spirits of the woods," Bondarenko muttered thoughtfully, "though they always told us at school that that's all bullshit, including God Almighty as well. On the other hand, they told us a lot of their own garbage."

Qergina stopped beating the drum and turned to the girls as they entered. "Did you do all the sacrifices, girls?"

"Yes, aunt Qergina, everything."

"Then have a seat."

"I guess it would be appropriate to have a drink?" Timoshkin suggested.

"Oh yes," Qergina willingly agreed. "Liquor is always appropriate."

She poured out some of the precious liquid into teacups, then raised her own cup, said something in Chukchi and turned to address the men in Russian: "Thank you, O Higher Being, you Sun and Dawn, you, Pehittin, and all other Merciful Beings, for bringing together male and female, forcibly separated for so long by the Evil Spirits, headed by the Big Moustache. With the help of you Merciful Beings, each of those separated halves has now found its other half and partner."

After their supper of deer meat and blood soup, Qergina announced that they should dance as part of the thanksgiving ceremony, and beat her drum again. While the others danced, Yatta sang native Chukchi melodies. Trofimov danced with Lena, Bondarenko with Natasha, Goldberg with Tanya, and Timoshkin with Zhenya.

"You dance well," Trofimov told Lena, and she smiled.

"Well, you know, I have been in town, at their Palace of Culture. They have a dancing group there, so I learned the polka and the foxtrot, though not the waltz."

"So you've been in the Soviet Palace of Culture?"

"And why not?

"Just interested. Those Palaces of Culture are Soviet institutions, and Qergina said that you're not at all Soviet-minded, and not a Young Communist."

"Oh, no, I'm certainly not in that League of Young Communists,"

Lena assured him. "And I never will be. Young Communists have to reject all their family's magic charms and even destroy them. You're even made to spy on your parents, and your brothers and sisters. I'd never ever agree to do that."

"I think we understand each other," Trofimov smiled.

14

When they were tired of dancing, they sat down on the deerskin rugs.

Yatta turned to Qergina. "You know, I guess it's time for the performance."

"Yes," she agreed. "Just let me relax and concentrate."

"Are we gonna have a shamanistic ceremony or somethin'?" Bondarenko asked.

"Yes," Natasha whispered. "Aunt Qergina is a great shaman, the last of them left alive."

"Come on, my girl," Qergina smiled. "I'm not a great shaman, nor even a real shaman. My father was, though, and there were some other real shamans around here. But none of them are alive now." She paused. "But I do know how to talk to the Beings and the Spirits, and I've got to talk to them now."

"Will you summon them here and talk to them in our presence?" Trofimov asked.

"Yes, my boy, that's what the shaman's art is all about."

Trofimov threw a questioning look at Lena.

"Yes," she said, "I'm a witness: aunt Qergina has done it many times."

"Can we see these spirits?"

"Not really. They appear only in the dark. But you can hear them."

"Well, that's somethin' interesting, ain't it?" Bondarenko looked from one to the other.

"Forgive me, Lord," Timoshkin muttered, crossing himself. "It may be a sin to listen to these pagan demons."

"C'mon, Zakharych. That's no great sin." Bondarenko reassured him. "We're here in their land after all. It's quite in order to listen to their local masters. It ain't mean worshipping them. Later on you can confess to a holy father and get absolution when we reach America."

"Well, maybe you're right," Timoshkin murmured.

"Let's move to the sleeping room," Qergina announced.

It was fearfully hot in the small square sleeping space, and everyone became sweaty in the sticky heat. Yatta and the women stripped off all their clothes down to their loincloths. Trofimov and Bondarenko bravely followed their example. As Trofimov looked at Lena's naked, bronze-coloured body and saw her ample breasts, well-developed thighs and slender waist, he became aroused, a sensation he had not experienced for a long time. Goldberg and Timoshkin looked at the naked company around them but made no move to strip. Bondarenko gave them a cheery grin.

"Aw, come on, guys. Never seen naked girls before?"

"No," Goldberg replied earnestly, "Never, except for my wife."

"I never even saw my wife nude, she always wore her underwear," Timoshkin said.

"Then take a look at these girls and enjoy it. Where else are you gonna see so many at one time? Bondarenko asked. "The only thing I'd like is a bit more light."

"You're a regular old goat, Mikhail." Goldberg threw him a shy grin.

"You bet. Why not?" Bondarenko said.

"You know, folks, can you move closer together?" Qergina said. "I need more space."

They crowded closer together. Trofimov found himself pressed against Lena and getting more and more excited by the proximity of this young female body. He tenderly stroked her breast, and she smiled at him encouragingly.

Qergina settled herself by the rear wall, lit herself a large pipe and inhaled the smoke for a while. Then she beat her drum and sang. She beat more and more rapidly, the sound blending with her voice to produce a loud and mysterious noise. At times she interrupted herself with cries of "Ah, ya-ka, ya-ka, ya-ka!" and then resumed her singing. At various intervals, Yatta and the girls joined in with cries of "Hic, hic! Quaivo!" The men sat bewitched and overwhelmed by the strange music that distracted them from even the girls' flesh next to them.

Suddenly voices emerged from the cacophony. They sounded harsh and unnatural, sometimes resembling the cry of an animal, sometimes like nothing ever heard before. The sounds did not come from Qergina. They floated all around, some apparently drifting in from afar, others exploding in one's ears, some descending from the ceiling or somewhere even higher, others thrumming and then melting away deep underground. It became hard to tell which sounds came from Qergina's drumming and singing, and which from elsewhere. A chorus of many voices filled the tent.

"D'you hear?" Trofimov whispered to Lena. "Someone's walking around, but I can't see anyone."

"It's the spirits. They're here. Here's one." She pointed in front of her, where one could clearly hear the tramp of dancing feet.

"Yes! Here he is," Trofimov instinctively stretched out a hand to touch the creature. Lena grabbed his hand and pulled it away.

"Oh, no!" she exclaimed. "You mustn't do that. You must never touch the spirits. The spirits hate it. If you touch them, they'll turn the whole yaranga and all of us to ashes."

"Oh?"

"Yes. Sit quietly." Lena commanded.

All of a sudden, Qergina fainted and fell to the floor, muttering unintelligibly.

"Just look at her," Bondarenko exclaimed. "She's worked herself into such a frenzy, she's gone and collapsed."

Goldberg sprang to his feet. "We've got to help her. Maybe she's had a stroke or a heart attack."

"Oh, no. Sit down and keep quiet." Tanya grabbed him by the shoulders and made him sit down.

"D'you want her to die?"

"Calm down, Yakov," Yatta urged him. "Everything's fine, you know. She's simply possessed by the spirits." Yatta took Qergina's drum and beat it slowly.

"What does it all mean?" Trofimov asked.

"Aunt Qergina's soul is away from here," Lena explained. "She's visiting the Spirits and talking to them in the places where they live."

"Where's that supposed to be?" Bondarenko enquired.

"The old folk say it's in the land beyond the sunset," Natasha replied.

"That means somewhere in the west, from where we are?" Bondarenko concluded.

"I don't know." Lena gave a shrug. "But you know, you mustn't worry. Qergina does this all the time, and she always returns and brings back news."

For a while Qergina remained unconscious, then she slowly rose again and took her drum back from Yatta. She beat it again, slowly this time, and sang in a low voice. Finally she laid the drum aside.

"I have finished," she announced.

"All this is beyond my imagination, Qergina," Trofimov exclaimed. "I never saw anything like this."

Qergina smiled. "You know, my father or some other great shaman would have done it much better. But still, you know, I achieved what I wanted. I summoned my spirits here and talked with them about your plans. Then I made a journey beyond the clouds to the land of stars, and I got all the answers I wanted from them."

"Come on then, aunt Qergina. Please tell us." Lena pleaded.

"You know very well you shouldn't interrupt me, you silly girl." Qergina silenced her in severe tones. "Wait! Anyway, I obtained from all the spirits a blessing on you girls and men coming together. They also gave their blessing on all your hopes. Your union will result in the conception and birth of lovely healthy children, so that none of your home spirits will fade away after you. But the spirits have sent several warnings as well."

"What are these warnings, aunt Qergina?" asked Natasha.

"First of all, everything that happens between you girls and these men must be kept in strictest confidence. Nobody except the eight of you must know anything about it. No one. Ever! You girls must keep in mind that your men are not safe. Remember that well. If these men fall into the Big Moustache's clutches, they'll suffer a most painful death, and that's against the will of the Merciful Beings. Therefore, only if these men safely reach and cross the sea all the way to the other shore, and only when they arrive there, will you girls give birth to the children you dream of, the next in your line. You must do everything to help provide for the men's safe journey. And a final warning to you: what you have to fear most is that through your fault they might fall into the claws of the Evil Ones." Qergina raised her voice. "In that case you will never have children, never. Instead you will all miscarry. And even if later on you have other encounters with other men, they'll result in miscarriages. Therefore when you die, the hearths of your homes will be without masters, your families' guardian spirits will fade away, and your unprotected souls will fall into the claws of flesh-eating demons. Do you understand?"

"Yes, aunt Qergina, we understand," Natasha and Lena whispered.

"But, you know, if you keep this secret well, and if these men overcome all obstacles and safely reach the other shore, then you needn't worry or fear anything. All your dreams will come true. You'll get pregnant and give birth to lovely children who will be your joy, your support and your continuation. You and your children will live under the protection of the Higher Being, the Sun, the Dawn, the Stars, and of your guardian spirits."

All the time Qergina spoke, everyone remained silent.

"However," said Qergina, resuming a more practical tone, "let's discuss some other things. Do you want to have your meeting here, at my place, or at yours?"

"I think it would be better at our place, if the ladies don't mind," Trofimov replied, looking at the girls. "It doesn't seem a good idea for us to be in Qergina's way in her own home for such a long time."

"Whatever you think convenient," Lena readily agreed.

"But we must take some precautions," Qergina suggested. "It would be better for you not to see the way there. That way, if you don't know, you don't know. So what do you think if I blindfold the four of you?"

The girls looked surprised, but did not object.

"Don't be upset, girls," Qergina urged. "This way it's better for everybody. No matter what, you'd never be able to show the Big Moustache's underlings the way."

15

Trofimov lay on his stomach on the hot, wet floor of Qergina's bathhouse. By his side knelt Lena, naked. She lashed his bare back with a bundle of birch twigs.

"More, please. And do it harder."

"Harder?" Lena grinned. "You want me to lash you like a restless and unruly reindeer?"

"Yes. That's exactly what I am. I'm a restive buck who's mad about a girl." He stretched out his arm and fondled her thighs.

"Hey!" she laughed. "You want me to lash you, don't you? Hold still."

Trofimov obediently stretched out on the floor and Lena resumed whipping him with vigour and passion. "Yes, I know," she laughed, "you Russians like it rough. It's your old custom, right?"

"Yes, I always enjoyed it like that."

"Where did you get all these scars?" she asked. "From the war?"

"No, from our own MGB, the Big Moustache's henchmen."

"Yes, Evil Spirits always torture people. Aunt Qergina says the Big Moustache is the greatest of all the Evil Spirits."

"Maybe he is now," Trofimov said, "after defeating Hitler. When I was in Berlin—"

"Oh, Berlin. My fiancé was killed in Berlin," Lena said with a sigh.

"You had a fiancé?"

"Yes. Aniqai and I were engaged when I was fourteen, and he was sixteen, the same year the war started. But two years later he was drafted. We planned to marry when he came back. But, you know, he never did. We got a notice saying he was killed in action."

Trofimov sighed. "That's a common story all over Russia. Hundreds and hundreds of thousands of Russian wives and brides and mothers got those 'killed in action' notices. In Berlin alone I lost half of my battalion."

"Oh, were you such a big boss?"

"Not so very big. I ended the war as captain in command of a battalion. But you said your fiancé was killed in Berlin?"

"Yes, did you know him?"

"I don't know. I did have a young Chukchi in my battalion. I can't remember his name. He was an interesting chap, and he often told us your Chukchi legends."

"Yes," she sighed, "Aniqai knew lots of our legends. How did he die?"

"The lad I'm talking about got killed by a German shell when we forced our way into the city centre. It was during an attack."

"You didn't send him to his death, did you?" her voice had a pleading note.

"Yes and no. I led the battalion into the attack, but I was with them all the time. I could have been killed as easily as any of the soldiers."

What a peculiar set of circumstances, thought Trofimov. That poor guy, if it really was her fiancé Aniqai, died like thousands and thousands of others in that vicious war, and now his battalion commander is about to sleep with his bride.

"Captain," Bondarenko's voice suddenly interrupted Trofimov's thoughts. "D'you feel like a drink?"

"Do you hear, Lena? We're invited for a drink. Would you like some?"

Trofimov and Lena emerged from the bathhouse and joined the rest of the company in the corner of the tent.

"Well, here's to our meeting and reunion once again," Bondarenko announced, raising his flask.

Later that evening the four men and their new girlfriends reached their destination. Here, in the woods, in a tent lit by a burning fire, the eight gave themselves up to that most ancient of earthly pleasures granted to living beings by Mother Nature.

Nothing else existed for the four men, neither the powerful state with its terror machine, nor the security police in their blue epaulettes, nor the labour camps, nor the savage north with its frosts and blizzards. The only reality now was these fresh and voluptuous young women, so completely exposed to them, yet still so mysterious.

For the girls, far, far away were their daily chores and wearisome duties on the collective farm, and the sad, frustrating years of their youth. All that was gone, abandoned in their village, dozens of kilometres away. The only reality now was these men, the partners for whom they had yearned for so long. The girls and the men were for one another like newcomers from another world, a world free of misery, toil or danger, and they were eager to have more and more of each other to satisfy their insatiable craving for life.

Amid this all-engulfing delight only one person felt uncomfortable. Shy and monogamous by nature, Goldberg had never imagined having any woman other than his lawful wife, the mother of his children and his life's companion. He felt out of place, as though he stood stark naked on a crowded square. He would have refused this pleasure if he could, but he dared not, fearing to look ridiculous in his comrades' eyes, especially Bondarenko's. Even more, he was afraid of disappointing this lovely young girl Tanya, who placed so much hope in him. He tried again and again to become aroused. He admired and touched Tanya's fresh, resilient body, then tried to conjure up an image of his beloved wife Roza. Tanya did her best to relax and arouse him, but in vain. While his comrades close by made love repeatedly, he was unable to start. Finally, exhausted and frustrated, he lay prostrate on the deerskin rug and succumbed to his desire for sleep.

"I know you're sleepy," Tanya murmured tenderly. "We'll try again later."

Bondarenko, who lay next to Natasha, heard Tanya's words and whispered to his partner, "Poor Yakov. He can't do it. He's so shy. Not even fighting at the front has altered him. I can hardly believe he was an artillery captain."

"And poor Tanya. She's never going to have a child." Natasha whispered in answer.

Bondarenko grinned. "Well, in that case, maybe I could do the job."

"You shameless stud." Natasha giggled and punched him playfully in the stomach. "I won't let you. You belong to me now."

"That was fantastic!" Trofimov exclaimed the following day, after they had taken the girls back to Qergina's and returned to their forest camp.

"Not quite as good as with my Anyuta," Bondarenko said with a grin, "but still very good. Only our Yakov ain't so lucky, are you, Yakov?"

"Piss off, Mikhail," Goldberg snapped.

"Why are you angry?" Bondarenko grinned again. "I'm just commenting. Your girl expected you to work like a bull with a herd of cows, but you didn't quite do that. Or did you manage it finally?"

"Not everybody's a king stud like you," Goldberg retorted. "I need to get close to a woman first, and get to know her better."

"Donna talk bullshit." Bondarenko laughed. "That might work in Moscow, or wherever you're from, but not now, not out here. We're fugitives and we could get whacked tomorrow. Do you want to be the only man to die fasting?"

"Talking about death again, Mikhail?" Timoshkin said. "With Gold's help, we'll make it to Alaska. You donna need to pick on poor Yakov. He feels unlucky enough without your jokes."

16

The days came and went, and eventually spring approached. At first nothing seemed to change, but the frosts gradually became less severe, and the sun blazed brighter. It slowly got warmer, and during daytime the men could dress more lightly. They had the snow goggles as a gift from Qergina, and they too helped.

There was plenty of work for all of them. Flocks of birds returned from the south—ducks, ptarmigans, mountain finches, snipes. The birds gathered in large flocks and began their mating, aware only of their would-be partners and of real or potential rivals. A sentimental nature lover, released from other cares, might have spent hours watching them, but that was not the case with Trofimov and his comrades, who had to think of providing for their forthcoming journey across the winter tundra. The arrival of the birds meant an abundance of work for them. Day after day they spent catching dozens and dozens of them, using nets, snares, darts or their bare hands. They plucked, butchered and stored them in the ice cellar they had prepared. Only once did they interrupt their bird hunt to visit Qergina, bring her their pelts and collect summer sealskin boots. They did not know where she obtained them: evidently here too a taiga black market flourished out of sight of the authorities, like a mountain spring bubbling beneath the winter's ice.

Finally, when the last birds had returned and completed their mating and settled down for the summer, the men broke off to enjoy some rest and relaxation. They were surprised to discover that spring had really arrived. There was no snow on the ground, fresh grass sprouted, and early flowers emerged in profusion, scattering the scene with splashes of bright yellow, pink, blue and violet. The larches covered themselves in tender green needles, making the woods look denser and full of life. The short northern warm season rushed into blossom, as if to beat the deadly arctic frosts that would inevitably return and suppress its splendour.

"Well, guys," said Trofimov one morning as he admired the landscape around them, "this is our first spring since we became free men again."

"I can't believe it," Bondarenko exclaimed. "I wonder whether we'll be alive and well next spring, in America. Well, we ain't there yet, but at least we're alive and well."

"Touch wood," said Trofimov.

"We're doing fine, aren't we, guys?" Timoshkin, as usual, needed reassurance.

Goldberg smiled sadly, "As I look at the grass and flowers, I can't help recalling springtime in Leningrad. You really felt that life was starting anew."

"Well," Trofimov pondered, "in Leningrad, Moscow, the Urals, the warm summer days are here."

"Yeah," Timoshkin said, "the time when sowing begins. Right now all our villagers will be busy as hell. The collective farm managers are anxious to be first to finish sowing. Out here you couldn't sow a damn thing in this permafrost."

"But even here, spring is quite something," said Goldberg. "Back in the camp I hardly used to notice the difference. Spring meant two more hours of work each day. Here you get a sense of everything coming back to life. You feel that life goes on, that you have a path to follow, and there are a thousand hopes."

"This is a stopover, before we celebrate next spring in America," Trofimov said with a pensive smile. "This spring marks our freedom. The next one will mark our victory."

They had barely managed to complete mending their boats and nets when the ice broke and the ice drift started. On Yatta's recommendation, they did not go to the river before the ice drift ended. Often large sharp floes of ice carried away whole sections of the bank together with trees and even animals unlucky enough to be caught there.

After a few days, the river cleared and the fishing season began. They spent day after day on the river, fishing as intensively as they had earlier hunted the birds.

During these days, Qergina and the girls visited several times. Although there was a lot of work on the collective farm in spring, the girls arranged opportunities to visit their newly acquired partners. On these occasions, the chores of the day were followed by nights of desire and passion and eager expectation.

"Hey, Yakov," Bondarenko threw Goldberg a playful wink on one such morning. "I guess we can congratulate you at last."

"You shameless goat." Goldberg turned red. "You've no sense of other people's need for privacy."

"C'mon, don't be shy. It's really somethin', ain't it?" He turned his head and exchanged glances with Tanya.

"Yes, I aroused his virility," Tanya smiled. "Some spirits had bound and chained it, and it wasn't easy to release. But I managed."

"You're quite the girlie," Bondarenko exclaimed. "Let's hope this is one more step for this guy on his road towards a new life."

"Yes," Lena agreed and turned to Goldberg. "You've been brought back to life. Making love means life and freedom. The Spirits of Darkness had suppressed your virility, but now it's back with you. May it never again abandon you."

Goldberg shook his head. "Just look, Sasha, how goddamned shameless they are."

"C'mon, Yakov," Trofimov grinned, "This isn't Moscow. Out here things are simpler. Once we get to America, you'll have all the privacy you want."

"Right, Captain," Bondarenko grunted. "Let's drink to Yakov's success." He raised his mug with a wink to the others.

17

Time passed and summer came to an end. Most of the time, the men busied themselves hunting and trapping. In exchange for the pelts, Qergina supplied them with necessities for their forthcoming journey: sleds, reindeer and winter clothes.

Herds of wild reindeer lived on the border of the forest and the tundra. In summer they moved to the tundra, where there were fewer flies and other parasites; in winter they moved back to the forest, where there was more food at this time of year, reindeer moss and young shoots. The reindeer herds moved by the same route with very little variation. They crossed the rivers always at the same fords and shallows. For centuries this regular routine had created a great opportunity for local hunters, who intercepted the animals at the river crossings and killed enough of them to provide a supply of meat for the coming winter. Trofimov and his men planned to take advantage of the reindeer migration to stock up for their coming trip.

One August afternoon, they sat around the bonfire outside their tent, looking at the spread of grass, the banks of the creek, and the stockade of tree trunks that encircled them. It was evident that summer was coming to an end. The larch needles had turned from green to amber and would soon shed, leaving the trees grim and bare for the eight or nine months of winter. The flowers too quickly faded, and fewer and fewer remained each day. While the sun was up it remained warm, but the sunset came ever earlier, and soon it was twilight only a few hours after noon.

"Well, men," Trofimov looked around them, "looks like our last few days of summer."

"We'll be on our way soon," Timoshkin said.

"It's rather sad, you know," Goldberg joined in. "I've rather got used to this hospitable place, and to Qergina, and Tanya and the other girls."

"Me too," said Bondarenko, shaking his head. "Especially to my

Natasha."

"Maybe we'd prefer to stay here for a while more?" Yatta asked. "There's no desperate urge to leave right now."

"It's too risky," Trofimov said. "We could stay here this winter, and then for another summer, and then for another winter. But eventually they'll track us down. Qergina and the girls will suffer because of us."

"Who knows?" Timoshkin wondered. "Some folk back in the camp said many runaway convicts lived up to a dozen years in the forests."

"Sure, one can do that, no problem," Bondarenko said. "Our partisan unit stayed in the woods for all three years of the German occupation and survived. We had to change location about half a dozen times, but we were never caught. And those woods were nothing like the size of these forests."

For Trofimov too, the temptation to stay was hard to resist. He had become strongly attached to Lena, to her subdued charm, femininity and passionate lovemaking. The prospect of relapsing into a monkish state was less than appealing. Who knew how long it would last—just for the immediate future, or perhaps for the rest of his life? And again, who knew how long he had to live? On the other hand, to stay here for another year was risky. Sooner or later, the collective farm manager or someone would notice those girls were absent far too often; people would see their rounded bellies, draw their conclusions, and begin spying on them. Even if the girls managed to escape, this short-term paradise was doomed to end. Besides, the hard journey to the Bering Strait was something they had to go through with sooner or later.

"No," Trofimov said firmly. "Even if we never got caught, we'd spend the rest of our lives as outlaws. It's not the way out for us, unless we plan to start a rebellion or a partisan campaign. But the time for that hasn't yet come. We have to sort out our lives, and we can do that only in America, or in some other free country."

"I think Qergina and the girls should come with us," Goldberg proposed. "Especially Qergina. She could be in danger if she stays."

"That's not such a bad idea, Yakov," Trofimov said.

"It's a great idea," Bondarenko enthused. "They're all strong women, with lots of native skills. Qergina knows how to shoot and use knives. Maybe the girls could learn to shoot. I'd be willing to teach them."

"Yes, but they may not be willing," Timoshkin interrupted.

"But why?" Bondarenko wondered. "D'you really think they prefer slaving away on that collective farm? And what about Qergina? Even if nobody ever finds out that she helped us, they could still get her for practising shamanism."

"Well, people get attached to their homeland," Timoshkin said. "I used to think that I'd never leave my home village. When I left for the war, I dreamed only of returning to my woman and my kids if I didn't get killed."

"But you said that later on you didn't want to leave Germany, and it was only those English bastards that handed you back to the Soviets," Bondarenko reminded him.

"Only because I knew what they were gonna do to me. Qergina and the girls aren't facing any threat."

"Anyway, guys," Trofimov summed up, "we'll ask them. As for ourselves, at the moment we've got to think about the autumn hunting. How soon will the reindeer arrive, Yatta?"

"In about a week or so," he said.

The following day, their party moved closer to the Yeropol River, a few miles from the spot where, according to Qergina, the wild reindeer herds would make the crossing. They did not move down to the riverbank before the hunt, since this might increase the danger of their running into someone. One of them would spend the day sitting on the rock beside the reindeer ford with binoculars at the ready, watching for the reindeer to approach.

One morning, Yatta was on watch, perched high on a rock, when he noticed in the far distance, close to the horizon, something that resembled a moving grove of bushes. It was the herd. What looked like moving bushes was the reindeers' antlers. Yatta took off for the tent and woke his friends. Without wasting a minute, they picked up their guns and spears made from bayonets mounted on long wooden poles, took their two boats and hurried to the riverbank.

"This year, you know, they've come three days earlier than usual," said Yatta when they were on the move.

"It was a good idea to start looking out as soon as we did,"

Bondarenko remarked.

Trofimov, Timoshkin, Yatta and Goldberg hauled their boats closer to the river, but hid them in the bushes so as not to scare off the game. As they watched from their hiding place in the trees, a large herd emerged from the grove on the opposite bank and waded into the water. The men waited till all the animals were in the water before breaking cover and moving forward.

Once the animals had moved sufficiently far from shore, the men hauled their boats to the water, launched them and overtook the swimming herd.

The animals tried to dodge the boats, but the current was strong, and there were too many of them. The front animals veered away, colliding with those that were still moving forward, and chaos resulted. The men intercepted the panicking animals and stabbed one after another with their homemade pikes. Animals that reached the shore were shot by Bondarenko with his machine gun. The shore and water became stained red with blood, and the air was filled with the animals' cries.

Finally, when some two dozen reindeer lay dead in the water and a few more on the shore, Yatta gave the signal to stop. They turned to lassoing the floating carcasses and steered them toward the bank, by no means an easy task because of the strong current. Eventually, however, the job was complete, and the hunt was over.

"Ugh! What a disgusting hunt," Trofimov shook his head.

"That was a sin to kill so many of God's creatures," Timoshkin said and crossed himself. "We aren't gonna eat all of them, are we?"

"C'mon, Zakharych," Bondarenko said. "We're in no position to be merciful. I'll bet we not only eat 'em all, but there's probably not gonna be enough. Isn't that right, Yatta?"

"Well, I think that's about the right amount for us to survive in the tundra," Yatta replied. "There's going to be one blizzard after another, so we'll have to spend a long time in the tent without any chance to hunt."

"Anyway, it's not too much to have a decent reserve supply," said Trofimov.

"I wonder, though, how are we gonna carry all this load," Timoshkin wondered.

"Qergina promised us two more sleds with a pair of reindeer for each," said Yatta.

Shortly afterwards, while they carved up the carcasses, they had a pleasant surprise.

"Hey!" a young woman's voice broke the stillness of the forest. Lena, Natasha, Tanya and Zhenya appeared in the clearing carrying baskets of berries.

"Is it really you?" Trofimov called.

"As you can see," Lena smiled. "Aunt Qergina brought us up to your place, but you weren't there. Then she said you must be here, hunting. And here you are."

She hung on Trofimov's neck, and hugged and kissed him.

"We've been missing you," Bondarenko exclaimed happily.

"As you can see, we've not come to see you empty-handed," Natasha smiled. "Here's our present for you, wild berries."

"Well, that's saved us a lot of work. Thank you," Trofimov said.

"I see you're busy," said Lena. "We'll help you."

Goldberg said. "We thought we'd have to work till very late at night."

"Well, with nine pairs of hands, we'll finish sooner," Lena laughed.

Some hours later the meat had been separated from the rest of the carcasses, cut into small strips, and these strips hung up on the dozens of wooden racks they had prepared. Eventually the five men and four girls stood by the results of their work, looking proud, smeared with blood and fat.

"Now let's swim and wash the grease off," Lena suggested.

"In this cold?" Timoshkin put on a show of shivering.

"Well, you know, we're used to swimming at this time of year," said Tanya. "It only gets cold next month".

"Well, it's as you wish," Lena laughed. "I want to go for a swim."

She stripped naked, exposing her strong succulent body with its by now visibly rounded stomach. The other girls followed her. They all looked several months pregnant.

"Look," Bondarenko exclaimed, "they've all got tummies. We did a good job." Then, looking at Tanya's belly, "My congrats, Yakov."

"Piss off, Mikhail," Goldberg snapped, and everyone laughed.

Goldberg eyed the four girls. "How can you swim in such cold water when you're pregnant? Won't your babies freeze to death?"

Natasha laughed by way of answer. "Maybe there's some danger for you white folk, but not for us. It'll only make our babies healthier."

"Come on, let's swim, girls." Lena hurried them. "The boys can follow us if they choose."

With that, she took a run and hurled herself into the river, followed by the other girls. They swam and splashed with ringing shrieks of pleasure and laughter. The men stood bewitched and enchanted by the spectacle.

"Well, Captain," Bondarenko winked at Trofimov, "are we fuckin' brave enough to try this?"

"Surely. Come on," Trofimov cried.

They launched themselves into the river, but the next moment rushed back out, scalded by the ice-cold water.

"Brrr!" Bondarenko yelped.

"Cold, eh?" Timoshkin laughed.

"Abso-bloody-lutely. My guts are frozen, and so are my balls."

Timoshkin shrugged. "Well, if you young guys can't stand it, how can I risk freezing my old bones?"

"Holy Spirit! Just look at 'em." Bondarenko pointed at the girls and Yatta, swimming and having fun in the water. "Can you believe it? Not afraid for their tummies or their pussies."

"Hey! Come join us," Lena shouted from the water.

"Yeah, in a while. We got to get warm first," answered Timoshkin.

Bondarenko appealed to Timoshkin and Goldberg. "Zakharych, Yakov, come on. Get in there and cool yourselves."

"Well, Zakharych, what do you think?" Goldberg looked at Timoshkin.

"Let's try it." Timoshkin finally decided to venture in. He and Goldberg hurled themselves into the river and came rushing out, shrieking. Meanwhile the girls emerged from the water, all laughter. Lena nestled against Trofimov and then dragged him toward the water. Trofimov resisted and they lay on the grass, where he caressed her wet, naked body.

"Well, thank you again for the berries and for the help," Trofimov said as they dined with the girls by the campfire in front of their tent.

"You're very welcome," Lena smiled. "But you know, we were thinking you ought to be on your way soon, and we should see you once more and help you a bit, so you can rest before you set off."

"Yeah, we'll soon be on our way," said Trofimov and decided to broach the subject discussed earlier. "That's what we wanted to talk to you about." Lena and the other girls gave him curious looks. "Well," he continued, "do you know where we're going?"

"Yes, you're heading across the Strait," Natasha said, "to where the skies meet the land."

"Right. And I wanted to suggest that the four of you go with us."

"Go with you? To the land beyond the sea?" Lena looked astonished.

"Exactly," said Bondarenko. "Why are you so surprised? There's a land there where people live. Yatta told us some of your people are there. They fled there to get away from the collectivization. Is that right, Yatta?"

"Yeah, about ten or fifteen score of our Telqap people are there."

"Well, I guess they're a different tribe," Trofimov continued. "But they're still your own Chukchi people, and you speak the same language."

"Yes, the tongue's the same," Natasha confirmed. "But they're of different kin, and they've long been enemies to us, folk from the Upper Anadyr."

"But that's all in the past," Bondarenko said. "Now you all suffer from the same enemies, the Soviets, so why not go with us?"

"No," Lena shook her head.

"Why?" Trofimov asked.

"It's an alien land, with different folks and different gods and spirits. We can't take our home spirits with us."

"Yes," Natasha added, "and we have parents and other older relatives here. It's a bad thing to leave them alone. We used to have elder brothers, but none of them returned from the war. Our younger brothers and sisters are under age. Our parents are getting old. They ain't feeble yet, but they will be in a few years, and life is hard as never before, people wear out quickly."

"Yes," said Zhenya, "and we're their only hope."

"Well, it's up to you," Trofimov sighed. "But you're going to be in danger from the authorities if they find out that you've seen us."

"Yes, but fate can strike anyone," Lena nodded. "And you know, we've got to stay and keep the home fires burning, and take care of our old folks and rear our children. Your children, that is."

Trofimov took a deep breath. Unlike Bondarenko, he doubted from the outset whether the girls would be willing to go with them. The more so since he was not sure whether in their pregnant condition they could withstand the hardships of the journey, let alone the problem of what to do with newborn babies. But at the same time he hoped in his heart of hearts that they would be willing. It was hard to part forever from Lena, for whom he had deep and tender feelings now that she carried his child. Unlike his comrades, this was to be his first child, and he was in his late twenties, exactly the age when a man matures enough to become a father.

"So ... is that your final word?" he asked

"Yes, you know, I'm afraid it is," Lena replied.

Trofimov and Lena lay together on the reindeer skin rug, and he stroked her stomach.

"Can you feel him moving?" Lena whispered.

"Not yet," he smiled. "Why do you think it will be a boy? Maybe it's a girl."

"No, I know he's a boy," Lena insisted. "I want him to be a boy, and he'll have light brown hair like you, and he'll be nice and strong and smart like his father."

"What will you tell him about his father?"

"I don't know. Maybe I'll tell him the truth, that his father was a strong man who was pursued by Big Moustache and his men and had to go away to the land beyond the sea."

"No, you can't tell that to a little kid. He could blab, and then you'd be in trouble with the authorities."

"Never mind, I'll find what to say to him while he's little. Later on I'll tell him about you, when he grows up." She paused. "Do you have other kids from other women?"

"Not to my knowledge. I had girlfriends at the front, but I never heard of any of them getting pregnant."

"Then this is your first child. Don't forget him. Think of him regularly when you're in the Land on the Other Shore, and he'll be happy, and so will I."

"Surely I will." He hugged her again, enjoying the warmth and freshness of her body.

18

The winter had returned. The larches shed their needles, and a short while later, the snow began to fall. It was only left for the rivers to freeze before the men would be on their way. A few days after the first snowfall, they visited Qergina to bring her pelts and to collect the sleds and reindeer to haul them. She was as good as her word. There were six new sleds, with two reindeer for each, so they could sit and drive the sleds instead of moving along on skis the whole time. Trofimov thanked her wholeheartedly.

"Well," she smiled, "I think we've settled everything. The sleds are ready, and the reindeer you can take. Otherwise you're all set for your trip, aren't you?"

"Indeed," Trofimov said. "We've got enough dried meat and enough yukola. And now, thanks to your help, we'll be traveling in luxury like lords. That's something barely credible for a set of runaways like us. Thank you, Qergina, for going to so much trouble for our sakes," Trofimov said.

"Well, you know, that's no big deal, my boy," she said. "I just follow the old laws of hospitality. And with you and your friends it's something special. Yatta has been my man for several years. How can I not help him and his friends?"

"Well, thank you again. And there's one other thing I want to say," Trofimov said.

"What's that?"

"Maybe you'd consider going with us? Yatta's your long-term companion, and you could settle with him in Alaska, or wherever. Here you'll be constantly at risk, and if anyone learns that you helped us, you're doomed."

"Yeah, Qergina," Yatta joined in, "I wanted to say the same thing. We're together again, and we've left our troubles behind. I don't want to leave you here alone at the mercy of the Big Moustache's men."

"That's kind of you." Qergina smiled sadly. "But you know, I cannot. I'm bound by my oath."

"What oath?" Trofimov asked.

"I pledged to my folk that I'd never abandon them, and they in turn vowed never to betray me to the Soviets. They've been true to their word all these years, so how can I break mine?"

"What a strange thing," Bondarenko exclaimed. "The girls don't wanna go with us because of their parents, and you don't want to because of the village folks. As a result you might fall into the hands of the men in blue epaulettes."

"Well, in that case that's my fate, my dear man," she shrugged. "But at least I'll be true to my word. If I betrayed my folk, I'd lose the support of the Higher Being and the Merciful Beings."

"Well, that of course is serious. I understand you, Qergina," said Yatta.

"It's for you to decide," Trofimov sighed. "We're not leaving till next week. Maybe you'll change your mind by then."

"But no, I'm not going to change my mind ever," she answered. "Now let's go to my tent and have a meal. I bet you're hungry."

Finally the day of parting came. The five men were at Qergina's home, standing ready with their sleds and reindeer, all prepared for the journey.

"Well," Yatta hugged Qergina, "Farewell, Qergina, my dear woman. We shall never see each other again."

"Farewell, Yatta. Farewell. May the Merciful Beings help you on your way. Whatever happened between us, you're part of my life forever."

"You still don't want to go with us, Qergina?" Trofimov asked for the last time.

"No, there's no way I can do that."

"Then farewell, and thank you for everything."

"Farewell, my good man."

"Goodbye, hostess," said Bondarenko, his voice cracking.

"Farewell, and God bless you." Timoshkin made the sign of the cross over her.

"Goodbye," Goldberg added. "We'll never forget you."

Trofimov looked at his watch. "Well, it's time to go."

"Indeed," Bondarenko agreed.

"Wait one moment," Qergina said. "I've got amulets for you."

She went inside the tent and returned with several small wooden figurines that resembled animals or humans, or something in between, and strings to hang them round one's neck.

"This is for you," she said, presenting Trofimov with a small figure with a large head, straight body, and a bunch of reindeer skin strips instead of legs. It might have appeared ugly, but to him it seemed friendly and benign, like every gift that came from the heart.

"These are for you." She handed another figure to Goldberg and the other three men. "These figures represent the Noon, the Sun, the Dawn, and the Raven, the Higher Being's assistant," she explained. "Keep them on you, and don't take them off on the way, not even at night, and you'll be safe and successful."

Trofimov placed the amulet around his neck and hugged her warmly.

They formed a train with the two driving sleds in the lead and the other three behind. The front deer on each sled was tethered loosely to the sled ahead of it. Yatta hissed at the reindeer, and the column moved off sending up a small cloud of snow. Qergina receded into the distance, getting smaller and smaller until she disappeared, yet another person who had helped them on their trek, a woman they would never see again, and whose future fate seemed as obscure and uncertain as their own.

19

Although they could afford to rest in the moving sleds, for much of the time they ran alongside on skis, to avoid freezing. The frosts were no keener than in the woodlands, but strong winds blew virtually all the time, sending up a constant cloud of snow and piercing their bodies despite the warm deerskin coats they had acquired from Qergina. They rested in the sleds as long as they could stand the cold, and skied behind the column until they got warm and exhausted.

Only rarely could they afford the luxury of stopping and making a bonfire, since the endless snow-covered tract was almost barren, with only a few bushes and dwarf birches growing by the side of frozen rivers. Moreover, these birches were so deeply frozen that it was impossible to set them alight. The only solution was to cut and keep them in a special reindeer skin bag where they could thaw and serve as firewood a few days later. When they slept, their tent was warmed not by a campfire but by a "kolymka" lamp that used reindeer marrow for fuel. This lamp served also for cooking. It provided some warmth, but they were forced to sleep fully clothed.

The day's schedule had to be altered to suit the tundra conditions. They rose before dawn, had breakfast and prepared to move on. By the time everything was loaded, the cold winter sun was already in the sky, though it seemed more like twilight than daytime. It was light enough to see the way, and for seven hours or so, until mid-afternoon, they continued on the move. By then, it grew dark, and it was impossible to see the way ahead, especially in the snow squalls that constantly gusted. So they halted, set up camp and ate their main meal of the day.

Because they could not make a bonfire, they could not cook or eat outside the tent. They remained constantly on the alert so as not to be caught unawares by pursuers, and to keep wolves and other predators away from the reindeer. One of them had to remain on guard not just at night, but during breakfast and dinner as well. The man on watch had nowhere to keep warm. Because of the winds, watch duties were an ordeal for all except Yatta. Several times Yatta suggested he remain on guard at least half the time in order to relieve the others, but Trofimov, ever a champion of fair play, rejected that idea.

At the end of their first week in the tundra, a severe blizzard blew up, and the travelers were forced to make a long stopover. This came as a great relief, since they were becoming increasingly exhausted. Furthermore, the snowstorm relieved them of having to keep guard: at such times both predators and human enemies were forced to remain in their dwellings or their dens. During the first days of the blizzard, they slept for hours on end. They lost count of time and could determine neither how many days had passed, nor whether it was day or night outside. Furthermore, Trofimov's watch had stopped. Fortunately, they had food and tobacco with them in the tent, so they could eat and even smoke without leaving its cover. Trofimov tried winding and resetting his watch, but since no one knew the correct time of day, they left it at three forty, as it was when it stopped. They could thus keep count of the passing hours without any notion of the real time.

During the days when they were snowbound, they spent time in endless conversation. They retold each other the stories of their lives, learning about one another in minutest detail, and probably discovering more than they had ever known about even their closest relatives. On one such occasion Timoshkin told them the story of his repatriation.

By the time of V-Day, Timoshkin's prisoner-of-war camp near Kassel turned out to be in the British occupation zone. At first the British officers declared the Russian prisoners were free, and fed them well after their years on a starvation diet in German captivity. Although they were not released from the camp, they enjoyed substantially greater freedom of movement. They could travel to the city a few miles away as often as they wanted. Some of them even began finding jobs in neighbouring German households and farms, for which they received additional food and other small items.

The life was pleasant and even cozy, and few of these former German prisoners thought much about the future. They had heard from the German camp administration that all POWs were regarded as traitors by the Soviets, and they faced the prospect of imprisonment if they returned. It was hard to say whether the men believed this or not. It sounded absurd, yet most of them were peasants who had already suffered many unpleasant surprises at the hands of the Soviet authorities, and the idea of being punished for falling into enemy hands sounded not implausible. However, during those endless days of German captivity, the idea of ever returning home had seemed remote indeed.

At the end of the war, the question of repatriation became a major problem. There were increasing rumours that after the Yalta Agreement the British administration intended to hand them all back to the Soviets. The British officers in charge of the camp fervently denied this, but suddenly tightened the regime so they were allowed out of the camp only for very short spells. Finally, even these excursions were banned.

At that point Timoshkin realized that something unpleasant was in store. He and a few other men tried to escape to the south, to the American occupation zone, from where, so they had heard, there would be no enforced repatriation. They moved during the night, sleeping in haystacks during the day. On the fifth day they were caught by British troops and returned to the camp. A month after that, they were loaded into railroad freight cars and transported to the east, through Soviet-occupied East Germany, Poland, and straight to the Soviet border. There, like thousands of others in his position, Timoshkin, the honest Russian peasant and soldier, whose only guilt lay in having been wounded and taken prisoner, was put through a procedure that involved interrogation by SMERSH officers, sentencing for treason, and transit by cattle car to the Soviet Far East. It was in that transit that he met up with Trofimov who happened to be sharing the same cattle car.

"Yatta, now you tell us somethin' interesting," Bondarenko requested, after all their life stories were exhausted. "Tell us a legend, or a fairy story, or somethin' about your people."

"Yes, please do," Trofimov said. "I remember you once said the Chukchi were never subdued by the Soviets until the collectivization in the thirties. Is that true?"

"It's true, all right," said Yatta. "And before that, under the Sun Chief, we never paid tribute to him."

"And how did a small people like the Chukchi manage that against a huge country like Russia?" Timoshkin asked.

"Well, you know, we lured the Cossacks deep into the hills and rocks, and there they lost their way and exhausted their food supplies," Yatta explained. "Our winters were too cold for them, and when they were weak from cold and hunger, we attacked them. That's how we captured Yakunin. He was the cruelest of all the Russians. We called him Aqa-tei-nnilin Yakunin—the cruel murderer Yakunin. He killed old folks and children. He hacked our men to pieces, axing them between the legs. He raped the women and then tore them in two like yukola. Some men he seated with a noose around their necks and the other end tied to their cocks. Then he poked a red-hot iron in the man's face, so he jerked back and ripped off his own cock."

"Good God!" Trofimov could hardly believe his ears. "That's like the Spanish conquistadors when they conquered America."

"I read about that too," said Goldberg. "They were cruel. But Russians doing something like that? I could never imagine it."

"And you managed to capture this bastard?" asked Bondarenko hopefully. "Or did he flee?"

"Oh, you know, we captured him."

"And I bet you made things painful for him in return." Timoshkin said.

"Yes, we did. The old folks say that the elders and warriors couldn't decide for seven days what to do with him. Finally, some say, they roasted him over a fire, and his roasted flesh was cut off piece by piece. Others say, though, that he was stripped naked in the frost and forced to run around with a wooden club tied to his head, the way we do with restive reindeer. As he ran around, the club clouted his head, while our folk beat him with whips and tent poles till his skin got torn off together with the flesh."

"God, how cruel men can be to one another." Goldberg exclaimed.

"Well, it fuckin' well served him right," said Bondarenko. "He deserved that much twice over."

"Yes," Yatta concurred. "But it wasn't so often that our people did that to anybody. Even murderers were usually just exiled from the tribe if the victim's relatives didn't demand blood revenge. Though those that killed old folk, or children, or raped little girls, had their throats slashed, the way Russians do with their cattle."

"I wonder where the name Yakunin comes from," Trofimov said. "Maybe he was actually called Yakov?"

"Well, you know, some called him Pavluchka," Yatta added.

"Pavluchka? Perhaps he was Major Pavlutsky. He headed an expedition to the east during the reign of Catherine the Great," Goldberg surmised. "He perished in a war with the local natives. There's a monument in his honour in Anadyr, and in another village there's a magnificent cross to his memory. The village itself is called Mayor-Krest, Major's Cross."

"Hell," exploded Bondarenko. "As always, the fucking bloody bastards collect honours and distinctions from the tsars and other rulers."

"I donna think that could have been much consolation to him,"

Timoshkin smiled wryly. "I wouldn't want to be roasted on a fire and then hacked to pieces, even if they put up a dozen crosses to me after that."

"You're right, Zakharych. I can just imagine how they'd roast your old bones," Bondarenko joked. "Or my younger ones, for that matter. That's what the Nazis would probably have done to me if they'd caught me. And the men in blue epaulettes all but did the same thing. Almost like what they did to the captain with their rods and crowbars."

"So," Trofimov went on, "you say, Yatta, that the Russians never subdued your people? That surprises me, because on all maps of the old Russian Empire, Chukotka was shown as part of Russia."

"Well, there was a treaty with Russia a long time ago. Russians could come and trade with us, hunt on our land, and even establish settlements, but in exchange they pledged never to exact tribute from us. After that the wars between us ended."

"You sure are tough guys," Bondarenko marveled. "And to this day you don't wanna be Sovietized and rat on one another, and you still have your own gods."

"Yeah, there aren't many of us Chukchi who would report on one another. But you know, otherwise we're still trapped. Some of us tried to resist, but what could anyone do against machine guns, tanks, or those iron birds that they have?"

"Yeah," Timoshkin sighed, "there's little that ordinary men can do against tanks and planes."

"There was one time—just one moment—when we could have done something," Trofimov said. "Right after the war. But everyone wanted to go back home to enjoy the wonderful future prepared for us by the kind offices of Comrade Stalin."

20

The blizzard finally ended, and the five men were on the move again. Once more they were confronted by the endless plateau with occasional hills and valleys, ascents and descents, and by frozen rivers with sparse brushwood along their banks. It seemed inevitable that they would lose their way in this endless snow-covered desert, but Yatta remained confident and seemed to know the way well. These were places where his tribe had once roamed for years on end.

One day as evening approached and the sky grew dark, Bondarenko exclaimed, "Look!"

"What is it?" Trofimov looked round behind him.

"No, up there." Bondarenko pointed to the sky.

The eastern half of the sky was taken over by a bright flame with tongues of red and orange, amber, green, and blue that collided and recoiled, sometimes blending and creating incredible new colours, then disintegrating into numerous small lights that resembled festive garlands.

"Stop for a moment," Trofimov suggested. "It's the aurora borealis."

They stood with their eyes glued to the spectacle in the heavens.

"Incredible," Goldberg exclaimed. "So that's what it's like."

"It's beautiful," Timoshkin was fascinated. "I heard about these northern lights, but I never knew they were like this."

Bondarenko lit one of his home-rolled cigars. "Well, I guess this must be a good omen. It's in exactly the direction we're heading. It must mean we'll get to America alive and well."

"It must mean just that," Trofimov agreed.

"But you know, it really is a good omen," Yatta said. "It means we have the good will of the Heavenly Beings and of the Deceased."

"The deceased?" Bondarenko frowned.

"Yes, that's Heaven," Yatta explained, "where those who died an honest death now reside." He pointed towards the aurora. "You see the band on top? That's where Lii-vilit, the good dead, live. Those are the ones that died a natural death. Then you see the next one? It's thicker. Those are the 'kyele dead', those whose lives were taken by Evil Spirits."

"That must be the largest band," Trofimov observed. "This land abounds in evil demons."

"But you see the other band, in the direction of the dawn?" Yatta continued. "That's where the 'bloody dead' live, those who were killed."

Bondarenko looked disappointed. "If those are bands of all the dead, then it must be kind of a really bad omen."

"No." Yatta countered. "That's the place where the deceased live a happy life. Only those favoured by the Merciful Beings live there; the others live in the underworld. When they show up, it can only mean that they regard us favourably."

"So what we see is paradise," Timoshkin concluded, "and paradise is something we dream of going to. It can't be a bad omen. It means the Lord looks on us with favour."

"Who knows, Zakharych, what it means?" Bondarenko said. "He may indeed look on us with favour and therefore summons us up there double quick for that very reason."

Timoshkin crossed himself. "Well, then, that's God's will. And we can't go against that, can we?"

"Surely not," Bondarenko grinned. "You know very well, I'm always ready to die. That's fucking fate."

"Cross yourself, Mikhail." Timoshkin ordered him. "You shouldn't indulge in indecent talk in the face of a divine vision."

"Sorry, Zakharych. Forgive me, Lord." Bondarenko crossed himself. "I shouldn't blaspheme."

"Anyway, travelers and explorers regard the aurora borealis as a good omen," Trofimov said. "And so do the natives. So it really does look like a good sign to us. In which case, maybe we should stop here for the night?"

"Sure," said Bondarenko. "It's getting dark anyway."

Trofimov, Bondarenko and Goldberg dug away the snow to clear a space for the tent. The other two drove stakes into the ground a short distance away to tether the reindeer.

"Holy shit," Bondarenko cursed with a note of terror in his voice.

A dark, stained skeleton emerged from beneath the snow like an evil phantom.

"Look. There's another one here," said Goldberg, peering into the hole he had dug. Another skeleton appeared under the snow—a skull and part of a shoulder blade.

"Looks like a mass grave. Let's dig a bit more," Trofimov suggested. Very shortly, they uncovered another skeleton and then several more.

All in all, they uncovered the remains of about thirty humans.

Some were complete, with skulls, vertebrae, arms and legs in one piece. Others had disintegrated, dismembered by time or by tundra predators. Skulls lay without bodies, and other bones also lay separately. They stood and gazed at the bones.

"What's wrong?" Yatta detected trouble.

"Come and look at this, for Chrissake," Bondarenko called.

Timoshkin and Yatta tethered the last of the deer then walked over to the campsite.

"O Lord," Timoshkin crossed himself vigorously. "God save our souls."

"Maybe it's a native burial site," Goldberg suggested.

Yatta looked at the bones carefully. "But, you know, this ain't a Chukchi grave. We bury people separately, one by one, and usually at different sites. And we sacrifice a couple of reindeer and mark the grave with their antlers. There's nothing of that here."

"Look at this." Trofimov pointed out one of the skulls. In the back of the skull was a round hole with slightly jagged edges. They examined the other skulls and found that almost all of them had similar holes.

"Well," said Bondarenko, "it's fuckin' clear to me what this is: an execution site."

"God save their souls. Poor wretches." Timoshkin crossed himself again. "I wonder who they were."

"Who knows, Zakharych? Maybe convicts like us. Or maybe locals who refused to work on the collective farms, or workers who built some airfield or other fuckin' secret installation, and then they were liquidated to get rid of all witnesses and evidence."

"But you know, some of them are Chukchi, but there are more Russians," Yatta said. "There are a few women too."

"What are we going to do with them?" Goldberg asked.

"Let's move a kilometre or so away from here," Bondarenko suggested. "It's a bad sign to spend the night in a place like this."

"I'm not so sure we can move on in this darkness," Trofimov said.

"It would be un-Christian to leave them here like this," Timoshkin added. "We've got to bury them properly, ain't we?"

"You're right," Trofimov said. "Put our tent a little way from here, and we'll bury them in the morning."

"What a horrible place," Goldberg exclaimed as they had dinner.

"We've been away from the camps for more than a year, and I've got out of the habit of seeing such things."

"You're too fuckin' quick to get out of the habit," Bondarenko said with a menacing edge in his voice. "Don't forget we're still in Soviet territory. It's a long way to America."

"But we're far from Kolyma, the land of death," Goldberg tried to argue.

"Yeah, but this is so-called Dalstroy territory, the site of all those Soviet Far Eastern construction projects. It stretches all the way to the Strait. In Dalstroy territory you can expect to find blood and bones."

"It doesn't look recent," Trofimov observed. "This is a permafrost region, and still only the skeletons remained."

"You're right, Sasha, you know," said Yatta. "These remains are ten, or maybe fifteen years old."

"Maybe victims of Garanin's executions," Bondarenko speculated. "The old-timers in our camp said that a third of the camp population were whacked at that time."

"But you know, there are Chukchi among them," said Yatta. "During the collectivization many runaways hid in the woods, and the soldiers used to catch and kill them. The locals used to help them."

"Well, whoever they were, let's drink to the peace of their souls. God bless them."

The following morning they hacked out a shallow grave in the permafrost and buried the remains. When they had filled in the grave mound, Bondarenko asked, "Shall we leave it like this, or make some sort of cross or whatever?"

"We've nothing to make it from," said Yatta. "There's not a single tree."

"We could use a couple of our poles," Goldberg suggested.

"But we can't do that, otherwise our yaranga won't be firm enough against the blizzards."

Then Trofimov pointed to a small boulder. "We'll use this as a gravestone."

With a lot of time and effort they shifted the stone from its place and rolled it into position on top of the grave.

"O Lord, for the sake of their martyrdom, forgive these poor people's sins." Timoshkin crossed himself.

"Well, Captain, what d'you make of all these omens?" Bondarenko asked. "Don't they contradict one another?"

"Puzzling. Maybe they mean we're going to go to paradise by stepping over other people's corpses, which, incidentally, has already happened. We've left enough of them in our path already."

"Yeah, we did that," said Bondarenko. "But those guys were our enemies, and these corpses we found just now were just victims."

"It might mean that we go to paradise and leave our bones here too," Goldberg joked.

"Shut you up, Yakov. Donna ruin our morale," Bondarenko snapped. "And even if it does mean that, we've still got to behave like good fighting soldiers."

"I'm sure, though," Trofimov said with assurance, "that those northern lights are a good omen."

21

At last they had crossed the Anadyr Plateau and reached the foothills of the Iskaten mountains. Below these mountains the river Amguema, the last large river on their route, curled along its course beneath a thick crust of ice. They had to make a decision about their further route: move along the river or cross the mountain range. The first route would be easier and promised more comfort: there were groves along the river, which meant firewood, hot meals and warmth, but this route was more risky since the river valley could easily be cordoned off by troops. The mountain route was thus the more sensible: more arduous but much safer, for no amount of troops could cordon off a whole range of mountains. This was the route Trofimov was inclined to take, but they needed firewood, and he pondered whether they should risk a brief sortie into the valley to collect some. However, even that seemed dangerous, since they could be ambushed along the way. Yatta scrutinized the valley with

Trofimov's binoculars.

"No," he concluded, "we can't risk going down there."

"Are you sure, Yatta?"

"Oh, yes, Sasha. The birds are flying too high, which means they're scared of something, and it's like that all the way along the river bank."

"Maybe they're afraid of wolves," said Timoshkin.

"D'you want to run that risk, Zakharych?" Bondarenko as ever preferred caution.

"Mikhail's right. We can't take such risks."

"You mean to say we've gotta set off over those rocks and crags without firewood?" Timoshkin objected limply.

"We have no choice," said Trofimov. "If they're patrolling the valley, we can't even move in daylight. They might spot us. We'll have to travel by night."

The dark was virtually impenetrable, but they could not risk using their flashlights. At any moment they could stumble, fall and plummet down the mountainside, but Yatta was an excellent guide. He knew the location well and could see perfectly well in the dark. For him it was never really dark in that snow-covered area. Gradually they moved uphill, helping the deer by pushing from behind. The frosty wind lashed their faces, and all the while they longed for a square meal and the chance to rest up in a warm tent.

In a narrow gorge deep in the Iskaten mountains, the five travelers rested and shivered in the icy, gusting wind.

"Lord, what awful cold." Timoshkin clenched his teeth.

"You gotta be tough, Zakharych," Bondarenko said. "We can't risk making a fire."

"I know that," Timoshkin sighed. "Only it's harder on me. My bones aren't as young as yours."

"Yatta's even older," Bondarenko pointed out.

"But that's Yatta. I bet he could walk naked through the snow. I ain't a native here."

"Was it any easier at the front in winter?" Trofimov laughed, with a shiver. "Remember the winter of 1941-42? Guderian's tanks were approaching, so Zhukov ordered us not to make bonfires that might attract Nazi bombers. Later, when we joined the Siberians for a counter-offensive, we hid in the woods without fire for ten days. I suffered like hell from the cold. The Siberians had their fur coats, but I hadn't any warm clothes."

"Oh, yeah," Timoshkin relaxed somewhat. "It was the same on the Leningrad front. We were on the banks of the Neva taking cover from their shells but unable to fire back since that would have attracted the Germans' artillery fire."

"The same in the forests," Bondarenko added. "Once our unit was running from a German brigade, and we had no time to make any dugouts. Their spotter planes were right over our heads."

"Okay, guys," Trofimov said, "we all had our share of freezing, and we lived to tell the tale. So cheer up. This is just another episode."

A month later, they approached the Yultin trail, the only one that ran across the Chukotka peninsula. Here the vast peninsula narrowed to a tongue of land only two hundred kilometres wide. A trail ran from the port town of Egvekinot on the southern coast to the small town of Yultin in the north. Trofimov had no doubt that this trail would be cordoned off by troops: his only hope was that it would be impossible to post soldiers every two kilometres. He assumed that there would be small units—a squad or platoon—every twenty kilometres. The trick would thus be to squeeze through a gap far enough from either side to avoid being noticed. Since there had to be communication between neighbouring military posts, it was unwise for five men to cross in clear weather, when sled tracks would be easily visible. As they approached the trail, Bondarenko and Yatta were sent ahead on reconnaissance.

"What's to report?" Trofimov asked when the scouts returned.

"We can't cross here, Captain, there's a unit posted just at the bottom. The other units are placed every ten kilometres."

"How large is each unit?"

"Fifteen men, all armed with submachine guns, plus one fixed machine gun, and two tracker dogs."

"Do they have radio sets?"

"Yeah."

"Yatta, is there any path between the cordons that can't be seen from either side?"

"Yes, Sasha, there is. I can lead the way."

"That's good. We follow Yatta's lead. Each sled team will cross one at a time, with one of us behind. Go cautiously and be as quiet as you can. Yatta, are you sure it's going to snow tomorrow?"

"I'm sure."

"We can't cross when it's snowing, so we go tonight, while it's dark." Trofimov paused and looked at his comrades. "One more thing. With God's help, we'll avoid them, but if they detect us and we have to fight, our first target is their radio set. That's your task, Mikhail."

"No problem, Captain."

"Yatta, the dogs will be your responsibility. Any questions?"

The path was extremely narrow. First it rose through a narrow gorge between two high rocks then it descended all the way towards the point where it crossed the trail, which wound its way between two mountain ranges. At that point, a few meters to the left, another path began, leading up into the mountains on the opposite side.

When they finally descended, Yatta led the first sled across the trail. Then the second team crossed, led by Bondarenko. Then the third. Still there was no sound. Trofimov was the last to cross, after which their procession moved up into the mountains on the far side of the trail.

"Looks like we made it," Goldberg commented with relief.

"Touch wood," Bondarenko hissed. "They're too close for comfort. They could be after us at any moment."

Private Ivanov made his way along the trail with a dog and lantern. They plied this route every two hours. One soldier was sent along the trail halfway to the next unit then turned and came back. This method of patrolling was suggested by Colonel Vardanyan, the head of General Nikishev's operational department; he had come to the conclusion that Trofimov's notorious gang was steadily moving east, and it logically followed that their intended destination was Alaska.

At first, Nikishev had refused to believe Vardanyan's theory, but when the latter laid out all the facts, he agreed that it seemed plausible. It was therefore most practical to intercept them here on the Yultin trail, which they would have to cross in any event. The trail was therefore cordoned off and patrolled as densely as possible, with half a platoon posted each ten kilometres. By dispatching soldiers regularly to inspect those sectors of the trail between each unit, they managed to maintain almost regular surveillance of the whole of it. This patrolling had been going on now for two months, so far with no results.

Ivanov continued along the trail, shivering. He had already covered about three kilometers and had two more to go, then he was to retrace his steps all the way back. It was dark and only a few bleak stars glowed in the sky, obscured every now and again by clouds then reappearing, just like his own hopes of success, he thought to himself. There was no special landmark where he had to turn; his only indicator of distance was the master corporal's watch that was issued to every soldier dispatched on these inspection trips.

At times Ivanov felt weary and hungry, and he had the idea of resting somewhere halfway to his destination, then going back and reporting. It would be hard for the lieutenant or master-corporal to expose him. But as soon as such thoughts arose, he felt a crushing and invincible fear of going against the will of the all-powerful Soviet state, which was forever on the alert and ready to annihilate anyone who even slightly violated its supreme will. From books and movies, newspapers and other sources of information, he knew that no one ever successfully cheated the state. Even smart guys such as Trotsky, Zinovyev and Bukharin had failed. So how could some ordinary private from a small town in Bryansk Province hope to succeed in deceiving it without being caught? And if he were caught, service in a penal battalion was the least terrible fate that would await him.

Besides, there was the slim but seductive chance that he might be the one who succeeded in tracking down the gang. In such case he would certainly be generously rewarded, maybe even with a few weeks of home leave. But the chances of that were slim.

Hell, what a terrible wind. At least, on the way back it would be blowing from behind.

But look. What was that? His tracker dog suddenly barked and dug at the stone-hard snow. Ivanov brought his lantern closer to the trail. No, there was nothing to see, the snow crust was too hard. But … but … Here, barely visible, but still quite definite: tracks left by sled runners. Could this be them? He set off at a run in the direction of his unit.

Lieutenant Korneyev sat by the fire in the shelter of a rock together with deputy platoon commander Parfyonov, an army veteran, and fourteen soldiers of his special task force. For almost two months he and his unit had been among the troops assigned to patrol the Yultin trail.

It was just half a year since Lieutenant Korneyev graduated from the MGB cadet college, but he suffered from a terrible inferiority complex at having been born too late to fight in the war. Ever since his wartime childhood he had been determined to serve in the military and defend his Soviet motherland like the heroes of Moscow, Stalingrad and Kursk. When victory came in 1945, he had another year of high school ahead of him. Bitterly disappointed, he was determined to link his life with the glorious Soviet Army. He was vigorously involved in DOSAAF training, got good recommendations, and was admitted to one of Moscow's military colleges. Just last summer he had graduated with the rank of lieutenant. He had heard about anti-Soviet armed gangs at large in the Baltic republics and Western Ukraine and requested to be posted there. Instead he was sent to the Far East, where fortune seemed to smile on him. He knew all about Trofimov's gang, which had broken out of a labour camp and roamed the Kolyma forest. They had already brutally killed several Communist Party members and others. But the gang was far away from Egvekinot, where his battalion was stationed, and he thought his chances of participating in their capture were slim. Even so, his service in the Far Northeast seemed important. After all, there were several labour camps in Egvekinot, with more than a thousand enemies of the people imprisoned there.

It came as a pleasant surprise to young Nikolay Korneyev therefore, when he and his platoon were summoned to cordon off part of the Yultin trail in anticipation of these notorious bandits' attempt to cross it. It was by no means certain that the gang would try crossing the trail, and the chance that he and his soldiers would encounter them were not more than one in twenty, but this was the closest chance of a real fight that he could hope for. The days went by and nothing happened. Like his men, he suffered in the frost and piercing winds, and fought fatigue and boredom with liquor and tobacco.

"What's the matter, Ivanov?" Korneyev looked hard at the patrol soldier who had returned well ahead of schedule.

"Comrade Lieutenant, there are sled and reindeer tracks."

"What? Where?" the lieutenant's heart pounded in his chest.

"A couple of kilometres to the north."

Korneyev was suddenly gripped by a happy trepidation: could this really be that accursed gang, and did he now have the chance to capture them?

"Attention!" he shouted at his men. "Follow me."

The half-platoon mounted their reindeer and took off along the trail with their lieutenant in the lead. They reached the spot where Ivanov had seen the tracks, and Korneyev's lantern revealed the obvious signs of sled runners and reindeer tracks.

"Right! Looks like this really could be them. Follow me."

While Bondarenko kept watch on the path and rocks behind them, the other four men made a brief stopover in the gorge atop a high mountain pass.

"Well, guys," Trofimov smiled, "if nothing happens before the end of the night, it means we've passed the most dangerous stage of our trip. Our next goal is the Strait.

"Well, with the Lord's help, we made it." Timoshkin crossed himself. "Can we make a bonfire?"

"No, not till tomorrow night," Trofimov said.

Suddenly Bondarenko appeared, running towards them.

"Alarm! They're coming! Looks like a whole unit!"

"Quick! Get up! Move!" The approach of danger immediately reawakened Trofimov's instincts as a former combat officer.

They were away in seconds. The path ran down into the ravine, wound its way around a rock and then uphill again. They negotiated the ravine, but on the way up they were suddenly bathed in the powerful beam of a searchlight.

"Get down!" Trofimov commanded and all five of them threw themselves flat on the path.

"You there!" the lieutenant's voice roared through a megaphone. "Come out! And get your hands up!"

"Don't answer." Trofimov ordered.

"Can't you hear? Come out with your hands up."

Silence was his only answer.

"Hands up and come out!" the voice became impatient. "I'll count to three, and then we shoot."

"Target the searchlight and fire," Trofimov ordered.

Five long bursts of gunfire followed, and a hail of bullets hit the pursuers' searchlight and radio equipment, shattering them. Some men and deer were killed as well.

"Quick!" Trofimov gave his next orders. "Unharness a sled. We'll make a barricade."

"Which one, Captain?"

Trofimov calculated which of the sleds could be sacrificed. Not the one with the tent poles, nor the other with the cover. Not the one with the cans of reindeer marrow fuel, or the one with their tools and other essential equipment. It had to be the food sled. They could always kill another reindeer for meat.

"The food sled," Trofimov called. Following his order and crawling on all fours, they unharnessed the sled and turned it on its side across the path. At first the enemy fired at them sporadically but hit no one. Then the firing ceased.

"Looks like they can't see us," Trofimov said. "Let's try and get away. Lead the deer on uphill.'

After a short while Korneyev ordered his men to fire again, but there was no response from the other side.

"They've gone."

"Shoot at the area uphill and ahead of them," suggested the master-corporal.

"But the orders are to take them alive."

"That's hardly possible, comrade Lieutenant."

"Orders are orders, Parfyonov."

"Yessir."

Lieutenant Korneyev's half-platoon took off in pursuit of the bandits. They moved more slowly: some of the saddle reindeer had been lost in the exchange of fire, and five soldiers had to move on foot. Unlike a good horse, a reindeer could not carry two riders.

Trofimov's group advanced, but halfway towards the mountaintop, one reindeer after another fell on their knees with exhaustion.

"Shit!" Bondarenko cursed. "Looks like we're stuck."

"Yeah, we'll have to stand and fight." Trofimov remained calm and businesslike. "Unharness the sleds, put them all together, and take up position behind them. Don't fire till I say."

Very shortly the soldiers had approached close enough to be visible in the dim moonlight.

"Fire!" commanded Trofimov.

Three soldiers fell dead. In the moonlight, the lieutenant and his men picked out the barricade of sleds. Korneyev gave orders to use their grenade launchers, and within a few seconds a shower of grenades flew in the direction of the barricade. The grenade launchers' range was insufficient, however, and most of the shells exploded short of their target, scattering splinters around.

Korneyev attempted another advance, but machinegun fire from the other side forced him back. The lieutenant realized that he had virtually no chance of capturing the bandits alive. But order or no order, better a dead enemy than one who had made his escape. He therefore gave orders to open fire with the fixed machinegun whose range was adequate for the distance. A long machinegun burst followed, and a shower of bullets hit the sleds.

"Looks like we're finished," Goldberg said with a grimace.

"Not quite," Trofimov said. "We still have enough ammunition. We can carry on and hold out for several more hours. If and when we run out of ammo, we can use this to finish ourselves off (he pointed to his pistol). There are seven bullets in it, enough for us all."

Trofimov noticed Timoshkin's silence. "What's with Timoshkin?"

Bondarenko looked at the motionless body then shook his head. "I'm afraid … killed outright. Shot in the head."

"Our first casualty," Goldberg said in a low voice. "

"Don't lose heart, Yakov, we're not finished yet." Trofimov searched his mind desperately for a solution. He took in every minute detail of their surroundings, checking to see what advantage they might possibly gain in this situation. He had had to do the same many times on the German battlefront, and he realized there was little they could do against an enemy armed with a heavy machinegun. If only they could capture that goddamned machine, that would give them a decisive advantage. But how?

His eye fell on the rocky overhang above them. If the soldiers were to place their gun right beneath it, then someone on the rock might manage to jump down on top of them, kill the gunner with his bayonet and take control of the gun.

"Listen, Yatta," he said. "Is there a path to the top of this rock?"

"Yeah," said Yatta, "there's a narrow path half a verst up from here. It's steep, but we could manage it."

"Holy shit. Why didn't you tell me before? Now listen. You, Mikhail and Yakov, hold out here for a while, then retreat a few hundred metres further up. Give them a chance to occupy the spot where we are now. In the meanwhile Yatta and I will go up the path and take up a position on the rock. If they place their machine gun here, we can try and attack them from above and seize it. This may be our only chance. If you see their machine gun turn and fire on them, then you weigh into the attack as well."

"Very smart, Captain." Bondarenko immediately understood his proposal. "We'll hold 'em down firm and hard."

"They've gone silent," Lieutenant Korneyev said. "Maybe they're finished off."

Parfyonov the master-corporal shrugged then called out, "You there. Surrender. Come out with your hands up."

The response was silence. Korneyev felt uneasy and sensed he was losing control of the situation. He had lost six soldiers out of fourteen, but was no closer to catching the bandits. He also realized by now he could not capture them alive. Still, even if he had corpses that could be identified, it could be counted a success. Finally he issued a command. "Sidorenko, Barkhatov, and Matunin move up and try to reach them. Be careful. They can still shoot."

The three soldiers crawled cautiously forward towards the half-destroyed sled barricade.

Korneyev, seeing that there was no shooting, gave his unit the signal to move forward. Just as they reached the remains of the barricade, Parfyonov called out.

"Comrade Lieutenant! Two of them are up there on the snow."

"Shoot at their legs," ordered Korneyev.

The machinegun fire hit Goldberg in both legs. He fell flat in the snow just at the same moment as Bondarenko reached the cover of a large boulder. Goldberg tried to crawl on, but his legs were paralyzed. The three advancing soldiers rushed Goldberg. It was at that moment that Bondarenko, who had taken up position behind the boulder, realized what was happening.

"Fuck. Poor Yakov," he muttered.

Trofimov and Yatta continued crawling up the path. It was extremely steep and in places almost vertical. They hauled themselves up by their hands, struggling to maintain their grip.

"Is it far, Yatta?" asked Trofimov.

"Just a few yards more."

Lieutenant Korneyev moved his men up under the cliff. They seized the badly injured fugitive, tied his hands behind his back and seated him between them, leaning against a boulder.

"So," Lieutenant Korneyev turned to his prisoner, "are you going to answer or not? Where are your cronies?"

"No point in waiting, comrade Lieutenant," Parfyonov urged when the prisoner remained silent. "Beat the shit out of him."

The lieutenant was hesitant. On the one hand, regulations allowed him to use "methods of physical pressure," but on the other, in the Soviet heroic literature he had stuffed his mind with, it was usually the others—bandits, Whites, or Fascists—who resorted to brutality, carved red stars on their enemies' backs, or buried them alive. Soviet commissars were harsh yet noble and humane as heroes are expected to be. Five months of service in the Special Task Forces had slightly amended that romantic picture. With part of his soul he would have liked to remain like the commissars in those books, yet it seemed he had little chance of avoiding brutality with this fucking bandit.

"Get talking, or we'll beat the hell out of you," he shouted at the prisoner.

"That will be on your conscience, Lieutenant," replied the prisoner quietly.

"You aren't gonna teach me. I tell you, either you speak—"

"I don't know the answer," the captive said firmly. "I didn't see where they went. It was dark."

Korneyev turned to Parfyonov. "Okay, if that's the case, go ahead."

"Bilibin! Over here." ordered Parfyonov. One of the soldiers walked over to the prisoner and propped him against a rock then beat him.

This scene was watched both by Bondarenko, concealed behind the boulder, and by Trofimov and Yatta from up on the cliff. Bondarenko cursed in a low voice, but there was little he could do without running the risk of killing Goldberg along with his tormentors. Trofimov up above stared into the darkness. Against the snow he saw the silhouette of soldiers and of Goldberg as they battered him.

"Yatta, you can see better in the dark than me. Which one have they got, Mikhail or Yakov?"

"Yakov."

"Damned scumbags." It cost Trofimov an effort not to curse loudly and thus disclose their position to the enemy. "Listen, Yatta. I'm going to try and jump them now. I'll deal with the machine gunner, if you give me fire support from up here. Use short bursts. Watch for who aims at me and zap 'em quick, understand?"

"Yeah, Sasha."

At that moment, Trofimov with bayonet in hand jumped from the overhang some twenty feet above and landed square on the gunner's back. The next moment the blade hit the man's neck, and a second later the muzzle of the machine gun was turned on the soldiers, belching a long and deadly burst.

Within seconds, before the enemy realized what was happening, half of the soldiers were dead. Two of them turned their submachine guns toward Trofimov, but two short bursts from Yatta dispatched them on the spot.

At the same moment Bondarenko emerged from behind his boulder, shooting dead the two or three that had survived Trofimov and Yatta's attack. The lieutenant and master-corporal were still alive. They leaned against the rock, pushing Goldberg in front of them as a shield and holding a knife to his throat.

"Listen, you scumbags," the lieutenant yelled. "Make one move and your friend dies."

Trofimov rapidly assessed the situation. What could be done? Shoot them? But that might kill Yakov. Negotiate? Offer them a free pass in exchange for Yakov. They would hardly believe him. He himself would never do that: it was clear that as soon as they got Yakov back, nothing could prevent them from shooting the lieutenant and his assistant dead. Most likely the lieutenant realized that. If he were in their place, Trofimov would have tried to retreat using Goldberg as cover. That meant Yakov would be doomed. But still, let's try negotiating.

"Listen," Trofimov began. "Let him go, and we'll let you go back."

"How do I know you won't shoot us?" the lieutenant answered.

At that point two submachine gun bursts from up on the cliff hit the lieutenant and his master-corporal. They both screamed and slowly collapsed into the snow, releasing Goldberg. In the next instant, Yatta made his way down the cliff.

It was all over. The army unit was destroyed. The wounded lieutenant and master-corporal were tied together. Trofimov approached Goldberg, now unconscious, blood streaming from his mouth. Yatta bent over him to help.

"Yakov, poor guy. What have they done to you?" Trofimov exclaimed. "Scumdogs."

Trofimov stepped over to the lieutenant and kicked him in the stomach. He grabbed him by the collar and shook him fiercely. "You're going to pay for Yakov, you milksop. You'll pay for Chrissake."

He turned to Yatta and Bondarenko. "Mikhail, check whether any of them are alive. Yatta, how's Yakov? Take care of him. Do your best."

"I'm doin' what I can. He ain't bleedin' no more."

Trofimov inspected what was left of the sleds and reindeer. Four of the sleds were still usable. Five of their dozen reindeer had been killed. However, six of those belonging to the army unit were alive. Their things were scattered all over the slope and had to be gathered up and repacked on the sleds.

"Yatta, free up one sled for Yakov."

"Yes, Sasha." Yatta took their tool bag off its sled and made a bed of reindeer skins. He laid Yakov on it and covered him over with a warm deerskin.

They retrieved their scattered possessions and ammunition, packed everything away in the bags and loaded up the sleds and two of the enemies' reindeer. Finally they replaced their own slain reindeer with the army's animals, and tied the carcasses to the rear of the sleds.

"I think it's best to lash Yakov down on his sled, otherwise he could fall out. Not too tight so it doesn't cause him any pain," Trofimov suggested.

Yatta nodded and helped him secure Yakov on the sled.

"Everythin's loaded, Captain," Bondarenko announced.

"Have we got the tent?" Trofimov asked.

"Ripped to shreds. And the poles are all splintered."

"Too bad," Trofimov shook his head.

"But, you know, there are caves on the way. We can spend a few nights in them," Yatta said. "Also we can find some dwarf birches on the way for new poles, and they've left a big chunk of tarpaulin that we can use as a tent cover."

"And now for these two bastards," Trofimov nodded towards their two captives. "They can't walk, and there's no room for them in the sleds or on the deer."

"Why the fuck should we care about them?" snapped Bondarenko. "Tie 'em to the reindeers' tails. That's good enough for them."

"I hope they'll survive somehow," Trofimov grinned. "I'm afraid we'll have to tie Timoshkin in the same way. It's the only way we can take him with us. We've got to give him a proper burial."

"Surely," Bondarenko sighed. "It makes little difference to him now, poor old guy."

"Right, you take care of it, and then let's go. We have to get as far as we can before it snows again."

22

They were on the move the whole of the following day and half of the next night, halting only briefly for short rests, and to eat and smoke. By now they were all dead tired. Around midnight they reached a large cave and stopped.

With the remains of the two broken sleds they could make a decent fire. First of all they prepared a bed of three overcoats for Goldberg. Yatta sat beside him all the while, giving him melt water to drink and watching to make sure the bleeding did not start again. The injured captives, still tied together, were put by the wall near the cave entrance. Only then, when everything was arranged, could Trofimov and Bondarenko sit down by the fire and rest.

"Well, Captain," Bondarenko inhaled with relief, "that idea with the cliff was fantastic."

"Well, I had four years of war experience after all. That counts for something." Trofimov grinned. "And that youngster is fresh from college, never seen a battle in his life."

"Yeah," Bondarenko agreed, "old war dogs like us aren't that easy to crush, are we?" He sighed, "Only poor old Zakharych is done for."

Trofimov remained silent for a moment. "And who knows whether Yakov'll make it?"

"Yatta's a magician. Let's hope."

"I'm not sure whether Yakov can stand all this traveling, but we have to keep moving for another couple of nights, to some remote place where we can stay until Yakov gets better."

"What are we gonna do with these two scumbags? Interrogate them? I'll bet they know quite a bit."

"Sure," Trofimov agreed. "Will they talk, or play at being Stalin's heroic little eagles?"

"Just let 'em try. I can get the bastards to talk. I managed it with the Nazis."

"So," Trofimov maintained an arrogant expression as he addressed the hostages, who looked worn out and dispirited.

"Yeah, comrade … Mister …" the master-corporal muttered.

"I see. So now I'm both 'comrade' and 'mister' to you, am I?" Trofimov chuckled. "I know that if you ever got the upper hand, you'd be addressing me as 'scum.' I have questions for you. Whether you live or die depends on your willingness to answer. First of all, who gave the order to cordon off the trail?"

"General Nikishev," the master-corporal replied quickly. "The order came down through our own Colonel Sukhov."

"Good. And do you know where the other patrols and ambush parties are positioned?"

"I don't know that," the master-corporal answered. "That's a top military secret, I'm too low a rank to know that sort of thing."

Trofimov then rounded on the lieutenant. "You must know more than that, junior?"

The lieutenant remained silent.

"I'm waiting for your answer," said Trofimov.

He said nothing.

"Well," Trofimov's voice became harsher, "it's up to you whether to talk or give up your life for Stalin and the Soviet motherland."

"You've no right to talk about our Great Leader Stalin, you fascist scum," hissed the lieutenant.

"I'm no fascist," retorted Trofimov. "I'm a Russian officer, one of those that defeated Hitler. And it wasn't me who betrayed the Soviets, it was the other way around. And you," he grabbed the lieutenant by his collar and brought his face close to his own, "you're not even a man, are you?"

The lieutenant blushed.

"Not yet a man, but already a dirty little communist tyrant. You didn't hesitate to beat our friend into a coma." He smashed the lieutenant in the face.

"Come on, finish me off then. What are you waiting for?"

"There's one tiny thing," Trofimov retorted. "I pledged to these four men to lead them alive out of this hell. At any price. And much as I'd like to have my revenge on you, I'm ready to sacrifice that feeling. If you answer my questions, I might restrain myself from finishing you off. What's more, when we take off out of here, we'll leave a good chunk of meat for the two of you, and then it'll be up to God to decide whether you live or die. But if Yakov dies, I shan't leave you any food."

"Fuck off," the lieutenant snapped after a long silence. "I'm a Soviet officer," he announced. "You'll never make me break my oath."

"In that case, I'll finish the two of you off with my own hand. It'll be a real pleasure." Trofimov drew his pistol.

"Okay, come on. Do it."

"No. I'll leave the two of you till tomorrow morning to think it over," Trofimov concluded and went back to join his comrades by the bonfire.

"Did he tell you anythin'?" Bondarenko enquired.

"No."

Bondarenko grinned. "I thought as much. Those Young Communists are tough. Same as the Nazis. They understand it when you get tough, though. Fists and boots and rifle butts work well on them. Then you can untie their tongues."

"Forget about that," snapped Trofimov.

"I knew you'd say that," Bondarenko sighed.

"Then drop the subject. Let 'em think till morning, and then we'll see."

"As you say, Captain. Come and have a bite to eat. You must be hungry."

"Sure am." Trofimov took a piece of freshly fried meat.

After supper, Trofimov fell asleep, and Bondarenko followed suit. Yatta stayed at Goldberg's side. In a couple of hours Yatta woke up Bondarenko.

"How's Yakov?" Bondarenko asked as he opened his eyes.

"Not good. Sometimes he regains his senses, you know, but then he falls unconscious again. I'm still hoping."

"Good. We should let him have a good rest. And we'll …" His lips curled in a cruel smile, "we'll talk to those bastards ourselves. By morning they'll fuckin' well talk. By the time the captain wakes up, we'll have that information."

"But you know, he'll realize we did it," said Yatta cautiously.

"'Course he will. So what?" Bondarenko chuckled. "He'll swear and curse at us, that's his right as leader. He may even bop us one on the snout, but we're used to that, aren't we? But he won't turn down the information we extract from them, will he?"

"No, you know, I don't think so."

"That's the main thing," Bondarenko paused and looked at Yatta. "Just remind me what your kinsmen did to that Cossack."

"They stripped him naked and whipped him for a bit, then they held him over a fire."

"Hmm, I don't think we need to go that far," Bondarenko grinned, "though stripping them naked is a good idea."

Yatta got up and hurried to Yakov's side. "He's bleeding again."

"Okay, stay with him. I'll deal with those bastards myself. I'll try the methods we used in our partisan unit."

"Take them further away, towards the entrance. Yakov shouldn't hear them screaming."

"Good point," Bondarenko agreed.

The prisoners sat by the wall, their hands and feet tied. Bondarenko grabbed the lieutenant by the shoulder and dragged him towards the entrance where the roaring of the blizzard drowned out all other sounds. Then he dragged out the master-corporal.

"What are you gonna do to us?" the master-corporal asked in a trembling voice.

"What the fuck d'you think I'm gonna do to a couple of bastards like you? Somethin' like what you did to poor old Yakov." He paused. "And to start with you're gonna answer all my questions."

"Not a single one." snapped the lieutenant.

Bondarenko gave a nasty laugh.

"C'mon, youngster, I know how to untie your tongue. And I'll do to you, Young Communist, what I did to the Nazis. Or, rather, I'll start with you, man." He turned to the master-corporal and took out the map that had been found in the lieutenant's pocket. "Now," he said, "show me the location of the cordons and patrols."

"For Chrissake, I don't know," the master-corporal protested, shivering.

"In that case, we'll try a different approach." Bondarenko untied his hands and feet. "There you are. You're free to fight. Misha Bondarenko never hit a man with his hands tied."

With that Bondarenko swung his fist and clouted the master-corporal full in the face. The prisoner collapsed. Bondarenko stripped him to the waist and punched and kicked him.

"That's for Yakov, you motherfucker. And that's for Yakov. And that's also for Yakov."

The prisoner moaned.

"You gonna tell me now?" Bondarenko asked, pausing for a moment.

"Spare me, man. I've got a wife and three kids," the man pleaded.

"Oh, you've got a wife and kids?" Bondarenko taunted. "And who cared about my wife and kids when you people put me in the jug fresh from the war? Who?" he yelled. "Yakov has a wife and kids, but you lot couldn't give a flying fuck about them, could you? Back in the thirties your crowd pushed thousands and thousands of innocent folk into cattle cars and shipped them off into the tundra. Together with their kids and old folk. Did you care about that?"

Bondarenko kicked him in the groin.

"I don't know what you want to know. I don't know," The man pleaded, writhing. Bondarenko grinned and continued kicking him.

"Lieutenant, for Chrissake," the man screamed. "Tell this bastard what he wants to know. I can't stand any more."

"Hey, what's that? You really don't know?" Bondarenko asked with an evil smile.

"No. Not a fuckin' thing."

"So much the worse for you. Take what's yours, you bastard. For Yakov and Zakharych too." With that Bondarenko grabbed his bayonet and slashed open the master-corporal's throat.

"Now it's your turn, Young Communist." Bondarenko turned to the lieutenant and untied the thongs that bound his hands and feet. "Start talking."

"I told you already, scum, I am not talking."

Bondarenko shrugged. "In that case you're not gonna complain."

One blow followed another. "Here's another one for Yakov, and this one's for Zakharych, and this one's from me … You fuckin' Komsomols have been sucking our blood for years. You seized our grain. You left our kids swollen with hunger. A Young Communist whelp like you sent me to the camps as a reward for fighting the Nazis. Till now I've finished off only those Nazi fascists, but now at last I can have a go at you, Young Communist." Bondarenko slowed down slightly. "So, gonna talk? If so, I'll just shoot you tomorrow. No more beating."

"Fuck off, you bandit," the lieutenant yelled.

The beating resumed, and Bondarenko went on and on with the boundless energy of his rage. He stopped only to go back into the cave and returned with a crowbar.

"I'll crush your fuckin' bones."

The lieutenant moaned but said nothing.

The blow of the crowbar across the prisoner's right collarbone made a crunching sound that mingled with a scream.

"Like it?" asked Bondarenko. "In a moment I'll do the same on the other side. And then I'll smash each of your ribs, and when I've finished all of them, I'll smash your balls. You're not gonna need them any more anyway."

"Mikhail," Yatta called.

"Yeah, Yatta? How's Yakov?"

"Not good. The screaming disturbed him. He mustn't know what you're doing, or he'll get worse."

"No problem." Bondarenko picked up a piece of deerskin rug and plugged the lieutenant's mouth. "What about Yakov? Is he gonna live or not?"

"I don't know." Yatta looked at the lieutenant and then at the corpse of the master-corporal. "Why did you kill him?"

"'Cos he didn't know anythin'. This youngster does, but I ain't cracked him yet."

"Try using fire," suggested Yatta. "But you know, I can't help you. I can't leave Yakov for long."

"No problem. You go and do your best to save Yakov. I'll manage on my own."

"What was that? Who screamed?" Trofimov emerged from the darkness holding a torch. The next second he saw the battered lieutenant and the body of the master-corporal.

"What the fuck does this mean?" he exploded. "I'm asking you. What does it mean?" Trofimov grabbed Bondarenko by the chest. "I told you. No torture!"

"Calm down, Captain. This guy ain't gonna crack otherwise.

You want to let him die the death of a heroic Young Communist, and take the information with him to hell?"

"Enough. I gave you an order, and you, you bastard, defied that order."

"We've got no fuckin' choice," Bondarenko snapped back. "Do you want to pity this whelp and have us caught in the first fuckin' ambush?"

Bondarenko appealed to Yatta. "Look at him, Yatta. He's so obsessed with his fuckin' humanism that he can't see the facts. I'd not be surprised to hear talk like that from Yakov. But from you, Captain?"

"You know, Captain," said Yatta in a calm voice, "you're wrong. That boy is our enemy. He's one of the Big Moustache's henchmen. He butchered Yakov, one of us. He deserves harsh treatment. We'd never crack him otherwise."

"So the two of you are in this together," Trofimov shouted, "conspiring behind my back."

"No, hell. That ain't conspiring." Bondarenko shot back. "We're just not gonna be hostages to your fuckin' stupid humanism. Go and have a rest for Chrissake, and leave this one to me. When he cracks, you might get back your powers of leadership." He paused. "Or try questioning our Young Communist here. Maybe he's ready to crack."

Trofimov stepped over to where the lieutenant lay. He knelt down and pulled the rug out of his mouth.

"You'd do best to answer my questions." He took up the map again. "Then we can leave you here alive."

"You fascist. I'll die a Soviet officer."

"Well, did you hear that?" said Bondarenko. "Maybe now you'll get smart."

Trofimov looked Bondarenko in the face then stared at the lieutenant. It was a hopeless deadlock. The lieutenant was intransigent, and there was no doubt that Mikhail would never leave him in peace. As soon as Trofimov's back was turned he'd torture him again. There was only one way to break this impasse. Trofimov looked into the lieutenant's defiant face again, drew his pistol and pulled the trigger. The shot thundered and echoed inside the walls of the cave.

"Fuck!" yelled Bondarenko. "You really are off your fuckin'

head. Look at him, Yatta. He shot the youngster. He's silenced him once and for all. D'you understand what you did for Chrissake?"

"I did what I had to do. I will not allow acts of butchery."

"But you know, that was a very stupid thing to do, Sasha," Yatta was clearly distraught. "We may all pay for that."

"Stupid ain't the word," said Bondarenko. "I don't know how the fuck to describe it. What were you thinking? Now because of you we're all gonna be fuckin' finished. What the fuck were we thinking, electing you as leader?"

"Is that so? Then you don't want me any more?" Trofimov swung round to face them. "Maybe you want to whack me too? Just try it. I can tell you, I shall fight. I'll be no match for the two of you together, so what are you waiting for?"

"Shut up!" Bondarenko snapped. "Cut this crap. You can think of me however you fuckin' well want, but I'm not a piece of scum, and I'll never spill the blood of a comrade-in-arms. Never." He paused. "And as for your pity for this shitty little Communist, we'll all have to pay for that. We agreed to be together, and we'll stay together until they finish us off. That's all I have to say."

Trofimov smiled in reply. "Then I'm not mistaken about you, Mikhail."

"And, overall, in the big picture, I ain't mistaken about you either." Bondarenko tried to smile back, but failed. "At least, we won't win this fight without you."

"Nor without you either," Trofimov replied.

"Did you see the map?" asked Trofimov.

"Sure," said Bondarenko. "It shows nothing, just the territory. No ambush points, patrols, cordons, or whatever."

"Did you try reading it close to the fire?"

"Sure. How else could I read it in the dark?"

"You're not getting me. Did you hold it for a while near the fire? It could have hidden cryptography."

"What d'you mean?"

"There are special kinds of ink that reveal nothing to the naked eye, but you can see them if you hold them close to a source of heat."

"Holy shit," exclaimed Bondarenko. "Why didn't you never tell us that before?"

"Well, now you know."

"Let's give it a try." He almost dragged Trofimov towards the campfire but they stopped, petrified. Close to the fire was a large pool of blood. Yatta knelt next to Goldberg's motionless body.

"Yakov ..." Yatta began in an apologetic voice. "He tried to get up. He began bleeding, and collapsed."

"And you, you bastard, weren't watching him. Instead you helped Mikhail to torture those two."

Yatta stood silent, his eyes downcast.

"C'mon, Captain," Bondarenko took Yatta's side. "He isn't guilty. How d'you think could he spend every single moment with Yakov? After all, he needed to go for a piss, didn't he? And Yakov had somethin' on his mind too. God knows what. It often happens with sick people."

"He got up because he heard their screams," Trofimov said.

"All right," Bondarenko said, "you ain't need to make me feel guilty. When I get to America I'll make a pilgrimage to a Russian Orthodox monastery and sacrifice a month's income so the monks will pray for forgiveness of my sin."

23

The surviving fugitives were left in a sorrowful mood. The blizzard raged with full fury, so they had no alternative but to stay in the cave. Even were it to end soon, however, they could not move immediately, since it seemed unlikely that Goldberg would survive another move. He remained unconscious, and it looked as if he might die despite Yatta's skills. He breathed and swallowed water, so they nursed a faint hope.

On the evening of the second day, Bondarenko remembered the map and suggested to Trofimov that they examine it. Trofimov agreed, and they went to the entrance of the cave, lit a small fire and settled down with the map.

"So," Bondarenko began, "you said you can read somethin' by the fire with a magnifying glass, right?"

"Yes," said Trofimov. We'll try the binoculars. Hold the map with both hands close to the fire, and I'll look through the binoculars."

Bondarenko followed his directions, and Trofimov leaned over the map and examined it through the binoculars. His guess was right. By the light of the fire he saw markings all over the map, signs of infantry units, tank platoons, artillery pieces, and ambush dugouts. They were all there.

"Here they are," Trofimov exclaimed. "They're all here. Everything's marked—mounted squads, platoons and even infantry. Tanks too. Look at this sign: the cross marks the site of dugouts."

"Let me see," Bondarenko asked urgently.

Trofimov took the map and held it close to the flames. "Look through the binoculars."

"Holy shit. There's points and crosses and little squares, whatever the hell they mean. It's clearly good to be an officer. You know secrets that a bumpkin like me would never guess." He handed the binoculars back to Trofmov and held up the map again while his friend continued examining it. The map showed that all the valley passes were cordoned off. They could only go through the mountains along the Iskaten range.

"Sasha!" Yatta called.

"Yes, Yatta! What's happening?" Trofimov answered.

"Yakov has come round. He wants to talk to you. Come quick before he faints again."

Trofimov rushed to Goldberg's side. He was pallid and grey in the face, but his eyes were wide open. Trofimov knelt down by his head, and their eyes met.

"That you, Sasha?"

"Yes, Yakov. How are you?"

"Not too bad, you know. Almost no pain. Only it's hard for me to see. I … I'm almost gone."

"What have those bastards done to you?"

"I don't know. At first I was racked with pain, but now it's gone. I just feel feeble."

"Well," said Trofimov with grim satisfaction, "they've paid for it."

"Yes, I heard. Mikhail did something dreadful to them. They screamed so loud."

"Well, you know, Yakov, Mikhail was so outraged, he couldn't help but take vengeance."

"And are they—?"

"Yes, they're dead. I shot the lieutenant, and Mikhail killed the second one."

"Poor bastards. I know you were always mad at me for pitying our enemies, but that doesn't matter any more. They're dead, and I'll be following them soon."

"C'mon, Yakov. You don't want to bury yourself ahead of time, for Christ's sake. You know, Yatta's a magician."

"No, believe me, I'm in a really bad way. Give me some water, please."

"Just a second." Trofimov poured some warm water into a mug. Goldberg gulped it feebly. Drops of red from his mouth mingled with the water."

Trofimov heaved a deep sigh. He would have gladly kept the two Soviet soldiers alive and allowed Bondarenko to do whatever he wanted with them, so long as he gagged their screams so as not to bother his wretched comrade.

"What date is it today?" Goldberg suddenly asked.

"The twentieth of December. Why?"

"The beginning of Hanukkah."

"What's that?"

"The Day of the Second Temple. It's when candles are lit everywhere, and Jewish folk all round the world celebrate. On this day in 164 BC, the Second Temple was opened with great festivities."

"The Second Temple? So there was a first one?"

"Yes. The First Temple was built by King David and destroyed by King Nebuchadnezzar of Babylon."

"Is that when the Jews were taken to Babylon as captives?"

"Right. Jerusalem was destroyed, and King Zedekiah tried to flee." Goldberg choked and blood ran from his lips. "He was caught and brought before Nebuchadnezzar, and his sons were slain in his presence, and then … his eyes were put out." He choked again.

Trofimov looked at him with deep sorrow.

"Anyway," Goldberg continued a moment later. "At least I'm not going to die in their hands. And … I wish you luck. By the way, when was it we had those Chukchi girls?"

"Some time back in March."

"Then … that means they're about to give birth."

Goldberg's face lit up in a smile. The next moment he fainted again.

For another half hour Trofimov wandered around the cave, towards the exit where the two soldiers' corpses lay together with Timoshkin's body, then back to the fire where Goldberg lay with Yatta seated by his side. He could not dispel a sense of deep melancholy, he who had seen so many dozens of men die, many of them in great pain. But that was war. Their deaths were something normal, just as they were in the camps. But they had spent a year without any of their company dying, and he had cherished the hope that they would all reach safe haven alive and well. That dream was shattered.

Bondarenko approached him and proposed that they study the lieutenant's documents. Trofimov agreed, hoping this might partly dispel his sorrow. They sat by the fire at the entrance to the cave and looked through the documents. The first was an officer's ID card.

"Korneyev, Nikolay Grigoryevich," Trofimov read, "born July 31, 1928. Place of birth, Saratov. Hmm ..." The card stirred a memory.

"Did you know him?" asked Bondarenko.

"Maybe. I'm not sure."

"How come? You've never been to Saratov, and he's too young ever to have been at the front."

"I was in Saratov in hospital in 1943," said Trofimov. "I gave a talk to some high school students one day. The Young Communist leader of the class was named Kolya. He said he planned to enter military college after high school. I don't remember his surname." He continued reading: "Lieutenant, Special Task Force of the MGB— fucking whelp." He spat.

"Yeah, those Special Taskers spilled our blood like water," Bondarenko concurred. "They hunted the guys from our village who took off into the woods back in the thirties. They shot any villagers they suspected of sympathizing with them. And they came after the villagers again as soon as the Nazis had left. A double dose of shit."

Bondarenko took up another paper and gave a gust of malicious laughter.

"What's so funny?" In the last few days there had been no laughter at all among their group.

"Just read it." Bondarenko proffered the paper to Trofimov. It was a letter:

29 September 1949
Saratov

My dearest beloved Kolya
I received your last letter the day before yesterday. I'm glad that everything's all right with you, although I certainly realize how hard things are in the service. I also know it's your choice, and indeed someone has to protect our country on those remote frontiers. You aren't one to shirk your duty. That's one of the things I admire in you and that I love you for.
Our life goes on as usual, with nothing new. I am graduating next spring. I can hardly wait till that day comes, and at last I shall be able to come to your faraway frontier to join you and share your hardships and toils. I've started registering to make this move in spring: they say it can take more than a year. But I'm quite ready for that. Such is our life, hardly anything is achieved without toil. One just has to deal with that, like you are doing out in those icy regions.
I kiss you. You should always remember that my love is with you. May that memory support you there and help ease your hardships. And this photo will be a living reminder of that.
With love, Your Lena.

"What shit." Bondarenko spat in disgust. "I can't stand it. Just like in that song about little Katya and her Special Tasker. One of those who made our lives a misery, butchering us and breaking our bones and feeding us to the mosquitoes. And this little chick pledges her love for one of that lot." Bondarenko giggled maliciously. "No, girlie, you're gonna wait and wait, and your darling ain't ever gonna come."

Trofimov glanced at the body of the man whose name was Kolya. Was he the same Kolya who had looked on Trofimov with such admiration back in 1943, and pledged to join the military?

This young lieutenant whose corpse lay unburied had the same first name and the same probable date of birth as that teenager.

Trofimov could not recollect his face.

24

"Sasha! Mikhail!" Yatta called.

"What is it, Yatta? Is Yakov—?"

"Yes. He's dead."

Trofimov and Bondarenko walked over to where Goldberg lay. His eyes were half closed, as if he were meditating about something that had made him tired. Reluctant to believe that Yakov had gone, Trofimov took his hand. Bondarenko looked at him questioningly.

"There's no pulse." Trofimov was surprised how steady his voice was as he spoke those tragic words.

"Well," Bondarenko heaved a deep sigh, "his sufferings are over. If there is a heaven, he'll surely get his reward."

The three men took off their fur caps and bowed their heads.

"Let's lay him next to Timoshkin." Trofimov was first to break the silence. Together they lifted Goldberg's body and carried it towards the entrance to the cave.

"We have to give them a decent burial," said Trofimov.

"Of course," Bondarenko nodded. "How can we do otherwise?"

"We'll mark their tomb with a boulder."

A day later, when the blizzard finally ended, the three of them went out to bury their perished comrades. Yatta led them to a relatively level part of the slope, where there was soil above the rock. They dug into the frozen ground with crowbars and spades. They worked solemnly and silently, since there was little they could say. Casual conversation was inappropriate, and they were too tough to weep and show their grief.

"Looks like it's deep enough," Trofimov said when the pit was one metre deep.

"Yeah, that's deep enough," Yatta agreed,

They brought Timoshkin's body, which felt surprisingly heavy, and carefully laid it in the pit. They laid Goldberg at Timoshkin's side.

"God save your souls, Yakov and Zakharych," Bondarenko crossed himself. "Farewell. Go peacefully on your way, and don't nurse grievances against us."

"Sleep peacefully, brothers," Trofimov's voice choked. "Forgive us for not being able to do more for you." He turned to Yatta and Bondarenko. "Can we afford a gun salute?"

"No," Bondarenko shook his head. "It could give away our position, although it'd be very appropriate," he sighed. "Well, let's fill it in. You throw the first clod of earth, Captain."

Trofimov took a handful of icy earth and dropped it into the pit. Bondarenko and Yatta did likewise, then all three filled in the grave with their spades.

They chose a large boulder and with great effort rolled it on top of the grave mound.

"Looks good," said Bondarenko. "Can we write something on the stone?"

"We can't write their names," said Trofimov, "but we could draw something. How about a cross and a Star of David side by side?"

"Oh, yeah, I know what you mean. The Nazis forced Jews to wear them," Bondarenko recalled.

"Do you have any of your berry paint, Yatta?"

Yatta nodded and brought a small skin bag with a flask full of red paint. Trofimov found a small stick and daubed a Russian Orthodox cross and a Jewish star next to it.

"Maybe we could add somethin' else," Bondarenko suggested.

Trofimov agreed and painted two crossed guns framed by a chain broken at one link.

"That looks good," Bondarenko admired the artistry. "They were our brothers-in-arms, and together we broke our chains. A good picture for a soldier's grave." He paused and chuckled. "My late father would have been pissed off to see the Orthodox cross and Jewish star together on one grave, but it's normal to bury soldiers of different beliefs together. Anyway, Dad, Yakov wasn't among those that crucified Christ. He himself was a victim, and they showed precious little pity for him." He paused and became lost in his thoughts, then spoke again: "You know, it's unfair that it had to be him who suffered such pain before his death, and not a hardened guy like you and me. He wasn't suited to making war.

But he had courage. They tortured him, but he never betrayed us. He was a real hero."

For a few minutes they stood in silence over the tomb and then left to prepare for their onward journey.

The purplish-red noonday sun, high in the lilac polar skies, shed its rays on the tomb, illuminating the picture on the stone, a monument to two ordinary men of different races, united in their struggle for life and liberty. Years, decades and centuries would pass, generations would come and go, states and governments and regimes would rise and fall, but hopefully this grave would remain. Some day someone would find it and try to understand whose tomb it was, and who those men were who had found their final rest just here.

PART IV: THE LAST PUSH

1

Trofimov, Bondarenko and Yatta lay flat on their stomachs on top of the mountain ridge, gazing down into the valley. They surveyed the area, passing the binoculars from one to another. As far as the eye could see spread a vast treeless valley dotted here and there with small hillocks, the entire landscape covered by a thick white shroud of snow. A casual observer might have assumed that the valley was deserted, but as hunted outlaws they were inclined to distrust their first impressions.

This was the Ulyeveyemskaya Valley, which cut across the mountain plain from the centre of the Chukotka Peninsula to Koluchinsky Bay in the north. A few days ago, as their group of three reached the rocky approaches, they had seen a large company of troops concentrated in the valley, equipped with machine guns, artillery and tanks. Obviously General Nikishev's operational department had laid special plans to meet the gang of bandits who for more than a year had so offended his self-esteem. The troops were concentrated at the western descent into the valley. The military authorities had failed to camouflage these preparations, although, as Trofimov realized, it would have been virtually impossible to conceal so many troops and weapons. It was clear that the entire valley was cordoned off, and for this reason, they would advance northwards along the mountain ridge toward Koluchinsky Bay. They would then attempt to traverse the Bay on the ice in order to reach the mountainous eastern shore.

On the fifth day, their party reached a place from which it appeared that the valley was free of troops. Nevertheless there were suspicious signs—the birds were flying high, which suggested human presence on the ground. In the bright daylight they surveyed this part of the valley, trying to decide whether they should risk the crossing.

"Those hills could provide cover for a cordon," Bondarenko said.

"I agree," said Trofimov. "I'd be highly surprised if they left this gap open for our convenience, though they might be short of troops. How big is the valley, Yatta?"

"About five score versts from east to west, and about the same from north to south."

"That's a hundred kilometres each way," Trofimov calculated.

"A hundred kilometres of flatland."

"Well, you know, it's not all that flat," Yatta corrected him. "There are occasional rocks and hills."

"I'd swear they've got ambushes set up down there. They'd be complete numbskulls not to," said Bondarenko.

"Most likely," Trofimov agreed. "We'll have to take an alternative route. What do you think, Yatta?"

"Well, you know, there are two ways. One is to go southwards again, then turn north and make for the next large valley."

"I bet they've cordoned off that valley too," said Trofimov.

"Or we can move northwards, make a large loop around another valley, the Eturerveyem, then move up towards Koluchinsky Bay. Then we'd go across the bay over the pack ice, straight into the Genkany Mountains. And they go all the way to the Strait," Yatta explained.

"But isn't it risky to cross the ice?" Trofimov queried. "It's so flat. We'd make perfect targets out there."

"No, in fact, it isn't at all flat. It's very rugged and ridged all over with ice hummocks," Yatta said. "Some of them are quite high, and they'd provide good cover."

"If the ice cover's that rugged, then that's the best way for us."

"I think so too," Trofimov agreed. "I doubt whether they're patrolling the bay. Is the ice thick enough, Yatta?"

"Oh yes, although sometimes it cracks open. I donna know why. Maybe the Chukchi Sea gets into a rage and throws up big waves, or something."

"Well, we'll have to take the risk," Trofimov concluded. "Still, before going that way, let's reconnoiter. Who knows, there may be a gap in their cordon, so we might just get through?"

"I'm ready to go," Bondarenko said.

"But you know, Sasha, I think I should go with him," said Yatta. "Mikhail really doesn't know this place and he could get ambushed. But I've crossed this valley many times."

"Oho, so you donna trust my skills?" Bondarenko laughed. "Remember, I was a scout for three long years."

"Yatta's right," said Trofimov, "and the two of you can achieve more together. If you do land in an ambush, you'll be twice as strong to fight back. God forbid, if one of you got shot, the other might manage to get back."

"How you gonna stay here on your own, Captain? Aren't you scared?"

"What are you talking about?" Trofimov grinned. "With all this ammo? I'm almost invulnerable up here. Anyone trying to come up here will be a sitting duck."

After supper, Bondarenko and Yatta set off and disappeared into the darkness.

Trofimov sat alone and leaned against a boulder, a Kalashnikov resting across each shoulder and the machine gun beside him. The night was calm and clear with bright stars and a shining moon. Everything was still, the rocks and the valley beneath, and the only sounds were those of some small animal scuttering nearby.

Trofimov looked at his watch. Four o'clock in the morning, and still no sign of them. It didn't mean they were in trouble—he would have heard shooting—but he desperately wanted to sleep, and at one point even thought of going to the tent for a short nap. He dismissed the idea. Too risky. What if "they" decided to explore the mountain rocks and seized him while he slept? He shivered at the very thought of being caught. His old scars from Razzhivin's torture chamber hurt again, and then there were memories of how other convicts had ended up in the ice cellar, or tied to the larches. Brrr!

Trofimov abandoned any idea of sleeping and rolled a cigar from their supply of twist. Smoking helped one stay awake. He looked at his armoury of machine and submachine guns and the heap of grenades. Truly, he was next to invincible. He grinned. What a difference it made to have a supply of tools for killing. He no longer felt like a vulnerable creature of flesh and blood but almost like a one-man army that no enemy could destroy without suffering heavy losses. He took out his flask of liquor and took a sip. A pleasant warmth coursed through his body. Now let the bastards try coming here. They could hardly get him with ordinary gunfire. To defeat him they'd need shrapnel or mortar fire. This was just like the battlefront in wartime, something he was perfectly used to. He smiled and enjoyed the feeling that the worst he had to face would be death in battle, not a painful lingering demise in the hands of an infuriated enemy.

He checked his watch again. Five o'clock. Well, maybe the guys had found plenty to explore down there. After all, they hadn't set any time limit, so they might continue reconnoitering till the next evening. Surely they'd do that rather than return without a complete picture of what was going on.

Suddenly two bleak figures emerged from the darkness and climbed the rocks. "Wolves back from the hunt?" He called out the agreed password.

"And with prey," came the answering phrase from Bondarenko.

Trofimov smiled with relief. "Any success?" he asked as they finally approached.

"Well, as you can see," Bondarenko gave his usual grin, "we're back, and without any fuckin' enemy tailing us. Everything was as you predicted, Captain."

"So there are ambushes in the valley?"

"It's packed with 'em, even artillery, all well entrenched and camouflaged under the snow."

"They're obviously serious about getting us," Trofimov chuckled. "And I bet they're hoping we'll take the bait."

"No fuckin' doubt," said Bondarenko.

"Then we've no choice," Trofimov concluded. "We'll cross the bay."

For ten more days they moved northwards along the steep mountain slopes. Down in the valley troop detachments were easily seen, interspersed with long stretches that showed no sign of human presence. Trofimov chose not to risk exploring, convinced there were camouflaged ambush parties everywhere along the valley

If there were cordons at Koluchinsky Bay as well, they would have to postpone their plan to make direct for the Strait and instead seek refuge in the mountains. However, one factor worked in their favour: the authorities could hardly have the manpower to cordon off the valley and the bay and Strait as well. According to Trofimov's calculation, that would require more forces than the Far

Eastern regional command ever had at their disposal. So, if they had the valley tightly closed off, that meant the way across the bay ought to be relatively free.

At last the valley at the foot of the rocks gave way to a large inlet covered solidly with mounds and ridges of pack ice. Powerful waves smashed the original ice cover into floes, after which polar temperatures quickly froze the water again, creating a new encrustation of impacted ice hummocks that rose above the surface like gigantic camel humps.

Trofimov sent Yatta and Bondarenko out again to ascertain there were no ambush points on the bay shore. The information they brought back was encouraging: there were no troops either on the shore or on the bay. Apart from which, this part of the bay formed a deep inlet well away from the northern coast proper, where a further concentration of border troops might be expected. With nothing to impede their passage, the three men therefore set out across the ice field covering the bay.

2

They had maneuvered their way between the ice hummocks for two days. At night they found shelter under one of the larger ice escarpments and set their tent up there. Although the north border region was fairly distant, Trofimov was anxious that aircraft might fly over and locate their reindeer and sleds. During stopovers they buried the sleds under the snow, and each evening they built a large igloo and kept the animals inside with their hind legs bound. There was of course no food on the ice for the reindeer, but their provisions of yukola, or sun-dried salted fish, came in very handy. Surprisingly, the reindeer ate it.

In the morning of the third day they were caught by a blizzard, which gave them a chance for a rest. As usual, Yatta foresaw its approach well in advance, so there was time to put up their tent and construct an igloo for the deer.

"Well," Bondarenko said on the second day of the blizzard, "it may be awfully boring sitting here trapped for days on end, but just think how lucky we are compared to those less well equipped. I wonder how many folk perished in blizzards like this without any chance of surviving."

"We'd be in the same boat if we didn't have Yatta."

Yatta smiled. "Well, the skills I have are what every Chukchi inherits from his forefathers."

"But it's thanks to you that we're benefitting from them, Yatta," said Bondarenko. "What would we do without you? And to think that at first I didn't wanna take you with us. Why, I even had a set-to with the captain about it."

"I understand," said Yatta without betraying the least sign of offence. "You didn't trust me. But, in the camp nobody trusted nobody."

"Right," Bondarenko nodded. "And we didn't really know you, despite your good deed when you brought the captain back from the dead. But you were a trusty, and I thought someone in that position would never want to risk escaping. Anyway, I want to ask your forgiveness. Now I see what kinda guy you are."

"That's all fine," Yatta smiled. "But what made you trust me?"

"It was that conflict with those bandits, the other orderlies," Bondarenko said. "Especially when they decided to whack you for I donna remember what, and you asked for our help. We couldn't refuse you, 'cos we owed you so much."

"Yeah, and I owe you guys plenty," Yatta replied.

"And that made us kind of sworn brothers. I realized you'd have to escape too, or those scumbags would have finished you off. All that put paid to any further doubts."

"How long ago was that?" Trofimov wondered. "It seems like a century ago. We've changed as people since then."

"'Course we've changed," Bondarenko agreed. "Then we were just cons; now we're free men, sort of. And no one's gonna bag us again all that easily."

"That's true," Trofimov said. "But there's more to it than that. I don't know how exactly to put it. All this, all that's happened to us, all we've done, including fighting together, has formed a link between us that's as tight as any blood bond. The death of Timoshkin and Yakov brought us even closer together."

Bondarenko sighed. "I especially pity old Yakov. Zakharych was shot dead on the spot, but Yakov suffered a lot. And now he'll never see the promised land of America. Whatever you say, Captain, I'm glad I beat the shit out of those bastards. That was my revenge for Yakov."

"Well, you know my position on that," said Trofimov. "And it hasn't changed. But maybe God himself punished them by your hand. In which case I'm not going to argue with you. They deserved it."

"I think so too," said Yatta.

"I know you do." Trofimov paused. "Let's talk about the future instead, about when we get to America."

"Well," Bondarenko smiled, "maybe we'll recall all of this, how we broke our backs in the mines, how we fought and endured." He sighed. "But who knows? I had the same sort of thoughts in our partisan unit: I thought the war would end, and a new life would begin. I guess you had the same sort of ideas running through your head at the front, eh, Captain?"

"I did," replied Trofimov. "I thought about how I'd sit and recollect these days at the front when peace was declared. It never occurred to me I wasn't ever going to enjoy a peaceful existence, and that there would be even more suffering than before. So I agree: it's rather hard to think about the peaceful life we'll lead if and when we get to America."

"But at the same time, it's already about a year and a half since we escaped," Bondarenko said. "By any normal expectations for runaway cons, they ought to have nabbed and finished us off long ago. But we're still here. We ain't frozen, we ain't starved to death, and we ain't been caught, though we've been chased by all the troops in the Far East. Now we're quite close to Alaska. That's really somethin', ain't it? A few hundred more kilometres to go, and then we cross the Strait."

The following day they reached the eastern shore of Koluchinsky Bay, and a day after that climbed up into the Genkany mountain range, the final barrier on their route towards the Bering Strait.

3

It took them a month more to reach the legendary Cape Dezhnyov, easternmost point of the Asian continent. The cape consisted of a large mountain descending to the sea on three of its four sides. In its northern foothills lay the town of Uelen, which under the tsars and for a decade following had been a centre of local trade. Chukchi people from all over the land came there to barter goods with the coastal Eskimos in return for the sealskins they needed for their summer boats and raincoats. Traders from the Alaskan shore came too, to trade Winchester rifles, gunpowder, bread, sugar and liquor. Uelen was at one time the site of an annual fair that boomed with a polyglot hubbub, partying and dancing.

That was a thing of the distant past. The border was effectively closed off and guarded by border patrol units armed with machine guns, artillery, armoured personnel carriers, as well as an air force squadron. This was put in place to prevent foreigners from penetrating, and to prevent defectors from leaving the Soviet Union and making their way across the Strait.

Trofimov, Bondarenko and Yatta passed the town of Uelen on the southern side following a mountain path. They halted on the eastern side of the mountain that descended directly to the waters of the Strait. Trofimov sent Bondarenko and Yatta ahead to reconnoiter and check how heavily the coast was patrolled or cordoned off.

After their safe return, they reported to Trofimov. "This is the situation, Captain," Bondarenko said. "All the shore south of Uelen is cordoned off, and there's an observation post about every five kilometres."

"Damn," Trofimov cursed. "And I guess the visibility's excellent?"

"Not that good, fortunately. But still …"

"Well, we can't even try approaching in clear weather, not even at night," Trofimov said. "On the other hand, we can't go in heavy snow either. The best thing would be if we could set off in fog with light snow falling. I hope, Yatta, that sea fog isn't too rare around these parts?"

"Yeah, it occurs every so often," Yatta replied.

"Then that's the best way for us," Trofimov concluded, "though only if they don't have radar."

"What the hell is this 'razor'?" Bondarenko asked.

"*Radar*, not razor. It's a sort of lamp that produces special rays, like light rays only they're invisible. These rays feel out where objects are."

"You mean it helps them to see in the fog?" Yatta asked.

"Exactly."

"Well, that's modern science for you. Damn it." Bondarenko snapped irritably. "I never imagined they could do that in real life. I thought it was only in fairy tales."

"Well, don't you remember that famous Soviet song 'We're born to make a fairy tale come true'?" Trofimov grinned. "Nowadays there's a lot of that sort of thing going on around the world."

"Can this razor, or whatever they call it, be used to find out where we are?"

"Yes, unfortunately it can."

"If they've got that damn gadget, we're finished," Bondarenko said angrily.

Trofimov shrugged the matter off. "Well, we have to take the risk. It's not switched on all the time anyway. Let's hope we can sneak through unnoticed. Besides, it won't be easy for them to chase us down among those ice ridges and hummocks. If we're quick enough, we can get away from them, especially if it isn't good flying weather."

"What about your kinfolk, Yatta?" Bondarenko asked. "They crossed the Strait, didn't they?"

"Yeah, they sure did."

"At that time it was easier, wasn't it?" Trofimov asked. "There were no border guards, or at least not so many as now. Now, as they proudly claim, the border's firmly locked and sealed."

"Yeah, you're right," Bondarenko said dreamily. "How nice it would be if there weren't any water, and we could just walk across to America. We wouldn't have half as many problems then."

"It was like that at one time," Trofimov said. "There used to be a land bridge where the Bering Strait is now, and the American Indians are believed to have crossed over that way from Asia."

"You know, our old folk say there was land there a long, long time ago," said Yatta. "There's even a folktale about it."

"A folktale? Oh, let's hear it," Bondarenko said.

"Well," Yatta began, "in olden times the coast of Chukotka and the opposite shore weren't separated by any sea. There was land with two mountains on it, and in between them was a little creek. And across the creek there used to be a bridge made of the backbones of whales. Our people lived in those places then. They hunted seals and walrus, and some of them even had reindeer herds away in the tundra.

"The richest man among the Aiwans was a man named Tepkelin. He was rich and powerful. He hunted lots of game, and his storehouse was always full. He lived there with his wife, but had no other relatives. Once, in summer, Tepkelin was out at sea in his kayak hunting. The weather was fine, and ribbon seals emerged from the water one after another. He didn't attack them with his harpoon because he was waiting for the thong seals. None of them appeared anywhere near the shore, so he went farther out into the open sea. Soon he could barely see the shore and his home village, so there Tepkelin stopped and waited for the thong seals to appear.

"After a while a large thong seal emerged from the water in front of him. Tepkelin hurled his harpoon and lodged it in the thong seal's neck, then he threw his bladder float into the water. The thong seal tried to dive, but the bladder held it up on the surface. Tepkelin chased after the seal in his kayak, until eventually the animal weakened, and he then fastened it to the float.

"Meanwhile it was getting dark. Tepkelin made haste towards the shore, but he was still at sea when darkness fell. Suddenly a monster sprang up out of the water and gripped Tepkelin's back with its talons, and it was impossible to tear himself free. He paddled towards the shore with all his strength. The beast tore at his coat with its claws and he paddled even harder. After ripping his coat to shreds, this monster tore at the flesh on his back, and Tepkelin almost dropped his paddle in pain.

"Once again he tried to get the beast off his back, but without success. Tepkelin was bleeding profusely. He had to reach the shore as quickly as possible to save himself. He paddled furiously despite the pain, and at last he had almost reached the shore, where the folk were sitting waiting. Tepkelin was getting weaker and weaker, and he called out to them, 'A beast is clutching at my back! Get it off me, but make sure you don't kill it! Keep it alive!'

"The kayak finally reached land. The men lifted Tepkelin out and saw this beast clinging to his back. Finally it released him and was about to return to the sea, but the folk seized it and brought it to Tepkelin's yaranga.

"'We've caught your tormentor, Tepkelin,' they said. 'What do you want us to do with it?' Tepkelin told them to skin the beast alive and throw it back into the sea.

"Later that night all the folk were asleep, including Tepkelin. Suddenly he woke up and heard the roar of surf close by. A strong wind blew, and the waves had risen and covered the lowlands near the village. Tepkelin dressed and stepped out of his yaranga. The waves had already reached some people's tents, and people tried to reach safety by climbing up the mountain. Dogs barked, people called out and the surf roared. Soon the waves reached Tepkelin's yaranga. He ran inside and told his wife to dress, and they set off to climb the mountain. At that moment a huge wave came, smashing the yaranga and dragging the people away. Tepkelin and his wife were washed out to sea.

"All night the storm raged. Many people perished, many dogs were drowned, and many yarangas were washed away. A tiny strip of land remained above the water. At dawn the wind blew even stronger and the rocks were engulfed in cloud. It was only towards evening that the storm finally died down. The people who survived looked down from the mountaintop at the remains of their village. When the sun rose, they saw that the water was everywhere. The entire land where they had once lived was covered by the sea.

"And that's how the Bering Strait appeared. Only two mountains remained above the waters, and they now form two islands."

"Well, well, God certainly got mad at that guy for skinning his beast alive, didn't he?" Bondarenko commented.

"Yeah, that was God the Creator," said Yatta.

"You know, our Christian God is also referred to as the Creator," Bondarenko said. "So maybe you and us, like, worship the same God."

Next morning, as if in answer to prayer, a thick fog descended on the coast. Trofimov decided to waste no time and set off. Their party slowly descended along the path, hardly visible in the fog.

"Are you absolutely sure that there's no cordon or ambush party down there?" Trofimov asked.

"Yeah, unless they set it up in the last few hours," said Bondarenko.

In a couple of hours they reached the bottom of the mountain, and in another half hour stepped out onto the sea ice.

"The last lap," said Bondarenko in a low voice.

"Indeed. Although it could well be the hardest stage of all. Pray that they don't have radar."

4

The caravan of reindeer and baggage moved slowly across the pack ice negotiating the frozen ridges and hillocks. Trofimov constantly checked the compass.

"We have to go as straight as we can," he urged, "or we could end up at Ratmanov Island, and that's Soviet territory."

"What about the others? What about Inetlin?" Yatta asked.

"That's what we call Kruzenstern Island, and that's American. The borderline runs exactly between them."

"And they're somewhere about half way across, aren't they?" Bondarenko guessed.

"More or less."

"Then we could reach this American island by tomorrow night," Bondarenko concluded.

"Theoretically, yes. But we shouldn't risk it. In this fog we could run up against the Soviet island and walk straight into the arms of the Soviet border guards. We'll head for the American coast. If the American border guards are efficient and well equipped, we won't even have to go the whole way. They'll spot us and come out to meet us with a helicopter or a small truck."

"I hope they don't shoot us first." Bondarenko chuckled.

"I doubt it. They'll order us to surrender, and if we obey, they'll pick us up."

"And then you talk to 'em, right, Captain?"

"Yeah, I'll tell them we're asking for political asylum. Then we'll be interned for a while."

"What the hell does that mean?"

"Temporary detention," Trofimov explained. "I don't think they'll send us to jail. They're more likely to keep us some place until all the bureaucracy gets done."

"Are you sure they won't hand us back?" Bondarenko looked uncomfortable.

"No," Trofimov replied. "They could do that if they had an extradition treaty with the Soviets, but I'm sure they have none. Only friendly states have treaties like that. Political asylum is hardly ever refused to refugees from hostile states."

"But maybe we could avoid the border guards and reach my kinsmen first?" Yatta suggested. "I know some of the local Aiwan tongue, and I can ask the way if need be."

"No," Trofimov objected. "If we avoid the border guards, they'll think we're spies, and it would be very hard for us to prove that we're not."

"As you say, Sasha."

When Masha Danilova, a junior sergeant and army radio officer, began her shift on the radar, a newfangled affair said to have been stolen by Soviet intelligence from West Germany or France, or wherever, all she foresaw was more boring hours in front of the screen.

To her surprise, it clearly showed an obscure collection of metallic objects moving along the surface of the ice at a good distance from shore. Considering that radar showed only metal, it could mean only one thing: people with a lot of metal, possibly weapons, were crossing the Strait.

No one had ever tried to cross the Strait from either side, and Masha, like all other personnel at border post number thirty-one, had long been convinced that illegal crossing of the frontier was a thing of the distant past. Anyway, what idiot would try to cross such a heavily guarded border? She picked up the telephone receiver.

"Hello. Get me colonel Lisyansky. It's urgent."

"Colonel Lisyansky speaking," his baritone voice sounded in the earpiece.

"Comrade Colonel, Danilova speaking. Radar shows someone moving across the Strait in an easterly direction."

"What? Who can it be? Are they armed?" the colonel asked.

"There's lots of metal showing."

"What's their bearing?"

"About 65 degrees 1 minute and 25 seconds north by 169 degrees, 25 minutes and 19 seconds west."

Lisyansky was chief of border control point number thirty-one, and immediately on hearing Danilova's message, he summoned his adjutant.

"Call up all frontier post chiefs in the region," he ordered, "and get them over here immediately."

"Is this an emergency, comrade Colonel?" asked the adjutant standing in front of the colonel's desk.

"You're not supposed to question your superior," snapped the colonel, then, after a pause and more calmly, "but I can tell you that it looks like that gang from Seimchan is trying to cross the Strait over the ice."

"Those five? That's impossible. They couldn't have crossed the Uljuveyem Valley without being noticed."

"No discussion. Carry out the order."

"Yessir."

Within half an hour the three captains in command of nearby border posts stood in front of Lisyansky, and he briefed them on the situation.

"So," he summed up, "each of you get a Jeep load of men with at least one machine gun in each vehicle. Kharitonov, you take control. Leave a deputy in charge of your post."

"Yes, comrade Colonel. I'll need the bearings."

"Here they are." Lisyansky handed him a sheet of paper. "Now off you go and get cracking."

"Yessir."

Once the three captains had left his office, Lisyansky took up the phone again. "Masha, get me Sukhin on Ratmanov Island." He waited for the barking voice at the other end. "Hello, Sukhin? Lisyansky here. Can you hear me? That Seimchan gang are crossing the Strait … Yeah, no shit! They've been located by radar … Bearings? About half an hour ago they were at 65/1/25 by 169/25/19. Have you got a Jeep? Fine, pack it with as many men as possible and get going. Cut them off from your side … Fine, carry on."

Within twenty minutes, three Studebaker armored Jeeps moved out in line formation across the ice.

5

Trofimov, Bondarenko and Yatta took a short rest. They leaned against a hefty ice block and smoked.

"Have we passed Ratmanov Island yet?" Trofimov asked.

"Not yet," said Yatta, "in a couple of hours maybe. About a dozen kilometres."

"Still a long way off," Bondarenko shook his head.

"But if the weather was clear, and if there weren't all these hummocks, they could have spotted us already," Trofimov said.

"Then thank the Lord. Sometimes it looks like He cares after all for us wretched escapees." Bondarenko grinned. "Although not for those that do nothing to help themselves. Whatever the priests say about 'Blessed be the meek' it's quite obvious that God really favours the brave and the adventurous."

"Not always," Trofimov gave a shrug. "He didn't save those three that ended up tied to the larches."

Suddenly their conversation was interrupted by the muffled rattle of engines.

"D'you hear that?" Trofimov turned to Bondarenko.

"Course I do. I ain't fuckin' deaf."

"Take off. Fast." Trofimov commanded.

They set off as fast as they could. The engine noise came closer and closer until it was no more than a couple of hundred metres behind them.

"Here, Captain, they're right behind us." Bondarenko exclaimed.

"Yeah," Trofimov listened hard, "and there's more than one vehicle—three for sure."

"How could they find us? It was snowing when we started off. I didn't think our tracks would stay that long."

"I'm afraid either someone saw our tracks soon after we left," said Trofimov, "or they have radar."

"If so, we aren't half in trouble. If only God would send us a blizzard right now."

Yatta looked up to the sky. "No, it doesn't look at all like heavy snowing."

The column of armored Jeeps slowly wended its way through the gaps between the ice hummocks, following the tracks of the sled party, which were now perfectly visible. In the front Jeep captain Kharitonov sat at the driver's side.

"We can see their tracks, comrade Captain," the driver observed.

"Good," Kharitonov smiled. "Can we go a bit faster?"

The driver shook his head. "No, comrade Captain. You can see, we can hardly get between these ice hills as it is. If we go any faster, we'll slam into one of them."

"So I see." Kharitonov picked up the radio intercom. "Calling Commodore, calling Commodore. Number six calling … We've picked up the tracks. The only problem is we can't move fast enough. The gaps are too narrow … Yes, yes …"

The Jeeps were close behind them. They passed a long stretch free of ice ridges, and then turned in behind another row of hummocks with their pursuers closing in.

"Hell," Trofimov turned to his comrades. "We've no choice. Get the grenades."

Yatta went to the sled with the weapons and handed them each a dozen or so grenades.

"Spread out in a line facing the enemy and lob one grenade after another onto the ice in front of them, but don't pull the pins. Wait till you've got just four left, then pull the pins and throw them. D'you understand the trick?"

"Got you, Captain. Then all the grenades go off together with the last ones, and there'll be a humongous crack in the ice. That's real smart. It wasn't for nothing they promoted you captain."

"You guys, stand there and there. I'll get behind this hummock." He pointed to the closest of them. "Can you lob your grenades above these bumps?"

"Yeah, sure," Bondarenko and Yatta both nodded and confirmed.

"You know, I think we should keep back a few grenades," Yatta objected. You never know. We might need 'em later."

"All right, do that," Trofimov agreed. "Get ready!"

The roar of engines was just beyond the ice ridge where they had taken up position.

"Now!" Trofimov ordered.

The grenades flew over the ice hummocks. One, two, three … Instinctively both Trofimov and Bondarenko several times almost pulled the linchpins and stopped themselves only at the last moment.

Kharitonov's Jeep had reached the small gap in front of the ice ridge separating them from their quarry. They had to slow to walking pace, since the gap between the hummocks was almost too narrow for any vehicle to pass.

"Look out, comrade Captain," the driver called out. "Something's landed in front of us from over the ridge."

Kharitonov strained his eyes.

"Looks like grenades. How come there's no blast? Don't their grenades work? Maybe it's just some crap and they want us to think they're grenades?"

That instant a powerful blast shook the surface of the ice, a crack opened up, and fountains of water spurted up from the crevasse.

"Stop! Stop! Fucking hell!" Kharitonov yelled.

Too late. The driver stood on his brakes, but the ice was awash with water. The Jeep slithered to the crack and plunged into it. Within seconds the heavy vehicle sank beneath the surface with its driver and passengers. The driver of the next Jeep stopped just in time, and the third Jeep also ground to a halt. Soldiers and officers jumped from the two vehicles.

"Shit," bawled Junior Lieutenant Tarasov who was in command of the second Jeep. "The bastards broke the ice."

"As we see," Lieutenant Shchukin said grimly. "I never imagined they had so much explosive. And poor old Kharitonov's done for."

"Maybe we can get round the crack," Tarasov suggested.

"How can we do that with all these ice hills?" Shchukin retorted. "And how're you gonna get a Jeep through a narrow space like that?" He pointed out the narrow clefts between the ice hills on either side.

"I guess we could look for a wider opening," Tarasov said.

"Ridiculous. While we manoeuvre around this crack, they'll have time to reach no man's land, and we've no right to chase 'em beyond that point. I'd rather just report the accident and have done with it." Shchukin boarded his Jeep again and switched on the intercom.

"Calling Commodore. Calling Commodore. Number six calling. The bandits have blown a hole in the ice ... How? With grenades. They've apparently got lots of them ... Yeah, and the current's opened one hell of a long crack. We've no chance of getting round it at the speed we can go over these ice ridges ... Right. Return? Yessir."

Shchukin got out of the Jeep and shouted a command: "Everyone back into the Jeeps. Orders from the chief. Move slowly back and get away from the crack."

Colonel Lisyansky turned to his chief of staff, Major Alibekov. "Akhmet Abdullayevich, bad news. The bastards have blown the ice. Kharitonov's vehicle's gone through the ice with every man on board."

Alibekov spread his hands in a gesture of dismay. "Those guys are very clever. Looks like they even know about the currents. How far are they from Ratmanov Island?"

"About twenty-five kilometres to the north."

"Then we set up an artillery barrage from the island. They're within range."

"We can't do that. It'll destroy Pavlukhin's Jeep and crew. He's set out to intercept them from the front."

"Ah, so there's still a Jeep on their side of the crack?" Alibekov queried.

"Right."

"Then they won't get far," Alibekov grinned. "The men in the Jeep have got two machine guns. Those bandits have got no chance."

"You know, I hear that noise again," said Yatta.

Trofimov stopped and listened hard. "You're right. Another Jeep ahead, trying to intercept us, and we can't avoid it. You were right, Yatta. A good thing we kept back a dozen grenades. Get down and dig in."

They dug a small trench in the snow.

"Build up the parapet with a barrier in front." Trofimov commanded. "You know how, Mikhail?"

"Of course."

"You, Yatta, watch me and do exactly the same."

They barely had time to build up a snow barrier before the chugging of a Jeep engine filled the air right in front of them.

"Lie still, and don't raise your head above the parapet. When the Jeep appears, chuck one grenade after another, all six of them."

The next moment a Studebaker Jeep emerged from behind an ice ridge ahead of them. A shower of grenades landed beneath its wheels. The evening darkness lit up again. Engulfed in flames, the Jeep sank into another crack that opened up in the ice. A few men jumped clear of the vehicle, just in time to be mown down by a burst of machinegun fire. Trofimov then listened for suspicious sounds, but the expanse of ice and seawater was silent except for the wind.

"Right, let's move on around this ice ridge," said Trofimov. "I hope there are no more armoured vehicles ahead."

"God protect and save us." Bondarenko crossed himself.

"C'mon, let's go," Trofimov hurried them.

In the radar control room, Masha Danilova sat closely watching the screen and registered both explosions. Her eyes filled with tears as she thought of the mothers, wives and fiancées that would now be receiving "killed in the course of duty" notices. She saw with her own eyes how right Comrade Stalin was when he announced that the class struggle would inevitably become more acute as the building of socialism progressed.

She wiped away her tears and reached for the telephone.

"Comrade Colonel, Danilova speaking. There's been another explosion. Looks like the other Jeep from Ratmanov Island has been destroyed." She glanced at the screen. "It's disappeared off the screen, which means it's probably sunk."

On hearing this news, Colonel Lisyansky slammed the receiver back in its cradle and turned to Alibekov.

"They've blown up the other Jeep and crew from the island." He clenched his teeth. "Now there's no other way. We have to have the artillery. Get in touch with Rogov and tell him to use all his guns. Saturation shelling. I'll get the exact bearings in a moment."

"Yes, Alexey Matveyevich."

6

"Well, Captain," said Bondarenko, "we pulled off another surprise job."

"Looks like they've probably run out of vehicles," Trofimov breathed a deep sigh.

"That's right. If they'd had more on the island, they'd not have sent just one Jeep."

"But you know, they could have more back on the shore," Yatta volunteered.

"Maybe," Trofimov agreed. "But with the cracks and narrow corridors between these ice blocks they're not going to reach us all that soon. And by then, we'll hopefully be on the American side."

At that point, his ear caught a whistling sound all too familiar to him from the war.

"A shell!" he yelled. "Get down!"

They threw themselves flat on their stomachs. The next second several shells whistled past a few meters over their heads, and a moment later they heard blasts beyond the ice hummocks.

"Fuck!" Bondarenko cursed. "Gypsy's luck, as they say."

"Indeed," Trofimov said. Once again they were on the brink of death, when just a minute ago it seemed as if dangers had been left behind.

"But you know," Yatta said, "let's wait a minute. Maybe they'll stop."

The men lay in the snow, praying for the shelling to cease. But no. More and more shells exploded around them. Two exploded just behind them, killing all their reindeer.

All three of the heavy artillery pieces on the island shelled continuously. The island commandant, Major Kirpichnikov, was an old-stager from the war. Back then he had been in charge of a part of the General Staff Artillery on the First Byelorussian Front that had broken the German defences in Byelorussia and Poland. He knew more than anyone what concentrated fire power meant: a well-aimed barrage could destroy the vast majority of enemy personnel and equipment. He also knew that even the most intensive fire could not wipe out all enemy personnel, since some would inevitably find shelter in dugouts, cellars or elsewhere. But those who escaped death usually became heavily demoralized, and thus rarely capable of strong resistance. This was an important fact of artillery warfare, the final stage always being left to the tanks and infantry.

But now things had happened in reverse order. It was the motorized infantry in Jeeps that first tried to intercept and catch the bandits, and they had miserably failed, losing two Jeeps together with their entire crews. Now it was the turn of Kirpichnikov and his artillery to say the final word. Maybe it would have been even better if that idiot Lisyansky hadn't tried to intercept the gang, and had entrusted the whole operation to Kirpichnikov and his men from the outset. Ten lives would have been spared. But those shitheads in their arrogance wanted to seize the bandits alive, whereas with a dangerous gang like Trofimov's their goal should have been elimination.

Now Kirpichnikov listened with pleasure to the roar of his cannons. His guys were doing their best. There was no way that bastard Trofimov and his merry men would escape from this fire trap. One shell or another would inevitably bury them in the icy waters of the Strait.

Trofimov, Bondarenko and Yatta sheltered in a narrow corridor between the ice hills, with shells exploding all around them.

"Looks like this fuckin' barrage is never gonna end," Bondarenko said. At that moment a shell hit the ice not far in front of them, blowing a huge hole in the ice crust. Drops of freezing water hit them in the face, burning their skin like hot resin.

It was obvious that the troops on Ratmanov Island had more than enough ammunition to maintain this barrage for days, and that was probably what they meant to do. If Trofimov and his comrades remained where they were, sooner or later one of those shells would score a direct hit and finish them off.

"If we sit here we're doomed," he said. "We've got to get out of their range."

"But how can we?" Yatta said. "We'll get hit as soon as we stand up on our feet."

"We'll crawl," said Trofimov.

"You're right," Bondarenko said. "There's nothing else we can do. Do we leave our stuff?"

Trofimov looked at what was left of their luggage—scattered poles, tools, and shreds of bloody reindeer flesh. One sled was intact.

"Pack some of the stuff in skin bags and pull it behind us. It'll be hard going, but there's no other way.

"Yeah," said Yatta, "we can try that."

They gathered up what was left of their belongings, including an axe and two knives. Bondarenko came across some of the tent poles.

"What about the poles?"

"By all means," Trofimov said. "They could come in handy. Tie them separately, along with the skis.

Their packing completed, they set off crawling along the narrow ice corridor, but soon found themselves facing a shell hole that covered the width of the passage.

"Go round." Trofimov ordered.

They crawled their way through to another defile between the ice ridges, only to meet another crater in the ice, and then another. Before they could detour, a shell exploded almost in front of them, breaching yet another hole.

"The poles," Trofimov shouted. "Make a bridge."

They laid the poles across the ice crater.

"Captain, you first," said Bondarenko.

Trofimov moved out across the flimsy bridge and safely reached the other side. Yatta and Bondarenko followed.

"We made it," Bondarenko exclaimed.

Barely had he said so when a shell exploded a few yards in front of him, and he found himself in icy water up to the shoulders. The water turned red. Trofimov and Yatta rushed and grabbed him under the armpits. They pulled him out of the hole. His overcoat seeped blood.

"How are you, man?" Yatta asked.

"Shitty," Bondarenko clenched his teeth and suppressed a moan. "My stomach's all burning."

"Come on, Sasha, help me." Yatta called out.

They undressed Bondarenko. More than a dozen bleeding shrapnel wounds perforated his chest and stomach. Trofimov and Yatta took cloth from their baggage, staunched the bleeding and bandaged him up.

"There must be a set of clothes somewhere. Quick, find it, or he'll freeze to death." Trofimov commanded.

Yatta delved into one of the bags and found a set of clothes that Qergina had given them for a special occasion. They dressed Bondarenko, who kept moaning.

Trofimov took out a flask. "Here, have a drink, Mikhail. It'll deaden the pain a bit."

"Thanks, Captain." Bondarenko drank a few slugs and the expression of pain on his face eased.

"Yatta, how are we going to carry him? On our shoulders?"

"No. Roll him up in reindeer skins and pull him."

They wrapped Bondarenko in their two remaining deerskins, tied him around with thongs, with two longer lengths to serve as a harness, and then moved further.

Shells continued to explode around them in the middle distance, breaking the ice.

"Hell. We can't cross by the poles now. Yatta, you get over to that side, and I'll push him towards you."

"Sure, Sasha, let's try that."

Yatta crossed the flimsy bridge of poles. Trofimov then laid Bondarenko on the poles and pushed him towards Yatta. Somehow it worked, but at that moment a shell exploded to their rear and Trofimov felt a sharp pain in his left leg.

"Shit!" He swore. "They got me too. It's my leg."

"Me too, in the shoulder," Yatta said.

"All three of us wounded. We'll have to bandage one another."

A few more shells exploded. Bondarenko muttered.

"What's that, Mikhail?" Trofimov lowered his face to hear what Mikhail was saying.

"Captain, finish me off. You two ain't gonna make it carrying me all the way. Fuck this pain!"

Trofimov shuddered. He had heard several such requests from wounded fellow soldiers during the war, and twice he had acted on them. Both times because the men were in desperate pain— one with his stomach ripped open and with his gut literally falling out, and the other with his chest and lungs torn open. Even then it was unbearably hard to do, and never would he have done so had he not been completely sure that the injured man was going to die, and that a few more hours of life would bring him nothing but agony. But what about now? True, Bondarenko was in pain, even severe pain. He had multiple shrapnel wounds, but none of his vital organs seemed to have been hit. Only a physician could determine his chances of survival. And as long as this was so, Trofimov's conscience would never allow him to take matters into his own hands.

"C'mon, Mikhail, quit talking garbage. We're your comrades and we'll carry you to the end if need be."

"Why for Chrissake?" Bondarenko retorted. "Do you two wanna croak as well? If you try to carry me, all three of us are goners. We'll all fall into the hands of that lot, and—Damn, that hurts!"

"Calm down, man. They're not chasing us any more," Trofimov told him. "And they can't get at us among all this ice. That's why they're shelling. They wouldn't be doing that if they still hoped to catch us."

"Then we'll all be shot to bits by these cursed shells," Bondarenko insisted. "You're wounded, and so is Yatta. How the fuck are you gonna make it, dragging me? Without me, you've got a chance. I … I don't wanna die in their hands, but I ain't mind being shot by a comrade, a brother in arms. If you ever get to America, just go to church and pray for my soul. C'mon, do it, Captain."

"If he wanna die, we gotta respect his wish," Yatta said. He turned to Bondarenko. "Mikhail, do you really wanna go up beyond the clouds?"

"Of course. I'm hardly gonna live anyway, for Chrissake. And you ain't gotta croak along with me."

"You hear, Sasha? That's what he wants. So you know, we gotta do it. I can do it in any case."

"Yeah, do it, Yatta. Shoot me." Bondarenko appealed.

Yatta lifted his submachine gun. Trofimov lunged and struck his arm. The Kalashnikov clattered onto the ice,

"Stop it!" Trofimov yelled.

"But he wanna it himself. And he has good reason."

"I'm in command, and my word's final. Neither you nor I are going to do that. No, no, and a thousand times no. We pledged complete loyalty to each other. If we get hit by these shells, then that's our fate. If that lot are about to seize us, then I'll shoot you, Mikhail, and then Yatta and I will shoot one another. If we get so weak that we can't move, and we're going to freeze to death, we'll do the same. But not until that moment. You're not doomed to die yet, Mikhail. American doctors are good, they can save you. How can I deny that chance to my comrade? How am I to live my life if I do a thing like that?"

"You're such an obstinate shithead," Bondarenko said and then fainted.

On and on they moved. Yatta and Trofimov's wounds sent stabbing pains through their limbs with every move they made. Shells blasted craters around them or struck the ice hummocks sending showers of tiny ice fragments that struck them in the face like sharp blades. The icy wind buffeted their faces and sent shafts of searing cold under their clothes. It seemed as if God in his wrath assailed them with heavenly fire on every side. What surprised them most each minute was that they were alive and moving forward. The way seemed endless. They lost all sense of time, and their minds were dulled and blunted. All they remembered was that they must keep moving and hauling the bundle in which Bondarenko was wrapped.

While a weaker person may be guided by a survival instinct

that leads him to avoid danger, a man of courage willingly faces danger, not because of any wish to die, but due to his skill and the thrill of daring and cheating death. In a desperate situation, a weaker person's preservation instinct fails first, so that both his body and soul surrender to impending death. The stronger man holds on to his courage and continues even an apparently fruitless struggle, grasping at the flimsiest chance to avoid what looks like an inevitable end.

1

The head of Wales Frontier Section, Captain Royce, sat in his office with his deputy, Lieutenant Davidson standing beside him. The two of them listened to the mysterious manmade thunder coming from the west, out in the Strait.

"What can it be, Lieutenant? Have they started another war?"

"No sir, the shelling's in their own territory."

"Then it must be military exercises."

"Might be, sir. Odd that they're shelling only in one direction."

"Where from?"

"North of Big Diomede, what the Soviets call Ratmanov Island."

"That is odd." Royce shrugged. "If it's not exercises, it can only mean one thing."

"Yes, sir?" Davidson looked at him expectantly.

"Someone's trying to cross the border from that side."

"Fugitives?"

"Yes, trying to reach our shores." He paused. "Though I doubt they're alive after such heavy bombardment. Get your planes up and explore our section of the Strait."

"All of them, sir?"

"All of them. We need to know what this shelling is all about."

"Yessir."

Yatta looked round at Trofimov. "Look, Sasha, they aren't

shelling us any more."

"They're shelling all right," Trofimov said, "but they're landing behind us. Than means we've crossed the border."

"You sure?"

"Abso-bloody-lutely. We're on American territory."

"How's that? Their land's beyond the Strait, isn't it?"

"Yeah, but the border runs down the middle. Half the waters are Soviet and the other half American. We're in American waters, or on American ice! They can't shell us here, because that would be a breach of the border. It could start another war. We're safe, Yatta!"

"But, you know, how can you divide the Big Waters?" Yatta shook his head.

"In our times we know how to do that."

Trofimov looked at Yatta with a big grin on his exhausted face. "We made it," he exclaimed. "Yatta, we made it to the promised land."

"Wait a little, Sasha. We're still over the water. There's still about two score kilometres before we reach land. Maybe we should try to reach Inetlin Island. You say it ain't Soviet territory any more, and that would be halfway to the coast."

"Hmm, that's to the south?"

"The southeast."

"No. We could easily lose our way and end up heading back into Soviet territory. I'd rather make straight for the shore. It's far, but there'll be no risk of getting lost."

"As you say, Sasha. But then we'll have to spend a night on the ice."

"We'd do better to do that. We can make a bonfire with the poles. There'll be no more shelling and holes in the ice. We'll do a few kilometres more, so we're well beyond Soviet territory."

"Yeah, that's wise," Yatta agreed. "If only you can walk with your injured leg."

"I got used to being wounded during the war."

In one of the American border reconnaissance planes the pilot, co-pilot and radio operator watched the shelling a few miles west of their flight path, just north of Big Diomede Island.

"I wonder what it means, for Christ's sake," the co-pilot said.

"I think the captain's right. They must be trying to stop somebody crossing the Strait from their side," the radio operator said. "It's incredible. I can't imagine any other nation putting up a barrage like that just to stop a bunch of guys from emigrating."

"Well, they take pride in the idea that their frontier is locked and sealed," the pilot grinned. "I talked to some Russians near Leipzig in '45, and they were emphatic about that."

"Calling Thirteen. Thirteen, come in." the radio suddenly came to life. "This is number One. Give us an update on what's going on. Over."

"Calling number One, this is Thirteen. Situation continues. Shelling on Russian side continues unabated. Nothing new. No sign of anyone on our side."

"Well, whoever those guys were, I guess there's not much left of them now," the pilot shook his head. "No one could get through a barrage like that."

"I guess you're right," the co-pilot agreed.

"I reckon we could make a stopover now," Trofimov proposed when the sounds of shelling were well to the rear of them. "We're clearly out of range now."

"It looks that way." Yatta agreed. "Shall we make a fire?"

"Yeah, but use half of our poles in case we need to stop again."

They stowed their luggage and settled Bondarenko beside it. Then they chopped up the poles and started a fire. It was no easy task in the strong wind, but they succeeded and then moved Bondarenko closer to the warmth.

"How cosy," Trofimov exulted in the warm glow that filled his cold exhausted body. "You know, I felt I was freezing to death."

"Yeah, we really need this now. Otherwise we won't make it to the shore."

Bondarenko opened his eyes and gave a moan. Trofimov took out the flask.

"Have a drink, Mikhail." He held the flask to Bondarenko's lips, and the injured man swallowed a little. A weak smile came to his face.

"Great thing, liquor. Warms the cockles of your heart." He

looked around and strained his ears to hear the shelling. "Where are we? Why ain't there no more shelling?"

"Because they don't want to cause a war," Trofimov smiled.

"You mean—"

"Yeah, buddy, I mean we're on the other side."

"No shit. Hurrah!" Bondarenko tried to move but groaned.

"C'mon, old guy, you've gotta lie still, you know," Yatta urged.

"Right. But that's great. Come here, guys. I wanna hug you to celebrate the occasion."

"Not with your wounds, Mikhail," Trofimov smiled at him. "It'll be too painful for you."

"Then we gotta have a drink," Bondarenko tried to shift nearer to them.

"You drink," Yatta said. "We'll wait till later."

"Why? How come?"

"You're in pain," Yatta said. "If Sasha and I drink our supply of firewater, there won't be none to treat your pain."

"At least have a sip," Bondarenko insisted.

"All right," Trofimov took the flask. "To our good fortune." He took a sip and passed the flask to Yatta.

"Poor Yakov and Zakharych ain't gonna see America," muttered Bondarenko. "Let's drink to their memory too."

"Right." Trofimov took the flask again and took another tiny sip.

At that moment the roar of an aircraft overhead aroused an all too familiar sense of danger.

"We gotta dig into the snow again, fast as we can," Bondarenko urged.

"No need for that," said Trofimov. "That plane came from the east, it must be American."

"Yeah," Yatta confirmed, "it sounds like it's from the east."

The plane emerged from the clouds.

"Yatta, you've got sharp eyes," Trofimov said. "Can you see what's on the plane?"

"How d'you mean, what's on the plane?"

"I mean the signs, the markings. Every state has special symbols for their air force. Soviet planes have red stars on the wings."

The plane, whose crew had obviously sighted their fire, made several low circles overhead.

"You know, it's got a five-pointed star on the wing," said Yatta.

"Fuck! A red star?"

"No, white."

"You sure?" Bondarenko asked.

"Yeah. You know, it has a white star inside a black circle."

"Then it's American." Trofimov relaxed. "That's the same marking they had in Germany."

"Calling number One. Calling number One. This is Thirteen. Over." The radio operator called urgently. "Our bearing is 66/25 by 168/54. Three persons sighted below us … Yeah, they're sitting around a bonfire, right on the ice. One of them's waving his arms, signaling us … Yes, yes, looks like one of them is sick or injured … Yes, absolutely sure … Roger."

On the ground Captain Royce greeted his unit commander, First Lieutenant Schneider.

"I've just got a message," said Royce. "Those men out on the ice are alive. Three of them at least. One of them's probably wounded."

"Have we got their exact bearings, sir?"

"Yes, one of the plane crews has just reported. Take two Jeeps and the ambulance, and get out there and pick them up. They must be defectors, unless it's a cunning trick to plant spies on us. I doubt that. You understand what to do?"

"Yessir."

After the American plane had circled several times and dipped its wings to acknowledge their waving, it flew off towards the east. Apart from the wind, everything was silent again as the dusk closed in. Trofimov and Yatta did not have enough tent poles, so they built an igloo, a tiny one.

"Well, guys," Trofimov announced, "hopefully this is our last night on the ice. By tomorrow night, I guess we'll be in some American barracks."

"God willing, Captain." Bondarenko smiled.

Trofimov smiled back. "Touch wood, there are no more serious obstacles. What can stop us now?"

"You know, it looks like you're right," Yatta agreed.

"I'm still worried though," Bondarenko said suddenly. "You know those Soviet bastards often break the borders and trespass on other territory. They did it in Poland and Lithuania."

"This is different, though," Trofimov reassured him. "Those were small countries, unprotected. America's a major world power. The Soviets don't want a war with them."

"Still, I'd feel a whole lot easier with a machine gun in my hands," Bondarenko said.

"Maybe. But then we'll look like terrorists. We mustn't arouse any suspicions." Trofimov remained unshakeable in his decision.

After constructing a tiny igloo, just big enough for the three of them, Trofimov and Yatta moved Bondarenko inside, wrapped in his deerskin covering.

"How about a big cig?" Bondarenko suggested.

"Sure." Trofimov rolled three shag cigars. "No point in economizing any more."

Bondarenko inhaled the smoke with a blissful smile. "Almost makes you forget about your wounds."

After an hour or so in which only the howling of the wind could be heard, there came a new disturbance.

"Attention! Attention!" the rasp of a radio megaphone broke the silence in English. "Whoever's in there, walk out with your hands up! Attention, those inside, come out with your hands up! I repeat: Hands up! Do not resist or we'll shoot."

"You hear that?" Yatta turned to Trofimov. "I donna know that tongue. Is it English?"

"Yes," Trofimov confirmed. "Let's go, Yatta. You stay here, Mikhail. I'll tell them you're too sick to move. Yatta, come on. Put your hands up."

Trofimov and Yatta crawled out of the igloo and stood up with their hands raised. Three vehicles stood between the ice hummocks. Floodlights mounted on the roofs lit the scene. A tall American officer of the border guards came forward to meet them, followed by several soldiers.

"Here are two of them," the officer said, and scrutinized them carefully. "There must be a third one here as well."

"Yes, Lieutenant," Trofimov said in his accented English, "but he cannot move. He is heavily wounded."

"Yes, we guessed that. We've brought an ambulance for him." The officer looked at Trofimov. "You speak English. How come?"

"After the war I spent half a year on the River Elbe near Leipzig with your troops."

"Oh, a former ally. That's good." The officer smiled. "I'm First Lieutenant Schneider."

"Captain Trofimov. Happy to meet you."

Schneider turned to his soldiers. "One or two of you get inside the igloo and help him. Be careful. He's badly wounded."

A handful of soldiers retrieved Bondarenko from the igloo and put him on a stretcher then carried him over to the white Jeep marked with a red cross. Trofimov and Yatta got in a Jeep with Schneider.

8

Fresh from the unit's medical centre, where their wounds had been dressed, Trofimov and Yatta sat in Captain Royce's office and gazed at a large portrait of the late Franklin Roosevelt hanging over his desk.

"Your names?" Royce began.

"I'm Alexander Trofimov, and this man," Trofimov pointed to his companion, "is called Yatta. He has no surname as far as I know. The other man, the wounded one, is Mikhail Bondarenko."

"And what is your purpose in crossing the American border?"

"We're fleeing from persecution by the Soviet state, and we're asking for political asylum."

"Are you willing to confirm and pledge that you are not Soviet spies?"

"Yes, of course."

"And you have never served with the MGB, Soviet military counter-intelligence, or Special Task forces?"

"No, never. None of us. Bondarenko and I fought in World War II. I was in the regular army, and he was a partisan in German-occupied territory."

"Fine, but you have to sign the pledge form. Where have you come from?"

"We escaped from a labour camp near Seimchan. That's about 1400 miles to the west of here."

"That's a long way to come."

"Yes. Yes, it is."

"Were you inmates in that camp?"

"Yes, we were."

"Then how come you were so heavily armed when you crossed the border?"

"We killed several camp guards and seized their weapons. Then on the way we twice fought off army pursuit units, and we took their weapons as well."

"Does that mean that you committed acts of terror?"

"I wouldn't call them acts of terror. We had no choice, we were heavily guarded in the camp."

"So you claim it was justified self-defence?"

"Yes."

"And would you face detention and execution if you were captured?"

"Without question."

"What were you imprisoned for?"

"All three of us on political grounds. I was accused of spying for British and American intelligence."

"Were there grounds for these charges?"

"Absolutely none. It was sheer fabrication. The real reason I was charged was because of my letter to Marshal Vassilevsky about war crimes in Latvia. As for Bondarenko, he merely expressed a hope that the collective farms would be disbanded."

"So you claim that you were prisoners of conscience?"

"Something like that, although we never used those words."

After their preliminary interrogation, Captain Royce made arrangements by phone for the new arrivals to wash and change clothes. A soldier invited Trofimov and Yatta to follow him and led them across the base to a two-storey wooden barracks. In a few minutes they found themselves in a small room with two iron beds.

"Here you are," the soldier smiled. "Real luxury. This is a sergeant's room."

"What was all that he asked you about?" Yatta asked Trofimov as soon as they were alone.

"The usual things. About our escape, about the camp. And, of course, whether we were Soviet spies."

"But you know, I donna like his voice," said Yatta. "He sounded severe, even threatening."

"Oh, don't worry about that," Trofimov consoled him. "He's just a military officer doing his job. That was a routine bureaucratic tone for the American Army. Not the worst kind, though, Soviet bureaucrats are far ruder."

"Did he say what they're gonna do with us?" Yatta looked anxious.

"As far as I understand him, we'll be taken to some sort of local military governor."

"When are they gonna let us go free?"

"I don't know. Usually they keep refugees interned until their plea for political asylum is heard. That might take some time. Maybe half a year, or even a whole year."

"Oh, that's too long. By that time I could have reached my kinsmen ten times over." Yatta said in despair. "Maybe we could try and escape and go join them? They'd willingly accept you as my sworn brother."

"No, Yatta, we can't do that," Trofimov tried to be persuasive. "I don't want to raise any suspicions. If we run away, we could be charged with spying and sent to jail for another dozen years."

"But what if they hand us back to the Soviets?"

"I can assure you they won't do that. After the war the Americans never handed our captives in Germany back to the Soviets. Not like the British and the French did. Don't worry, buddy, the Americans can be relied upon."

"C'mon, guys, get up," the jovial sergeant wakened Trofimov and Yatta the following morning.

"Is it morning already?" After the exhaustion of their journey, Trofimov could hardly recollect the events of the previous day.

"Is this really Alaska?"

"Where else?" the sergeant laughed.

"So we made it."

"C'mon, get up, get dressed," the sergeant urged without answering. "We've gotta go."

"Where are we going?" Trofimov enquired.

"You'll see," the sergeant grinned.

Outside, a snowmobile with a soldier in a fur coat at the wheel awaited them. The sergeant showed Trofimov and Yatta onto the back seat. They watched the road. At first the vehicle took them along the single main street of a small town, then along a barren stretch of snow-covered seashore.

"Did he say where we're going?" inquired Yatta.

The snowmobile ran along the shore, curving now to the right now to the left. Suddenly it turned out onto the ice, hugged the shoreline then crossed the mouth of a small river, or a narrow inlet, and turned up on the opposite shore. In another twenty or so minutes they arrived at a row of wooden houses, barracks huts and other buildings, and pulled up in front of a two-storey wooden cottage.

"We're here," the sergeant announced. "Let's go."

He led them to the cottage entrance and rang a bell. A soldier emerged in the doorway. The sergeant said something to him and entered the house leaving Trofimov and Yatta under the soldier's guard.

"Well, Yatta, looks like we're still in luck," Trofimov smiled.

"I think so too," Yatta said, "but I'm still worried. They're treating us as captives, keeping us under guard all the time."

"Oh, don't worry about that. We're internees now."

The sergeant re-emerged at the entrance to the cottage.

"Come on in," he announced loudly. "The colonel's waiting for you."

9

The colonel was a tall blond man in his late forties with the typical face of a war veteran. Trofimov recognized his own sort instinctively, no matter what their clothing or the expression on their faces, and he felt reassured. It was always easier to find a common language with such people.

"Have a seat," the colonel smiled and gestured towards a row of chairs by the wall. Trofimov and Yatta sat down.

"So you're our heroic fugitives?" he asked and smiled again.

"Yes, and there's a third one as well, only he's wounded," Trofimov said.

"Yes, I know all about him. I've given orders to have him admitted to our hospital."

"Thank you very much, Colonel," said Trofimov, already feeling somewhat easier.

"I'm Colonel McPherson," he said and opened a folder on the desk in front of him. "This is your dossier from Captain Royce. You apparently told him you're runaways from a Soviet concentration camp somewhere in the Magadan area, and that you've made it all the way from there to here. Is that correct?"

"Yes, it is."

"And you seized some weapons and repulsed their efforts to pursue and recapture you, correct?"

"Yes, Colonel."

"How large were these units?" McPherson asked.

"The first one consisted of about forty home army volunteers, not regular soldiers. The second had sixteen Special Task soldiers, well trained and heavily armed."

"And the three of you managed to fight them off?"

"We were five originally. Two were killed."

"In any case, that's impressive." The colonel looked at Trofimov. "And it can mean only one thing, that there was an experienced combat officer among you, and I believe that would be you."

"How do you know it's me?" Trofimov asked.

"First of all, I can tell from your bearing. One can always recognize another officer despite external appearances. Plus, you knew my rank, probably from the epaulettes, therefore you must have had some contact with American troops. And that could only have happened during the war, somewhere in Germany."

"You're right. I am a war veteran, a captain," Trofimov confirmed. "And I was in Germany, near Magdeburg."

"I can tell that too, from your good English," McPherson smiled. "I was on the Elbe myself, further north." He paused and looked at Trofimov. "Do you remember any of our officers that you met there?"

"Surely. I remember a Captain Wood, and First Lieutenant Hughes."

"Sam Wood?"

"Yes."

"Hah! He was my friend from college days," said the colonel. "He was a freshman when I was about to graduate. We fought together in North Africa and in Italy, then on the Western Front. He was transferred to another unit at the end of the war."

"I met him in Magdeburg. We used to drink together, and even embraced as old friends," Trofimov recollected.

"It was a fascinating time, wasn't it?" the colonel smiled as he recalled his own memories.

"It was," Trofimov agreed. "It seemed there were no more fascists or Nazis, and that a new and better life for everyone was just round the corner. We Russians and you Westerners were comrades-in-arms, and it was supposed to remain like that forever. We thought we'd take the best of everything from one another and start afresh. Now it's surprising that we could have been so naïve."

"Yes," McPherson sighed, "just five years later. Everything has changed. Drastically. The former comrades-in-arms are bitter enemies."

"For us Russians things have changed even more drastically. Those of us who embraced our allies on the Elbe were suspected. Many were purged as I was. I was tortured. They tried to make me confess that I was recruited by British and American intelligence. Look at my scars, Colonel. From the MGB." Trofimov opened his shirt.

"It's unbelievable. I thought only the Gestapo and Japanese counter-intelligence committed such atrocities."

"I used to think the same, but then I discovered our own MGB were more than a match for either of them."

"Well," the colonel sighed, "perhaps I'm lucky that I wasn't purged. I just had to come and serve here, in this remote corner of Alaska."

"You? Purged? Why?" Trofimov asked.

"Why? For the same reason as you. For being on the Elbe and embracing the Russians. Some time I'll tell you more," McPherson grinned. "Now, to get back to business. What do you intend to do next?"

Trofimov shrugged. "Apply for political asylum, I guess."

"Well, of course you've got a good case for that. Do you want to ask for asylum in the States?"

"I thought so. Where else could I go?"

"Do you have relatives, friends, in the States?" McPherson asked.

Trofimov pointed to Yatta.

"Yatta has kinfolk in Alaska. They fled here back in the thirties. But Mikhail Bondarenko and I have no one."

"Then I think the two of you should think about our neighbour, Canada. In America nowadays, you'll be suspected of being Soviet spies. The US is crazy about that right now. Canada's a calmer place. You'll certainly have a more modest income, but on the other hand it's a more peaceful country. Besides, it'll be easier for you to find a job, especially in the Canadian West. There are big construction projects underway there. Do you have professional skills apart from the military?"

"I finished one year at a technical college, and I worked for one year as a trucker."

"Then Alberta could be the best place for you. At least for the next few years you'll have a steady job there. Anyway, back to formalities. You have to compose a letter to the immigration authorities, appealing for asylum. They'll send you application forms. That will start the process. I think you can probably write on behalf of all three of you."

"I can do that. And where shall we live in the meantime?"

"I'm not sure. By law, refugee claimants crossing the border illegally are placed in special camps, but there isn't such a camp in Alaska. No one ever crossed the Bering Strait before you. I'll make enquiries. Maybe they'll transfer you to a camp, or maybe they'll let you stay here. I'd certainly be glad to host you."

"Thank you, Colonel."

"My pleasure, Captain. I can't refuse hospitality to my former comrades-in-arms. That is, of course, unless I get orders to the contrary. Anyway, Sergeant Graves will take you to your present residence. You'll stay there for several days at least. You can visit your wounded friend in the hospital if the medics have no objections."

The same afternoon, Trofimov and Yatta visited the hospital. As they entered the ward, they were amazed how clean and tidy it was, not at all like the hospitals they had seen back home. In Bondarenko's room were lots of instruments and mechanisms on the walls, several with buttons and special wiring. Trofimov could not figure out the purpose of all these things despite his technical background. There were just two beds in the room, and the second one was empty. Bondarenko looked pale and exhausted, but he was awake.

"Is that you, guys?" he muttered in a low voice. "Nice to see you."

"You too," Trofimov smiled. "How are you, buddy?"

"Better than one could expect. You see this ward? It's really somethin'. Could you find anythin' like this back in Mother Russia? They treat me like a general."

"This is civilization, buddy."

"Well, the quality's really somethin'." Bondarenko grinned. "See this button?" He nodded towards the wall. "If I need the latrine, I just push it. The nurse comes and wheels me over there. Can you imagine such a thing in a Soviet hospital?"

"Where is this button?" asked Yatta.

"Here." Bondarenko pointed to one of the buttons on the wall above his head.

"Oh, I'd like to try it." Yatta reached out his hand to the button.

"No." Trofimov grabbed his hand. "Don't do that."

"Why not?" both Yatta and Bondarenko were baffled.

"It's tactless. It's not acceptable in the West. Maybe the nurse is busy, or having a rest after working hard before she comes back on duty. And you want to call her just for fun?"

"I see. In that case you'll just have to believe me." Bondarenko winked at Yatta.

"I do believe you. How's the food?"

"Very good. Certainly not as tasty as my mom's or Anyuta's, but it's miles better than any Soviet canteen. Can you believe? They even served me tea with lemon."

"Like the best restaurants in Paris and Vienna," Trofimov joked.

"And it's so clean. Look at these sheets. I never had anything like this, not even at home."

"How d'you feel?" Trofimov interrupted him.

"Not too good yet. I'm still confined to bed, and I can't move. In the morning they cut out half a dozen pieces of shrapnel from my chest and stomach, but there's a lot of stuff still in there. If I lie here quietly, I'm okay. Oh, I forgot to tell you: they gave me some drug or other, I ain't catch its name, but I donna feel no pain now."

"Really?" Yatta sounded surprised.

"Believe me."

"Looks like they're real shamans here," Yatta exclaimed.

Trofimov smiled. "It must be morphine. Did they tell you how you're doing?"

"How could they tell me that when I donna know a single word of English, and they donna know no Russian?" Bondarenko shrugged. "Honestly, I don't even want to know. I ain't think I'm gonna pull through this, though."

"C'mon, buddy, you're alive and well. Why bury yourself ahead of time?" Trofimov objected.

"Ahead of time or not, I donna know. Sometimes I just feel that way. I've no strength at all."

"Cheer up, Mikhail. I've seen guys recover from far worse wounds than this," Trofimov said. On the other hand, there were dark circles around his friend's eyes, his eyelids were half-transparent and his cheek bones protruded. Deep down inside he had a sense of profound sorrow.

10

Trofimov and Yatta spent the following week in their room in the barracks. Most of the time they slept, restoring the energy they had lost in the previous months of extreme strain. Occasionally they walked around the unit buildings and the suburbs of the nearby town. They regularly visited the hospital and spoke with the physicians, who were still not sure of the outcome. They were not always allowed to see Bondarenko. He was evidently not progressing well, but his friends remained full of hope. Then one day Trofimov was invited to see Colonel McPherson.

"Well," said the colonel, "I contacted the Refugee Board and other institutions relevant to your case. Regrettably, I can't promise you any quick answers. The good news is that you'll stay here for the time being."

"I'd be only too happy. The more so, since you and I are fellow war vets."

"Yes indeed. Now, there are a few other things for us to discuss."

"Like what?"

"Well, I presume you need money," McPherson said. "You can have free accommodation and food, but all men have a few other expenses. You can apply to the local Red Cross and ask them for a few hundred, or maybe a thousand bucks. That'll be enough to keep you going for a while."

There was a knock at the door.

"Come in," McPherson said.

His batman entered.

"What is it, Snow?"

"There's a Mrs. Reeves to see you, sir."

"Just tell her to wait a moment," the colonel said, then changed his mind: "No, tell her to come in right now."

The batman left, and a tall woman in her early thirties walked into the room. She had beautiful chestnut hair, and her face and figure were delicate yet strong. She was a perfect beauty, or so she seemed to Trofimov, who had not seen a woman in months.

"Hello, Colonel," she greeted McPherson cheerily.

"Angela, glad to see you. Are you here on business?"

"Well, I was hoping to see the famous refugees who crossed the border."

"That's easy," McPherson laughed. "One of them, the only one who speaks English, is right here." He turned in Trofimov's direction.

"How do you do, ma'am." Trofimov bowed then looked her straight in the eye.

"Why so formal?" the woman smiled. "I'm Angela Reeves from the *Anchorage Sun*, and I'd like to talk to you."

"An interview?"

"Yes, if that's all right."

After a moment's hesitation he said, "I'm not sure about that."

"Why? Is there a problem?" she wore the same pleasant smile.

"How can I explain? If our escape gets a lot of publicity here, news could spread to the Soviet side, and that would harm my mother."

"Harm your mother?" Her smile disappeared.

"Yes. In the Soviet Union if someone commits an offence, their relatives can also suffer. Especially if the offender himself is beyond their reach."

"In this day and age? In the twentieth century?" she continued astonished. "It's unbelievable."

Trofimov shrugged. "Well, that's Soviet reality. That's how the Soviet government discourages its subjects from rebelling, even if they themselves have nothing to lose."

"I could interview you but not mention any names."

"Hmm, you know, I'd rather you didn't." Trofimov found it difficult to refuse such a charming young lady. "Or at least, you could maybe delay showing it to your editor."

"Okay, well, if not then not," she looked at Trofimov with a smile. "What if I talked to you off the record? Can I invite you to the Oceanside Café?"

"That could work," he agreed. "Do you promise no records whatsoever?"

"I promise. No notes. What time would be best for you?"

"Any time." He shrugged. "I've got a lot of spare time right now. You choose."

"What about this Friday at three o'clock, for a late lunch?"

"Fine."

"Good. I'll pick you up at a quarter to three."

"Is this café only fifteen minutes' walk from here?" he asked.

"Not quite," she smiled. "It's about three miles away, but I have a car."

"A car of your own?"

"Sure. Does that surprise you?"

"Back in the Soviet Union, only big shots have their own cars, people in high authority. Definitely not a journalist, especially as young as you are, ma'am."

"Do call me Angela. And to answer your question, in North America most people own a car if they have a full-time job. I can't imagine how one could get along without a car."

Trofimov grinned. "Well, in the USSR you can get around easily in the cities. There are buses and streetcars. They're overcrowded most of the day, but people get used to them. In the countryside you sometimes have to walk five or more kilometres. It's not too bad if the roads are dry, but otherwise you may have to wade through the mud."

Angela shook her head. "I wouldn't like to live like that. Anyway, I'll see you Friday."

"Bye. Nice to meet you."

"A charming woman, isn't she?" McPherson smiled as soon as she had left. He winked at Trofimov.

"Well, she's very good looking and pleasant to talk to."

"I guess all the soldiers on the front dream of such a woman," McPherson commented.

"Yes, very much so," Trofimov agreed. "Well," he rose to his feet. "I should go, if you don't mind. I have to work on all these papers you gave me."

"Okay, see you, Captain. Enjoy your date with Angela."

After Trofimov left, the colonel began work on a report to the general under whose authority he served. He barely had time to dictate a few words to his secretary, when his batman knocked and entered again.

"What is it now, Snow?" McPherson asked.

"A visitor from the Soviet shore, sir. He wants to see you

personally, sir. He got his documents and pass from Captain Royce."

"From the Soviet side? What does he want?"

"I don't know, sir. I guess something related to the fugitives."

"Call him in."

"Yessir."

The Soviet visitor was an MGB captain with the ordinary complacent face of a Russian peasant. He had a piercing gaze, so that even a hardened man like Colonel McPherson felt uneasy in his presence.

"I'm Captain Baluyev of the Dalstroy MGB administration," the visitor announced by way of greeting.

"Colonel McPherson, chief of the Teller Border District. What can I do for you, sir?"

Captain Baluyev took a paper package from the bag on his shoulder and placed it on McPherson's desk.

"I've come here on behalf of General Nikishev, the chief of Dalstroy, to demand the extradition of three deserters who came here two weeks ago."

"Extradition? But there is no extradition treaty or agreement between our countries, as far as I know."

"Nevertheless, the five bandits I'm talking about are classified as especially dangerous criminals, and there is an international agreement providing for extradition of such persons."

"Perhaps. Who are you referring to, sir?"

"I'm referring to three members, I do not know exactly which, of a group of five criminals: Trofimov, Alexander Ivanovich, Bondarenko, Mikhail Savelyevich, Goldberg, Yakov Moiseyevich, Timoshkin Pyotr Zakharovich and Yatta who has neither patronymic nor a surname." The captain snapped out each word as if rapping on the keys of a typewriter. "These individuals," he continued, "escaped from a corrective labour camp, killing seven camp guards, and on the way here killed about fifty other Soviet servicemen in the course of fulfilling their duties. We have evidence that the above-mentioned criminals are here on US territory."

Well, there you are, thought McPherson. They have the brass neck to come over here and make demands as though they were at home! C'mon, McPherson, this is a test of your resolve.

"Well," McPherson said calmly, "whether they are here or

not, what exactly are the grounds for your demanding their extradition?"

"They committed crimes on Soviet territory," Baluyev snapped, "and they must answer for them before a Soviet court of justice."

"Well, first of all, I have to remind you, sir," McPherson tried hard not to explode, "that there is no comprehensive extradition treaty between the USSR and the USA. There could be only one ground for extradition, and that would apply if those concerned were Nazi or Japanese collaborators. But that's not the case with any of these men. On the contrary, two of them are war veterans who actually fought against the Nazis."

"There is an international convention that provides for the extradition of criminals."

"Not of political prisoners," replied the colonel. "All three men were detained under the Soviet Article 58, which covers political offences. It doesn't refer to ordinary crimes, is that not the case?"

"These criminals murdered almost fifty Soviet servicemen on duty," Baluyev insisted. "That means fifty counts of·murder. Therefore they should be extradited as dangerous and violent criminals."

"As you said, those servicemen were fulfilling their duties," McPherson observed.

"Absolutely correct, and under Soviet law that is an aggravating circumstance."

"By 'fulfilling their duties' you mean attempting to seize these fugitives, correct?"

"Yes," Baluyev answered.

"Then the fugitives killed them in self-defence. In American law, that is perfectly justifiable. I don't know about Soviet law."

Baluyev exploded. "Do you mean to say, sir, that killing servicemen on duty can be equated with killing criminals in self-defense?"

"Absolutely, if in either case it means defending one's own life. And that's what it does mean in this case. They had to fight those soldiers or else be killed themselves."

"Not killed, returned to face trial." Baluyev argued.

"I presume that, under these circumstances, they would face execution. Am I right?"

"In this case, yes. Because they murdered seven camp guards."

"But they apparently had no other way. If they didn't run away, they were doomed to die in that camp." McPherson paused and looked straight into his opponent's eyes. "You know perfectly well, sir, that they would have perished there, from starvation, overwork, or execution on some trifling pretext. Do you think I'm ignorant of what your so-called corrective labour camps involve?"

"I would ask you, sir, not to interfere in our country's internal affairs, and not to repeat such offensive slander," Baluyev objected.

"Slander? I've seen the scars on one of the fugitive's bodies. A person with weak nerves would faint at the sight of them. Those scars are the result of torture that you inflicted on him. I'd remind you that torture is banned by the Geneva Convention of 1908. That ban was reaffirmed by the Universal Declaration of Human Rights a year and a half ago. There is also a ban on arbitrary purges. The Soviet state committed crimes against humanity in relation to these individuals."

"I would ask you again, sir," Baluyev blustered.

"You may ask whatever you wish, but I will not hand over these unfortunate individuals for you to slaughter them."

"Not slaughter. Bring to justice!"

"What kind of justice? Like this, for example?" McPherson produced a photograph that had been given to him by one of his CIA friends. It showed two men executed by being tied to trees and left to die of exposure. Although used to seeing ugly sights, that picture had deeply shocked him.

"This is despicable," Baluyev muttered, the blood rising to his cheeks.

"It certainly is. That's what you Soviets say every time someone catches you red-handed. You said the same thing when the Katyn Wood massacre was discovered. I well remember that. Anyway, sir, you may as well return to where you came from. There's nothing more to discuss."

"I shall file an official complaint."

"You can complain as much as you wish, but my word is final. Go back and tell your superiors that American officers don't cooperate with the Soviet terror machine."

Beluyev got up and left, slamming the door behind him.

McPherson returned to his work. No more than a few minutes

passed before he was aware of another visitor. He looked up and saw his chief of staff, Lieutenant-Colonel Sims.

"Yes, Sims?"

"I heard some of your conversation with the Soviet officer through the wall. I'd like to talk to you about it, McPherson."

"Oh, d'you think I did something wrong?"

"To say the least, Colonel, you were too hasty. If I were you, I'd invite the man back while he's still here."

"I don't understand you, Sims," retorted the colonel. "You think I should meet his demands?"

"That's exactly what I mean."

"And you, an honest American soldier, can say that?"

"Yes. I say it because otherwise we could all get into trouble. That officer will report the matter to his superiors, and they'll appeal the matter back to our general and even higher."

"And for that I should hand over fellow allied soldiers since the war, into the hands of those bloody butchers? Never."

"Be practical," Sims insisted. "By sticking to your emotions, you may cause a lot of problems both for yourself and for others."

"Really?"

"Imagine they're really Soviet spies, disguised as refugees."

"Bullshit!" McPherson snapped. "Why would they demand their extradition?"

"To pull the wool over our eyes and get these spies entrenched."

"You've got to be kidding, Sims."

"No, McPherson. I'm deadly serious. If we give them protection and asylum, and they turn out to be spies, our careers will be ruined. Yours will definitely be ruined after all that fraternizing and embracing with the Russians in Germany."

"That's enough." McPherson hit the table with his fist. "Don't make me doubt your military honour. I've no doubts about my own, and I'll never do anything to disgrace it. And that's final."

"But be reasonable," Sims insisted.

"I've made my decision, and I'm not going to budge. I'd rather put a bullet through my own forehead than betray war comrades." McPherson looked intently at his chief of staff. "And don't do anything behind my back if you value our friendship."

"I wouldn't do anything behind your back, for God's sake. I'm only expressing my point of view. You have the final word."

With that Sims turned and left.

11

Trofimov sat on a bench on the snow-covered lawn in front of the barracks, smoking a cigarette and waiting for Angela Reeves. He was just finishing his cigarette, when a Studebaker Jeep of the type familiar to him from the war, stopped in front of him and Angela stepped out.

She looked at her watch. "Five minutes late. I hope you'll excuse me."

"Of course," Trofimov smiled. "A lady should always come a few minutes late." He looked at her Jeep. "That's a nice car you have, very reliable. It takes me back to the good old days after the war."

"This one's not mine," she said. "My car's in Anchorage. I'm renting this one while I'm here."

"Renting?" Trofimov asked.

"Sure. What's so surprising about that?"

"There's no such thing as renting a car in the Soviet Union. A bike is about the most you can rent."

"Well, not here, thank God. Get in."

"Thanks."

Angela got in beside him and started up the car. "Today this is my invitation," she said.

"Thank you very much. It's certainly not our custom for a lady to pay for the man."

She smiled. "I guess you don't have any money just now, so there's no other way."

"I'll invite you back as soon as I get some money from the Red Cross."

"Fine. You can settle your debt then."

At the restaurant they ordered steaks. Angela ordered wine and Trofimov accepted it though he would have preferred vodka. Since she was paying the bill, he thought it would be ungracious to object. He didn't want her to think him a drunkard.

The place was practically empty, and this along with the candlelight at their table created a cosy, intimate atmosphere.

"Last time we met, I asked you for an interview and you refused," Angela said. "I'd still like to know something about you."

"You're very persistent," Trofimov grinned.

"It's a common sin of my profession. Would you agree to talk to me off the record?"

"If you give me your word of honour that nothing of this will be published, at least during the coming year."

"On my honour, not a word."

"Okay, then, ask your questions."

"Well, tell me about yourself."

"There's not much to tell," Trofimov shrugged the suggestion aside.

"C'mon, every person's interesting in some way, and you're an outstanding person."

"I'm not so sure about that."

"But I am. I'd like to know you better," she insisted. "For instance, who were you before you were imprisoned?"

"I was an army officer, a captain. After the war, I was sent to fight the Latvian 'Forest Brethren.' It was a terrible campaign. I wrote to Marshal Vassilevsky that I was weary of war and wanted to return home to civilian life. I didn't want to take part in punitive campaigns. Within a month, I was clapped in the jug and charged with being a spy."

"So you were purged for your unwillingness to help pacify the rebels of Latvia?" She looked at him with some degree of admiration.

"Right."

"Then you were a prisoner of conscience."

"That sounds pathetic."

"It's a regular term," explained Angela. "It appeared two years ago after the Paris Declaration of Human Rights."

"Two years ago? I'd already been in the camp for more than a year. I was at death's door at the time. I guess that would be in April. When was the conference?"

"In December."

"By December we'd already escaped and been on our way for

two months."

"So by that time you'd already killed those guards?"

"That's right."

"In that case you weren't quite a prisoner of conscience. The term presupposes absence of violence on the side of the prisoner."

"So what was I? A bandit, like the Soviets labeled us?"

"No, I'd say you were a political prisoner and an insurgent."

"'Insurgent' sounds honourable, I guess." He smiled.

"And what did you do before the war?"

"I'd just finished my first year at an automobile construction college."

"How old were you?"

"Not quite nineteen."

"That young?"

"Yes. I just finished high school and worked as a trucker on a construction site. I'm one of a generation of 'war youths.' We went to the battlefront fresh from school, or almost."

"At that time I'd just completed my undergrad studies at Harvard."

"Were you in the war as well?" Trofimov asked.

"Yes and no. I visited various fronts as a US Army newspaper reporter. I was in Africa for Operation Torch, then in Italy, then in France, and finally in Germany. I even spent a week in Soviet occupied territory."

"Where, may I ask?"

"In Berlin."

"In Berlin! When?"

"May and June, 1945."

"Just when I was there," Trofimov exclaimed. "I spent a few days in Berlin, then our unit moved west, towards the Elbe."

"I was there too," said Angela. "In Magdeburg."

"Oh, I was just a few kilometres south of Magdeburg. Wait a moment. My friend Kolya Denisenko went to Magdeburg, and he said he got to know a nice American woman journalist."

"Kolya … that's Nikolay," Angela figured out. "I met a Nikolay. He was a senior lieutenant."

"Was he dark-haired and of medium height?"

"Yes."

"And you met him in Magdeburg?"

Angela nodded.

"Then you're that same American journalist," Trofimov exclaimed. "What a coincidence."

Angela smiled. "It seems it's only by accident that we didn't meet there, in Germany."

"Yes, I even asked Kolya to introduce me to her—I mean you. He promised, but then we never got a chance."

"Then let's toast our surprising acquaintance at last, in such a surprising place," Angela proposed.

"A good idea. Cheers!"

During the rest of the meal, they chatted like good old friends, and felt closer and closer, as if that meeting in Magdeburg promised by Kolya Denisenko had taken place then. As with Colonel McPherson, he felt the same solidarity with her as with other old "fellow Elbenites." The feeling incorporated many things, including their joint struggle against a powerful and vicious enemy, a shared sense of triumph at their victory, and common hopes for a new and better time to come, hopes that were so bitterly dashed and frustrated. With Angela there was more than a sense of solidarity. She was a woman.

"How about instead of going back to the barracks you drop in at my place first?" Angela suggested as they got into her Jeep.

"With the greatest pleasure."

"Great. I'll give you a lift back later."

Back in her motel suite, they opened a bottle of sherry and continued to chat.

"So you left all your family back there in Russia?" she asked.

"Depends what you mean by family," he answered. "I'm not married, I never had time. As for my parents and siblings ..."

"What about them?"

"There were five of us, my mother and father, myself and my two brothers, one older and one younger. I went to an officers' college as I was a high school graduate, and then straight to the battlefront as a lieutenant. My brother Mikhail was killed about a month before I arrived at the front. Kostya, my little brother, volunteered in 1943, when he was barely seventeen. As mum and dad wrote, he was anxious not to be the only one of us three who wasn't in the war."

"I hope he survived."

"Until almost the end of the war. He was killed in the storming of Berlin, a couple of weeks before Germany surrendered."

"So your parents had two sons killed and the third …"

"Exactly. The third is also dead in a way, at least as far as my mom and dad are concerned. They were waiting for me to return from Germany, but instead I went more or less straight to Kolyma. Dad couldn't stand the shock of that, and had a heart attack while driving his truck."

"What an awful tragedy," Angela sighed. "There were cases like that in the US, when families lost all their sons. But they were rare."

"Not in Russia," Trofimov said. "It's a common phenomenon. The official estimate was seven million killed, but in reality it might well be three times that number. Many veterans who survived the war, like myself, were purged afterwards. I'm not sure what was better, sudden death or a long slow one in the camps."

"Your escape means that you've been kind of resurrected from the dead, almost like Christ." She smiled.

"It's a rather strange analogy."

"Well, here's to your resurrection."

Trofimov raised his glass then looked at his watch.

"It's nine o'clock, evening drill time for the regiment. After that they don't let anybody back into the barracks."

"That's no problem. Why don't you stay here with me?" Angela suggested.

"If they check and don't find me there, they might be alarmed."

"I'll call McPherson and tell him."

"Are you on such friendly terms with him?"

"I am. Wait a moment. I'll use the motel office phone." She took her coat and left.

Five minutes later she was back. "Well, McPherson doesn't mind. He said that I'd be responsible if you ran away. You wouldn't do that, would you?"

"Surely not. Not from you."

He stepped close to her and wrapped his arms around her shoulders with his face buried in the cloud of her hair. He rubbed his cheek against hers, and then their lips met. He sensed her response with great satisfaction. Her body nestled against his, her fingers stroked his shoulders and back. They were a normal man and a normal woman, free and unattached, with no obstacles to their natural desires and mutual attraction.

The following morning they lay in bed side by side.

"Alex, are you asleep?" Angela's lips touched his shoulder.

"No. What time is it?"

"Ten o'clock," she replied.

"So late? It seems like yesterday evening was just half an hour ago."

"I'll make coffee." She got out of bed naked, and he watched her almost perfect body with admiration mixed with re-emerging desire. The next moment she put on her bathrobe and went over to the percolator.

They drank coffee and then made love again. It was afternoon when Trofimov was finally ready to go back.

12

At the entrance to the barracks a sentry greeted him.

"Are you the Russian guy who crossed the ocean?"

"Actually I only crossed the Strait," Trofimov corrected him.

"Anyway, the colonel's anxious to see you."

"Anxious?"

"Yeah. You're to go straight up and see him."

He went to McPherson's office, feeling slightly alarmed as he anticipated their conversation.

"I guess you had a good night." McPherson smiled when Trofimov appeared.

"Yes."

"I'm glad to hear it." The colonel threw him a wink.

"I thought you were about to put me in the punishment cell," Trofimov grinned. "The sentry at the gate said you were anxious to see me."

"I do want to see you, but it's nothing to do with punishing you. I spoke with a Soviet messenger yesterday. He demanded that I turn you over. I showed the bastard the door."

"I'm grateful to you, Colonel. I'm beginning to believe in people's decency once again."

"Well, you're not subject to extradition according to US law," said McPherson. The authorities in Anchorage or even higher up could reverse my decision, but that's highly unlikely. His superiors could appeal to the Alaska State Court, maybe even the Supreme Court, but neither of them would extradite you, I'm sure."

"I'm glad to hear that."

"Now, there's something else to deal with," McPherson continued. "An FBI officer came to screen you. He turned up without warning."

"What does it mean?"

"Oh, just a routine screening," McPherson reassured him. "All fugitives who cross the border go through it. They want to satisfy themselves you're not a spy."

"When do I meet him?"

"Right now. He's in the next room. You can go in."

Trofimov entered the room. A portly officer in a type of uniform he had not seen before sat in the armchair. He nodded to Trofimov by way of greeting.

"You are Alexander Ivanovich Trofimov?"

"Yes."

"And the two men who crossed the border with you are Mikhail Savelyevich Bondarenko and Yatta of the Telqap?"

"That's right."

The officer motioned to Trofimov to take a seat on the opposite side of the desk.

"The three of you crossed the border at the coast near Fort Wales two months ago, on February 21, correct?"

"That's correct."

"And you claim that you escaped from a Soviet concentration camp in Siberia?"

"That's right."

"Were there others with you?"

"Yes, two other men."

"What happened to them? Why didn't they cross the Bering Strait with you?"

"They perished in a battle with government troops."

"What were their names?" The FBI man looked at Trofimov with an expression of some doubt.

"Their names were Yakov Moiseyevich Goldberg and Pyotr Zakharovich Timoshkin."

"And why were the five of you detained?"

"What do you want to hear?" Trofimov inquired. "The formal charges, or the real reasons?"

"Tell me the formal charges first."

"I can't remember all the articles involved. Bondarenko, Goldberg, Timoshkin and myself were all charged with treason, and Yatta—I don't know the charges against him. He escaped from internal exile, and for several years lived illegally in the woods until he was caught."

"I see." The officer still sounded suspicious. "And you're claiming that these charges were false?

"Yes."

"Did you have any criminal charges against you besides that?"

"No."

"When exactly did you escape from the camp?"

"In October, 1948."

"What were you doing between that time and this February?"

"Making our way to the border."

"Do you mean you travelled in winter?"

"Yes."

"But that's impossible." The officer frowned. "You'd have starved and frozen to death unless someone helped you."

"But that was precisely so. Yatta is a native Chukchi. The Arctic is his natural habitat at any time of the year." Trofimov went on to tell the story of their escape with emphasis on how they contrived to survive.

"Does this Yatta speak English?"

"No."

"Then we'll need an interpreter," he paused and looked at Trofimov again. "Do you have any proof that you're not spies?"

"Yes." Trofimov made an effort to control his mounting irritation. "First of all, if we were spies, why would the Soviets have created such an artillery barrage when we were crossing the Strait? Bondarenko was severely wounded in the course of it."

"Well, that could have been staged." The officer shrugged off that argument. "Any other proof?"

"Have a look at my body, and you'll see it's a mass of scars from the torture I was subjected to in early 1947."

The officer looked at Trofimov with interest. "Let's have a look."

Trofimov bared his chest and stomach.

"Hmm, that looks really nasty. What kind of torture did they use?"

"Various sorts. I was beaten by four men standing in different corners of the cell—that's the so-called 'fifth corner' treatment. When that didn't work, they hoisted me up on a rack and beat me with ramrods."

"Good grief," the officer exclaimed.

"Yes, and these scars are from those rods," Trofimov confirmed.

"Well, okay," the officer said, "I guess that's it for now. I'll see you again if necessary." And with that he left.

"How did it go?" McPherson asked when the FBI officer had gone.

"Oh, it was tedious," Trofimov sighed. "He asked about this and that, and he couldn't believe that we survived the winter all by ourselves."

"Don't worry," McPherson smiled encouragingly. "It's routine."

"I know. I realize that."

"Just take it easy. There's a lot of evidence in your support. Captain Royce and the other officers confirmed what a furious artillery bombardment went on while you were crossing the Strait. They can't ignore blatant facts, and in Royce's unit there are several career officers in the artillery who would confirm that that kind of shelling simply couldn't be faked."

"I'm happy, Colonel, if that's the case."

"And they can't ignore the marks of torture on you either. A medical examination could determine the approximate time when the scars were inflicted. When were you tortured?"

"Winter of 1947."

"Well, a qualified medical expert could easily determine that those injuries were inflicted not earlier than late 1946, after the war.

There's no way that could be the work of the Nazis or Japanese." McPherson sounded confident.

"Well, my congratulations," McPherson told Trofimov a few days later. "The three of you passed your FBI screening."

"So they don't think we're spies any more?"

"Well, it's not quite that straightforward. You'll always be under some slight suspicion all the time you stay in American territory, and they'll keep you under some form of surveillance. Such are the times we live in. Since you're not spies, then in principle you're eligible for political asylum."

"That's reassuring."

"It doesn't mean you'll be set loose on your own in the near future," McPherson continued. "The application process takes several months. You'll have to stay here."

"Well, I don't mind that. It's not at all bad here, with you."

"I hope so," the colonel smiled. "And it has some advantages. While you're here, you can enjoy life and not worry about anything. But once you get your residence permit, the first thing you'll have to do is look for a job." He paused. "By the way, have you chosen the country you want to live in yet? As I told you, maybe Canada would be better for you than the States."

"Yes, I remember. I don't understand why, exactly."

"At present the US is plagued with McCarthyite madness. Hundreds and hundreds of people are suspected of being communists and Soviet spies. The grounds for suspicion can be various, though most suspects are leftists. But not all."

"What do you mean?"

"Look, I trust you, so I'll be frank with you," McPherson said emphatically. "Why do you think I'm up here in Alaska? After all, I'm a decorated war veteran, and a cavalier of the Legion of Honour."

"Some kind of exile?" Trofimov guessed.

"Self-imposed. As one of that old company on the River Elbe, I would have fallen victim to the next round of purges."

"Arrested?"

"No, not as bad as that. After all, this isn't the Soviet Union. Here we still have the rule of law. I would have been kicked out of the military. It was unthinkable. I'm a career soldier. I've served in the Army for almost a quarter century. I'm not as lucky as you. I don't have any other skills or a profession. I'd have to work as a petty clerk, or something menial."

"That's disgusting," Trofimov exclaimed.

"Yes. After all, what am I guilty of? Fraternizing with the Russians? They were our Allies. There was no ban on fraternizing and embracing them. I never had anything to do with politics, and I never had any sympathy for the communists. But for those bastards in the FBI that's no argument. I had to do something to stay in the military, so I applied to be sent to Alaska. They won't kick me out from here. There aren't many officers of my rank who'd want to serve up here, on the edge of nowhere," He looked at Trofimov. "That's why I seriously advise you to try Canada. You'll have fewer troubles."

"If it's really like that here, then Canada's certainly preferable, though I can decide only for myself. Yatta wants to join his kinsmen here in Alaska. And Mikhail's so sick."

"Yes, Bondarenko." McPherson gave a sigh. "You know, I keep in touch with the hospital, and they're not at all optimistic. They think he's not likely to survive. They can't stop the inflammation."

"Is that the doctors' opinion?" Trofimov asked.

"Yes. They all think so."

"Did they tell you how long he's going to live?"

"The chief said maybe a couple of months, maybe more, maybe less. I'm sorry to be so blunt."

"So."

"Yes, I'm afraid you're going to be on your own. But there are a lot of Russians in North America."

Trofimov took a deep breath.

"So, what shall I do? I guess I'll try Canada."

13

Trofimov and Angela sat on a boulder by the seacoast.

"Spring at last," Angela said, looking at the grass and first flowers that were appearing. "The winter was so long."

"Not as long as in Siberia. It's still winter at this time. But you know, this spring is really special for me."

"It must be." Angela smiled. "It's your first spring as a free man, isn't it?"

"Not quite. Last spring on the Upper Anadyr we were already free men."

"But that's different. Being an outlaw isn't real freedom."

Trofimov shrugged. "Well, yes and no. Of course, we were fighting for our lives all the time. Like any fighting, it was hard going. Even so, fighting is better than slaving in a labour camp."

Angela chuckled. "You're not a very good Christian, my dear."

"No, I'm not. I'm not sure I'm a Christian at all. I was in the Young Communist League from the age of fourteen, and then I joined the Party at the battlefront. As you can guess, I was raised a militant non-believer."

"Are you still?"

"No. I don't know what I am. I became a good soldier at an early age, and being a good soldier is hardly compatible with being a good Christian. Although in tsarist times they referred to the army as a band of 'Christ-loving warriors.' Something of a contradiction, isn't it?"

"Indeed. So you're my 'non-Christ-loving warrior'." Angela hugged him tenderly. "Anyway, it's spring now, and the sun's shining, and flowers are blooming, and there's no more blood being spilled." He responded with a passionate kiss.

That evening they lay in bed in Angela's motel suite, half covered in blankets.

"How many men did you have before me?" Trofimov asked her.

"Come on," she laughed. "Every single boyfriend asks the same question."

"But still, I want to know," he insisted playfully.

"What's the need? I'm not an innocent. You never thought I was, did you?"

"No."

"Then what's the problem? Yes, I had a few men, apart from being married."

"I understand. After all, you were at the front. Almost all women there had affairs, the same as the men who could find a partner. What about your husband? Was he killed in action?"

"No, he's alive. We were divorced soon after the war."

"Why?"

"Well, it's a common story. He returned from the war, well, a changed person, a sort of emotional cripple. He went off his head for no reason. He even beat our kid, and he tried to beat me. With me it wasn't so easy. We were taught hand-to-hand fighting at the front."

"I get you. I know the story. Three or four years of war was more than many guys could take. Was he wounded?"

"Twice. Then he had shellshock."

"A well-known scenario. And the two of you have a kid?"

"A boy. He's in Anchorage just now. I left him with my friends, so he doesn't miss school."

"Listen," Trofimov said suddenly. "You told me you were a Harvard graduate. How come you're stuck up here in the wilds of Alaska? Did you choose this place?"

"Sort of, but actually I didn't have any better prospect just then."

"Why?"

"I was on the FBI's black list."

"For what reason?"

"For the same reason as everybody else," Angela sighed. "For being too left wing. I joined a left-wing student group at Harvard. They might have been willing to forgive me that, but not for the fact that I was on the River Elbe in 1945."

"God help us!" Trofimov exclaimed. "You're in trouble for it, just as I was. It seems there are people all over the world getting into trouble for those few wonderful months."

"We veterans of the Elbe have got to stick together. Just like we do." She embraced Trofimov, and in response he kissed her ripe, thrusting breast.

14

The days passed in monotonous succession, with no news and no change. One day an invitation came for Trofimov, Yatta and Bondarenko to appear before the Alaska Territorial Immigration and Refugee Board. It seemed that at last their ordeal was at an end, though there was still a slim chance that their refugee claim could be rejected. At least theoretically, that meant they could be deported to the Soviet Union. Formally it was not extradition, but in terms of the consequences there was no difference.

Bondarenko, who was about to be transferred to one of the city hospitals in Anchorage, could be exempted from deportation on health grounds.

Arrangements were made for Trofimov and Yatta to sail to Anchorage aboard a small steamship, accompanied by a military escort in the person of a Private Green.

Most of the time Trofimov spent on deck, watching the boundless sea. At first a lazy wind made ripples on the slight swell, but eventually the wind and waves became more agitated and the small ship pitched and tossed like a tin can. He watched the sunrise and sunset, unlike anything he had ever seen on land, and he looked up into the deep night sky with its swath of stars spreading to the horizon.

On the morning of their arrival in Anchorage, Trofimov and Yatta were in their cabin drinking tea when Private Green entered.

"Alex, come with me a moment," he said.

"Where to?"

"Just for a moment. There's something I gotta tell you."

Trofimov followed Green.

"Let's go to the bathroom," Green said.

"But I don't need to. What—"

"C'mon, let's go." Green tugged Trofimov by the sleeve.

In the bathroom, Green locked the door.

"What's this all about?"

"Hush! Nobody's gotta hear us," whispered Green. "Colonel McPherson told me to give you something."

Green thrust a hand in the inside pocket of his jacket and took out a paper packet. He showed Trofimov the contents, which consisted of several small pills.

"Keep quiet about this," Green warned him in a whisper. "It's potassium cyanide. He said there might be an occasion when you may want to do yourselves in. This is the easiest way."

"Guess what?" Trofimov told Yatta as soon as he returned to

their cabin.

"I dunno. What is it?" Yatta shrugged.

"Look," Trofimov showed him the pills. "A present from the colonel. Potassium cyanide, a deadly poison. To do ourselves in, in case we're to be deported."

"Oh, that's very kind of him," Yatta exclaimed.

"Yes, that's what camaraderie means among war vets. We'll go ahead with our escape plan to the Rockies, but if we're about to get caught, we'll use this stuff."

Next morning, the ship reached harbour in Anchorage. Green handed them over to another guard from the local garrison who was to be their final escort.

15

Trofimov and Yatta stood before the local Immigration and Refugee Board. The board consisted of three men. The chairman, a tall, fair man dressed in black jacket and tie, read out the verdict:

"The Immigration and Refugee Board of Alaska, having considered the application for political asylum from Alexander Ivanovich Trofimov, Mikhail Savelyevich Bondarenko and Yatta of the Telqap, has resolved to comply with the request of the said persons in accordance with United States federal and international laws on political asylum."

Trofimov broke into a broad smile and shook Yatta's hand in delight.

"Can you believe it, old man?" he exclaimed a few minutes later, as he and Yatta walked along the street. "Can you believe it? Everything's turned out right."

"Yeah, we've been very lucky," Yatta agreed. "I was worried all the time. I thought they wouldn't make such a fuss for so long, if they really were friendly to us. I thought all that delay meant something bad for us."

"Well, fortunately, you were wrong. Now let's buy a good bottle of vodka and go straight to see Mikhail."

"Sure," said Yatta.

They bought a bottle of Smirnoff vodka then took a taxi to the Anchorage Military Hospital. Smiling happily, they entered the lobby and Trofimov asked the receptionist how to find Bondarenko.

"Bondarenko?" the receptionist repeated.

"Yes. Mikhail S. Bondarenko."

The receptionist shook her head. "I'm afraid you may not be let in to see him. He's in very poor condition."

"As bad as all that?" Trofimov felt the blood rush to his temples.

"I don't know. You can go in, but I'm not sure you'll be allowed to see him."

Yatta and Trofimov went up to the third floor where they were met by the nurse on duty.

"I don't think you can see him. He's dying."

"What?" A spasm in his throat choked off any further words.

"I'm terribly sorry," she said. "He's been getting worse since yesterday morning. A Russian Orthodox priest heard his confession and gave him the last rites. After that he lost consciousness, and he hasn't come round since."

"But maybe ... maybe we could just look in and see him?" Trofimov felt his voice failing.

"Yes, you can do that if you wish. If he regains consciousness, he might want to see you." She went into the ward and returned a minute later. "Come in. He's waiting for you."

The first thing that struck Trofimov was the deathly pallor on Mikhail's face. His teeth protruded slightly from his mouth. This, he recalled from the camps and from the war, was a clear sign of approaching death.

"Is that you, guys?" Bondarenko whispered, and tried to turn his head.

"Yes, Mikhail." Trofimov gazed into his face. "It's us. We've brought you good news. They've answered our request for asylum, and we can stay."

"I'm glad, guys," the patient murmured. "Then we can ... but I'm dying ... you see ..."

"I ... I don't know ..." Trofimov found no words.

"C'mon, Captain, I know I am. And I ain't afraid. I never was, you know."

"Is there something you wonna us do for you, Mikhail?" Yatta asked.

"What can you do?" Bondarenko said. "I've got everythin'. I even confessed to the Holy Father. It was weird. He told me to repent, and that was difficult. I forgot all the prayers. But then I relaxed … and then … it was … very good. I've got rid of all the anger in me … even with that League of Young Communists. Let the Lord deal with them." He coughed, and then continued: "What month is it?"

"July," Trofimov said.

"July. And when was it we … we met those Chukchi girls?"

"Last March."

"Then … then that means our kids are over half a year old."

"Yes," Trofimov said.

"That's great, eh?" A smile bloomed on the face of the dying man. "Now I've got three kids. The eldest is twelve, and the youngest half a year. The family line will continue. In that case, it ain't so bad having to die." He choked and then continued, "Anyway, guys, you two carry on living, and have lots of fun. Hopefully, we'll meet again there, beyond. I'm glad to die here, and not back there." Then his voice cut short.

Trofimov looked into his eyes. They expressed a tranquility and calm so untypical of this restless man while he was alive.

The funeral was simple. They did not know anyone in Anchorage, so Trofimov, Yatta, the priest from the Russian Orthodox Church and two gravediggers were the only ones in attendance. Trofimov and Yatta carried the coffin, and the priest performed the rites of the faith, a faith in which the deceased was never too firm, but which he had professed all his life.

In the evening, after the funeral, Trofimov and Yatta wandered the streets of Anchorage. According to custom they should have held a funeral banquet, the *pominki*, but there was no one to invite. Instead they went to a city park and drank a bottle of Smirnoff.

"Well, Yatta, it's just us two now," Trofimov said as they wandered the streets again, the commander and the guide, the ones who were supposed to have led the others to safety.

Yatta sighed. "Now, you know, Mikhail's gone beyond the clouds to the place of the Blood Dead. He'll find relief with Yakov and Zakharych. All three are looking down on us, and they'll be our guardian spirits if we need them."

"Maybe, but I'm still very sad," Trofimov murmured. "More than that, I feel guilty."

"Alex. Yatta." A voice rang out next to them. "My congratulations on the happy outcome," Angela said. "I read about it in the *Anchorage Star*."

"Angela, thank you," Trofimov said quietly.

"Why so sad?" she asked, looking from one to the other.

"Mikhail's dead," Trofimov explained.

"Oh, I'm sorry. I'm very sorry." She looked at Trofimov. "Look, I have to run right now," she said, "but can you come round to my place tomorrow night? I gave you my card with the address, didn't I?"

"Yes, you did."

Angela and Trofimov sat on the sofa in Angela's apartment, drinking and smoking.

"My sincere condolences, Alex," she said.

"Thank you, Angela,"

"Let's drink to the peace of his soul."

Trofimov poured the vodka.

"I know how you feel," she said, after swallowing down some of the fiery liquid. "This is something you have to get through, and you do have to go on with your life."

"That's easy to say. But you know, I feel so guilty. These guys, Mikhail, Yakov and Timoshkin, trusted me to lead them to freedom and safety. They relied on me, and I relied on them. Mikhail was the one who killed that screw in the camp. But for all of them, I wouldn't be here. Now I'm alive and free, and they're all gone."

"But what is your actual guilt?"

"I don't know. Maybe I should have done better, so they could have survived."

"Hardly," she said and shook her head. "That was such a difficult undertaking."

"It was. But still, I feel most uneasy. How can I carry on living and owing my life to them, if they're gone?"

"C'mon, you're sliding into a self-destructive mood." She hugged him slightly. "You can't bring them back. You have to go on with your own life, like all of us. Try and put these tragedies behind you."

"Forget them?" Trofimov felt the anger rise within him.

"No, not forget. Leave them behind somehow, otherwise—"

"Leave them behind?" he exploded. "My best friends? My brothers-in-arms? You say that to me?"

"Yes, I say that. Because it's common sense."

"Common sense?" He shouted. "That's how you see it? These men are not your friends. They're not your sworn brothers like they are mine."

"Don't yell at me or I'll refuse to talk to you," she said harshly.

"What the fuck do you know about life anyway?" he bawled. "What have you seen of it? Have you seen shells tear your comrades to pieces? Have you seen women strung up and hanged? Kids thrown down wells? That fuckin' Lieutenant-Colonel Razzhivin with his torture chamber and his ramrods? Goners covered in ulcers from scurvy and dying on their bunks? Guys stripped and tied to trees with their jaws hanging loose and their mouths dry as dust, and mosquitoes swarming all over their bodies? Have you seen any of that? No, you never have."

"Stop accusing me, or—"

"Or what? What can you threaten me with after I've lived through all that? After I've been in hand-to-hand combat with the enemy dozens of times? After I've buried my friends innumerable times? After I was tortured and almost kicked the bucket in a labour camp? After I crawled across the sea ice with barrages of shrapnel landing all around?" His voice finally choked. "Yeah, I know you don't want to share my sorrows, nor anyone else's either. Not even of your own husband, the father of your kid. 'He became ill-tempered,' you said! You didn't want to think what he might have gone through at the front, did you? No! And it's always like that: good men go and suffer and get killed, and people like you sit at home and enjoy life, and—"

"That's enough!" Angela slammed the table with her fist. "I thought you were a good, normal guy, but you turned out to be another psycho. I don't want you here any more. You're not welcome."

"No love lost," he snarled, then rose and left, slamming the door.

16

By the time Trofimov returned to their motel suite, Yatta was fast asleep and snoring. He went straight to the night table and, without switching on the light, opened the drawer and took two of the pills that Green had passed him from Colonel McPherson. He left the room, carefully closing the door behind him. He had already made his decision on the way back from Angela's place, and all that concerned him now was to prevent Yatta from waking and trying to stand in his way.

The deserted street lay in darkness. He looked at his watch. It was one o'clock. There were no buses until morning. It didn't matter. He could easily reach his destination on foot in less than an hour. Anchorage was a small city.

He cast a final glance at the motel where Yatta, his last remaining friend, slept, then he set off through the empty streets of the nightbound city.

As he walked he gazed at the streets with their one- and two-storey houses, and mentally took his leave of them. In an hour or so he would no longer be on this earth, and that was fair enough. He had no right to live, particularly no right to enjoy what he owed to his three dead friends. They had paid for his life with their own, a victory in the best tradition of Stalin and Zhukov. Victory bought at the price of mountains of dead. And victory for whom? It was time to expiate that sin. It was no difficult thing to do. For a long time now he had had no fear of death.

All the time he walked the empty streets, pictures and scenes from his short but intense life unfolded before his eyes: his childhood in the Urals; the days on the battlefront; his old enemy Lieutenant- Colonel Razzhivin in that hellish torture chamber; the endless days in the camps; their incredible journey of almost fifteen hundred kilometres. That had been the most exciting and most unusual part of his life. They had achieved the impossible.

He reached the Russian Orthodox cemetery and walked along the narrow paths. Few ordinary folk would have had the courage to wander through such a macabre place in the dead of night, at a time when supposedly the ghosts came out of their graves. Trofimov had no fear of them. He had seen too many living ghosts. He was something of a ghost himself, a ghost of sorrow and repentance.

Finally he reached the fresh grave. The bright moon shed its light on the new black cross on Mikhail's tomb. Trofimov squatted in front of it and spoke to the grave.

"Forgive me, Mikhail. And you, Timoshkin. And you, too, Yakov. Very soon everything will be over and finished. Maybe there really is an afterlife, and I'll join you there. It would be great to see you again, eh? But if not, never mind. I'll at least expiate my guilt."

He looked at the cyanide pills. How funny! Each of them was enough to transform him into an inanimate object. He, who had made the journey from Kolyma to Alaska and had not been hit by a thousand bullets and fragments of shrapnel. When the sun rose, he would lie here, numb and cold. Yatta would be the only one to mourn him, although McPherson would perhaps be sad when he learned the news. And maybe Angela, that naïve and giddy woman.

The Soviets would almost certainly hear the news and rejoice. Why was he, of his own free will, giving them grounds to rejoice? Some smart MGB officer might even prove that it was he who had dealt with that accursed Trofimov in America. He might even receive a decoration or another star on his epaulettes, the goddamned bastard. No, Trofimov wasn't going to provide them with such pleasure of his own accord.

Hell, he still hadn't fulfilled his promise to old Ganin. He had pledged on his honour to have a requiem said for him and he would do that no matter what. Those Soviet bastards would not be allowed to triumph. He had defied them many times, and they had failed to break him. He and the few men who defied the tyrant should live. Maybe they would be needed for some future fight for freedom. Come on, Trofimov, grit your teeth and live.

He put the cyanide pills back in his pocket and bowed low before Bondarenko's grave.

The next day, he ordered a requiem mass for Ganin and Bondarenko in the Russian church. When the day of the service came, for the first time in the life of that former Young Communist, he stood before the altar together with Yatta and some local parishioners, listening to the moving sounds of the choral requiem mass. He felt something, maybe not a religious feeling, but a sense of the importance of every human life in the face of eternity, and he became almost convinced of the existence of an afterlife, probably the only thing that could reconcile a man with the tragedy of death.

17

A few days later, Trofimov saw Yatta off. He was going back to Nome, and from there to the Unalakleet district to his kinfolk who had lived there since the 1930s. Trofimov was headed for Alberta in Canada, where oil had recently been discovered and extensive construction of oil facilities was in progress. To do that, he had to obtain the approval of the Canadian consulate, and that would take yet more time.

Trofimov and Yatta walked along the pier and watched the ships moored around the harbour, ships large and small, passenger boats and freighters. Most of them were American, but some were Canadian, British and French. No Soviet boats, however, although probably at least one of the ships moored here would sail to those cold and cruel shores across the Bering Strait, where convoys of ships with human cargo brought countless unfortunates to their final ordeal, an ordeal that had linked the fates of both these men.

"So here you are, Yatta." Trofimov smiled at his friend. "At last you'll reunite with your kinfolk."

"Yeah, Sasha. They'll come in a large skin boat, and then we'll sail home."

"I'm happy for you. At least your immediate future is clear, unlike mine."

"But they invited you to that office, didn't they?" Yatta asked.

"Yes. Tomorrow I'm going to the Canadian consulate. If I'm very lucky, I'll get a visa. I'll probably go straight there. I've got no idea where the hell I'm going to end up."

"But, you're young and strong," Yatta emphasized. "You'll find your place in life, I'm sure."

"Attention please!" the megaphone on the deck roared. "We shall be casting off in five minutes. Any persons not embarking please leave the ship."

"Well, buddy, goodbye." Trofimov hugged Yatta.

"And Sasha, I know you wanted to kill yourself after Mikhail's funeral," Yatta said suddenly.

"Hell. You found out?"

"Well, you know, every hunter is a good observer. So I wanna tell you, you mustn't do that. There are only two of us left, so we have to live not just for ourselves, but for Pyotr and Yakov and Mikhail as well."

"I know. I'll never think that way again. That would only please the Soviets. Well," he winked, "hopefully it's not the last time I see you."

"No," Yatta smiled back. "You coulda come and visit me when you earn enough money. You know where to look for me. And before that, you coulda write to me in Russian. Goodbye, my dear friend."

The men embraced again, then Yatta walked up the gangway and boarded the ship. In a few minutes the vessel cast off, and Trofimov watched it sail away until it vanished over the horizon. Only a gray cloud hung over the violet surface of the sea to mark its passage and the end of a chapter in Trofimov's tough and eventful life.

The following day Trofimov visited the Canadian consulate. There he received the necessary papers including his Canadian work permit. Now that the Canadian West was booming, there was a demand for new workers, and there should be no problem finding a job there.

He left the consulate, stopped at the nearest bus stop and lit a cigarette. When he had smoked about half of it, a Volkswagen Beetle pulled up in front of him. The door opened, and he saw Angela inside.

"Hi, come on, get in. I'll give you a ride," she called.

"You, Angela?"

"As you see," she said with a smile. "I hope you're not still so mad at me as to refuse?"

"No, not so much." He sat down beside her. "I want to apologize. I was really rude."

"'I' apologize too," she replied. "You were brokenhearted, and I didn't show compassion."

"Well, we're all set for a reconciliation then, aren't we?" Trofimov smiled.

"I'd say so. And by way of reconciliation, I propose that we drop in at a bar and have lunch together."

"A good idea."

They ordered lunch for two and talked all the while.

"I've just got my Canadian papers," he told her. "I'll be leaving for there in the next few days."

"Where are you going in Canada?"

"To central Alberta. I hope to find a job on one of those new construction projects to do with the oil industry. I'm a certified truck driver, although of course my certificate and licence are back there."

"That's no big problem. They'll just give you a test," she said. "Do you have any plans beyond that?"

"I don't know. What do you mean?"

"You're a bright guy. Get some college or university education."

"Oh, no," he shook his head. "I'm too old for that."

"C'mon, you aren't even thirty."

"The sort of things I've gone through make a person much, much older than I really am," Trofimov said.

"You're still living in the past though. Try to look forward, towards the future. Anyway, when you settle somewhere, write to me, just a few words. I'd like to know how you're doing."

"With pleasure," he agreed. "Are you going to be here?"

"Until next summer at least," Angela said.

"And then?"

"I applied for a job in Seattle. If I'm lucky, I'll move there next summer. I'll write you from there. You can visit me. It's just a two-day trip from Edmonton to Seattle. How are you going to reach Alberta, by the way?"

Trofimov shrugged. "I'm not sure. Planes are too expensive. I thought I'd go by ship to a West Canadian port, then take a train or bus."

"If you're a good truck driver, you can save a lot of money by hitching a ride," Angela suggested. "Take the Great Alaska Highway. Highway One joins it at a place called Tok-Junction. The long distance drivers would take you along with pleasure, to share the driving. You won't have to pay."

"Sounds good. Thanks for the advice."

"There won't be too many trucks going all the way to Edmonton," she continued. "They usually go just three hundred miles or so. But there'll surely be another truck, and another pair of drivers going the next three hundred miles, and so forth." She paused and recollected. "And by the way, Tom James and Dick Norton will probably be going to Whitehorse in the next few days. I'll try to contact them and ask them."

"Thank you, Angela."

A few days later, Trofimov turned up at a local truck station. Drivers stood by several parked vehicles smoking.

"Which of you is Tom James?" he asked loudly.

"That's me," a tall, dark middle-aged man replied. "You must be Alex."

"Right."

"Come on then, let's go."

Tom James and Trofimov made their way to one of the large trucks. Another short, stocky middle-aged man appeared from the other side of the vehicle.

"So here's our fellow traveler," he said surveying the newcomer.

Alex introduced himself.

"You're a driver, aren't you?"

"Yes, I am. But I don't have my licence with me."

"Doesn't matter," said James. "The main thing is that you know how to drive. You'll take over after Tok-Junction, okay?"

"Surely."

"Then let's go," the second trucker announced.

The three of them climbed up into the cabin, Tom James started up the engine, and the truck moved slowly out of the station. After traveling a few miles along a city street, it turned onto the highway with thick pine forests lining either side.

It looks very much like the Urals, Trofimov thought.

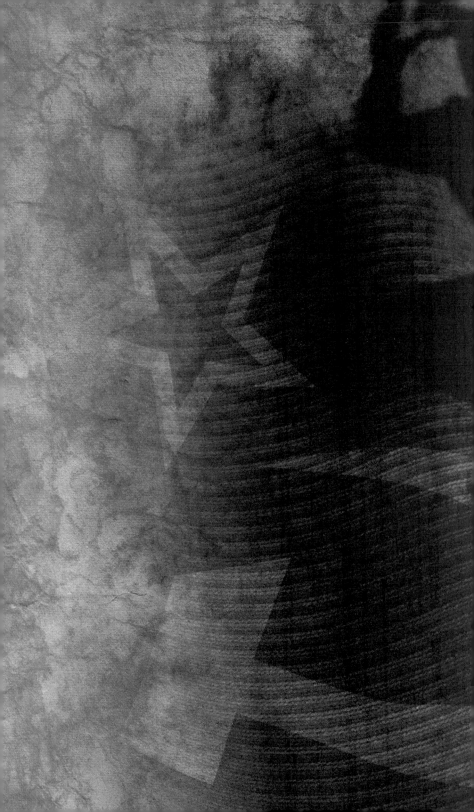

Afterword and Acknowledgments

Against Destiny is a work of fiction: its characters and events are inventions of the author's imagination. But it is also a historical novel, in two senses. First, its recreation of an accurate socio-cultural context in which the characters exist and their lives unfold is based on the author's inside knowledge of many aspects of life in the Soviet Union. Second, its plot unfolds under real historical circumstances, for whose presentation I used the following sources.

The description of life in Stalin's labour camps is based on the works of Alexander Solzhenitsyn (*The Gulag Archipelago, One Day in the Life of Ivan Denisovich*, and some other novels); on a less well-known collection of stories by Varlam Shalamov, *Kolyma Tales*, based on his personal experience of seventeen years as a prisoner in the Gulag; on the memoirs of Yevgenia Ginzburg, *Journey into the Whirlwind*; and on the memoirs of Oleg Volkov, *Sinking into Darkness*. Unfortunately, I cannot claim that I was influenced by Anne Appelbaum's *GULAG: A History*, but only because the first draft of my book was finished before her book was published. I was delighted to find out that her historically based descriptions of camp life correspond in many respects to the fictional descriptions in my book.

The description of the Chukchi way of life, cultural patterns and geographical placement is based on a fundamental monograph, *The Chukchi*, by a famous Russian ethnographer, Vladimir Bogoraz, and also on collections of Chukchi folk tales. The historical facts of Chukchi-Russian life, such as those referring to Major Pavlutsky and his atrocities, are well described in Bogoraz's work. Events referring to Bochkarev and his expedition are my recreation based on historical information about his role in the Civil War in the Far East, where he is described as one of the cruelest White commanders, and also on the references to him in novels by two writers: the Russian Soviet writer Andrey Aldan-Semyonov and the well-known Soviet-era Chukchi writer Yury Rytkheu.

The events of World War II described in the novel are common knowledge. There has always been a great controversy over the role of "Forest Brethren" in the Baltic States and other Western regions of the post-War Soviet Union. In Soviet historiography, they are depicted as fascists and ex-Nazi collaborators, whereas in literature from the "perestroika" period of the late 1980s, they are described as fighters against Nazi as well as Soviet occupation. They are mentioned with great sympathy by Solzhenitsyn in *The Gulag Archipelago*. Historiography in the time of Vladimir Putin has gone back aggressively to the Soviet interpretation of their role.

I want to express my deep gratitude to the people who helped me to bring this book to the point of publication. First of all I want to acknowledge the influence on my historical thinking of Professor Robert Johnston of the Department of History of McMaster University, under whose guidance I developed my views of Russian history from outside of Russia. Unfortunately he did not live to see this book.

My special thanks to Professor Christopher Barnes of the University of Toronto, who did a great job of carefully transforming my immigrant Russian English into standard English, preserving as much as possible of its verbal flare.

My great thanks to my literary agents Johanna M. Bates and Anne Bougie. Johanna at the very first contact expressed deep interest in the topic of my novel. This interest was based on her good knowledge of Russian literature, on her fascination with the movie *One Day in the Life of Ivan Denisovitch*, and also on her family history in the Netherlands during World War II, when her father helped to save Jews during the Nazi occupation. Johanna and Anne supported me endlessly and faithfully, bringing this book to the attention of potential publishers, with eventual success.

I am extremely glad to become one of the authors published by Kunati Books, a great author-friendly publishing house. My editor James McKinnon polished the text of the novel for publication, while the designer Kam Wai Yu created a fantastically expressive cover for my book. I am deeply grateful to them both.

And last but not least, I want to express my deepest thanks to my mother Inga Dolinina Hitchcock and my stepfather David Hitchcock for their unwavering support, help and encouragement during the years of my work on this book.

Alexander Dolinin

Alexander Dolinin was born and raised in Leningrad in the former Soviet Union, where he earned an MA in Iranian philology from the State University of Leningrad. He earned a B.A. in Honours History from McMaster University, with Russian history as one of his areas of specialization. *Against Destiny*, his first novel, joins his experience of living in the Soviet Union with a specialist's knowledge of the history, realities and circumstances that shape its main characters and plot. He has written several short stories, as well as a motion picture script based on *Against Destiny*. He is a Canadian citizen, living in Hamilton, Ontario.

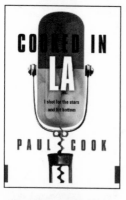

Cooked in LA ■ Paul Cook

How does a successful young man from a "good" home hit bottom and risk losing it all? *Cooked In La* shows how a popular, middle-class young man with a bright future in radio and television is nearly destroyed by a voracious appetite for drugs and alcohol.

Non Fiction/Self-Help & Recovery I US$ 24.95
Pages 304 I Cloth 5.5" x 8.5"
ISBN 978-1-60164-193-9

Against Destiny ■ Alexander Dolinin

A story of courage and determination in the face of the impossible. The dilemma of the unjustly condemned: Die in slavery or die fighting for your freedom.

Fiction I US$ 24.95
Pages 448 I Cloth 5.5" x 8.5"
ISBN 978-1-60164-173-1

Let the Shadows Fall Behind You ■ Kathy-Diane Leveille

The disappearance of her lover turns a young woman's world upside down and leads to shocking revelations of her past. This enigmatic novel is about connections and relationships, memory and reality.

Fiction I US$ 22.95
Pages 288 I Cloth 5.5" x 8.5"
ISBN 978-1-60164-167-0

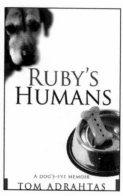

Ruby's Humans ■ Tom Adrahtas

No other book tells a story of abuse, neglect, escape, recovery and love with such humor and poignancy, in the uniquely perceptive words of a dog. Anyone who's ever loved a dog will love Ruby's sassy take on human foibles and manners.

Non Fiction I US$ 19.95
Pages 192 I Cloth 5.5" x 8.5"
ISBN 978-1-60164-188-5

The Unbreakable Child ■ Kim Michele Richardson

Starved, beaten and abused for nearly a decade, orphan Kimmi learned that evil can wear a nun's habit. A story not just of a survivor but of a rare spirit who simply would not be broken.

Non Fiction/True Crime | US$ 24.95
Pages 256 | Cloth 5.5" x 8.5"
ISBN 978-1-60164-163-2

Save the Whales Please
■ Konrad Karl Gatien & Sreescanda

Japanese threats and backroom deals cause the slaughter of more whales than ever. The first lady risks everything—her life, her position, her marriage—to save the whales.

Fiction | US$ 24.95
Pages 432 | Cloth 5.5" x 8.5"
ISBN 978-1-60164-165-6

Screenshot
■ John Darrin

Could you resist the lure of evil that lurks in the anonymous power of the Internet? Every week, a mad entrepreneur presents an execution, the live, real-time murder of someone who probably deserves it. *Screenshot:* a techno-thriller with a provocative premise.

Fiction | US$ 24.95
Pages 416 | Cloth 5.5" x 8.5"
ISBN 978-1-60164-168-7

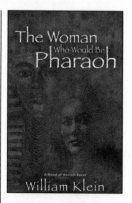

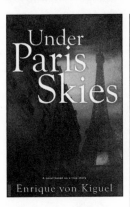
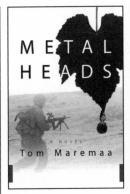